PRAISE FOR *STILLHOUSE LAKE*

"In this rapid-fire thriller . . . Caine spins a powerful story of maternal love and individual self-realization."

—*Publishers Weekly*

"Amazing."

—*Night Owl Reviews* (Top Pick)

"A chilling thriller . . . *Stillhouse Lake* is a great summer read."

—*Criminal Element*

"*Stillhouse Lake* is a true nail-biter right up to the end."

—*Fresh Fiction*

"Highly entertaining and super intense!"

—*Novel Gossip*

"What a fantastic book!"

—*Seattle Book Review*

WOLFHUNTER
RIVER

OTHER TITLES BY RACHEL CAINE

Stillhouse Lake Series

Killman Creek

Stillhouse Lake

The Great Library

Paper and Fire

Ink and Bone

Ash and Quill

Smoke and Iron

Weather Warden

Ill Wind

Heat Stroke

Chill Factor

Windfall

Firestorm

Thin Air

Gale Force

Cape Storm

Total Eclipse

Outcast Season

Undone

Unknown

Unseen

Unbroken

Revivalist

Working Stiff
Two Weeks' Notice
Terminated

Red Letter Days

Devil's Bargain
Devil's Due

Morganville Vampires

Glass Houses
The Dead Girls' Dance
Midnight Alley
Feast of Fools
Lord of Misrule
Carpe Corpus
Fade Out
Kiss of Death
Ghost Town
Bite Club
Last Breath
Black Dawn
Bitter Blood
Fall of Night
Daylighters

The Honors (with Ann Aguirre)

Honor Among Thieves
Honor Bound

Stand-Alone Titles

Prince of Shadows
Dead Air (with Gwenda Bond and Carrie Ryan)

WOLFHUNTER RIVER

A Stillhouse Lake
Thriller

RACHEL CAINE

 THOMAS & MERCER

Published by Thomas & Mercer, Seattle

www.apub.com

Amazon, the Amazon logo, and Thomas & Mercer are trademarks of Amazon.com, Inc., or its affiliates.

ISBN-13: 9781503902305
ISBN-10: 1503902307

Cover design by Shasti O'Leary Soudant

Printed in the United States of America

WOLFHUNTER
RIVER

PROLOGUE

Four days ago

When Ellie White's teacher, Mrs. Willingham, told her that her driver was coming early to pick her up from school, Ellie knew it wasn't the whole truth. Mr. Lou never came early to get her, not unless she was sick.

"Why?" she asked. She liked asking questions when things didn't make sense. She might only be six, but Daddy had taught her to ask if she didn't understand. Momma had been a little embarrassed by how much she'd taken to it.

"I'm afraid—I'm afraid that your daddy asked him to," Mrs. Willingham said. She was a nice white lady with a streak of gray in her brown hair, and she was a good teacher. She never treated Ellie any different from the others, even though Ellie's father had a lot of money. Even though Ellie had dark-brown skin, darker than any of the other girls here, who mostly looked as white as magazine pages.

"Daddy doesn't do that," Ellie said. "Something's wrong."

Mrs. Willingham was looking at her but not *at* her. "Well, your momma got sick," she said. "So he's sending a car to come get you and take you to the hospital where he and your momma are. Okay?" She helped Ellie put on her sweater, which Ellie didn't like to wear but didn't want to leave behind either. Then her backpack.

"Mrs. Willingham?" Ellie asked. She looked up at her teacher. "Are you crying?"

"No, sweetie. I'm just fine. Come on now. Let's get you out there, he's waiting."

"But Daddy said the code word?"

"He said the code word," Mrs. Willingham said. "The code is *blackbird* today, right?"

Ellie nodded. Thursday was *blackbird*. Every day was a bird of some kind, because she liked birds, and Momma always called her *little hummingbird* because she darted around so fast. But Sunday was *hummingbird*.

Mrs. Willingham went down the school steps first to talk to Mr. Lou, who was waiting inside the car on the loop that went between the steps and the big marble fountain. The rule was that Ellie was never to come to the car until Mrs. Willingham said it was okay. She and Mr. Lou were talking a long time. Mrs. Willingham kept crying.

It was hot today, and humid, but the fountain always looked so cool and pretty. The water sprayed out of a bunch of concrete shells into a bigger shell in the middle. Momma had told her there'd once been a pretty lady in the shell, but some parents had made the school take her out, so she was off in some storage closet now, which was sad.

Mrs. Willingham came back up the steps to take her hand. Ellie looked up at her. "Everything's going to be all right," her teacher said, but her voice shook. Her eyes were red. "I'm sorry, baby. But I have to do this. I have a family too."

Ellie felt sorry for her. "Is your family okay, Mrs. Willingham?"

She didn't mean to make the lady cry. "Yes, Ellie, they're going to be okay. Can you help me make sure they are?"

Ellie wasn't sure how to do that, but she nodded anyway. She liked to help, even if she wasn't really sure *why* Mrs. Willingham thought she could.

Mrs. Willingham opened the door and boosted Ellie up, which was Mr. Lou's job, usually. Then her teacher hugged her. "You stay strong, Ellie. You're going to be okay."

"But what about your family?" Ellie asked. "Aren't you coming with me so we can help them?"

Mrs. Willingham covered her mouth, and tears rolled down her cheeks, and she just shook her head. She shut the door, and that was when Ellie knew something was really wrong. Mrs. Willingham had just lied to her, but she didn't know why.

And then she realized it was worse than she thought, because this looked like the right car, but it didn't smell like the car usually smelled, which was a little bit like coconut, her favorite. "Mr. Lou?" she called toward the driver. The lock engaged with a heavy *thunk*. She could see him up in the front seat, a big man wearing a cap. She felt smaller than usual in the back seat, and as the car started to move, she quickly buckled herself up; Mr. Lou *never* started moving until she was buckled in. "Mr. Lou? What's wrong with Momma? Mrs. Willingham said—"

She stopped her questions because the man driving wasn't Mr. Lou. The eyes looking at her in the rearview mirror weren't his. "Put your seatbelt on," he said. Not Mr. Lou's voice. And Mr. Lou would have said *please*.

"I did already," she said. She was scared, but she wasn't going to show it. "Do you know the code word?"

"*Blackbird*," he said. "Isn't that right?"

"Who are you?"

"I'm somebody who's going to get you somewhere safe," he said. "Just like Mr. Lou would want me to do. All right?"

"I'm calling my daddy," Ellie said, and unzipped her backpack to pull out her cell phone.

It wasn't where she kept it. She knew better than to leave her phone somewhere. It was expensive, and important, and she *always* put it there in that pocket.

She felt tears well up and wouldn't let herself cry. *They'd* want her to cry, whoever took her phone. Whoever was playing this nasty game. "Who are you?"

"Nobody," the driver said. "Now sit there and be quiet." He turned the SUV onto a main road. She tried to watch where they were going, but quickly lost track; she never had to pay attention to that before. The school disappeared over a hill, and he made more turns, and she didn't know where they were at all.

She didn't know what to do. Daddy had always told her there were bad people, and she shouldn't go with them if they didn't know the code word, but he *did* know the code word, and she couldn't push "Emergency" if there wasn't a phone.

"Let me out," she said. She tried to make it sound like her momma would have: cool and confident. "You can stop up here."

"Shut up," the driver said. "Keep quiet. You start making a racket, and I'll tape your damn mouth shut."

That scared her even more than being in a strange car and not having her phone, but she wasn't going to show him that. She wasn't going to cry. She looked around and tried to think what else to do. The door wouldn't open. Neither would the window. The SUV had dark-tinted windows, same as Mr. Lou's car; they were to keep the sun out. But they also made it so people couldn't see in.

Ellie realized something awful. She was a shadow inside a black car behind tinted windows, no one could see her, and she didn't know what to do next.

When she started to scream for help at passing cars, the driver took an exit, parked under a bridge among the cool green trees, and put tape over her mouth and around her legs and arms. Then he carried her around to the back of the SUV.

It was empty except for a sleeping bag, one with Disney princesses on it. She was screaming underneath the tape, and wiggling, and trying to get free, but he put her on top of the sleeping bag and shook his head.

"Go to sleep," he told her, and wiped sweat off his face. "We've got a long way to go. You mind your manners and I'll feed you in a few hours. You'll be home in a couple of days with a real good story to tell."

Daddy had always told her, *If bad people get you, don't believe what they tell you.*

She didn't believe they'd take her home at all.

She got really scared when her nose started to get snotty and it was hard to breathe with the tape over her mouth, so she made herself stop and breathe, slow and regular. She was still scared, but she felt exhausted, too, and she finally just closed her eyes and tried to pretend she was somewhere else, back home with her momma.

She pretended so hard that she fell asleep, curled up in her momma's lap, and when she woke up, she wanted to tell him she needed to pee, really bad, but he was talking on his phone, and they were in the dark, in a forest.

He saw her sit up. He turned around. And she saw through the front windshield the turn ahead and the lights that were coming around it. The lights that were heading straight at them.

She tried to scream at him, to tell him to watch out for the other car, but he just frowned at her and said, "I told you to shut—"

And then the other car hit them, and everything rolled and crashed, and she thought she heard the man screaming.

Help me, Ellie wanted to say, but she was too scared and too hurt, and then the man stopped screaming, and there wasn't any sound at all.

1

GWEN

The wide, dark eye of the television camera reminds me of bad things. Very bad things. I try really hard to keep in mind why I'm sitting here. I'm here to tell my story, frankly and honestly.

Because other people have been telling it for far too long now, lying about me and my kids.

It's been all over the news for months now: Escaped serial killer abducts ex! Shootout in murder house! It's always written for maximum ghoulish effect, and contains at least a passing mention that I was arrested as his accomplice.

Sometimes they remember to say that I was acquitted. Mostly they like to forget that detail. There have been a hundred reporters swamping my email to the point that I just shut it down and ignored it. At least half of them have made the long trip to Stillhouse Lake to try to get me to open the door and *tell my side*.

But I'm not stupid enough to do it without knowing what I'm getting into first. This television appearance took almost a month of negotiations, of guarantees of what I will and won't be asked. I chose the *Howie Hamlin Show* because he has a good reputation; he's been sympathetic to other crime victims and an advocate for justice.

But as I take my seat in the interview chair, I'm still feeling unready. I didn't expect this rising level of panic, or to feel burning sweat on the back of my neck. The chair is too deep, and I feel fragile perched on the edge of it. It's the camera. I thought I was past this, but I'm not. Maybe I never will be.

The camera keeps *staring*.

Everyone else is so relaxed. The camera operator—just the one—is chatting with someone else, nowhere near the machine and its unblinking eye. The host of the show is conferring with someone offstage in the dimly lit and cable-tangled distance. But I feel pinned in place, and every time I blink, I see that other camera, the one set up on a tripod in a ruined plantation house in Louisiana.

I see my ex and his horrible smile. I see blood.

Ignore it.

This place is smaller than I expected. The stage consists of a short riser and three armchairs spaced around with a small, glossy table for accent. The table holds a couple of books, but I'm too nervous to study them. I wonder why three chairs. Are there always three chairs? I don't know. I can't remember, even though I watched this show beforehand to learn what to expect.

You can do this, I tell myself, and practice deep breathing. *You faced down not one but two serial killers. This is nothing. It's just an interview. And you're doing this for the kids, to make them safer.* Because if I let the media tell the story without me, they're only going to make it worse.

Doesn't help. I still want to bolt out of this place and never come back. The only thing that holds me in place is the sight of my kids, Lanny and Connor, watching from the greenroom. It's a worn waiting area with a soundproof window to the studio so the people inside can watch the action. Lanny gives me an excited thumbs-up. I manage a smile somehow. I'm sweating my makeup off, I know it. I'm so unused to wearing it now that it feels like a layer of latex paint, smothering me.

I flinch at a touch on my shoulder, and when I turn, there's a bearded guy in a ball cap with something in his hand. I nearly hit him. Then I realize it's just a small microphone with a long cord attached.

"I'm going to hand this to you; you run it under your shirt and clip it on your collar, okay?" he says. I guess he sees how jumpy I am, because he takes a step back. I shove the tiny mic under the hem of my blouse, and take it up to where it's supposed to be; he nods when I get it into position, then drops a battery pack behind me in the chair. "Okay, you're live," he says. I reply with a thanks I don't feel. The wire feels cold against my bare skin. I wonder if the microphone can pick up my shallow, rapid breathing. I fiddle with the placement, just to be sure.

"Two minutes," someone out in the darkness says, and I jerk upright. The host is still lingering offstage. I feel deeply alone and exposed. The lights blaze on, blinding me; I have to resist the urge to put up my hand to block the glare. I lace my fingers together to keep myself from fidgeting.

At the one-minute mark, the host steps up on the riser. He's a solidly built middle-aged white man, dark hair going silver at the temples. He's wearing a nice dark-blue suit, and I immediately wonder if I'm underdressed. Or overdressed. This is not me; I don't care about these things. Usually.

But then, I've never been live for a TV audience before either. Not of my own volition, anyway.

"Hey, Gwen, how are you?" he says, and we shake hands. His feels warm against my ice-cold fingers. "Listen, don't worry about anything. I know this is nerve-racking, but we'll get you through it, okay? Just trust me. I've got you covered."

I nod. I have no choice at this point. He has a warm smile, the same temperature as his hands. It's all a normal day at work to him.

I try another deep breath.

Thirty seconds crawl by, and then there's a countdown. The last three counts are silent hand signals, and then the host's smile lights up

9

on cue. He leans a bit forward toward the camera. "Hello, and welcome to this extraordinary episode of *Howie Hamlin*. Now, we'll be covering later in the program the shocking ongoing case of the abduction of little Ellie White, but before that we'll have an in-depth discussion of the case everyone has been talking about: Melvin Royal. There's been one very important voice missing from this media clamor, and we're so lucky to have her with us today: Gwen Proctor, or as she was previously known, Gina Royal. Gina Royal was the wife of the infamous serial killer Melvin Royal, who was recently shot dead in Louisiana during what can only be described as an unbelievably brutal attack on his—"

I can't stand it. I interrupt him. "Ex," I say, and bring Howard—*Howie*—Hamlin to a sudden halt in his polished intro. "I'm sorry for interrupting, but I'm his *ex*-wife. I divorced him a long time ago."

He takes a brief beat and says, "Yes, yes, of course, you're quite right, and that is my mistake. He was your ex-husband at the time this shocking incident occurred. So you'd like to be called Gwen Proctor now, not Gina Royal, is that correct?"

"That's my legal name." I've had it changed, officially, as well as the names of my children. Gina Royal no longer exists. She barely existed in the first place, looking back on it.

"Of course. So, Gwen, just to make sure our viewing audience is caught up on this incredible tale . . . when Melvin Royal was initially caught several years ago with a young woman's body still in the house you shared with him, you were *also* accused of helping him in his abductions. Is that correct?"

"Yes," I say. "I was acquitted."

"So you were!" He sounds smoothly approving. "But after that you went on the run, changing your name and location multiple times. Why do that if you were innocent?"

I have a vibe now, and I don't like it. Something's off. I sense this isn't going to be the softball interview I was promised. "I *am* innocent, but there were death threats being delivered to me and my kids on a daily basis. Internet harassment and threats of rape and violence constantly. I did what was necessary to protect my family." I don't mention that Melvin kept finding us too. Sending letters. That's a can of vipers I don't want to open.

"Didn't you go to the police?"

"The police are always reluctant to act on anonymous threats, which is an issue those with stalkers know all too well. I chose to take actions to be sure my kids were safe."

"I see. But why keep on moving, then?"

"Because one thing internet trolls are really good at doing is working together to find people and victimize them all over again. It's a game for many of them. I didn't realize it in the beginning, but my harassment was a highly organized effort. It still is, I'm certain."

"Then why are you here taking that risk?"

I pause. I want to get this right. "Because it happens every day. Not just to celebrities, or people like me who've drawn attention; it happens to ordinary people. Even to children. And our laws, and our law enforcement, haven't adjusted to deal with this problem at all. But I'm not here to save the world. Just my kids."

"From what, exactly?"

"Misinformation," I say. "Lies that take hold and gin up more outrage, more harassment. So I want to tell my story." Even saying that makes me shake inside. I've spent so much time running. This is, in many ways, the hardest thing I've done, being so . . . vulnerable.

"The floor is yours," Howie says. "That's why we've given you this time."

So I do. I tell him about marrying my ex, about our early life when I had no clue that the demands he placed on me in the home, in our bedroom, were anything but normal. I was too young and too sheltered to know better. I'd been told to be sweet, be accommodating, be what my husband expected from me. And once the kids came, it was too late to listen to my instincts. I was too afraid to look at the truth.

Until the truth crashed into Melvin's workshop—the one he never let me enter—in the form of a drunk driver. That was the day Melvin's gruesome, cruel handiwork first saw the light of day.

When I go silent there, remembering that moment and fighting that memory, Hamlin leans forward. "Gwen, let's get right to the point here. You *had* to know, didn't you? How could he bring these young women into your home and you *not* know?"

I try to explain about his locked workshop, his night-owl hours. Hamlin pretends to listen, but I can see he's just waiting for me to finish. When I do, he says, "You understand why many, many people doubt your story, don't you? They simply can't imagine that you slept side by side with a killer and never had a clue."

"Ask Ted Bundy's girlfriend," I say. "Ask Gary Ridgway's wife. Ask Dennis Rader's entire family. There might have been signs, but I couldn't recognize them for what they were. I *never* imagined he was doing these things, or I would have tried to stop him."

"Tried?" Hamlin repeats.

"He'd have killed me," I say. "And he'd have had our children to do with as he pleased. I can't even imagine what that would have been, and I don't want to. I survived, Mr. Hamlin. I did that for my children, and I will keep doing it, no matter what comes."

I'm fairly happy with the way I've phrased it, but I'm on guard now; why is he pushing me? This isn't what we agreed on. He's supposed to be helping me, not interrogating me.

"Let's go back to your husband, Melvin Royal. He continued to pursue you even while he was behind bars, that was your claim, wasn't it? Part of your harassment? Surely that part had nothing to do with faceless strangers on the internet."

Claim. I nearly snap at him. I feel like a prisoner in this chair, and I hate the feeling. I can't glance at the camera, but I know it's staring; the red ON AIR light is a smear in my peripheral vision. I try to focus on

Hamlin's face, but it's a blur. I keep seeing people moving around me, and I hate it, *hate it*. I don't like people sneaking up on me.

"Gwen?"

I realize that I'm staring at him with a blank expression, and I try to remember the question. *Melvin. He's talking about Melvin.* "My husband sent me letters," I tell him. "Someone inside the prison smuggled them out for him; we now think he's scattered them all over the country for people to send, even posthumously. There's still an investigation underway into that, as far as I know."

"And did you keep these letters? Show them to prison officials? The police?"

"The first ones," I say. My throat feels dry. My fingers twitch. "But he was already on death row. There wasn't a lot they could do to punish him."

"Hmm." He draws it out, and he's assumed a thoughtful expression. "And you have records of all of these internet threats you say you received?"

Why is he doubting me? What the hell is going on here? "Of course I do, including police and FBI records of the harassment. Look, there's no point in continuing this if you're—"

"Your contention is that it started out coming from the families of Melvin Royal's victims?"

I'm in the act of rising to walk away, but now I sit down again. I hadn't wanted to go there. In fact, I'd told the producer I wouldn't answer questions about the victims or their families. I need to head this off. "I don't want to talk about the victims' families."

"Why not? They were the original people who were angry with you, weren't they?"

I do *not* want to blame the families. I can't leave that as the impression. "I don't blame people who were dealing with an impossible load of grief and anger. I blame the complete strangers who piled on to satisfy their own needs."

"Did you bring any examples of this harassment we can show our audience? For the purpose of establishing your case, of course."

I feel color burning my cheeks and chin. My *case*? Am I on trial here? "No," I say. I try to keep it calm and level. "I didn't. And I wouldn't. They're vile."

"I believe our producer did ask you to bring some to share, isn't that correct?"

I'd tried. I'd opened up the file drawer where I kept those awful things, tried to find one that wasn't so personal and horrific that it brought bile to my throat, but I couldn't. Anything less they'd have dismissed as *She's blowing it out of proportion.* Anything that was truly horrible they'd have said was unsuitable for the air.

"I decided to protect my children," I say. "Many of those messages are about them, and I refuse to make those public. I'm not making their torment into public entertainment. I'm here to tell the truth, not publicize the lies."

I feel a brief, shining moment of calm as I say it; I'm in the right, I know I am, and I think the audience knows it too.

But then he turns on me.

"Gwen . . ." He slides a bit forward in his chair, angles toward me, a confessional in the making. "Are you aware of the documentary?"

I feel like the chair is melting underneath me, sinking me into the center of the earth. "What *documentary*?" I'm aware of the edge I've put on the word. I can't stop myself. "What are you talking about?"

It's subtle, but I see a little flicker of enthusiasm flash in his eyes. "We'll get to that in just a moment. But first, there was a video that briefly surfaced that seemed to confirm that you were involved in your ex-husband's case—"

What fucking documentary? I take a deep breath to calm myself, and say, "The video was an expert fake, and the FBI has confirmed that fact; you can look up the press release. The fact that there's even a question about this at all just points up the continuing harassment I have to face every day, as do my kids." I'm still trying to turn this disaster around. I can't think what else to do.

"Well, let's talk about that. Melvin Royal seems to have a significant and growing number of defenders assembling online who believe that either he had no real guilt in this entire crime spree, or that you share equal blame. Don't you think those people have a right to express their opinions?"

I want to smash my fist into his face. I want to scream. I want to *run* so badly my legs shake with the urge. "If their opinions include saying that I should be flayed alive and my children murdered in front of me, then no. I don't." My voice has the force of fury. I swallow a burn in the back of my throat. Taste bile. "What documentary are you talking about?"

"Yes, that's a perfect opportunity to introduce our other guest today. Mrs. Tidewell? Would you please join us?"

I realize that the people I'd been aware of moving in the background were the bearded microphone handler and the floor director, and as I turn slightly, I see someone new stepping up onto the riser. I know her, and it feels like I'm plunging off the edge of the world.

Miranda Tidewell. Rich, connected, and terminally angry. She's got reason to be; her daughter, Vivian, was my husband's second victim. But since the beginning she's believed that I shared the blame, that I should have known and stopped him, or that I did it right alongside him. She's been a knife in my back from the moment Melvin was arrested. It was principally her advocacy that made sure I was arrested, too, and tried, though the evidence was slim at best, and based on a cracked foundation of perjury by a neighbor.

Miranda wanted me on death row alongside Melvin. And from the look she gives me as she steps up to take the third chair, the chair I'd been wondering about . . . she still does.

The contrast between us is stark. While we're both white women, my hair's dark, my clothes plain and serviceable. She has upswept hair the color of pale gold, expensive jewelry, and she's wearing a designer business suit. She looks television-ready, down to her pitch-perfect makeup.

She doesn't even look at me, though I'm staring at her. She accepts Howie Hamlin's handshake and sits down in the chair with elegance and ease. "Thank you for inviting me to be on this morning, Mr. Hamlin," she says. "And for hearing our side. The families of the victims of Melvin and Gina Royal appreciate your outreach."

I need to get up and walk away.

She doesn't acknowledge my presence in the slightest. I don't have any idea how to ignore hers. The whole world has taken on an eerie, whispering unreality, as if I've sunk deep into the ocean.

"Of course. And the group you represent is called . . ."

"The Lost Angels," she says. "After the children, sisters, mothers, and more-distant relatives and friends that were taken from us."

"I understand that the Lost Angels have come up with the funding to launch the filming of a full documentary that you say will fully explain this case. But with Melvin Royal dead, and Ms. Proctor completely exonerated, what benefit do you see coming from this expense?"

I want to scream, throw something, get the hell off this stage, but I can't. I need to *listen*. Howie Hamlin, whether he intends to or not, is doing me a huge favor by alerting me that the Lost Angels—a group I haven't heard from in a long time—is active and working. I'd really thought they'd had enough, had moved on with their grief and their lives. But apparently not.

"Well, obviously we're not interested in a new criminal trial; Mrs. Royal was acquitted by a jury of her peers," Miranda says. "What we do believe in is the court of public opinion, which has been so incredibly effective in other miscarriages of justice when the guilty go unpunished. We will be laying out our full case for the public, in the form of this new, in-depth documentary that goes deep into the life of Gina Royal."

"Is this documentary finished?"

"It's just beginning," Miranda says, and turns her attention suddenly on me. The hatred in her eyes is just exactly the same intensity it was on the day she sat in the courtroom as I was acquitted and released. I haven't seen her since then, but it's like no time has passed at all.

This is all so monstrous that for a moment I can't even quite believe what I've heard. I can't move. I can't think. I just stare at this woman, who seems otherwise so *normal*, and I can't fathom how someone could be this . . . obsessed. For *years*. "You can't do this," I say. "You can't tear my life, the lives of my children, apart like this. Again."

"I'm not," Miranda says. "I'm simply funding a documentary, which will be released to the internet and film festivals all over the world when we're done. It's . . . a labor of love, if you will. To honor your husband's victims. Our children. And I look forward to hearing *your* opinion, Mrs. Royal. I think you'll quite like the actress we have playing you in the dramatic re-creations."

She wants a scene. She's here to provoke one. To make me lose my shit and choke her right here on this stage, with Howie Hamlin and half the state of Tennessee as the horrified witnesses. I need to play this game, and play it well.

So I sit back. "I'll look forward to it," I say. "And I'll be glad for the chance to put out my own statements correcting any inaccuracies. And as you probably know, not all the family members are on your side."

"No," Miranda agrees. "I'm afraid some of them believe in your particular brand of victimhood. It's too bad, really." She's probably talking about Sam, but she's being careful; the last thing she wants is to attempt to smear him right now. It would make her look a lot less legitimate, and a lot more vindictive.

"It's too bad that you haven't been able to find a positive way out of your own grief, Mrs. Tidewell," I say, and I mean it. "I'm sorry for what happened to your daughter, and I wish you could find peace with the justice that was already served. Her killer is dead."

17

"One of them," she snaps. "One to go." She recognizes that she's stepped on the line, if not over it, and she makes a conscious effort to put tears in her eyes, and put a hand over her mouth. A perfectly overwhelmed grieving mother, if you're not watching closely. "Forgive me, Mr. Hamlin. This is harder than I thought."

"Are you all right, Mrs. Tidewell?" Howie asks, as if he cares; he has tissues at the ready, and she dabs lightly at her eyes, careful not to smudge. "If this is too hard for you, we can take a break."

"What if it's too hard for *me*?" I ask him. I'm aware I'm angry, but I can't out-delicate Miranda Tidewell; she was born to manipulate, and I've never mastered that particular skill. "This woman spearheaded a movement to put my life and the lives of my children at risk from forces she has no hope of controlling, and she's threatening to do it again!"

"I'm not threatening anything," Miranda says. Her voice is even trembling.

What a brave woman, people at home will be thinking. While I look like an angry, coldly vindictive bitch.

"I'm just stating that we're making a documentary about our lost loved ones, and investigating the full scope of the case."

"Please bear in mind, ladies, that I'm not taking a side," Howie says, and his tone reminds me of a greasy tub of used lard my grandmother used to keep on the stove.

I can't help it. I snap.

"I don't have a side! I have the *truth!*" I half shout it at him. I can't keep it together anymore. "You brought me on this program to talk about the harassment of my family, and instead, you've given time and space to a woman who will do anything to destroy me and my kids. No, you don't get to pretend that's a *side*. That's not why I came here."

"Ms. Proctor—"

"No!" I stand up, unclip the microphone, yank it down my shirt, and throw the thing into the chair. I want to throw it in his face. "I'm done."

The camera tracks me as I charge off the riser and out of the glare of the lights. I want to shove the computer-driven machine out of my way, but I'm sure that would mean fines or charges, so I dodge it and head straight for the greenroom. I slam the door open and look at my two kids—my two beautiful, wonderful children, who are staring at me openmouthed. There are three other people in the greenroom now too: an African American man and woman and a white woman, all dressed for camera appearances. The black couple looks distraught and not sure what to make of what just happened. Behind me, Howie Hamlin is apologizing to viewers, and promising to continue the interview as soon as Mrs. Tidewell feels able. He cuts to a commercial, leans back to peruse some notes, and says, "Awesome. Mrs. Tidewell, I'll keep you for two more minutes; then we'll go to the Whites. Erin, have them ready."

The Whites. I remember his introduction at the beginning. These, then, must be the parents of Ellie White, the missing six-year-old. It's been days since she disappeared, driven off by a fake chauffeur in what was evidently a well-planned and professional abduction.

"I'm sorry," I tell them, and then wonder if they want anything from me, even sympathy. After that horror show, maybe not. They don't answer. I don't even know if they hear me, really.

"What the hell happened?" Lanny finally blurts. Her eyes are huge, her face pale even under the too-pale makeup she still favors. "Mom? Is that woman one of the mothers of . . . ?"

"It's all right, baby," I tell her. "Let's go. Right now."

Connor hasn't made a sound, but he comes to me and puts his arm around me. He's had a growth spurt in the past few months, and he comes up to my shoulder now. Lanny's still taller than he is, but not by that much.

I want them out of here while Miranda is still on the air, unable to pursue. I nod to the Whites; the woman with them—middle-aged, with a utilitarian hairstyle and practical pantsuit—nods back. She studies me as I move my kids out of the greenroom and grab my bag on the way out the door.

I'm dialing my phone before we even hit the outer door. A staffer tries to waylay me, probably to persuade me to go back into the gladiatorial pit of idiocy, and I stiff-arm him out of the way and don't listen to a word he says.

Then we're outside, and Sam's picking up on the other end of the phone. "Done already?" He sounds surprised.

"You weren't watching?"

"I went to get coffee. What happened?"

"Tell you in the car. We'll meet you at the end of the driveway," I say, and we head down the slight slope of the walkway at a good clip.

As we do, I see that the giant monitor on the front of the broadcast building is silently playing the *Howie Hamlin Show* with closed-captioning beneath the action. There must be a time delay, because apparently Hamlin is just now apologizing to the audience for my abrupt departure. I'm sure the next step—because Hamlin's staff will have done their homework—is to let Miranda talk about how suspicious my behavior is. About the dead young women found last year floating in Stillhouse Lake, right outside my front door.

About how I got away with murder . . . except that it wasn't me. It was a man who wanted to frame me at the orders of my ex. Not that they'll ever believe that.

I shouldn't have to defend my very existence. My horrible past. The scars on my body and soul.

I can't believe I let myself get pulled into doing the show. I've let my kids down. I'm fighting tears, shaking. I thought I was going to end all our problems, and instead I've just made it another sideshow.

My phone rings as we round the curve. I see Sam's truck idling down at the end of the sidewalk with his emergency flashers blinking. I answer without taking my eyes off our escape route.

"Yes?"

"Ms. Proctor, this is Dana Reyes, the assistant producer of the *Howie Hamlin Show*. I'm so sorry that came off as such a surprise; we certainly didn't intend for it to be that confrontational." *Liar.* "Please come back to the set. We'll have the next segment set up for you alone, and I promise, we'll focus solely on your story"—I practically hear her check her notes—"about the stalking of your family. Obviously, we apologize if you felt offended by—"

I hang up on her. We pile into the pickup, and Sam turns the flashers off and pulls into traffic. It's a beautiful afternoon in Knoxville, Tennessee, hot and clear, the sky an intense blue. Sam is sending me cautious looks. He doesn't want to ask. I don't want to volunteer. The kids are sitting behind us in the extended cab, and they're uncharacteristically quiet too. Shocked, as I am, that such a nice day has turned so completely toxic.

What did I just do? I think. From Howie's lead-in about the *conversations on the internet*, Miranda's been stirring trouble for a while. I let the onslaught of reporters distract me from keeping track of all the threats out there, and that was my mistake. I didn't know that this was building against me, against *us*. But I should have.

Conspiracy theories have been multiplying insanely for years now, ever more ridiculous and far-fetched. Chemicals in contrails. Antivaxxers. Climate-change deniers. And all those are almost precious compared to the toxic horror of the 9/11 and school-shooting truthers who reduce the worst nightmare of any parent's life to fakery, and rip the survivors' lives apart.

Trust Miranda Tidewell to realize that it's just the right environment to destroy us with a minimum of effort. Make a slanted documentary, launch some outrageous claims, find something that *feels* true about them, and sell it hard and often. The delusional and the emotionally disturbed will find something in it to comfort them. The lazy will rely on it as unlikely but *possible*. And in a year or two, the lazy will convince themselves "better safe than sorry" and pass it along as truth.

She's smart to do it this way. A documentary—even peddling half truths and lies—has a certain amount of built-in credibility.

People will believe it because the same mind-set insists that my innocence, my horror and grief, is just an act. That I had to know, be part of it. Because if they had to admit it was real, that they could be vulnerable to the same terrifying, random events that hit me like a wrecking ball . . . that's far too frightening.

Better to fight an imaginary demon than face real ones.

The more I think about it, the angrier I get. I *do* want to go back into the studio, and I want to rip that smug host's ears off with the volume of my yelling.

That's a good reason not to go back.

"Hey. You okay?" Sam's voice is quiet, and it steadies me out of the vibrating rage and into something a little less violent.

"No," I say. "It was an on-air ambush. I suppose you know Miranda Tidewell."

I see him stiffen. The glance he throws me is wide-eyed and shocked.

"Holy shit," Sam says. "She was in the studio? *With you?*"

"Absolutely. She's saying the Lost Angels group is making a documentary," I tell him. "About me. I suppose they can't avoid dragging you into it too."

"Oh my God." Sam looks absolutely wrecked. I wonder if he's met Miranda; he might have, after coming back from Afghanistan. He'd missed my trial and acquittal, so he came into the horror show late in the game. Miranda would have wanted him on her side . . . and I remember with an uneasy twinge that Sam *was* on that side for a while. At least the side of those who believed I was guilty. "Okay. We need to get out of here and go straight home." If he wants to tell me *I told you so*, he holds back, for which I'm deeply grateful. He'd warned me not to rely on the goodwill of television personalities. He'd been right.

I'd promised the kids a fun day in Knoxville after the show. But I know that ship has sailed; the last thing I want to do is have them vulnerable out in public, with at least some percentage of the city on alert for us after that disaster. Some jerk won't be able to resist the bait, and I am *not* having my kids harassed. "Yes," I agree. "Sorry, guys. I know I promised we'd stay the afternoon, but—"

"You're looking out for us," Lanny says. Connor, predictably, doesn't say anything. "We get it. But, Mom . . . we can handle things." She says that with the absurd confidence of a fifteen-year-old, and I'm terrified that she means it.

"Well, I can't handle things right now," I say, because that way I'm not insulting either of them by pretending that they haven't been through hell and back. "I know this is a long trip for nothing. I'm sorry. I really didn't see this coming." I should have. If I'd been on guard, watching the internet like I should have . . .

"It's okay," my son finally says. "We understand."

That's sweeter than I deserve, and suddenly I'm even angrier that there are people out there treating us like paper targets. My kids are as real, and as incredible, as they come. And I will fight for them to the end.

Sam says, "How about some ice cream for the road?"

"Ice cream!" Connor says, suddenly animated. "Oreo ice cream?"

"Whatever you want, my dude," Sam says. "Lanny?"

I look into the rearview mirror. She's wrinkling her nose, but she says, "Sure." A concession. "Mom? Are we back at DEFCON One, or what?"

"I don't know," I tell her. "Sweetie, I just don't know. But for now, I think we have to be very, very careful."

◆ ◆ ◆

We make the drive back to Stillhouse Lake and our house without incident, though I'm hyperalert for anything. The ice cream is good, and Connor is in an expansive mood after wolfing down both his and half his sister's; I'd worry about his eating habits, but the morning pastry is an anomaly, and my son's metabolism keeps him rail-thin anyway. He's putting on height and muscle, a process that's slow now, but I can see that it'll accelerate soon. Good. It's an unfortunate fact of our lives: I need my kids to grow up faster than normal. That's been true since the day our lives blew up. Burn in hell, Melvin.

The past few years haven't been easy for Lanny and Connor. Or me. But I'd thought we were easing into some kind of peace, finally. We had Sam, who was as fiercely protective of them as I was, who'd followed me up into the wilderness to win them back. We had a home. We had at least a tentative kind of acceptance from friends and some of the neighbors.

But after this . . . I don't know. I just don't.

"Let me out here," I tell Sam. "I'll get the mail. You guys get dinner going, okay?"

"Okay, but you know this means you lose your vote."

"You hold my proxy vote," I say. "Something healthy?"

"Boo," my kids say in chorus. I roll my eyes and wave them on up the hill.

I used a pretext of checking the mail, but as I stand there, I pull out my phone and dial. When the answering service picks up on the other end, I tell them I need an immediate callback from Dr. Marks. They're cool and professional, the people in that office; they've heard it all. I suppose I should have put more distress into the message, but Dr. Marks knows me. She'll understand the message.

It's only a few minutes later when the call comes. Katherine Marks. "Gwen," she says, and as always, her voice is crisp, calm, oddly soothing. "How'd the television appearance go today?"

"Did you watch?"

"No, I'm afraid I couldn't. I had clients."

"Well . . ." I shift a little, reluctant to admit it now that I'm actually on the phone with her. "Not well. I had the . . . the thing we talked about."

"You reacted to the camera?"

"Yes." Paradoxically, the second I admit it, all the memories come tumbling back. I thought I was past this, though Dr. Marks had warned me that this particular kind of post-traumatic stress might keep rebounding on me. It goes deep. That day and night at Killman Creek, I'd believed, really believed, that I was going to die as Melvin Royal's victim. Tortured to death for an audience paying to see it happen, and all of it, *all of it*, happening in front of the unblinking eye of a video camera. "I kept seeing it all over again. I couldn't . . . I couldn't control it."

"Do you want to come see me?"

"I can't," I say. What I mean is, *I don't want to.* I want to hide here, at home with my family. "I was hoping you might be able to just . . ."

"Talk you through it?" she finishes, just a little wryness in the tone. "You've been remarkably reluctant to dig deep into this. Are you saying you're ready to do that now?"

"Yes," I say. What I really mean is, *No.* Or, *I don't know if I can.* I close my eyes. The breeze is warm and damp as it rushes over me, and I breathe in slowly, then out in a rush.

I open the door to the memory, and the first thing I see is my exhusband, Melvin Royal, lying next to me, smiling at me as I wake up. I'm *there*. I feel the crowding, heavy Louisiana humidity. Smell the rotting wood of the house. The damp, stiff nightgown sticking to my skin belongs to a dead woman.

I feel the shackles biting into my wrists.

No. NO.

"Gwen?"

I open my mouth. Nothing comes out. I turn from the memory, shove it deep, slam a mental door and lock it with a cartoonishly large imaginary padlock. But I still see his Cheshire-cat grin, and the glassy dead eye of the camera watching me.

I watched him beat a woman to death. Beat her until there was nothing left of her. I can't go back there.

"I'm sorry," I tell her. My voice sounds small and defeated. "I can't—"

"It's all right," Dr. Marks says. "You pushed too fast. Let it go. Step back. Listen to your heartbeat. Breathe. You don't have to do this until you're ready, and you'll feel it. Until then, you need to protect yourself from something that hurts. There's no shame in that."

I do as she says. I'm almost panting, but as I slow down, I'm back here, at Stillhouse Lake. The air is familiar. The fresh smell of the trees cuts the memory of rancid decay. I open my eyes and stare at the peaceful, soft ripples of the lake.

I'm not there. But in a way I never left. Maybe I'm not ready to leave it behind yet.

"I'm sorry," I tell her again. "I just—I thought I could do it today. But I almost lost it."

"Almost," she says. "But you didn't. You need to forgive yourself for human weakness. No one's strong all the time."

I need to be, though. I have enemies, just as much now as ever. Strength is the only thing that stands between those faceless threats and my children.

I make an appointment with her in two weeks. We'll sit for an hour, and I'll try to get this poison out of me. But today's not the day.

When I hang up, it's not quite sundown, just a shady late afternoon, and I enjoy the silence for a minute before I head to the mailbox standing at the bottom of the drive. It's painted a cheery yellow with flowers on the lid, and though the kids wanted to put our names on it, I told them no, very firmly. I let them sign the work with their initials. I figured that was a compromise. I focus on the painting, on the peace it represents, and I tell myself that I'll get through this.

I pull the door down and see a blur just before I hear a rattling hiss. Instinct makes me jump back just before the snake strikes. I take several fast, stumbling steps away; snakes can reach almost their full body length, and this one misses me by a few inches, retracts, and begins to slither angrily into a knot inside the box.

A snake. In my mailbox.

I try to control my racing heartbeat and instant shakes. It's a nasty-looking bastard, mottled gray and brown like the forest floor, with the distinctive head of some kind of viper. I don't know snakes, but I know if they rattle, it can't be good. I don't know if I've let out a scream. Probably.

I dial the Norton police officer I know best—Kezia Claremont, one of the few people I trust with my kids—and must reach her in the car, because her voice comes in close and tinny, rumbled by road noise. "Hey, Gwen. What's up?"

"There's a snake in my mailbox." My voice sounds remarkably flat. "I think it's some kind of rattlesnake."

"*What?*"

"Rattlesnake. In my mailbox." I glance around and grab a fallen branch that's lying nearby, making sure I look for any friends the snake might have first. I use the stick to flip the door of the mailbox shut, trapping the snake inside . . . and then I begin to wonder if this branch might have already been used for this very purpose. Too late to worry about fingerprints, if that was even possible to get from rough wood. "My kids could have opened that, Kez. Jesus *Christ.*"

"Is it poisonous?"

"It *rattled.*"

"Are you bitten?"

"No. No, I don't think so." Now that the adrenaline is starting to recede, I feel sick and woozy. I check my hands and arms for any bites, but I'm clean. "I'm okay. But someone needs to come get this thing out."

"Okay, here's what I want you to do: keep that box shut. Tape it shut if you need to. I'm sending a specialist to come get it." There's a pause. The road noise lessens. "You think someone put it in there? Deliberately?"

"The box was shut when I got here, Kez. And the mail was inside. That snake arrived *after* the mail. Unless vipers have figured out how to close doors behind them, it sure didn't seal itself in there on its own."

Kezia's quiet after that for a few seconds. I hear clicks; she's switched over to texting. I can hear the distraction in her voice as she replies. "Okay, here's what we're going to do. I've got the snake guy and forensics dispatched. As soon as the snake's gone, forensics is going to process that mailbox. If we're lucky, somebody's left us a print."

I can't imagine anyone fool enough to do that, but she's right—it's worth a shot. "Okay," I tell her. "I'll wait here until they arrive."

"I'm on my way."

Lanny comes back down the hill as the vivid blue sky fades to faint orange above me, and the trees give up their daytime green and become sharp black points. The wind's died down, and the lake is still. Most of the boats are gone.

I'm standing six feet from the mailbox, and I don't take my eyes off it.

"Mom?" Lanny says.

"Go back in the house," I tell her. I'm staring at the mailbox, maybe a little obsessively. "I'll be there in a bit. I'm waiting for someone."

"Uh, okay?" She doesn't know exactly what I'm doing, or what to ask. "Should I go ahead and start the chicken or what?"

"Yes," I tell her. "Go ahead. Thanks, honey."

"Okay." She doesn't leave. "Mom, are you okay?"

"I'm fine." She frowns at me. "Honey, I just . . . I need some time, okay? I need to work through some things. You go on. Tell Sam I'm okay." Because I know Sam will be down here next.

She knows damn well I'm not telling the whole truth—and I'm not, because I need to keep her safe—but she goes, finally. I like that instinct in her, to question everything. It will serve her well in the future, even with me. And I'm glad she didn't stay. I'm very aware—hideously aware, as night begins to fall—that I'm standing out here alone, exposed, and a snake in my mailbox is hardly the only threat out here. What if the person who put it there comes back? What if they're behind me *right now*?

I give in. I take a fast look around as my daughter heads up the hill. No one around. No threats I can see.

But it doesn't mean they aren't there. Waiting.

2

GWEN

The man arrives first about ten minutes later. He's a rough specimen who looks like he's just spent weeks out in the woods, and I don't like it. Or him. Or any of this. He says, "Hey. I'm here for that snake."

"ID," I say. He blinks.

"What?"

"Show me some ID. I don't know you, and I'm armed." I've set my feet in a solid fighting stance, centered my weight, and loosened my knees. I don't know if he recognizes that, but he eyes me warily. I wonder if he's thinking I'm paranoid.

Well, he'd be right.

"Okay." He holds up both hands. "Sure. Reaching for ID, okay?"

"Slowly."

He does, never taking his eyes off me. He reaches back behind him, and I'm bluffing about the gun because I've left it in the goddamn truck's locked glove compartment, and right now I'm kicking myself for that, but when his hand reappears—slowly—it's holding a wallet. He opens it and pulls out a thick white business card.

"On the ground," I tell him. He crouches and puts it down halfway between us, as far as he can reach.

I step over and pick it up in one quick, fluid dip, then raise it so I can read it while still watching him.

It's a nice one, pure white with official black lettering and raised ink. Professor Greg Maynard. He works for the University of Tennessee. Goes to show, you can't judge a woodsy hermit by his looks. He's a full tenured professor of biology. How odd.

"Snake?" he asks again.

I point to the mailbox. "Sorry about that," I tell him. "I just—I don't know who did this. You understand?"

"Maybe it was just meant as a joke?"

"Open it."

He gets a cotton sack and a stick with a hook on the end and flips the box open. The snake strikes. The professor doesn't even flinch, but then, he's standing at the exact safe distance. "Timber rattler," he says. "Wow. Cool. You were lucky, that is definitely not a joke. Not a good one, anyway." I watch, fascinated, as he coaxes the snake out of the mailbox, and it winds down the metal pole of the box to the dirt. From there, he efficiently pins the snake down just behind the head, and picks it up barehanded with an amount of calm I find amazing. The snake rattles and thrashes a bit, but it goes into the bag, and he cinches it shut and ties it securely.

I almost let my guard down until it runs through my mind that it would take someone with these exact skills to put a timber rattler *in* the mailbox.

"Are those local around here?" I ask him.

He nods. "Sure, out in the woods. Sometimes I find one of them down this far, but it's not too normal. We see more cottonmouths and copperheads around the water." Maynard's thorough. He examines the inside of the mailbox with the light of his cell phone before saying, "Okay, you're clear. I'll get this little beauty back to my lab."

"Lab," I repeat.

"I'm a herpetologist. I milk snakes. That's how we make the anti-venin," he says. "There's always a demand for it out here in the country. You see any more of them, or any other kind of viper for that matter, you give me a call. I'll find him a good home back in the woods where he won't bother anyone once we're done with him."

I nod, still not taking my eyes off him. Professor or not, he's now my primary suspect. Though what the hell he'd get out of scaring the shit out of me, or seeing me bitten, I have no idea. He doesn't seem to have any personal grudge. I'm not getting any vibe like that from him at all.

He's loading the snake into his truck when the forensics team—well, one middle-aged guy in a baggy windbreaker—rolls up in an old Jeep. The forensics guy shows me ID without me asking for it, in a move so natural he probably does it in his sleep. Speaking of that, he looks dog-tired, but he asks me intelligent questions and writes things down, and he's dusting the mailbox for fingerprints, when Kezia Claremont pulls up just a couple of minutes after. She's driving her personal car without the lights and sirens, and I'm glad about that; our neighbors are surely already gawking at the parade of activity. I'd rather not give them more to gossip about if possible.

"Hey, Beto," Kez says to the forensics guy, and he waves without looking up. She's still wearing what I think of as her work clothes: a plain navy pantsuit and a white blouse, with her detective shield clipped to her waistband. Gun concealed under her jacket. If she'd been home already, she'd have swapped out for jeans and a comfortable T-shirt. "Snake's gone, I guess."

"Off to a happy home, according to—" I check the business card. "Professor Maynard. What do you know about him?"

"Why?" she asks, then answers her own question. "Skill sets. Right." She shakes her head. "Take him off your list. There are at least two dozen hillbillies around here who handle snakes just fine, and they're more likely to be mad at you."

There's no point in asking why, but I do anyway. "Any particular reason?"

She shrugs. "Well, let's start with you being from out of town and go from there."

"I've been living at the lake for—"

"I'm an outsider, and me and Dad moved to this place upward of twenty years back," she says. "If you weren't born in these parts, you're not from here. For some that's enough. Then add on the rumors, the internet bullshit . . . I'll be honest, it could be anybody."

"Great." I'd been hoping to end this day less paranoid, not more.

Kez moves forward to study the mailbox. "It fastens securely, right?"

"Yes."

"No way that thing got in there accidentally."

"Nope. And it could have bitten Sam, or the kids. It was just good luck I was the one who opened it. If it had been Connor or Lanny . . ."

"It wasn't," she says. "So let's focus on what did happen, not what didn't. At worst, someone just tried to kill you, though I expect the county DA would plead that right down to criminal mischief. He isn't your biggest fan."

"No kidding," I say. "I'm surprised he hasn't indicted me for standing here too long."

"Well, you know what they say about a good DA: he can get a grand jury to indict a ham sandwich. Lucky that ours just isn't that good."

I have to laugh, because Kezia doesn't usually smack-talk law enforcement, but she has a special contempt for District Attorney Elroy Compton. So do I. He's a silver-haired white man whose trial record consists almost entirely of convicting black defendants in a county racked with a mainly Caucasian-driven meth and prescription-drug trade. He pleads out the white offenders, naturally. They're "good people at heart," and other such shit, no matter how violent and depraved their crime. Their church members will vouch for them. Their parents are fine Christians. The usual refrain.

It reminds me painfully of those years I blindly believed in my monstrous ex-husband, unable—or unwilling—to see the truth right in front of me. Sometimes I think half the world has sunk into the same state of denial. And that makes me angry.

"Any idea who'd want to scare you like that?" Kezia asks.

"Are you serious? Most of Norton still believes I got away with the *local* murders, for a start. And that's not even counting all the trolls, the stalkers, the families of Melvin's victims . . ."

"Criminal hackers from the Absalom collective who slipped the net," she finishes. "Yeah, I know. I was hoping for a more specific enemy, because *pretty much everybody* doesn't narrow it down that much."

"I know. But right now, it's what I've got."

She taps her pen against the pad of paper she's using for her notes. "Yeah, not sure you helped with what went on TV today. What about the woman? The one from your interview?"

I don't want to believe that, but the fact is, the most die-hard fanatical harassers were, for a while, the family members of Melvin's victims. Including Miranda.

"Miranda Tidewell? She might put arsenic in a mint julep, but snake handling? I really don't think so," I say. "But . . . she might hire someone to do it. Just to scare us."

"She did seem like she was on a mission to prove you were . . ."

"A monster? Yes. She's always been, since my trial. I just thought—well, I hoped—that she'd moved on."

"These days we've got obsessive freaks for everything," she says. "Especially if it's complicated and stupid. Sorry. Hate to say it, but, Gwen—"

"Yeah, look out for myself. I know. I'm on that."

She studies me. "You forgot to carry, didn't you?"

"I didn't forget. I left it in the truck while I came to get the mail."

"Truck's up there," Kez says. "And you're a sitting duck out here, you realize that?"

"I did once I was stuck watching the snake."

She nods. "Good. Don't do that again. Most jackasses around here, I wish they'd leave their damn guns in the safe. But not you. You actually do need one. So make sure you have it."

I give her a smile—thin, because I know she's right, and I'm smarting a little from that. "Message received," I tell her. I realize how dark it's gotten. She usually walks her father uphill to his cabin well before this. "Did you get Easy home already?"

"Yeah, that's why I wasn't here first," she says. "Sorry, but I had to see him safe."

"Good. And you're heading home?"

"To Javier's," she says. Javier is her lover, maybe even (though I haven't asked) her long-term partner, but they still live apart. "Hey, Beto? You done?"

"Done," he says. He's closing up his kit. "Didn't get a lot; a few good prints, but they'll probably be either the family's or the postal worker's. Maybe we'll get lucky."

"Maybe," Kezia says. "Thanks, man. Get home safe."

"You too."

Her gaze suddenly shifts and focuses as he moves to his truck. She's looking uphill, and I follow her gaze to see Sam heading down toward us.

"So you've got some explaining to do," she says. "Good luck, girl, I'm rolling. Javier's waiting dinner." She's gone before he gets there, and he watches her drive away as he comes to a stop just a couple of feet away from me.

"So," he says, "Lanny said you lied about being okay, next thing I know Kez is here plus two more cars . . . What the hell is going on?"

I sigh. I'd been hoping to avoid this. "Let's go inside," I tell him. "Better I catch everybody up at once."

I make a detour to the truck and retrieve my firearm; the instant I have it, I feel steadier. I know that's wrong; the gun doesn't make me any safer, just more capable of retaliating. PTSD, lying again. I'm going to have to train myself out of using a weapon as a comfort blanket. It's a necessary evil for me, but that shouldn't mean I *need* it.

"Gwen?" Sam's concerned. I give him a smile I don't really feel.

"Ready," I say. I'm really not.

As soon as we come into the house, I lock the door and set the alarm to *stay*. Lanny stands with her arms crossed, hipshot. Connor even looks up from the book he's reading. They're waiting for an explanation too.

"How's it coming?" I ask, trying to sound normal. It doesn't work. Lanny keeps frowning at me, Connor shakes his head, and Sam's look says that I am failing miserably at reassurance. "Okay," I say. "So there was a snake in the mailbox."

"A *what?*" Lanny blurts out. I've surprised the frown off her face. Sam stops stirring.

"What kind of snake?" Connor asks. "Was it a copperhead? I've seen a copperhead before."

"Not a copperhead. I don't want you to worry . . ." My voice fades, and I realize that I have to do this. "I'm lying—I *do* need you to worry. I need you to understand that after the day we had, things are not going to be the same. You need to be extra careful. And from now on, Sam and I will get the mail. Okay?"

"Mom, we're always extra careful," Lanny says. "Come on. You know that."

But they're not. *They're not.* And it makes me feel sick all over again to think about Connor opening that mailbox, or Lanny, or even Sam, though his reaction time is even better than mine. My kids think they're paranoid enough.

They never can be. Not enough to prevent everything that might come for them, and that overconfidence could be deadly.

Sam's watching me very steadily. "Hey. Kids. Give us a minute, okay? Connor, go stir the beans. And you owe me a salad, kid."

"Okay." For me, Connor would have sighed as if the weight of the world had landed on him, but Sam just gets a compliant mood and instant acceptance. I envy that.

Lanny checks her phone. "The chicken's almost done," she says. "Like, three minutes."

"Then take it out when it's ready," Sam tells her, and disarms and unlocks the front door. "Gwen?"

I follow him out. I don't like being on the porch right now, and I turn out the lights. We're plunged into darkness until my eyes begin to adjust.

"What's going on?" he asks me.

"I don't know," I say. "Snake in the mailbox has me on edge, obviously. So does what happened today. I just feel—"

"Exposed?" he asks. Puts his arms around me. "I'm sorry. I really am. I know you didn't want to do that damn show in the first place, and I'm sorry I didn't warn you off it harder. I had a bad feeling, and I'm sorry to be right. I still didn't think they'd dare pull that, not after all the agreements."

"Neither did I, or I never would have been there." I relax into his warmth. His strength. I can disarm for a moment here with him, even if it is out in the open. "Maybe we'll get lucky. Maybe somebody left a fingerprint on the mailbox."

"You never answered the kids," he says, and tips my chin up. It's dark, but not dark enough that I miss the look in his eyes. "What kind of snake was it?"

"Timber rattler."

"Jesus, Gwen!"

"I know." I rest my head against his shoulder. "I'm fine. The snake's fine, even. No harm done."

He has a lot to say about that, I can sense it, but he holds back. I can tell he brought me out here to talk about something, but I doubt it's the snake in the mailbox. Odd. He usually doesn't hesitate to bring up uncomfortable things.

I think about how strange this is. Every once in a while, it hits me: Sam is the brother of one of Melvin's victims. By any logic at all, he shouldn't be here, and we shouldn't have . . . this. It didn't start that way; I didn't trust him, and he believed deep down that I was guilty. It's taken time and work and pain to get here to this moment of trust, of peace. And it's still fragile, even though we've built that bridge. It isn't steel. It's glass. And sometimes there are cracks.

After a long moment of silence, he says, "Listen, about Miranda Tidewell. Did she . . . did she say what she was really planning?"

"Just some kind of documentary. For release everywhere, I guess, or as wide as she can manage. I'm going to guess it won't be flattering." I try to make that sound light, but it isn't. It can't be. Miranda Tidewell is filthy rich and brutally angry, and if she can't take an actual hatchet to my life, she'll do it with a metaphorical one instead. She understands the power of the medium.

"Gwen." He moves his hands from my waist and cups my face, a wonderfully gentle gesture, something that makes me catch my breath. "How are we going to do this? Tell me. Tell me how we protect the kids from this."

"I don't know," I tell him. I feel tears prickle at the corners of my eyes, and blink hard to keep them from forming. "Maybe we can't. Maybe we have to help them learn to live with it instead."

"God," he says, "I hope you're wrong. I really do."

When he kisses me, it's sweet and gentle, with an ember of heat beneath it. A little desperation too. I feel that. We're always, ever standing on the edge of a cliff with some long, dark drop below. Right now that cliff feels especially precarious.

"Food's ready," he says. "How scared do we all need to be?"

"Very," I say. "I need you and the kids to be on guard." I hate that. I hate taking away the small bit of normality we've carved out for the kids. But they're going to have to understand what might be coming.

We lay it out over the dinner. It's rosemary chicken, my favorite. That was sweet of them. The chicken's delicious, the beans done just right; the salad is a mess but my kids are trying. None of us really taste any of it, I think, as we talk about the possibility that Stillhouse Lake may get more and more hostile for us. We talk about awareness, and staying with friends and adults we can trust. We talk about what to do if things go wrong. It's not a fun conversation, but it's necessary.

The kids don't protest. I see Lanny's mutinous anger; she's just gotten to an age where she wants her life to get bigger, not smaller. Connor's less bothered. He's been introverted since well before this, and I don't see that changing anytime soon.

But I have to keep close watch on my daughter.

They ask to be excused. I let them go with their plates half-finished, and Sam and I clean up the kitchen. I keep glancing over to be sure I've set the alarm to *stay*. He notices, but he doesn't comment. I wash the plates and pass them over, and he dries and puts them away. It's done in a comfortable, easy silence, but my mind keeps going back to the studio, the frozen horror, the way I lost it on live television. It's like touching a hot stove, but I can't stop.

I'm almost grateful for the distraction when the home phone rings. I keep a landline for safety reasons; nine times out of ten it's some recorded voice trying to scam me, but landlines don't go down nearly as fast in a crisis as cell phones, and they're not reliant on either battery or house power.

I feel better having it as a fail-safe.

I reach for the phone, then pull back. I don't recognize the number, so I listen as the recorder catches the call. Old-fashioned, but this way I can screen calls and pick up if I recognize urgency. I've got the volume low, and I'm prepared to walk away. But after the greeting starts, a real human voice on the other end says, "Uh, hi, I'm looking for . . . for somebody named Gwen Proctor?"

I get a sick feeling in my stomach. I've fielded lots of abusive phone calls, of course. Nameless strangers who want to kick me while I'm down, shouting insults. Nameless men who tell me in detail about their fantasy of raping and murdering me, or my children, or both. A creepy more-than-few who tell me they loved me at first sight and knew we were destined to be together, if only I'd just *understand*.

Then that hesitant female voice continues, "Please, I'm begging you. Please answer me. I don't know where else I'm supposed to turn."

And I know it's one of *those* calls.

It started with a random call, the distant friend of a cop who had my number. A woman crying months ago, begging me to tell her what to do because she didn't know how to stay alive. She was the mother of a fourteen-year-old boy who'd abducted, raped, and killed a neighbor's five-year-old. Who'd hidden the body under his bed for three days. She'd found it. Reported it. Turned in her own son to the police.

She hadn't been prepared for the terrifying truth: people blamed her too. Blamed her for raising a killer. Blamed her for not knowing. Not stopping him.

I'd spent an hour trying to help her find ways to deal with what she was going through. In the end I looked up a domestic violence shelter where she could at least hide out for a while. I don't know what happened to her. But she told someone else who'd contacted *her* about me, and how I'd helped. And so on.

For the past three months I've been getting these tragic, disembodied voices begging me for help and answers I don't have. The best I could give most of them was understanding and the cold comfort of knowing they weren't alone in this nightmare.

Sam's watching me, and his expression says *don't*. And he's right, of course. We don't need more trouble. I almost let it go. I can hear her breathing. Hear her choking back a sob.

"Okay, then," she says, and I hear the dull defeat in it. "Sorry I bothered you. I'll hang up now—"

I grab the receiver. "This is Gwen," I say. "What's the problem?"

There's a deeply indrawn breath on the other end of the line. "Sorry," the woman says. "I figured I could get through this without being such a . . . a damn mess. I guess I'm not like you. You seem pretty near made of steel, from what I'm told."

I still have no idea who this is, or what it's about, but I have an instinct that I should listen. "Oh, I'm not, believe me," I tell her. "It's all right. Take your time. What's your name?"

"M-Marlene," she says. "Marlene Crockett. From Wolfhunter." Her accent is pure rural-Tennessee drawl. "It's up around—well, up 'round the backside of nowhere, I guess." She laughs nervously. It sounds like cracking glass. "Never heard of it, right?"

She makes it a question, so I'm honest. "I haven't. What do you need from me, Marlene?"

She doesn't get right to the point. I recognize the tendency; she wants to circle around the point, work up her courage. She tells me about her town, about her frustrations with her job, about the patch of grease she just can't scrub off her wood floor. I wait her out. Sam finishes the dishes. He writes me a note and slides it over. *Got some work to do.* He heads back toward our shared office. We have partner desks in there now, set a decent space away from each other. Sam's both working freelance as a laborer on construction projects, and running a couple of small commercial jobs for a firm out of Knoxville; I'm maintaining an online accounting business that takes a few hours a day, with some graphic design on the side. I'd be more financially secure with a day job, but then again, I like being home with my kids, especially during these epic long, hot summers. And I like the idea that I can—even now—drop everything and run at a moment's notice. It'll take a while for me to gear down from that impulse. If I ever can.

I finally judge that she's winding down, so I cut in. "Marlene? How did you get this number, exactly?"

"A lady said on social media about how you weren't no monster like some say, and you helped her. I asked her if you might help me too. She said you might and gave me your number."

"In the open? On her *social media*?"

"By email," Marlene says. She sounds even more nervous. "Was that wrong?"

At least it wasn't posted on the internet, but still: I need to change this number. Or get rid of the landline completely. "Who was it?"

"Don't know her real name, but she goes by Melissa Thorn."

Melissa and I are going to have a talk. "Okay," I say. "Can you tell me what's wrong?"

I expect her to say something about her boyfriend, her husband, someone else in her family. Even a friend. But she says, "It ain't wrong with *me* exactly. It's more . . . it's more like it's this whole damn town. Well, some people in it, I guess. Though this place here has never been good land. Got blood soaked in it from the jump."

This is going nowhere, and I'm starting to think I'm being played. Maybe she's just a lonely time-waster. "I'm giving you one more minute to tell me what I can do for you. Then I'm gone and I won't take your call again. Understand?"

She pauses. "I understand." But she doesn't go on. Silence stretches. She finally says, all in a rush, "So if something bad's happening around here, what can I do? Can't go to the police, no way. What do you do if you don't trust folks in town?"

"I can help you with some state agencies to call, if that's what you're asking, but you'd better be ready to tell them what your problem really is," I tell Marlene. "First, are you in any physical danger right now?"

"I . . . I don't think so. But it's just . . . it's hard. I don't know what to do about it, or where to go. I just don't want to get myself in worse trouble than I'm already in." She sighs heavily. "I'm a single mother, and my girl, she's a handful, you know? I got no people here. Nobody to help out. I got to be careful. It's real complicated."

It always is complicated, from the inside. People on the outside looking in seem to think it's simple to cut ties, walk away . . . but there are so many ropes holding a person down. Children. Extended family. Friends. Jobs. Money. Obligations. Guilt. And fear, so much *fear*. The most dangerous time in any woman's life is when she's separating from a partner, particularly an abusive one. Women instinctively know that, even if they've never seen the blood-drenched statistics. Sometimes it feels safer to endure the devil you know.

"I know it can feel like you're in a trap with no way out," I tell her. "But that's not true. You always hold the key to your own cage, okay? You just need to find the courage to use it. Is the problem with your husband?"

She sniffles, as if she's on the verge of tears. "No. He's dead."

"A boyfriend? Someone you dated?"

"No."

"Okay." That's pretty new. Most calls I get are about husbands or domestic partners. Occasionally about unknown stalkers. "So specifically, who is threatening you right now?"

"It ain't . . . it ain't threats. Not exactly. And I can't say no names," she says. "It's just . . . if I tell somebody, and it comes back on me and my daughter, it'll be real bad, you know? And if I don't tell nobody . . . I don't know how I live with that."

"I'm sorry," I say. Gently as I can. "But I'm not a therapist, or a lawyer, and whatever you tell me might cause legal problems for you in the future if you've been part of something illegal. Understand? If you want to talk about something that frightens you, but isn't a crime, let me put you in touch with a psychologist or psychiatrist—"

"I'm not going to any *shrink*!" She sounds offended. Small, rural towns haven't exactly embraced talk therapy.

"Okay, if you think it might be criminal, Marlene, why do you think you can't go to the police?" She doesn't answer that. Just silence on the line. "Are you afraid of them?"

"I'm afraid of everything," she says.

"What about the state police?"

She sucks in a breath, then lets it out. "Maybe. Maybe that'd be okay, I guess. Not sure if they'd believe me about this, but I could try."

"Then I urge you to make that call. Sometimes lives can be lost if you wait, and then you have to carry that responsibility forever." My mind is racing to fill in the blanks: Is she talking about a neighbor under threat? A friend? Something else? I can't tell.

"Yeah," she says. I can hear her pacing restlessly. "Yeah, I know that. But this is a small place. Hell, half the town is related. I guess I have to figure this out myself and—" She stops on a dime, and I don't even hear breathing. When she talks again, it's in a hushed, rushed whisper. "I got to go. Sorry."

"Marlene, if you can't tell me what's going on, I don't know how to help you."

"Come up here," she says. "Come up here and I'll show you everything. It ain't far where they buried the wreck. You decide what to do about it." *The wreck?* Buried? That doesn't make any sense.

"You mean, come to Wolfhunter? No. I can't." No way am I going to some isolated rural location. Armed or not, ready for a fight or not . . . No, the risk isn't worth it. Not anymore. "Call the state police. Will you do that?"

She doesn't answer. With a quiet click, she's gone. Call ended. I shake my head as I hang up. It's unsettling, but I don't know what I could have said or done differently. Whatever's going on with her, it's strange, and I can't help but be suspicious. I just found a snake in my mailbox. Now a mysterious caller is trying her best to get me to drive off into the lonely hills.

I'm not getting drawn into a trap. I've got enemies.

Today only confirmed that.

I linger near the phone, waiting for a callback, but it doesn't come. I finally head toward the office. I stop along the way and pop my head into Connor's room; he's reading, which is exactly what I expected, and I don't bother him. It's hardly a surprise to find that Lanny is texting, and she barely glances up when I knock on her open door.

"Hey," she says, "who was it calling?"

"Someone who wanted advice," I say.

Her fingers stumble and pause, and she transfers her attention to me. My daughter's pretty, but more than that, there is character in her face, and strength. A fair bit of sharp stubbornness too. Can't imagine where she gets it. "What did she want?"

"Honestly? I'm really not even sure. She doesn't seem to be in too much trouble, though. Not in fear of her life, at least not enough to really accept help."

"K." She goes back to her glowing screen, thumbs working with furious precision. I love the way she attacks things, with all the intensity of a life-and-death situation. My beautiful Atlanta, never moving at less than full speed. "I hate this, you know." She's talking about the danger, the restrictions, the way her life keeps drawing inward.

"I know," I tell her. "We'll try to make it better."

When I get to the office, I find an open bottle of wine, and a full glass on my desk. Sam's got one of his own. He's got his cell phone cradled between his neck and shoulder as he searches in a drawer for paperwork. I take the glass and mouth *Thank you* as I slip into my own chair. I check my email box.

It's a damn disaster. I suppose I should have expected that, in the wake of the Howie Hamlin debacle, but I hadn't, and seeing the huge increase in abusive, anonymous emails makes me regret having dinner first. I ignore those for now; most are repetitive anyway, like they passed around a script. *Kill yourself, you ugly bitch. Do everybody a favor and join your husband in hell. Start a barbecue and crawl inside.* That kind of thing.

Once I clear those out and into a FOR EVALUATION folder, I get rid of the flood of reporters wanting me to comment on the upcoming documentary. Someone's helpfully signed me up for a Lost Angels newsletter. How nice.

Apart from those, there are four more messages, each containing automated web searches that I've programmed to archive monthly to my in-box. I've slacked off the Sicko Patrol for too long. Obviously. At first I was recovering, and then . . . then I convinced myself that with Melvin gone, Absalom gone, things would just . . . get better. That I didn't need to worry as much anymore.

I was an idiot. And I'm paying for that brief, stupid burst of overconfidence.

I start as far back as I can find and open the report. It's just an archived list of links mentioning either Gwen Proctor, Gina Royal, or any of the other briefly used false names I'd hidden out under. The date is soon after the events at Killman Creek.

Seems normal enough. If you can call mutilation, rape, and death threats normal. And of course, there are a lot of them. Hundreds.

What's more ominous is that when I open each of the reports, I can see the cancerous growth, charted out in ever-proliferating links to videos, discussion boards, new Facebook groups dedicated to stalking me, Twitter hashtags. And that's just on the public side. The dark web is mostly inaccessible to me now; I have a Tor browser that grants me anonymity, but the dark web is a who-do-you-know network, full of shadowy contacts and hidden agendas. I used to rely on the hacker collective known as Absalom to navigate that world, but back then I didn't know who—*what*—Absalom really was, and really wanted. Without that easy access, the searches I can run in the deeper levels of the internet are very limited.

But I can see the surface, and the growing monster: day after day of commenters feeding off one another's fear, paranoia, hate, and easy judgment. There's a link to the Lost Angels website, finally. I click it, but I can only get to the public home page of the site, the one with all the photo montages for each of Melvin's victims. It's difficult for me to come here at all, looking at the calm, smiling, hopeful faces of young women just starting their lives. The innocent babies and children they once were before my ex got his hands on them. I keep scrolling. There's usually a news section at the bottom beneath all this heartbreak where members of the Lost Angels community—families, mostly, though some close friends too—will put updates they feel are important.

This time it isn't just a post recalling a birthday, or a graduation; it's a full press release, dated only a couple of weeks ago.

It announces that filming on a Lost Angels documentary is underway. Not just about the victims, but about the killings themselves. About Melvin Royal.

Most especially, about the woman who might have gotten away with murder: Gina Royal.

I feel sick. I understand their pain, their rage, their need for some kind of relief, and I've never hated them for despising me. The one thing I can be grateful for is that at least so far, there's no mention of Sam in connection to the making of this film.

A significant number of people got on board for this project. Almost ten thousand of them, pledging hundreds of thousands of dollars. It's matched by the nonprofit that Miranda Tidewell started for her murdered child. I feel even sicker, staring at the announcements. And the promise of *more to come soon*.

They're really doing this.

They're really coming for me.

Sam finishes his conversation, and I hear him call my name, but I don't immediately respond. I can't. In an effort to get my mind off the Lost Angels, I've clicked another link. Now I'm staring at the message

47

on my screen that says, OPEN SEASON ON MURDERERS, and it's a surveillance picture of me, Lanny, and Connor laughing together in front of our cabin, unafraid. There's a target drawn over us, and painstakingly photoshopped bullet holes in our bodies.

Sam comes around the desk, and I quickly minimize the picture to the desktop—but not soon enough. He leans over and commandeers the mouse. Brings it up again. Studies the image. I know that silence. Sam's currents run deep, fast, and sometimes dangerous.

"What are you thinking?" I ask him.

"I'm thinking this gets printed out and taken straight to the police," he says. "And to the FBI." We have friends in both places, thankfully. "And I'm thinking that whoever took this was right here, watching you. And I want to know who the hell that is."

"The original photo could have been taken by a journalist," I tell him. "They've been after us from the day Melvin went down." Since I never gave much in the way of interviews, they shot a lot of pictures, usually grainy long-lens shots like this. "It doesn't mean this photoshop hero who changed it has been, or is, anywhere close to us."

"It doesn't mean he isn't either," Sam says. "Sorry. I take this seriously."

"You think I don't? This isn't even the worst of it."

He doesn't quite look at me. "That's what I'm afraid of."

I'm going to have to let him in on all this. I've hesitated, because there are some particularly awful things in my Sicko Patrol file. Things that feel, even now, too intimate to share. But he needs to know. "Okay," I say. "You want to sit down and look at the rest of what I've got?"

I see the flicker of shock go through him. He pulls his chair over and leans forward, elbows on his knees. "Sure," he says. "Let's go."

He thinks he's ready.

But I register the revulsion and horror in his eyes as I scroll.

Nobody's ever really ready. Not for this.

3

SAM

Just knowing that Miranda Tidewell ambushed Gwen on the show this morning was bad enough, but hearing about the documentary she's planning sets off a storm of white noise in my head. I can't process that Miranda Tidewell and Gwen Proctor can occupy, however briefly, the same space. I've held them completely separate in my head, in neat, contained boxes. Never to meet.

But life doesn't work like that, and now that Gwen's told me about the Lost Angels documentary, I feel like I'm starting a slow fall down a deep, dark well. There's an impact coming. And it's going to be deadly.

All I can do for now is pretend it isn't happening. I'll keep living my normal life, my *real* life, for as long as I can. Because what Miranda represents . . . it's dead, as dead to me as Gwen's marriage is to her. I tell myself that, even as I recognize that Melvin's ghost has never stopped haunting either one of us. Dead doesn't mean gone.

Watching the sick parade of trolls and their dark, inventive ways to hurt her . . . I'd like to say that it surprises me. It doesn't, exactly. It feels all too horribly familiar.

By the time we're halfway through, I'm numb to most of it. I'm sure that's her default these days. We agree to cherry-pick the worst offenders and take them in tomorrow to Norton PD; at the very least, Kezia Claremont will be on our side, and Detective Prester, while not the warmest man I've ever met, is fair. He feels a little sympathy for Gwen's situation, and that counts. We should make best efforts to have law enforcement watching our backs right now.

Our little community at Stillhouse Lake doesn't have its own police force, except informally in that Kezia Claremont moved into the neighborhood up the hill and across the lake from us, not far from her dad's place. Ezekiel—Easy, to his friends—Claremont is a charming, feisty old guy who needs the help, though he still insists he doesn't. I stop in every other day or so, have a beer with him down on his jury-rigged and likely illegal deck, pick up things he needs. He's been up on this hill for a long time, no doubt resented by all his rich, white neighbors until the economy tanked, and most of them moved away. We came in after that . . . Gwen, to rehab a trashed house and make it her own. Me, to watch her and prove she wasn't what she said she was.

Except I was wrong. Gwen is exactly what she appears to be. She is one of the most fierce, honest women I've ever met. That wasn't a simple adjustment to make, realizing that, but once I did it, I felt . . . free. Like the rage that had possessed me for so long had lifted.

It scares me to think it might not have left . . . just circled. Maybe all that anger I let loose in the world is still out there, and headed straight back for us.

In the morning, we head for the police.

Norton's a typical southern small town a few miles from Stillhouse Lake, and it's clinging to the edges of an economic hope and prayer. The boarded-up stores tell a story. So do the potholes in the roads. Nobody fools themselves into thinking this town's got a bright future, but they're grimly determined to make it work. I personally like Norton; I like the preservation of the buildings, even if they're standing empty. It's a place that has some style, even if Gwen often thinks of it as a lost cause. She tends to see the darker side. I try to look for the light, or at least, I've been making it a mission lately.

The police headquarters hasn't been substantially remodeled since the eighties, and it's due for it, but at least the parking is generous. When we walk in, we immediately get the look from the woman behind the desk, or rather, Gwen does: blank and suspicious. It isn't that Gwen's a stranger. It's that she's Gwen, and the woman on the other side of that desk knows all about her past.

I lean in and interrupt the staring contest. "Hi. We're here to talk to either Detective Prester or Detective Claremont."

The woman shifts her stare to me. It warms slightly. "And may I say why?"

"It's confidential," I say, and give her a smile. It seems to work. She picks up the phone and dials. Gwen looks at me and rolls her eyes. I shrug. Not everything needs to be a dramatic face-off, particularly not with people we're actively trying to recruit as allies.

In about a minute, Kezia opens the door between the counter and the rest of the police station, and waves us through. She's a polished young African American woman who's lately taken to wearing her hair in a thick, natural Afro around her head, and it looks proudly spectacular, especially out here in the sticks. The individuality of hairstyle contrasts sharply with the conventional tan pantsuit she wears; it almost conceals the shoulder holster. Her badge flashes on her hip as she turns, and I hold the door for Gwen as she follows Kez into the detective area.

It isn't impressive—not surprising, considering the size of Norton. But as in all small, rural towns, this one's battling drug cooking, addiction, and the associated crimes. It doesn't prepare her for the discussion we're about to have.

"I'm guessing this isn't a social call." Kezia gestures us to the worn chairs on the far side of her desk. "About the snake?"

Gwen sighs. "Not entirely. You saw the *Howie Hamlin Show*."

"Yeah," Kezia says. "They kneecapped you live on air. I'm sorry."

"Me too."

"This documentary they were talking about . . ." Kezia leans back for a moment, considering. "They'll be coming here. You get that, right? They'll want town footage, local interest, probably talk to some of the locals who aren't your biggest fans. And there's nothing we can really do about that. You might go to the city and try to get some kind of injunction, but I doubt it'll work."

"Yeah, we didn't come about that," I say when Gwen doesn't answer. "I have news about the snake, though. We found a fingerprint, matched it to Jesse Belldene. Jesse's one of those hillbillies I told you about, good at catching all sorts of critters. The problem is, Jesse says he didn't do it, and a single fingerprint doesn't get us where we need to be to charge him even for criminal mischief." Kezia shakes her head. "The Belldenes are a nasty bunch, and it looks like they've taken a dislike to you. Any reason why . . . ?"

Gwen says she doesn't know. I don't immediately answer, because . . . I think I do. And I think it's my own fault.

I clear my throat. Both of them look at me. It feels like two spotlights hitting me at once. "Belldene," I say. "This Jesse. Does he happen to come to the shooting range much?"

"He did once," Kezia says. "Then he got banned. He came in drunk a couple of weeks ago, and someone on the range took his gun away and laid him out flat when he tried to get it back. He didn't file charges, but I heard they had to fix some teeth. Why?"

I slowly raise my hand. "I'm the one who slammed him face-first into the counter," I tell her. "He was acting crazy and unsafe. Javier was up front or he'd have handled that better. I guess Jesse holds a grudge."

"Wait," Gwen says. "You mean . . . it wasn't about me?"

I raise my eyebrows. I don't remind her that not everything is. She gets the point, and puts a hand to her mouth to cover what I think might be a laugh. I'd told her about the incident when it happened, but when the mountain man—Belldene—had bolted out of the shooting range, I'd never gotten his name. And I didn't know I'd broken his teeth.

Kezia must have caught the relief from Gwen, because she says, "Well, I wouldn't get too comfortable, Sam. The Belldenes sure love to mess with people. I don't expect this will be the last you hear from them."

"Anything you can do about them?"

She shakes her head. "Catch them in the act. You've got surveillance, right?"

"Of the house, not the mailbox."

"Point a camera that way, is my advice. If they mess with it, at least we'll have evidence."

I like that a lot better. But it doesn't solve the immediate problem. "Thanks for that, but . . . it isn't why we came. We came about the threats. You think the Belldenes might be behind those too?"

Kezia sits forward again. "Hit me."

Gwen takes the folder out and slides it across. Kezia flips open the folder, and her instant focus is on the photoshopped picture. She studies it for a moment, then deliberately turns to the next page. That's a death threat against Gwen for being Melvin's partner. It's long, and it dwells way too much on how they plan to exact justice.

The next accuses both me and Gwen of being some kind of fakes carrying out a government conspiracy to convince the public that serial killers are real. It threatens to kill the kids (also actors, apparently) if we don't come forward and confess about the government's secret agenda—which they then go into great detail about, including rants about the secret cabal of the ultrarich and the chips in our debit cards. That one is full-on unhinged, and clearly the work of someone with serious mental issues.

There are a lot of threats that Gwen's gathered, and Kezia studies each one in silence before she closes the folder. "Wow," she says. It seems like an understatement. "How long a period is this?"

"I just took the last weeks' worth," Gwen says. "I expect it'll ramp up now that the Hamlin segment is available on the internet for people to pass around. That always cranks the crazy up several notches."

"Uh-huh," she agrees, and leans back. "So. I can put in for warrants and traces on these IPs, but you know how it is: not a lot of chance they're doing it from an open account that's easy to find, and if we do get them, there won't be much in the way of charges. If there are charges, there probably won't be a trial. So in the end . . ."

"Costs a shitload, is a ton of time and money to investigate, and probably doesn't do any good," I say. "So your advice is . . . wait until one of them shoots one of us in the head and there's a real crime to investigate."

"I didn't say that," Kezia says, and I recognize that she's broken out her professionally soothing voice now. I must have sounded like I was taking it personally or something. "Look, I'll do it. I'll follow up. I'll order more patrols around the lake for a while. But the fact is, none of this looks like the work of locals, especially the Belldenes."

"So nothing's going to happen to stop it," I say. "We spend the rest of our lives looking over our shoulders. The kids grow up living in fear."

"Sam . . . ," she starts, but I'm not having it.

"No, Kez, don't pour sugar on a pile of shit and call it breakfast. You're leaving Gwen and the kids unprotected when people clearly *want them dead.*"

"Blunt question, then: What do you want me to do about it? Twenty-four-hour guards? Bring in the FBI? They've got a division that specializes in internet threats, but they're 24/7/365 busy at it with a staff of probably less than a thousand people for the whole country, so those kids are gonna be grown by the time you get their attention. I'm trying to help. I'm also being honest. Lord knows, laws haven't kept up with threats. But I'm a law officer. I can only do what the law allows."

I'm angry. I hadn't expected to be, but I wanted more out of this. Gwen, on the other hand, seems to be the one keeping her cool this time.

"Sam," Gwen says, "she's being practical. I didn't expect anything different. And you know how brave the internet makes some people, at least when they're behind a screen."

She meets my gaze, and I look away. I used to *be* one of those anonymous angry people, typing rage at her through the vague haze of the web. We've never discussed any of it in detail, never identified specific screen names or threats or anything else I might have done during that dark, dark period. It's easier to get past it when we don't break open the scars. "Anyway. Thanks for your time, Kez. Really, I just wanted to make you aware of the situation so you can be prepared when something comes up." When, not if. I note the sentence construction.

Kezia flips back to the first photograph, the one where Gwen and the children are perforated with fake gunshot wounds. "This one concerns me," she says. "More than the others."

"Why that one?" I ask. There are other photoshops in the packet. Many are worse.

"It's different. Doesn't waste time on ideology or fantasy." She cocks her head and studies it closer. Picks it up and frowns down at the image. "Look, most of these assholes will draw a ton of wounds, right? The bloodier the better. It's designed to shock and scare. But this one?" She turns the photo toward us. "What do you see?"

We're both quiet for a few seconds. I finally say, "Kill shots."

"Right," she says. "Head and chest. Head and chest. Head and chest. And if you look at where the shots are located, they're very nearly instant kills. Someone knows their stuff. I'm going to worry about that."

"So am I," I say.

Because there are very few things more dangerous than a sniper who knows what he's doing.

◆ ◆ ◆

"She's probably right," I say on the drive back. "They're just desk warriors. But I want to reach out to Mike and send him the image just in case he's seen anything similar, or can find something. I'd really like to know if this guy's for real or just another shithead with a keyboard."

Gwen's not a desk warrior at all; she's survived worse than most people can imagine. I'm not afraid of a fight either. But strength and courage aren't a defense against a sniper bullet.

"Check with Javier at the gun range," Gwen says, and the next second I'm kicking myself for not thinking of it first. "Snipers have to practice, right? Maybe he knows somebody local who's putting in the time?"

"I'll go now," I say. "Drop me off at the truck. I should probably check a couple of job sites too."

"Will you be back for dinner?"

"Depends. Is it meat loaf?" It's a running joke right now; for whatever reason, Connor's decided he can't get enough meat loaf, and it seems he asks for it at every other meal. Gwen tries not to indulge him too much. But the kids have been through so much, a little excessive serving of meat loaf seems like a small price to buy some happiness.

"Not tonight," Gwen says.

"Then I'll be there."

I lean over to give her a kiss before I slide out when she stops the SUV; it turns long, and sweet, and I start reconsidering going out to the range. But then I remember that every second I don't track this down could put her in more danger.

So I go.

My truck's seen hard use bouncing over country roads, but it's a real workhorse, and I love it . . . except when I get calls. Between the engine noise and the clatter, it's a bad connection waiting to happen.

I don't recognize the number that lights up my cell as I climb the hill toward the gun-range parking lot, but I recognize the area code. Washington, DC. I answer and raise my voice to be heard over the engine noise. "Yeah?"

"Changed my number," says Mike Lustig. "Thanks for picking up, my man. Jesus, what are you driving, an F-15?"

"Beat-up Chevy," I tell him. "Sounds about the same, right?"

"What? I. Can't. Hear. You." He overly enunciates all of it, but he's just yanking my chain.

"Then you won't hear me calling you an asshole who hasn't been in touch," I tell him. "How long has it been?"

"According to my call log? Four months, give or take."

"My point exactly. Some friend you are."

"Settle your pasty self down, I had an undercover assignment. You'd have liked it, I got to learn how to print money."

"New retirement plan?"

"Way things are going around here, might just be," he says. "Government service is never exactly fun, but it's a special flavor of shit now."

"Preacher says this too shall pass."

"We got very different preachers."

"So . . . you called? You just bored?"

"No," Mike says. He sounds less light now. "Gwen just couldn't keep her damn self off the news, could she? You realize what all that means now. Creepy crawlies coming out of the woodwork again for her, you, the kids. Damn, all she had to do was keep her head down."

"You got any idea how much the press was on her? She needed to get in front of it and try to put it to rest."

"And how'd that work out?" He pauses for a few seconds. "Miranda goddamn Tidewell was on there. Did you see her?"

"No." I'm glad I didn't. I haven't looked at the YouTube footage either. I can't.

"You don't need me to tell you that you need to stay the hell away from that, right?"

"I don't, in fact. But thanks for thinking I'm a first-class idiot."

"Coach class," Mike says. "No way your cheap flyboy ass pays for an upgrade."

"Fuck off, my taxes pay your cushy government salary. Bet you don't hear that often enough."

He has a low voice, and a lower laugh; it vibrates the phone speaker. "Man, you can really channel your inner white boy sometimes. Listen, serious for a second: this thing you got with Gwen . . ."

"Don't. Don't start it."

"Sam, it ain't gonna go well. You have to know that. Sooner or later somebody's getting hurt. Probably her. And we both know why, don't we?"

By this time I've arrived at the gun range. I get out of the truck. I'm silent for a little while, leaning against the rough concrete blocks of the building. The parking lot's crowded, but there's nobody outside, just me and the frogs croaking somewhere in the trees. "Yeah, I know," I say. "I hear you. But right now, she's in trouble. I can't just . . . go."

"Gwen Proctor's a survivor."

"You think I'm not?"

"I think you used to be, until you let your guard down." Mike hesitates for a few seconds, then sighs. "Listen, I gave somebody your number. Take the call, okay? It's important."

"The hell are you getting me into?"

"Nothing you can't handle," he says. "Be safe, Sam. I still care. Why, I'll never know."

"That's sweet, but I'm still turning you in for counterfeiting. What's that, a solid twenty in the federal lockup?"

"See, now you're just being mean." He hangs up. I replace his old number with the new one, and I stay where I am for another long moment. He's right. Bad times are coming between me and Gwen;

Miranda's reappearance ensures that. And I really do need to consider what that can mean. But not now. The longer I can avoid that particular problem, the better.

I go inside and ask Javier if he's seen anyone suspicious. It doesn't make me feel better that he hasn't. Too many targets on our backs, and not a damn thing I can do about any of them. The range is packed right now, not a single lane space open, so I just hang out. I like Javier. He's a retired marine, still young, and he's got that gravity that makes people pay attention when he talks, no matter how quietly. He can defuse tension on the range just by walking in; whatever disputes people are having, they generally vanish the second he appears.

If I'd gone to get him when Belldene started his shit instead of handling it myself, he probably would have ended it with a staredown instead of a smackdown.

"You want me to keep an eye out for strangers," Javier says when I get ready to leave. We can hear the steady, muted hammer of gunfire on the other side of the concrete wall, but neither of us pays much attention. It's when the firing *stops* that you have to worry at a gun range, because it means everybody's paying attention to something, or somebody's hurt. "Trust me, I will. How are the kids?"

"Good," I tell him. I know he still feels guilty that Connor *and* Lanny managed to sneak out of his cabin and get into trouble after Gwen entrusted them to his care. "They're fine. And they miss you coming by."

He nods, but there's a certain set to his expression that I read as reluctance.

"She doesn't blame you," I tell him. "Not at all. You did your best to keep them safe."

"Yeah, it wasn't good enough, was it?" he says. "I know she doesn't blame me. Kind of makes it worse, man." He glances at me, then away.

"Well, I left them," I tell him. "How do you think that makes me feel? You were there for them. And I wasn't."

"They love you," he says. "You made them believe in the idea of having a dad again. Don't shove that off, it's important."

It is. It's also scary as hell. I don't want to hurt them, not ever, and right now . . . right now I can't see a way of avoiding that.

I don't expect the call Mike mentioned to come quite so fast, but it does, right then. I step outside to take it. Another unknown number, but this time from Florida. Miami, it looks like. I accept the call and say, "Sam Cade."

"Mr. Cade," says a calm woman's voice on the other end, "please hold for Mr. Winston Frost."

I don't know the name, but he sounds like he thinks he's important. It's only about thirty seconds of silence before the line clicks and a voice with a London West End accent says, "Mr. Sam Cade, hello, very good to speak with you. Thank you for taking my call today."

"Sure," I say. "What's this about?"

"Mr. Lustig mentioned that I'd be calling?"

"He said someone would be."

"Well, the thing is, I happened to have had the pleasure of meeting Mr. Lustig recently, and he heard that I was seeking a pilot for our corporate jet. He thought you might be interested in the opportunity. I understand you've taken some time off from the business, though, so—"

Flying. I feel a little jump in my pulse rate. It isn't deliberate. I don't *want* to react this way. But I've missed flying in ways I didn't even realize until this moment. "There have to be a lot of other pilots out there who'd kill for a slot like that," I say. "You're calling all the way to Tennessee for a man you've never met? Whose records you haven't even reviewed?"

"How do you know I haven't?"

"Trust me, those records would show my flight hours aren't exactly current."

"You're speaking like a man who isn't interested in coming back to the pilot's chair."

I am, and it's a lie. I want to get back to flying about as bad as I've wanted anything. *As bad as I want a home? A family? A life with Gwen?*

It rips me inside to even ask myself the question.

"Let me get back to you," I say. I'm aware that means *no*, most likely. I expect him to tell me to go to hell.

Instead, he says, "Of course, you'll need time to think it over; you'd need to move to the Miami area, of course, in order to be on call when we need you. The salary will be somewhere on the order of one hundred fifty thousand per year. The usual full-benefits package. We're not in any hurry, and I do realize that in order to recertify your standing, you'll need to devote some time to retraining. That is not an issue for us. We're happy to hire you conditionally while you complete that program."

The salary is suspiciously high, considering I don't even have real private-jet experience, though I can easily get it in training. "Would I be your only pilot?"

"No. We employ three pilots on standby at all times. Your position would be salaried, plus overtime should your flying time exceed eight hours in a day. So regardless of flight time, your compensation is secured."

I pause, and turn to stare off toward the horizon. "What kind of company?"

"Sorry?"

"What kind of company keeps three pilots on standby at all times and pays that much money as a starting salary?"

"A profitable one," he says. "You're more than free to research me and the company, of course. My assistant will be in touch in the next few weeks to hear your decision. Thank you for your time, Mr. Cade."

"Thanks for calling," I say. He's already gone by then, and I stare at the screen until the power goes off.

Who the hell did Mike recommend me to? And what am I going to do about this? Take an interview? Lie to Gwen? *Leave Stillhouse Lake?*

Honestly, in this moment, I don't really know. But one thing's for sure: I'm checking this guy out.

◆ ◆ ◆

Winston Frost research takes five minutes of time sitting in the cab of my truck with my cell phone. He's the CEO of Frost Industries, a major manufacturing outfit with plants around the world. Based out of London, but with a second home in Miami and a third one in Shanghai. Pictures of him all over the web, mostly at charity events; he has the usual detractors, but he seems to be legit.

I send Mike a text about it, but I don't get one back, at least not immediately. I want to know *exactly* how Mike knows this guy, and what he knows. Winston Frost's number tracks back to the Miami offices, so that's legit. I even redial and get the same cool-voiced assistant, thank her, and hang up.

Frost wouldn't be the first rich, evil businessman I've run into since meeting Gwen.

But damn. A steady job, steady pay, *flying*.

I don't want to want this, but fact is: I do.

4

LANNY

I'm sitting cross-legged on the bed, laptop open, waiting for Dahlia to pick up my Skype call. It rings and rings. And I start freaking out, the way I always do. *What if she woke up today and doesn't love me anymore? Is that why she's not talking to me?*

I know that's dumb. I've been through enough therapy to know I have some issues, subscriptions, volumes, libraries—whatever you want to call them. I'm always scared that I'm going to get hurt, even when nobody wants to hurt me. Which is why I reject people hard, first. I'm trying not to do that anymore. I fell in love with Dahlia; she makes my heart race and makes me want to cry inside when we're separated, and that's what love is, right? I *want* to be with her all the time. I'm practical enough to know that's not going to happen.

I end the Skype call and check her on social media. Her Instagram shows she's at someone's birthday party, looking bored under the poses. But at least I know she's not ducking me. At least, not today. *Don't be clingy,* I tell myself. *Be cool.*

I don't know how to do that. I've tried not to care for so long that slowing down seems impossible. At least I'm not jealous. I'm not, right?

I hear the front door open, the alarm warning sound, and the rapid keypad code beeps. Door shuts and locks.

Mom's home. But I don't hear Sam with her. They're usually talking when they walk in.

"Teriyaki chicken prep! Anybody want to help?" she calls.

I sit where I am, staring at the screen. Does Dahlia look happy, posing with that group of girls? She's got her arm around a boy in the next photo. Dahlia's mom said—when we weren't supposed to hear it—that the two of us were just *going through a phase.* Maybe she's right, as far as Dahlia's concerned. But I don't think that's me. Loving someone isn't a phase.

"Hey," Mom says. She's in the doorway now. "What's up?"

"Nothing," I say. I shut the laptop. "I was going for a run."

"Not by yourself," she says.

"Mom. It's not even close to dark. I'm just doing the lake."

"Not alone, you're not. I'll go with you. I could use the stretch."

"You'll slow me down," I tell her. She rolls her eyes. "No, seriously, you do."

"Well, I'm old," she says. "And I'm still coming."

"What about the dinner stuff?"

"I'll do it," my brother says. He's coming out of his room across the hall, headphones around his neck. Mom puts her arm around him, and he doesn't even stiffen up. He did for a while, but he's better now. At least, I think he is. We don't talk as much since I found out he was sneaking out to call our dad. I don't know what to do with that, or how to talk to him about it. It pisses me off that he did it at all. I can't even begin to guess why. And I don't want to ask.

"Garlic and ginger, green onions," she tells him, and smooths a part of his hair that's sticking up in the back. "Small dice on the garlic and ginger, okay? And remember to wash everything *before* you cut."

"I will," he says. It's probably wrong that I worry that he likes using kitchen knives. I mean, he's thinking of being a chef, right? Chefs use knives.

So did our dad.

Mom goes to her room to change, and I open the laptop again and look at myself. I'm thinking of posting a mood selfie. I like my hair today; it's at a funky angle, and the blue-and-green streaks I've put in through the black are still bright. I muss it up a little and try a pose for Operation Make Dahlia Remember I'm Alive, but my heart's not in it. I slam the lid again and put on a sports bra and oversize ancient tee over leggings with blood drops running down the sides. I'm tying my running shoes when Mom comes back. She takes one look at my leggings, and I know she's about to tell me to change, but then she checks herself.

One thing about my mom: she tries. She knows that I have to deal with the shitty past in my own way. I can't do it the way she does, at least not all the time. And I love these leggings.

I raise my eyebrows. She sighs and shakes her head. "Okay," she says. "Let's go."

Connor's in the kitchen when we leave, with a knife and cutting board and all the ingredients he's going to need prepped. Mom reminds him not to answer the door. He waves. We all know the drill.

"See ya, runt," I say.

"Hey, weirdo? I have a knife."

I flip him off on the way out. It's a typical joke between us. Some tiny little part of me still doesn't find it funny.

I'm the one who sets the pace around the lake, but I try to dial it down. I've been working at it hard. Mom used to be the fast one, and I wasn't in shape for it; but now I am. My legs are longer, and when I open up for speed, she has to work to keep up. I'm merciful. I don't totally humiliate her.

It should take about half an hour for us to run the full circuit, which is perfect, and we've picked the right time of day. The sun's behind the trees, breaking into pretty rays that hit the water and bounce. As we pass Sam's old cabin, Mom slows down. I fall back to match her speed. "Something wrong?" Sam doesn't live there now. It's fixed up, and now it's a constant stream of day-trippers who stay there. I'm naturally suspicious about people who don't stay put when they *could*. I think about all the nights I cried myself to sleep before moving again to find some temporary safety.

I don't cry anymore. Not about that.

"You thinking about something?" I ask, and Mom shakes her head, digs in, and settles into a longer stride. I easily catch up. We round the next turn, shadows drifting over us, and have to veer around a day-tripper putting a crappy boat into the water, loaded down with a cooler that I doubt is for fish.

Mom doesn't want to talk, obviously. We just run, matching strides. I'm already feeling the rush, my body working like it's made to, my mind soaring on a flood of happy chemicals. Half an hour is a tough pace around the lake, but we keep it up . . . until I see Ezekiel Claremont sitting on his little makeshift lakefront deck, made out of some pallets he's joined together. He's an old man, fragile, with wrinkled skin that's a still little darker than his daughter, Kezia's. Short gray hair. He has a camp chair and footstool, and he comes out every day to use this spot if the weather allows, and if his bad hip isn't acting up. Technically, it's probably not legal to have all this out here lakeside, but nobody bothers him about it that I know of. Maybe that's because he saved a girl's life a few months back by calling 911 when her canoe overturned in choppy water and she decided—stupidly—to take off her life vest and swim for shore. If the local lake patrol hadn't made it to her, she'd have vanished into the lake completely.

"Hey, Mr. C," I say, and we ease down to a walk. "What's going on?" I like Easy. I like his daughter, Kez, too. He's not funny, exactly, but he's sharp, and easy—like his nickname—to talk to when I feel like I need that. I come over here sometimes, and talk about my dad. He just listens and nods, mostly.

"Word is your mother got into some trouble on TV the other morning," he says. "You all right, Gwen?"

"Sure," she says. "Just another day in paradise, Easy."

"You think so?" He studies her, then shakes his head. "That other woman, she said a lot of things. People might listen."

"They might," Mom agrees. "I've been through it before."

"Not like this," he says. "Those *documentary* people, they're already here in town. Staying up at the Vagabond outside of Norton."

I draw in a sharp breath. Documentaries mean cameras. People asking questions. People invading our lives. I'd thought maybe it would all just . . . go away after the *Howie Hamlin Show*; I'd thought maybe the blonde lady who'd been so vicious to Mom would stop what she was doing. I've seen her picture before. She's the mother of one of Dad's victims. And she's got a lot of money to spend on making us miserable.

"They're here?" Mom's voice is sharp, and I blink. She sounds alarmed. She immediately changes that, but it's too late—I caught it. "I mean, I didn't expect them to be here for a while. If ever."

"Been here two days," Ezekiel says. "So says my daughter, and she ought to know. She keeps an eye on strangers."

"Funny," Mom says, "she didn't bother to mention that to me when I talked to her this morning."

"You went to see Kez?" I'm a little surprised. Mom didn't say a thing to me. "Why?"

She ignores the question and focuses on Easy. "You've seen these film people?"

"They been out here today," he says, and points a shaking, gnarled finger down to a nearby pull-in where visitors park. "Set up a camera and filmed the lake awhile."

"That way?" Mom points. He nods. "The lake . . . and our house." She sounds pissed off. I can't blame her. "They were filming *our house*."

I feel as shocked and invaded as she does. My bedroom faces the lake. Did they see me? Did I have my windows open? *Oh my God*, did I close the curtains before I changed into my running gear? I can't remember. I always do, don't I?

People watching us, again. That's not new, I guess, but I was a kid for most of that time. Now I feel . . . vulnerable. And I don't like it at all.

"Well, maybe," Easy says. "Don't think you were home then. You and Sam left before they got all set up; they were gone when you came back." He chuckles, but it doesn't sound like he finds anything too funny. "Fools tried to ask *me* about you."

"What did you say?" I ask, because Mom won't. His light-brown eyes focus on me, and he blinks a couple of times.

"I told them I mind my business, Lanny, what do you think I told them? They want more, they can go fish for it."

Mom looks frustrated. "Easy. You didn't call me? Because I know you have a cell phone in your pocket."

"Now, don't make me tell a tired old joke nobody wants," he says, and smiles slowly. "I didn't call 'cause I didn't want you and Sam charging out there and getting yourselves in trouble. The film people were here. Film people left. Satisfying as it might feel to beat the stupid out of them, you two'd get arrested, and they'd have even more to put in their damn film. Leave them alone. Best advice I got."

He's not mentioning that I might have come and kicked over a camera, but I sure would have. I will, next time they show up. And I won't tell Mom before I do it, either, because he's right: she and Sam would get arrested. If I do, no big deal. It's not like I'd get jail time. I'm just a dumb kid.

"What's in the cooler?" I ask Easy. It's sitting beside his chair, small enough for him to manage on the way up and down the hill.

"Why, you want a beer, girl?"

"I know you're not offering, and she isn't taking," Mom says. Easy pulls out a small bottled water and pitches it to me, then hands one to my mother.

"Have a little faith," he says. "And keep your cool, Gwen. Gonna be a long, hot summer around here."

We drink our water up fast, and chat some more; it's worth breaking up a run to talk to Mr. Claremont. He's an interesting man, and I like him a lot.

My mom finally eyes the horizon and checks her watch. "Sorry. Got to get home and make dinner. You going to be okay out here? It's going to get dark in the next hour."

"I know. Kez is coming home in a bit. She'll help me on up the hill."

"All right. You call if you need us."

"Much appreciated," he says. "You watch your step, ladies."

"Thank you, Mr. C," I say. As we set off, I hear him pop the top on a bottle that doesn't have water in it, and when I glance back, he's sipping a beer and lost in the view of the lake. As we ramp back up to speed, I say, "Mom? Did you know he used to be famous?"

"What?"

"Mr. Claremont. Used to be famous."

"Famous for what?"

"He won a bunch of medals back in the Vietnam War," I say. "He testified to Congress about some of the bad stuff that went on. Lots of people hated him for that. Lots of people loved him, too, but I think he understands what it's like to be hounded. Like us."

I can tell she didn't know, and I admit, I'm surprised. If background checking was an Olympic event, she'd have more gold than Michael Phelps. My brother, the nerd, would definitely be going for the silver. I feel kind of good that I surprised her. And for a change, it isn't a *bad* surprise.

From Easy's lakeside mini-resort, we kick it hard and race each other the last quarter of the way around the curve; I feel the burn building in my calves and thighs as the road begins to slope and we pull close to home. Mom's exhausted, I can see it; I wonder if she slept much. She's so exhausted, in fact, that she forgets the mail, or maybe she expects Sam to get it today, I don't know.

When she realizes I'm not coming with, she stops and looks back.

"Go on," I tell her. "I want to talk to Dahlia."

"Five minutes," she says.

I nod. As Mom heads up the incline to the house, I perch on a rock on the other side of the road, next to the lake, and hit FaceTime.

It rings. And rings.

Dahlia doesn't pick up. Again. This is the third time in a row, and it's killing me. *Why isn't she talking to me? What's she doing? What did I do wrong? Oh God, is she with somebody else?*

I'm so preoccupied with that, I forget that I'm not supposed to open the mailbox. I'm pulling down the door when I remember, and then it's too late, and I jump backward in case there's a snake inside.

There isn't. I check with my phone light and everything. Mom's going to kill me, though. She'd just said not to do this.

Too late now. I restlessly pick through the mail. Junk, junk, political junk. Some bills. And two other things: a flat manila mailer addressed with a printed label to SAMUEL CADE. It has a return address out of Richmond, Virginia, and a bunch of stamps on it. And a plain white letter, also stamped, no return address, with Mom's name on it.

I freeze, because I recognize the handwriting. It's my father's.

Dad's dead.

How can he possibly be writing to Mom? I feel sick and dizzy for a second, and I'm in danger of dropping mail all over the place . . . but then I take some deep breaths and shove the letter down the side of my leggings.

I know I should give it to Mom, but . . . for years, she kept his letters away from us. From me. She took all of that on herself. I've seen one of them, just a glance, really. Mom's trying to forget about Dad, and this will hurt her, I know it will. Whatever's in this letter, he *means* it to hurt.

I'm not letting him keep on abusing her. She took so much and never let us know what it cost her; I do know now.

I'm old enough. I can do this for her, especially after seeing what that stupid TV show did to her. I *hate* that people keep hurting her. She wouldn't like it, but . . . I'm strong enough.

I'll just tear it up and throw it away. She'll never even know.

◆ ◆ ◆

I put the rest of the mail on the counter and tell Mom, who's talking to Connor, that I'm going to hit the shower. She tells me not to hog all the hot water, she's sweaty too, and Connor says something I don't pay attention to because the letter I've hidden in my leggings feels like it's burning my skin. I hear the pickup truck outside as I shut and lock my bedroom door. Sam's back. I take the letter out and put it on my bed, then step back to stare at it.

I didn't imagine it. There's a letter there, an envelope with Dad's handwriting on it. So either I'm full-on crazy, or my dead serial-killer dad has got writing materials in hell.

And stamps.

I pace back and forth. I check my curtains—closed—and strip off my sweaty running clothes and dump them in the laundry basket. I change to soft cotton pants and a sweatshirt. It happens to have skulls on it. Sort of appropriate, I guess.

I intend to tear it up, and I try, I really do; I grab it in both hands and start to twist it, but the second I feel the paper start to give, I stop.

What if there's something important in it?

I can hear my mom's voice. *Nothing your father has to say is impor-tant. It's just cruel.*

But . . . what if there's a clue to what he's planned, and by tearing it up I miss it? No. I have to look. Just quickly. Just to be sure.

I sit down on the bed and—before I can talk myself out of it—I rip the top open.

Inside, there's a letter. Several pages long, folded in half. I remember how my mom used to put on latex gloves before handling his letters, but I don't have any. I pull the letter out.

Dear Gina, it starts, and I feel my mouth dry up. My dad tried to kill my mom. He nearly succeeded. She killed *him.* And here he is call-ing her by the old name, the name she hates.

It's like nothing happened. Only everything did.

My hands are shaking. I feel cold. I can almost, *almost* hear his voice, looking at his handwriting. I can picture him sitting in a cell writing this, but I can't see his face anymore. It's just a blur, an impression. Mostly it's just eyes. He always had these eyes that could change from nice to cruel in an instant.

I put the letter down and wipe my hands on my pants. They feel damp. And I can't get them to stop trembling. *What if it's poisoned?* I think, but that's dumb, that's some bullshit you see on TV, poisoned paper that kills you for touching it. But in a way, Dad poisoned everything he touched.

I've been thinking a lot about you lately, as my situation changes, he writes. Does he mean, while he was out of prison? On the run? I don't know. I want to stop reading now, and I've only read one sentence. I'm afraid. Really afraid. *I've been thinking about how I once thought you could save me from myself. It's not your fault you didn't. Nobody could.*

That isn't so bad. It's almost like he's apologizing. Almost.

> No, that's not what I blame you for, Gina. I don't even blame you for running away, taking the kids, changing your name. Pretending you never knew me. I understand why you did that.
>
> But you know what I don't understand, you faithless bitch?
>
> I don't understand why you think you're special. You're not. You stopped being special to me even before the accident; you were just a convenient prop in the act. Like the kids.

It feels like my bed is plunging through the floor. Falling straight down. I'm dizzy. Sick. And I can't stop reading.

I was thinking about killing you. Thinking about
it every time I took a new one back to *our* home. *Our*
sanctuary. I fantasized that I'd bring you in there when
I had someone on the hook, show you, watch the horror come into you, and then make you take her place.
It entertained me between guests.

I stop. I just . . . stop. The paper falls out of my hand and drifts
down to the bed. *This is your dad. This is who he was. This is what he
thought about.*

I want to cry, but I can't.

I try looking around my room, fixing on things that make me
happy. My fluffy pink unicorn that Connor won for me at a school fair
last year. My posters. The paint I chose for the walls of my very own,
permanent room.

But it all feels like a nightmare now. Like nothing is real except the
paper sitting in front of me on the bed.

I pick it up again. I don't want to, but it feels like I have to get all
the way through.

I don't understand how you've justified whoring
yourself out to the brother of that last one I took. I
don't understand how he doesn't strangle you in your
sleep and blow his own brains out. Maybe someday.
Maybe if he knew more about how his sister died,
how much she suffered, how long she begged me to
end it. Something to consider. Maybe I'll send him
something special.

Sam. He's talking about Sam, oh my *God.* I cover my mouth one
hand. I keep reading because I can see the end coming, and *God* I want
it to end.

You don't know who he is, Gina. You don't know what he's capable of doing. I'm laughing at the thought that you only bring monsters into your bed. You deserve that.

He's saying that Sam is a monster. That isn't true. It can't be.

Someday you'll get what's coming to you. Maybe not from me. But one of them, one of them you trust . . . that will be rich.

Give my love to our children.

—Yours forever,

Melvin.

I realize by the end that I'm gasping, and I have to wipe my burning eyes. It hurts, it *hurts*, because I can hear him in my head, and now I know I can't *not* hear him anymore. Dad. My father. The monster.

This is who he was. Is. Forever.

I didn't think I had any illusions left to break, but sitting there shaking, with that letter spread out in pages in front of me, I know I had so many.

The thought comes to me then: *What if Mom lied? What if he's still alive?*

And it terrifies me so much I grab my pillow and hug it close and scream into it to try to let that feeling out.

I gasp out loud when there's a knock on the door. I'm suddenly, horribly convinced that it's *Dad* out there, dead and rotten and grinning. Here to get me and take me back as his *guest*.

Mom says, "Hey, I thought you were taking a shower. Are you done?"

I'm not sure I can even answer her. I hear her try the door. I manage to clear my throat and say, "Changing!" I hope my voice doesn't shake. I hope she hasn't heard me screaming into the pillow.

"Okay," she says. I know her Mom radar is kicking in. "Lanny? Are you okay?"

"Go away!" I shout, and make myself be angry, because it's the only way I can deal with this right now.

She doesn't go away. I imagine her standing there, concerned, hand pressed against my door. Not understanding what brought this on.

Then she says, "Is it Dahlia?"

Oh, thank God. I choke back a sob and gather up the pages and shove them back in the envelope. "Yeah," I lie. *Is Dad really alive?* I want to ask, but if I do, how do I know if she's telling the truth?

"Can we talk about it?"

"No!" I put the envelope in my top drawer, underneath the liner paper, and slam it hard. "Leave me alone!"

She finally does. I hear her footsteps as she leaves.

I huddle into as tight a ball as I can, pull the covers up, and scream into my pillow again and again and again until my head hurts and my whole body aches like I'm running a fever. He's made me sick.

I tell myself that Sam wouldn't have lied about Dad being dead even if Mom would. No, Dad's dead. For sure.

I still imagine him standing by my bed when I close my eyes.

And he's smiling.

I have to give this to Mom, I know that. I have to confess to her that I read it. But I can't, not right now. It's taking everything I have just to . . . just to *breathe*.

When Mom comes to tell me dinner's ready, it takes even more to pretend like the world's still normal.

Like I'm normal.

But like my dad . . . I'm good at pretending.

5

GWEN

I've been expecting a fracture in the all-too-close Dahlia/Lanny love affair; they've been burning too hot, and that doesn't last. But at her age, what crush does? I'm afraid that a breakup on top of the stress we're about to be put under may trigger some real problems in my daughter. She's tough, but she's not invulnerable, any more than I am.

If this documentary bullshit is real, if they're *here*, then I need to think very seriously about our future in Stillhouse Lake. It'd be nice if our neighbors banded together in a united front against them, but I can't see that happening; too many of them didn't like me from the beginning, and more of them didn't like how the thing with local cop Lancel Graham ended, though he definitely deserved it. Having microphones in their faces might just give them the chance to vent their grudges.

I can't have my kids in the cross fire, not again.

Teriyaki chicken's well underway, and Connor, Sam, and I enjoy the kitchen time together, even though it's close quarters. Sam manages to steal a kiss when I slide by him to put the rice on, and I return the favor on the way back.

My son just rolls his eyes as he finishes chopping cabbage for the sweet-and-sour salad.

"Lanny should be doing this," he gripes.

"She's having a hard time," I tell him. "You don't mind, right?"

He says he doesn't, but he does.

Sam says, "I checked with Javier. No new faces at the range over the past couple of months, other than the usual day-trippers. Nobody asking for long-range practice other than the hunters he already knows." He means there's no evidence that a sniper's come to town and is training to take us out. Of course, if there is, there's also no reason a sniper would *have* to go to Javier's range if he's a hired gun; he could practice somewhere else, far from here, come in and do the job, and drive away. There's not much comfort we can take from a negative, and we both know that.

While the chicken cooks, Sam leaves the kitchen, spots the mail that Lanny left on the counter, and shuffles through it. He takes out a large manila envelope and opens it up, peers inside, and pulls out a slim black-bound journal. He opens the first page.

Then he just . . . stops. It's his utter stillness that draws my gaze, and when he shifts, I see something in his eyes. Something I don't want Connor to see. So I force a smile and say, "Hey, Connor? Five more minutes on the rice. Sam?" I gesture to him, and he unfreezes enough to follow. He's still holding the manila envelope and journal.

I shut the office door once he's inside, and lean against it.

"What is it?"

"A diary," he says. "I recognize the handwriting. It's Callie's."

It's his *sister's*. I catch my breath and ask, "Did the prosecutor's office release it?" I pick up the envelope from him and check the return address. It's a post office box. No name. I feel gooseflesh start to rise on the back of my neck. *Something's wrong here.*

"I never heard of them even finding one," he says. "I suppose someone must have found it and sent it to me as next of kin?" He opens it and flips pages. Stops. "Here's where she talks about tracking me down and finding out I was on deployment. I have her first letter somewhere.

I kept all of them." I can hear how this unmoors him. I can't imagine, seeing these glimpses into a life that was full of bright promise, and so brutally and suddenly gone.

"Sam . . ." I don't know whether to tell him I'm sorry or not. I don't know if *he's* sorry. Maybe this is a good thing. Maybe it's something that will help him deal with old wounds. "Sam, maybe you should stop. We don't know who sent this."

He's not listening to me. He's reading, and he laughs a little. "God, she's bad at this. She skips weeks at a time, then writes a long thing about her dinner. Two more weeks, and she talks about a job interview." He turns more pages, reads, looks up at me. Tears in his eyes. "She writes about the first time we did the video call. I was such an idiot. I acted like it was no big deal, finding her. I should have—"

"Please don't, Sam."

"But it *hurt her,*" he says. He sits down in the nearest office chair: mine. "Jesus. I didn't realize how much it hurt her to think I didn't care. I made her cry, Gwen. Over nothing. Because I wanted to play it cool."

I go to him. Put my hands on his shoulders. Kiss the top of his head. "But you both got past that. Didn't you?" I feel awful inside, listening to this. He's thinking at the moment only of his sister, and her life. I'm already thinking about her death, and how it happened in *my* house. How *my* husband was to blame. These two dead people are always between us.

He takes a deep breath and lets it out, then turns more pages. He reads in silence, and I stay with him, because I know this is something he doesn't want to do alone. "Yeah," he eventually says. "We got past it. We were friends." He stops on a page. It's written in a looping, feminine hand in purple ink. Bold, confident, happy writing. "Shit. This . . . this is the last time we talked. She was going to write me a letter. I never got one. Gwen . . . he took her away just four days after she wrote this."

I have a premonition suddenly, and I want to grab the book out of his hands. I want to stop him here, in this place, sad as it is.

But I don't, and he turns to the next page.

Same purple ink.

Very different handwriting.

Sam's whole body jerks, a shock like someone has hooked him up to electrodes, and I recognize the writing in the same instant.

One second too late.

"It's him," he says. I know that. I've just understood what's happening, whose writing this is. Sam's voice is different now. Low. Harsh. Blank of emotion, but that's coming—it's coming in a horrible, violent wave next because I can already feel the shock running through him. And through myself. "Oh Jesus. *He wrote this.* In her diary."

"Don't," I tell him, and I grab for the book like I should have before. He turns away, staring at the pages. "Sam! You can't! *He meant for you to do this!*"

Melvin loved gaslighting. Loved games. I don't know how he's doing this, but I can guess: he had accomplices hold things for him, and gave them orders on which to mail out, to whom, and when.

That is what he was like; he'd have planned ways to hurt and control us even from his grave.

The only way to win this game is to walk away. But I know Sam can't help himself. He needs this. He hasn't been through this. He thinks he needs to know.

It's self-inflicted torture.

"Go," he tells me.

"No. I want to stay with you."

"I know. But . . . I can't do this with you here. Please. Go."

"I'm asking you not to read it," I tell him. "Sam . . . you'll only let him hurt you. You understand that."

"I know," he says, and turns to look at me. I want to take this pain away from him. But I can't. "Please go."

So I do. I leave the office. I shut the door behind me. I leave him to suffer in the hell that Melvin has created in that journal, because I can't follow.

But I *am* going to find the asshole who sent this to him. Richmond, Virginia, might seem like a big place to hide, but not when I'm done. I will find out who Melvin trusted to deliver his bitter gifts.

And I will stop it.

I put on a too-bright smile for Connor, and together we finish up the rice, dress the salad with the handmade sweet Asian vinaigrette, put plates on the table, get drinks. I pour wine for me and Sam, and Connor gets water, as he usually does. Lanny hasn't come out of her room. I go and knock; she's out in a few more minutes, and an almost perfect replica of her usual self.

Almost.

She picks water as her beverage, and as we sit down, she says, "Where's Sam?"

"He's coming," I tell her. I hope that's true. I dish out the rice and the thickly sauced chicken; it smells amazing, but I have no appetite. My stomach is in knots. I keep staring at the hallway as I fill up Sam's plate. We wait for another minute or two. The kids are looking longingly at their food, fidgeting. "You guys go ahead. I'll get him."

They dig in before I'm up from the table. I walk down the hall to the closed office door.

I rest my fingers on the knob for a long few seconds before I turn it and look in.

Sam's sitting with his back to me. The journal is lying on my desk, closed now. He says, in an unnaturally flat voice, "I'll be there in a minute, Gwen."

No point in asking if he's okay. I just close the door and go back to the table, and when Connor asks me where Sam is, I smile a little and say he's on a call. The kids talk about what they want to do this weekend. Connor's up for another trip to the town library, which he loves; Lanny wants to see a movie, and there's some kind of house party across the lake that they're definitely not going to attend. I don't want to scare them, to crush this fragile normality they've achieved. But I don't know what else I can do if they're to stay safe. It feels like we're standing in a small, warm spotlight, but the darkness is closing in all around us to swallow us up.

We should run. Get away now. Run fast. Those instincts have served me well for years, but now . . . now they feel out of tune. We could run. Move. Change our names, again. But is it going to change anything for long? People will find us. They always have. They always will. And ripping away friends and normality from the kids might be the wrong move, again.

Sam comes out of the office and takes his seat at the table. I meet his eyes, and I see darkness. I don't know what Melvin wrote, only that it was directed very specifically at him. I don't know if I really want to know, or if he'll even tell me. But the shadow passes, and he smiles at the kids, jokes about weekend plans, and eats his food.

I do, too, even though every bite tastes like tears and ashes.

We're all trying *so hard*.

And I realize, as if I'm standing outside of the spotlight, looking in . . . that it can't last.

6

Sam

They're always going to come between the two of us. The ghosts. I don't want to admit that, but right now everything feels raw and wounded inside me, and I'm *angry*. Melvin's reaching out from the grave to drag me over knives again. And Miranda. Miranda's out there, circling like a vulture. I know she's coming for us.

For Gwen.

I flinch from thinking about Melvin and what I read in Callie's notebook. Miranda's not a welcome thought, but at least she's safer. I never was Miranda's lover. In some ways that's worse. She's a toxic, bottomless well of hate, but hate is emotionally seductive, and it brought the worst parts of both of us out in the open when we were together.

I never, ever want Gwen to know about the details of what I did, especially to her, during that time of my life. She knows enough without having to face the cold facts.

We finish dinner, do the dishes, pretend everything is fine for the sake of the kids until they're both on the couch, a movie is playing, and the two of us can step outside onto the porch.

She turns and puts her arms around me.

"I'll get started on the backtrace of the address in the morning," she tells me. "I should have an answer in a few hours. Maybe even a name."

I don't say anything. Taking out my anger on some random guy Melvin hired to mail stuff seems . . . useless. But I know we need to find this out and stop whatever else is in the queue from reaching us. Once we have a name, an address, we can get the FBI into it. Maybe. But it feels like an empty crusade. He's already won.

I can sense the lingering fear and worry in Gwen, and I bury my nose in her hair and breathe in the scent of her. It cools something inside me and warms me at the same time. Steadies me. It scares me a little, this reaction. I've known a lot of strong, capable women, but Gwen is a unique blend of need and independence. She can and will fight like a tiger for those she loves. We have that bedrock faith in common.

We stand on the porch, wrapped around each other, content to be silent for a while. Finally, I say, "I know you're going to ask, but . . . I don't want to talk about it. Not about the diary."

"Okay," she says. She understands that, I know. "But are you okay?"

I pull back and look at her. Fit my hands around her face and kiss her gently. "Not remotely okay. But that's why I need the time."

She nods, and leans her forehead forward to rest against mine. "I wish I could kill him all over again," she says. "And then sometimes I wish . . . I wish I hadn't killed him at all. Does that make sense?"

"Absolutely." Killing someone isn't like in the movies, something you shrug off with a quip and a drink. It eats at you, even when the person you kill unquestionably has to die. And there's no way that her feelings about Melvin aren't, at the very deepest level, still complicated.

Like mine about Miranda.

Jesus, I feel the ghosts crowding even closer, ready to tear the two of us apart.

Gwen pulls free and takes my hand. She leads me over to the two chairs on the porch, and we sit. There's a corked half bottle of wine and two glasses; I pour for us. She sighs and takes a sip, gaze fixed on the dark lake rippling like black silk in the moonlight.

The porch lights are still off. By silent agreement we leave them that way.

"I've been thinking about the woman who called. Marlene. From Wolfhunter." She takes a sip of her wine. "I'm wondering if I should go up there and talk to her."

"No."

"Sam—"

"*No.* Not now. Things are too dangerous, and she didn't tell you why, did she? I'm not comfortable with you going off out of town, away from everything you know. You've got—" I almost say, *You've got your kids to protect*, but I stop myself because I realize that I've almost unconsciously taken a step back if I say it. As if they aren't my kids now, too, to love and protect. *You asshole,* I tell myself. I can't let Melvin drive that wedge. Or Miranda. Or my own deep-buried, visceral rage. So try to save it. "You've got too much at stake. *If* she was more specific about what she needed, you could try to send her some help. But if she wasn't willing to do that . . . you have to think about yourself first."

She takes a long drink, and finally shifts her gaze back to me. I don't like what I see there. It's as dark and quiet as the lake. "This is a change. You're more paranoid tonight than I am."

"Yeah." I drain my wine in two long gulps, barely even tasting it, and pour another glass. "Assholes from beyond the grave will do that to you." And Miranda. Jesus, I need to tell her about Miranda. I really do. "And you're still not bulletproof."

"Damn bullet resistant, though."

"If you intend on doing something that stupid, I can't let you do it alone."

"Because if you did, you wouldn't feel manly enough?"

I try to lighten it up. "Woman, I spend my days hammering nails and building strong walls. I'm plenty manly enough." She laughs, which was what I intended. It breaks her focus. I let my tone turn serious again. "Maybe we should think about getting out of here for a while. Just . . . somewhere. If we're gone, Miranda and her circus will move on."

"What about—"

"The job?" I shrug. "Construction's a one-day-at-a-time kind of business. I can call out anytime I need to."

"But that doesn't mean they'll hire you back."

"Honey? I'm one of the best they've got. They'll hire me back." I sit back and drink my wine for a moment before I say, "I'm thinking of making a change, eventually, though."

"To what?"

"I don't know." That's almost a lie. Almost. I need to tell her the truth. Tell her about the job offer, the restless need I feel when I think about flying again. Stillhouse Lake is great because *she's* here, because I love her and I love these kids.

But at the same time, it's like my life is on pause.

I feel deeply fractured and restless. Between Miranda's documentary and Melvin's hammer blow to my brain, it's stirred ugly shadows, messed with my head. And Gwen's pulling away, defensively; I've felt it happening. She's already strengthening the shields between us. So the easy answer is, *Maybe we should let this breathe for a while*, and I go and find my own way.

But it isn't what I want. I love this woman. I want to be here. I want to be part of this family, not a separate, replaceable piece that comes and goes at will.

"I think I'm going to ask you to marry me," I say. It comes out of nowhere, and I don't even know why I've said it; my instant, panicked impulse is to try to claw it back, laugh it off as a joke, but then I go still because I meant it. I *want* this.

Gwen turns her head to stare at me. "What do you mean, you think?" she says.

"I am," I say. "Asking."

"Just like that."

"We're not the sunset-cliff-kneel-down-ring kind of people. Are we?"

I risk a glance at her then. She's half covering her mouth with her wineglass. But she's smiling. And she looks at me, and our gazes meet and hold fast. She takes in a breath and lets it out slowly. I feel a flare of heat, and I'm so damn glad, because it burns away all my doubts, all the filthy residue of Melvin Royal's writing, all the sadness and grief and fear that Miranda's brought back into my life.

"Why?" she asks. "Why ask now?"

God, she's smart. And hits without mercy. "Because I don't want to lose you," I say, and it's the most honest thing I've said in my life. "Not to a bullet, not to some fanatic with a grudge, not to the two of us just . . . going separate ways. I want to be in your life, and I want you in mine. I want us to be together for as long as God allows." I pause. "How's that?"

Her face is flushed. Her eyes bright. "That's pretty damn good," she says, and drains her wine completely in two long gulps. She gets up, empty glass in hand, and turns to look at me. "Let's go to bed."

I hesitate for a second, then slam down the rest of my wine and stand up to face her.

I take her hand.

And we go together to the kitchen, set the glasses in the sink, and Gwen turns to tell the kids, "We're going to bed, okay?"

They don't even look at us. They just nod, pulled deep into whatever story is unfolding on the screen. I follow her down the hall and into the bedroom; before we get the door shut, I'm kissing her, and she's against the wall, and we're deep into it, into each other, and thank God my mind goes quiet and the vivid horror pauses.

She pulls free with a gasp. "Lock the door," she says. Her voice is shaking.

I close the door and lock it, and when I turn around, she's pulling off her shirt, and mine's on the floor a second behind. I realize I smell like sweat from the long day, that I haven't showered, and for a second, I hesitate. "I should shower," I say.

Her smile is as bright as sunrise. "I like how you smell," she says. "And we're not sunset-cliff-kneel-down-ring people, remember?"

Damn, that goes deep, and ignites something wild.

The sex is untethered and breathless and silent—a mom's habit, or maybe it's because she's so guarded even when she's letting go. And it lasts, the intensity of it burning bright, until we finally collapse together, shaking and sweating. It's astonishing, the fire we wake in each other. Precious and secret and completely right.

We're still joined together when she whispers something in my ear.

I'm not ready for that answer, coming in the heat of this moment. Not in the least.

Because Gwen says no, she can't marry me. Not yet.

We sleep next to each other, but there's space in the middle, and a lot more between us than that. I rise early and hit the shower; I run the entire night through my head, from reading her ex-husband's words to the exact moment that Gwen first melted and then shattered my heart, and I don't know how to process any of it. I really don't. We're off the map.

Here lie goddamn monsters.

7

Gwen

The next day still dawns, however unlikely it seems. When I wake up, he's already left the bed.

I hate myself, because I remember that exact moment—no, the second—that I broke Sam's heart. I feel like a horrible bitch, even though I knew exactly what I was doing, and why.

Sam does nothing without a reason . . . but sometimes he doesn't really recognize that. I do. The proposal was an impulsive, rash move, done partly because he meant it . . . and partly because it was a distraction from something he didn't want to face. From *Melvin*. I felt it then. I feel it now. I can't let him get himself into something as big, as important, as marriage without both of us being honest about why we're doing it.

And yes, if *I'm* honest with myself . . . I may not be ready. It took months for me to let my guard down enough to acknowledge I love Sam, and months more before I dared open myself up to any kind of physical needs between the two of us. It terrified me. It still does on some level, but that's the fundamental damage that Melvin did to me, and I'm working to correct it. But Sam doesn't need to be my therapy, or my life preserver, or my rescuer.

I have to be all those things for myself if a marriage between us is ever going to work.

Sam's making coffee when I come into the kitchen. I watch him anxiously for any sign that he's angry, upset, disappointed . . . but I see nothing. He's too guarded, and he's too good at hiding what he's really feeling. *God, I really did that. I said no to him.*

"Good morning," he says. No indication he's hurting. He pours me a cup. He's already showered and dressed in heavy jeans and work boots and a moisture-wicking tee. "I've got the roofing job today. Should be back by dinner. You?"

This conversation is almost painfully superficial. I take the cup and sip. "Not much," I say. "I might go to the range and do some target shooting later. It's good to put in the practice, right? Given the circumstances?"

"Absolutely," he says. "You're going to run down that address in Virginia, right?"

"Yes."

He leans in to kiss me lightly, and before he can pull away, I put my lips to his ear. It isn't that there's anyone else listening, it's just that I need to whisper this.

"I'm sorry," I tell him. "Please come home again." Because I'm actually afraid that when he walks out that door, he'll keep walking.

He slowly pulls away, and our eyes meet. We say a lot in that moment. Volumes. And he says, "I'll see you tonight."

That's as much comfort as there can be, I suppose. This time, when we kiss, it's not quite as perfunctory. And I'm not quite as afraid to let go.

I spend the next two hours focusing on how Melvin's managed to hit us again. The first step is easy; the address on the front of the envelope that held his sister's journal traces back to a Pack 'N Ship on the north side of Richmond. I call. No answer. I look up the store and get another phone number, different from the one that's listed on their website. This time someone picks up. "Pack 'N Ship. How can I help you?" The second part of this sounds resigned to being asked a stupid question. World-weary.

"Hi, I'm looking to renew box seven ninety-one," I say. If I ask who owns it, I'll never get the answer. "I might need to update the credit card too."

"Oh, okay," he says. "Hold on." Keys click. "Looks like it's not supposed to be renewed until the end of the year."

"Well, if you don't mind, I'd rather do it right now. I might forget. And I've moved, so . . ."

"Sure. Same card number?"

"Oh, and I got married, not sure if I updated the card yet for that," I say. "What's the name on the card you have?"

Sometimes people catch on, but I'm betting from his boredom and general resentment of the job that he's not a due-diligence kind of guy. And I score, because he says, "Uh, it's Dan O'Reilly." I don't recognize it.

"Oh, that's my husband's card, so it should be fine," I say, and make sure I sound breathless and a little frazzled. "It's just so hard keeping up with all the changes, you know? Um . . . and do you have our current address? We moved out of the apartment."

"Twenty-two hundred Alfalfa Lane," he says.

"Yes, that's right. Thank you so much. Well, if the card's correct, you can just charge it when you're ready."

"Uh-huh. I need to add you to the record, Mrs. O'Reilly. First name?"

"Frances," I say. "Fran, for short."

"Phone?"

"Same as his," I say. I'm enjoying complicating the life of Mr. O'Reilly a little. "Thank you. You've been very helpful."

"No problem," he says, and ends the call.

I take it back to the web and look up Dan O'Reilly's details, cross-referenced with the address.

He's a registered sex offender. I feel sorry for the fictional wife, Frances. When I pay the fee to get his records, I find that Dan likes rape, and likes his girls young enough so they can't fight back. It's nauseating. I find the link; his brother, Farrell, is currently incarcerated in the same prison Melvin was in. And on death row for abduction and murder.

Child predators run in the family sometimes.

I'm guessing that one of Dan's associates—if not Dan himself—will be on the visitor logs for Farrell; Melvin would have made lots of nasty friends while he was waiting his turn at the needle. He probably arranged for payments to Farrell, who smuggled things out of prison to his brother.

But then I pause. Because it's too easy. It took me all of two hours to trace this back to Dan's box. And why would Dan put his own address on the envelope in the first place?

Two answers. First: He didn't. Someone else did, with the intention of throwing me off the trail.

Or second: He did, believing he was fully camouflaged by a PO box, because criminals generally aren't genius masterminds. Dan's despicable, and his younger brother being on the same death-row block as my ex . . . that's persuasive. But maybe it's meant to be.

Maybe someone wants Dan O'Reilly to take the fall for this. I need a deeper dive, but I can only do so much.

I call Kez. I give her all the information, and tell her my misgivings about it. It feels like Melvin would have done better at covering his tracks.

Of course she asks what was in the envelope. I hesitate, because I can't turn over the diary. When I do, I look up. My daughter is standing in the office doorway, and she looks . . . strange. She's watching me, and shifting from one foot to the other. I smile at her, but she doesn't smile back.

"Come in, sweetie," I tell her. She does, but just a reluctant step. It'd odd. I wonder if she's had another crisis with Dahlia. "I'm on the phone with Kezia. I'll be just a minute, okay?"

She nods.

"Gwen?" It's Kez, reminding me she's still waiting. "Contents of the envelope?"

I lie. I have to. I can't ask Sam to give up the last piece of his sister's life to be put in an evidence bag, maybe never see the light of day again. Melvin's dead; he'll never pay for the pain he's caused. "It was a letter," I say. I know that's a dumb thing to say, because I've already turned over all the letters I got from him. Except the one I received right after coming back from Killman Creek, and that one is at the bottom of the lake.

"Mom," Lanny says. I glance at her. Her eyes are wide.

"I'm going to need that letter," Kezia is saying.

Lanny sucks in a breath, pulls back, and pulls something from the pocket of her hoodie.

It's an envelope. An open envelope. And when I reach for it and turn it over, I almost drop it. It's from Melvin. Addressed to me.

"How did you know? I'm sorry," she whispers. "I . . . I thought . . ."

I instinctively mute the call with Kezia. I want to tell Lanny it's okay. It's not okay. I feel a wash of absolute despair, absolute horror. "Where did you—where did you get this?" My voice is almost as unsteady as hers.

"It was in the mail. Don't be mad."

"I'm not mad," I tell her. "I'm just . . . When did this come?"

"Yesterday," she says. "I knew you wouldn't let me . . ." Her voice fades out. So does the light in her eyes, and I know why. I've felt what she's feeling. And I would have done anything, *anything*, for her to never feel that. "I just thought . . ." She wipes at her eyes. "Oh God, Mom. The things he said—"

I hug her as if I can protect her from everything, fold myself around her and take the pain of every cut, every vile word, away. But I can't, and I know that. I kiss her forehead and whisper, "I'm so sorry, baby."

Then I go back to the phone and unmute it and say, "Sorry about that, Kez. I have the letter." I look at Lanny as I'm saying it. "Come get it." Then I hang up.

I put the letter and the manila envelope from Sam's package on my desk. Lanny comes and sits next to my chair, leans her head against me, and cries quietly. I stroke her hair. We don't talk.

After half an hour, I say, "Get up." I pull her to her feet. "We're going to run."

She sniffles and looks at me with reddened eyes. Not quite believing what I just said.

"We need to run," I tell her. "*You* need to run. Go get ready."

She finally nods, throws herself into my arms again, and kisses me on the cheek. "I love you," she says, and then she's gone.

I sink down in my chair, staring after her.

I look down at the letter on my desk, the letter that has hurt my child so very much, and it takes every ounce of strength I have not to scream, not to rip it to pieces and fling it into the lake and drown it, drown *him*, silence his voice forever.

I don't do that. I stand up. I leave the room. I change clothes. And we run.

◆　◆　◆

Kezia comes by an hour later to pick up the letter. Javier is with her; it's his off day. He gets fist bumps from the kids. Javier asks for Sam, and I explain he's out at a job site. Javier nods. "Yeah," he says. "Can I get a word?" He glances at the kids. "Alone?"

We walk off toward the lake. Kez stays with the kids. Javier kicks around some rocks before he says, "Not sure I should even tell you this, but a guy came around this morning to buy 7-millimeter Remington Magnums."

"Which means?" I don't recognize the ammunition.

"Sniper rounds," he says. "He wanted sniper rounds. I didn't have any. I told him he had to order them in."

"Did you know him?"

"Spud Belldene. Jesse's uncle. He served in the first Iraq war."

"As?"

"What do you think?"

Not good news. "They'd *kill us* over a drunken fight?"

"They're Belldenes," he says, like it answers the question. "There's a chance that he's just buying ammo for practice. He likes to keep his hand in from time to time."

It's hot out here, and I'm still sweating buckets. "Weird timing, though. Considering we're looking for a sniper."

"Yeah," he says. "Which is why I brought it up." He rocks back and forth, heel to toe, arms crossed. "The feds raided their compound up there three months ago but didn't find anything; they thought the Belldenes were cooking meth. They weren't. At least, not there. But . . . thing is, if Spud meant you any harm, I don't think he'd buy his ammo from me. He knows we're friends. He knows I'd warn you about it." He rubs his hand over his head; it's freshly cut short, a sharp military style that makes him look ready for battle. "But shit, maybe that's what he intended. He just wants to rattle you. I don't know."

"This can't just be about Sam breaking the guy's teeth."

"Well," Javier says, "wars have been started for less up here. Never can tell what people take personally. Especially people like the Belldenes; they live on pride. Die on it too. Sam's a stranger to them, city folk. So are you."

"And it's not about my ex?"

"Doubt it. You, the kids . . . you're collateral damage to them. Leverage. They go after other men for their real sport."

It's ironic, really. For so long I've been under threat for what Melvin did. And here I am again, defending myself against strangers for something I had no part in. It's darkly, sickly funny.

"How do I stop this?" I ask Javier. I don't really expect an answer.

He shakes his head. "Don't know that you can," he tells me. "Maybe it's time to consider getting out of this town for a while. Between the Belldenes and this documentary everybody's talking about . . ."

"Everybody's talking about it?"

"This is hot gossip in Norton. And it's bringing up a lot of old bullshit, about you being guilty of murder. Some of them will jump on whatever paints you in a bad light."

Great. I suppose I should have assumed that. "And how do I fight it?"

"You don't fight the sea. You leave until the flood's over." He's uneasy. And that makes me uneasy. "Watch your back. I'll do what I can to cool things down."

We don't fist-bump. We hug. I love Javi. I trust him, just as I do Kez. He's had my back from the beginning, since the day I walked into his gun range, and I know he'll do what he can.

When they leave, though, I feel exposed. And helpless. It makes me angry.

We stay inside for the day. I watch from the windows for the white van, the film crew, but they're not here. Not where I can see them, anyway. It makes me itch to think they could be hiding in the trees right now, filming me, filming our house. After a while I try to concentrate on the book I'm reading, but I keep looking up, scanning the perimeter like I'm on a military post instead of my own porch. Looking for the flash of a camera lens in the trees.

Or the flash of a sniper's scope.

It feels like a normal day, but there's something underneath that I don't want to examine too closely.

I call the kids in, and propose a trip into town for cake and ice cream; they seem happy with that, though lately Lanny's been obsessing a little over calories. She just ran off about a thousand. I think she'll be fine.

When we make the drive into Norton, everything still seems normal. There's an old man driving a tractor down the middle of Main Street, throwing clods of dirt in every direction, but that happens at least once a week. I creep along behind him until we make the turn into the first stop. We usually start at the ice-cream store and finish at the cake place, but as I pull in and park, I spot a clean white van glide in after. It doesn't have any logos on the side, and from the sticker on the bumper, it's a rental. There are two people in the van, and as I turn off the engine, I keep watching them as they exit the vehicle and go to the back.

I don't know what I'm expecting them to do, but when I see that the taller African American man has a handheld video camera and the woman is plugging in a microphone, I realize *exactly* what's going on.

It's the camera crew.

They've found us.

"Mom?" Lanny, who's got her door half-open. "Something wrong?"

"Close the door," I tell her. My tone makes Connor scoot back from his exit too. "Let's just wait a minute."

"What's happening?" Connor starts looking around, and the cameraman fits the viewfinder to his eye.

He's getting a good shot of the back of my SUV, including the license plate.

"It's getting hot in here," Lanny says. "Can we just go in and get some ice cream now?"

"No," I say. "Sorry, but I think it's best we just go home."

"Why?"

From where they're sitting, they can't see the van. I might have told Lanny if we were on our own; my daughter understands things better than my son when it comes to our sometimes-precarious social standing in town. But I'm not yet willing to ramp up Connor's anxiety levels. He's wound pretty tight; the terrible experience with his dad not long ago has made him even more introverted. I miss the days when he was still hanging out with geeks his own age, enthusiastic for games and movies and Dungeons & Dragons tournaments. I still think those things are inside him, but I don't think he feels safe anymore expressing them.

Just another reason to hate my ex. Roast in hell, Melvin. Preferably on a slow-turning spit.

"I'll tell you once we're home," I say. I start the engine and back up. I have to pass the van to head for the exit, unfortunately, and that means the cameraman is perfectly positioned to see us. I have a faint hope that the kids won't see that, but of course Lanny does, right away.

She points straight at them. "What the hell are *they* doing?"

"Filming us," I say. "Put your hand down, please."

My daughter does not put her hand down. Instead, she turns it and effortlessly raises a proud middle finger. "Hope they got that," she says. "Assholes. Why are they doing that?"

I don't want to tell them this, but it's best they're prepared. "You remember the woman on the *Howie Hamlin Show*?"

"Miranda Tidewell," Connor says. "She's rich." When we both look back at him, he shrugs. "I looked her up. Since she was doing a documentary about our father. Why is she doing that?"

"People want to hear about him, unfortunately. And us. So we have to be careful."

"Yeah," Lanny says. "Which you'd realize if you ever got your nose out of your books."

They're fighting again. I wish that they wouldn't, but I know that's the standard sibling relationship, especially at this age. Lanny did handle Connor with kid gloves for about two months after I came back from Killman Creek and gave them the hard news about their dad's death—and that I'd had to be the one to kill him, which was hard—but the peace treaty never really lasts. In fact, there's even more of an edge to it now. We've talked it over, but I don't think Lanny can get over the idea that her brother was talking to their dad during that time. Melvin, damn him, had convinced our son to trust him, and Lanny just can't comprehend that. It's a wound between them, and I hope that eventually it will heal. But it damn sure hasn't yet.

We're at the parking lot exit now, and unfortunately there's traffic coming in both directions, so I'm stuck. The cameraman has walked off to the side, still filming. I'm sure he's tightly focused on our faces. I hate it. It feels like a violation of our privacy, even if it's not technically against the law. Or maybe it *is* against the law? I don't know what the rules are in this state for filming minors without consent. Might be something to look into.

I look at the oncoming traffic and wish everything would move faster, but there is yet another tractor rumbling toward us at an achingly slow speed. The dark eye of that camera at the periphery of my vision seems to get deeper, like the mouth of a well I'm falling into. I blink, and I see the camera in the Howie Hamlin studio, the feeling of being frozen and helpless.

I blink again, and I see a filthy, moldering Louisiana mansion. A room spattered with blood. Chains.

And a camera filming, filming, *filming*. Just like the camera Melvin had set up to show my murder to a waiting, paying audience of watchers.

I hear what sounds like an approaching scream.

"Mom!" Lanny's alarmed voice makes me mash the brakes, and I realize that I've drifted almost into oncoming traffic, and the scream was the horn of a passing truck. She rakes her black hair back from her face and gives me a worried look. "Are you okay?"

"I'm fine," I automatically tell her, because that's what I always tell her. And myself. But it doesn't take a paid psychologist to figure out that I'm *not* okay. I'm having flashbacks. Cold sweats. Nightmares. And now this filming, bringing it all back. I need to talk to Dr. Marks.

I take a couple of deep breaths and whip the wheel left when there's a break in traffic. Out of the corner of my eye, I see the man angle his camera to follow our path.

I don't really feel safe until we're over the hill, turned onto the main highway, and headed out of Norton.

Lanny fidgets in silence for a while, waiting for a fuller explanation I'm not willing to give; she finally puts her headphones on and stares out the window. Connor drops into his book and vanishes from the world.

I'm glad for the silence until Lanny shoves her headphones aside and asks, "You're not going to get married again, are you?" Well, that comes out of nowhere.

"Honestly?" I say. "I doubt it."

"Even to Sam?"

"Even to Sam."

"Why not? Are you guys breaking up?" I don't want this discussion. I glance around. Connor doesn't seem to be listening.

"We're not breaking up," I tell her. "Nothing's changed. It's just . . . I'm happy where we are, is all. I don't think there's any reason to be pushing it, do you?"

"As long as you're not breaking up." She shrugs, as if she doesn't care. I know better. She likes Sam a lot, and most of all, she likes how Connor is with Sam. It takes a lot for my son to trust people, but when he's with Sam, I see a kid who feels like he's . . . normal. Seen. Loved by someone with whom he feels safe. It's pretty special, and very necessary.

So I say, "Sam's always his own person, Lanny, and he makes his own decisions. But I don't see him leaving us anytime soon. If I do, I'll tell you."

Lanny just shrugs again, as if it doesn't matter to her. Headphones go back on.

We're almost home when I get a phone call from Sam. He's made it home. "Everything okay?" I ask.

"Fine," he says, but with such crispness I wonder. "You heading home?"

"Yes. I'm not far. Why?"

"Because we had a note on the door. A film crew was here looking for you," he says. "Also, we're out of oregano."

"Note? Film crew?" I repeat. At least I don't repeat *oregano*. "Jesus, they're getting bold. I just spotted them in town too."

He's silent for a few seconds. "We probably need to talk about this."

"Probably." I'm not looking forward to that talk, or the other one that we need to have.

◆ ◆ ◆

All through the evening I can feel it sitting between us like a stone wall, and I want to reach across it, feel him reaching back . . . but I don't know if I should. Or if that's even possible right now.

Time, I tell myself as we silently do the dishes, me washing and Sam drying. *Give him time.* But time could drive him away, and I don't know how to do this; nobody prepared me for how terrifying being in love, *really* in love, could be.

My landline phone rings, derailing me, and I'm caught between irritation and relief. I dry my hands and grab it because I recognize the number on the caller ID. It's Marlene, from Wolfhunter.

I get silence after my somewhat-brusque hello. Noise on the line. Breathing. I'm about to hang up when I hear a young woman's voice say, "Help me."

I pause, uncertain. "Hello? Who is this?"

"Vee," she says. "Vera Crockett. Momma said you help people. And your number was in her phone."

The accent is familiar, and so is the last name. Marlene Crockett was the woman who called me after the Howie Hamlin disaster. Who clearly had something on her mind, but couldn't bring herself to say what it was. Who'd wanted me to pick up and drive to a nowhere town to discuss it in person.

I'm instantly on guard. Using a kid, that's low. I have to resist an urge to hang up. "Put your mother on the phone, please."

"I can't," Vee says. She sounds strangely flat. "She's dead."

"Excuse me?" I'm turning to look at Sam, instinctively, lips parting. I shake my head to tell him I don't know what's going on, but the tone of my voice has alerted him to something odd. "When? What happened?"

"You should come," Vee says. "They're goin' to get me soon too. She's dead on the floor, and they'll come for me next."

"Vera? Vee? Are you saying that your mother is on the floor *right now*?"

"Yes."

I feel the world shrink around me, reality condensing into the voice on the phone. "Okay, I need you to call 911, Vee."

"If I do that, they'll kill me." She sounds calm, but terrifyingly disconnected. I don't know what I'm dealing with here. "Shoot me down like a dog right here."

I gesture to Sam, cover the mouthpiece, and say, "Get on the phone with Kezia. Tell her to get the Wolfhunter police over to Marlene Crockett's house. I don't know what's going on, but the daughter says her mother's dead."

He doesn't hesitate or ask questions; he grabs his phone and walks off to the corner to make the call.

"Vee," I say. "Your mother. Can you tell if she's breathing?"

"She's dead." No affect in her voice. None at all. Shock? Something else? I don't know.

"Can you check for a pulse for me?"

"She's *dead*." For the first time, I hear emotion. It's exasperation, and it jolts me. "She's on the floor, and—"

I hear Vee Crockett hesitate. Go silent.

When she speaks again, she's whispering. "They're comin' back."

"Vee? Vee!"

She's put down her phone, or dropped it. I hear something like footsteps, or banging, and then an ear-shattering bang that makes me flinch and stare at the mouthpiece, as if expecting something to come out of it other than sound.

I conquer that impulse in another second and put it back to my ear. "Vee? Vera! Talk to me! What's happening?"

Sam's still on the phone, watching me. I raise a hand helplessly. Vee Crockett isn't talking. But I can hear something. Movement? Distant shouting? Something like that.

And then, suddenly, her flat, calm voice is back. "That sent him runnin'."

"Vera, what just happened?"

"I fired the shotgun," she says. "Right through the door. Guess that one's headin' right for the hills."

"Are you okay?"

"Yes."

"Vee . . ." I don't know what else to do but keep her talking. "Vee, your mom said that she was worried about something. Was it about you?"

"No," she said. "My momma's never worried about *me*. Well, if she did, she sure gave up a while ago. Can't really blame her."

None of this makes sense. I don't know how to read this young woman. "Vee, how old are you?"

"Fifteen," she says. That hurts. I close my eyes briefly.

"I have a daughter your age," I tell her. "I know I'd do anything for her. I'm sure your mother felt that way too." I swallow hard. I need to keep her talking. *God, she's just a baby.* "Tell me about your mom, Vee. What happened the last time you talked with her?"

"I don't remember," Vee says. "Doesn't matter now. She's dead. She's dead, and I . . ."

She doesn't finish the sentence, but I feel a sick, crawling sensation. Was the end of that sentence: *and I killed her*? Marlene had been so vague about what was happening. She'd mentioned nothing specific, but maybe she'd been loath to admit she was scared of her own daughter. That would be an awful thing to face.

I hear something in the distance. Sirens.

"Vee? Are you still holding the shotgun?" I ask her.

"Yes."

"I need you to do something for me," I say. I keep my voice calm, assertive, and caring as I can manage. Sam hangs up his call and comes to stand across from me, drinking in my expression, my body language. There's nothing he can do, though. This is all on me. "I want you to put the shotgun on the floor. Do it now, please."

I hear movement. Rustling. A heavy *thunk*. "All right," Vee says, "I did that. But they're gonna shoot me anyway. They've been itchin' for an excuse."

"They won't," I say. "Now I want you to open your front door, hold up both hands real high, and stand there on your porch. You have a porch, don't you?" Most people do, in the rural south.

"Yes'm," she says. "But if I go out there, they're gonna shoot me dead."

"I promise you they won't if you raise your hands high."

"If I do, I can't hear you on the phone," she says. Perfectly reasonably, yet still with that odd, flat lack of emotion.

"Can you put me on speakerphone?"

"Oh. Sure." She does, I hear the change in environment, the way the world opens up into an indistinct fog around her. "Okay. I'm goin' to the front door." Shockingly, she giggles. "Man alive, I punched a hole clean through that thing! I can see all the way through."

I'm sick, thinking that there might also be a dead person on the porch on the other side of the door, but I don't say that. I just say,

"Okay, please open the front door, slowly, and raise both your hands. Are you doing that, Vee?"

I hear the creak of hinges. Vee's voice comes more distant now. "Yes'm."

"Step out slowly, and *keep your hands up.*"

This is the moment. I hear the sirens outside wailing to a stop. I hear car doors opening. I can close my eyes and imagine it in a spinning 360 degrees: Vee, on the porch. The hole blasted in the door behind her. Someone wounded on the ground, maybe, or even dead. Two—no, three now—police cars, which must be the full complement of Wolfhunter police, gathered around the place. Officers with guns drawn, nervous and ready to fire.

"Drop it!" one of them yells, and I realize he's mistaken the phone she's holding above her head for a weapon.

"Drop the phone, Vee," I tell her.

"Okay," she says, calm as a winter lake.

I hear the phone fall.

An impact.

Then three beeps, and the call goes dead.

There's not a lot of discussion about what to do next. I try calling the number back. It just rings and goes to an automated robotic greeting. I can picture the phone hitting the porch and shattering . . . and even if it didn't, it'll be in an evidence bag shortly, and no one will answer. Either Vee Crockett has been shot, or she's in handcuffs right now.

Fifteen years old.

I'm shoving a couple of changes of clothes into a duffel bag as I talk to Sam. "I have to go," I tell him. "Her mother called me for help. And now I'm in this as a witness whether I go or not. Vee called *me* before the police came; they'll need my statement on the record. I don't want them coming here and making a scene for Miranda's film crew to record."

I see Sam flinch at that. Or maybe just at the mention of Miranda. "You don't know that will happen."

"I do," I tell him. "These documentary people are circling like vultures. And they *will* seize on this if the police roll up to our door. Better if I handle it away from home."

I want to talk to him about Melvin's note in his sister's journal, about the awful shock of that and the emotional wreckage of last night, but I know that this has to take priority.

He shuts the bedroom door behind him. "Gwen. Stop."

I pause, at least. I look up at him, restlessly folding and refolding a shirt.

"You're a target," he says. He walks to me. "You can't put yourself in the middle of something when you've got no idea what's going on up there."

"I can't leave a fifteen-year-old girl out there by herself either. She called *me*," I tell him. "Her mother's dead. If it was Lanny—"

"But she isn't Lanny, she *isn't*," he says. He puts his hands on my shoulders, and I ache to be pulled into an embrace, but he doesn't do it. He holds me there, at arm's length. "You can't take on trouble in a strange town. You don't know the players, or the people. And you've got no stake in this thing."

"But I do." I meet his gaze, and he blinks first. "Sam, I know you're just looking out for me. I know the risks. *I know.* I'm not that much safer staying here. Leaving and avoiding the cameras . . ." I have a second of bone-deep panic, of losing my breath. I'm back in Louisiana, in a room with a camera and blood and a dead woman and my brutal ex. I'm on the Howie Hamlin stage, trapped in a nightmare.

If I face another video camera right now, I'll lose it completely.

"Goddammit," he says, but he's not angry. Just resigned. He leans his head against mine, foreheads gently touching. Then lips, in a sweet, quiet kiss, as if I hadn't shattered him just last night. "Okay. But you're not going alone."

"But the kids—"

"The kids go too," he says. "We all have to go, or you don't."

What he's not saying is, *We go as a family*, but I feel that. I need that. I kiss him again, more fiercely, and feel his hands drift up to cup my face. He brushes hair back from my forehead and looks at me like I'm something he's trying to memorize.

Then he steps back. "I'll tell the kids to get packed."

The kiss still lingers on my lips, makes me tremble inside, and I want . . . more. It scares me. I never expected to find this, not here, not with *him*, but Sam Cade is never what I expect, moment to moment. I want to heal the gulf between us. I need to.

I have the oddest feeling, though. I feel like he's relieved.

Like he wants to escape Stillhouse Lake right now as much as I do.

◆ ◆ ◆

"But *where* are we going?" Connor asks as I watch him stuff way too many books in his bag. "Someplace cool?"

"Probably not, kiddo," I tell him. "A place called Wolfhunter."

He pauses. I can tell he's never heard of it. "It sounds cool."

"I don't know. I've never been there. But it's at the edge of the Daniel Boone." The Daniel Boone National Forest is a huge swath of dark forest, and just saying it sets a mood. Connor's eyes widen. We've been there, of course; it was one of the first things I did with the kids when we moved here.

"Are we camping?" he asks.

"I sure hope not. There ought to be a motel we can stay at. I'm hoping it's just for a day or two."

He hesitates, then packs another book. I have to hide a smile. He's as bad about that as I am about self-defense equipment. The collapsible baton in the bottom of my bag weighs at least as much as three of his paperbacks, and it's far from the only thing I have in there.

"Why are we going?" he asks.

"You remember the lady who called me the other day for help?" He nods. "Her daughter's in trouble."

"How old is she?"

"Lanny's age."

"Oh. I thought maybe it was the other girl."

"What other girl?" I ask.

"The one from the TV show." He picks up his phone, and calls something up. He hands it to me. On the screen is a picture of a beautiful little African American girl of maybe six or seven, smiling for the camera and bursting with charm. "Remember? Her parents were on there. She was kidnapped from her school. They were in the waiting room with us."

I remembered now: the traumatized couple in Howie's greenroom. I'd barely registered them at the time, so intent on fleeing that I didn't care about anyone else's reasons for being there. I'd just wanted out. "Oh." I sit down on the edge of Connor's bed. "How long has she been gone?"

"Almost a week now," he says. "She's probably not coming back, right?"

I don't want him to know these things. Not at his age. But statistically speaking, he's on point; most young children who are abducted don't survive more than a few hours. "Didn't I hear there was some kind of ransom demand, though?" The details are filtering back to me. Abducted from her school in a slick, organized effort. Not an impulsive, need-driven act, but a planned and orchestrated one. That doesn't mean the girl is alive. But it indicates she has a better-than-average chance to survive.

Connor's eager to catch me up. He's clearly been following the case. "The discussion boards say that the dad paid the ransom, but nobody knows for sure," he says. "So maybe there was a *secret payment* to get her back."

"Back up, Connor: *Discussion boards?*"

Some of the brightness fades out of him. "Sorry. But I don't go to the ones that talk about my father. I promise."

"Don't go to *any* of them," I tell him. "And you know you can't believe what you read on Reddit," I say. "Stay off the boards, okay?"

"I don't post, I only read."

"Don't make me put them on the block list, Connor."

He gives me a frown. "I'm not some little kid. But you never want me to know anything."

I don't. Earnestly. Not about child abductions, and certainly not about the depths of horror that human beings have in them. Not about his dad, though I know he already knows much more than I think. "I want you to know things. I also want to be sure you're ready for it," I say, and mean it. "I don't want you to get a warped view of the world either." *Not like mine.* "People are good most of the time. Bad some of the time. Rely on the internet for how you look at the world, though, and you'll see the worst side of people represented far too much."

"That's not true, Mom," he says. "People put together big movements on the internet. They help each other. Strangers help strangers. It isn't all bad."

He's right, of course. My son's more well balanced than I am. "Okay. But I mean it. Do *not* fall for things that feel right, and sound wrong. Understand?"

"Like the lies my father was telling me," he says. "Yes. I know."

"I'm sorry, sweetie," I tell him, and he looks down at the book he's turning over in his hands. "He shouldn't have done that to you."

He shrugs, a loose circle of his shoulders. "Yeah, well, it wasn't as bad as what he would have done to you, probably."

I blink. I see a cold black camera lens, focusing on me. My throat tightens up, and I know I'm going to have to deal with this trauma sooner rather than later, and in a more constructive manner than pushing it away. But right now there's a girl in Wolfhunter who's all alone. A dead woman who asked me for help.

"I'm sorry about the little one," I say. "I wish I could help her too. But first we're going to see what we can do for this girl, okay?"

He nods, and adds more books to his already overstuffed bag. Connor builds his walls out of stories. As far as coping goes, he could do a whole lot worse. I have.

I check on Lanny. She's already packed, in one backpack. Less than what I'm taking. She's pacing in the living room, arms folded, and when I say her name, she jumps and turns with a smile that I know isn't real. "Hey! Don't sneak up on me like that." She seems genuinely distressed.

"Are you okay?" I ask her. That sets her back a step, and I see her put up her sarcasm shields to full strength.

"Oh, *sure*. I'm super okay with a sudden trip to nowhere, to do nothing, when I was going to see Dahlia tomorrow! You *know* how much I wanted to do that, right?"

I'd never leave her on her own, but I do briefly consider leaving her in the care of Dahlia Brown's mom, Mandy . . . except that if Lanny and Dahlia are having trouble, putting the two of them in the same house for a day or two might shatter that relationship for good. I don't want to be responsible for that. So I say, "Absence makes the heart grow fonder."

"Such bullshit."

"Lanny."

"Yeah, okay, fine. Let's go already!" My daughter is nerves and edges, and I wonder why. I want to ask, but I know her. This isn't the time. She doesn't want confidences. She wants to be on the move. I leave her pacing, gather Sam and Connor, and head back for the living room and front door.

We all stop when the doorbell rings. Sam's closest to the monitor; he steps back to look at the camera feed. "It's Kezia," he says, and I open the door.

Kez looks tired. She nods to me, and I step back to let her in. She embraces Lanny, bumps fists with Connor, and the kids are genuinely glad to see her. I'm not sure I am. I close and lock the door and cast a glance at Sam.

"Yeah, so, I thought I'd better come by," she says. "Y'all are going out there?"

It's not a huge deductive leap. The four of us carry bags.

"We are," I say. I'm half expecting her to object, but she looks relieved.

"Good, because my little chat with Wolfhunter PD didn't go so well. Good ol' boys seem to have declared this case open and shut, but they want you to get up there to give them a statement, not just about what happened tonight but why you were in touch with the dead woman in the first place." She wants to ask, but she also knows better. Kezia understands the kind of people who call me for help, and what their situations usually are: dire. She wouldn't want to discuss it in front of the kids. "Call me when you get there," she says instead. "Not sure I trust these . . . officers." If we were alone, she'd call them a whole lot worse. "Seems like there's only a couple of lawyers anywhere near Wolfhunter, so I texted you numbers for them. If you don't want to memorize them, put them on your arms in permanent marker."

It's a precaution taken by activists at marches. I start wondering exactly how bad a vibe she got from the Wolfhunter cops, and what the hell I'm risking dragging my kids into. I look at Sam, and I see the same reservations, but he's not going to let me go alone, and I'm not leaving them here to fend off this video hit squad that Miranda Tidewell has sent to destroy what's left of my reputation. Whatever comes in Wolfhunter, we'll handle it the way we've done everything: together.

I let Sam and the kids go ahead of me out to the SUV; I hand Sam my duffel as he passes, and he nods. He knows that I want a more private conversation. So I shut the door and turn to Kez. "You didn't tell me these so-called documentary filmmakers were in town when we came to see you," I say. "Why not?"

"I'm a servant of the public when I'm at work," she replies. "They weren't breaking any laws, and honestly, I didn't see setting your temper on fire would do anybody any good. You go at them, you'll just make their case, they'll win a bunch of awards, and your life turns to shit. Just stay away. That's the best thing you can do: Don't give them anything to work with."

She's right, of course. "That's another reason why it's good to get out of town," I say. "Because I can't guarantee that if they shove a camera in my face, I won't shove it up their asses."

"Yeah. That's kind of what I was afraid of." She studies me. Sharp as broken glass, just like her father. "You still seeing that therapist?"

"Why? Does it show?"

"Not to most people. You went through *hell*, Gwen. Give yourself a break. Let yourself heal up before you get yourself into another fight."

"I appreciate the concern, but you know I don't even have a choice."

She shakes her head. "Just try to keep out of trouble. Please. You know I'll back your play if I can, so will Javi, but there's a line I can't cross, and you're going to be way outside my jurisdiction."

"I know," I tell her. We hug. Two women wearing shoulder harnesses under our jackets, which says a lot about how we view the world. "Watch your back."

"You too."

I set the alarm, lock up, and head for the SUV as Kezia walks to her boxy, city-issued sedan. She trails us down the road to where it splits, right for the exit to the highway, left to keep heading around to the other side of the lake. Her headlights disappear off the other way, and we stop at the highway. Sam looks at the navigation on the phone mounted to the dash.

"Hour and a half out," he says. Glances at me in the light of the dashboard. "You sure?"

"I'm sure," I tell him. "Let's go."

As we leave Stillhouse Lake, I feel a tiny, guilty bit of relief. Like I'm running away from my problems, dumping them and escaping into the unknown, the way I had before.

But it's false, that feeling. Escaping was always temporary. Problems always caught up to me.

But, I remind myself, I'm not doing this for myself.

Not this time.

◆ ◆ ◆

The roads out to Wolfhunter are narrow and winding, and despite the moonlight, very dark. Headlights seem to go dim on these roads, and I'm glad Sam is driving, not me. The trees close in on either side until they're a solid mass. It feels claustrophobic.

We hardly see another car or truck along the way; a couple pass us flooring it past the speed limit, and a few more head in the opposite direction. An eighteen-wheeler rounds a curve swinging wide, and Sam slows down to let it clear out. This isn't a road friendly to large trailers. It's hard enough in a well-driven SUV.

There aren't any working gas stations, just a couple of spaces hacked out of the tree line with empty, weathered buildings and faded signs. We don't see much of anything else. Lanny opts to nap, head resting against the side window behind Sam; when I check the rearview mirror, I see that Connor's reading a book by the light of his phone. "You'll ruin your eyes doing that," I tell him. He doesn't even look up.

"That's not even close to true," he says.

"Says who?"

"Science."

"Hey, can you do me a favor?"

Connor looks at me, a little frown wrinkling the skin between his eyebrows, which are now raised. "What?"

"Look up Wolfhunter and see what you can find out about the town."

He puts his book down. "Seriously?"

"Yeah, seriously. I'd like to know what we're walking into. You're one of the best researchers I know."

"Wait, *one* of the best?"

"Well, okay. Maybe the best."

That pleases him, though he doesn't want me to see it. He puts the book away and starts tapping on his phone at lightning speed I can't even hope to approach with my older, broader fingers. Sam looks over and gives me a smile. I return it. Making Connor feel useful is important; he's spent so much time second-guessing himself recently. Getting his head into something else is good.

Sam's smile fades, and he turns his attention quickly back to the road. I know he's hurting inside, not just from what's between the two of us, but from that damn journal. Melvin wouldn't have arranged for it to be sent if it hadn't been a time bomb designed to harm, even destroy. And I don't know what it said.

I suddenly wonder if Sam brought it with him. The thought actually frightens me, that something Melvin's defiled might be traveling with us right now, like a parasite waiting to take hold inside us.

I can't ask. I can't start this conversation here with the kids.

Motel 6 looms out of the darkness like a neon oasis to the left; it's not in Wolfhunter, but it's close, a couple of miles from what looks like the center of town, such as that might be. We make the turn, and Sam parks in front of the office. "Two rooms?" he asks. I nod.

"Preferably with connecting doors," I tell him. "For sure next to each other."

"I don't think that'll be a problem," he says. There are only four cars in the parking lot, and most likely one of them belongs to whoever's working the front desk. It's a modest-size place, just one level and no more than fifteen or sixteen rooms set in an L shape around the lot. No swimming pool, but I think most motels have done away with them for liability reasons, and I don't want my kids attracted to lounging around one anyway. "Be right back."

He slides out and walks into the office. I wait, watching him inside through the dim glass, and I'm startled when Connor suddenly leans forward and says, too loudly, "Mom!"

"Oh come on, volume control!" Lanny moans, and pulls her hoodie over her face. "What the hell."

I turn to look at my son. He's ignoring his sister completely, totally focused on me. He holds out his phone, and I take it.

He's pulled up a blog. *True Crime* something, I don't really pay much attention to the site's title once I recognize I'm going to be dealing with an amateur's opinions . . . until I read the headline on the blog entry.

SECOND WOMAN MISSING IN WOLFHUNTER, TN. COVERUP?

Okay. It has my attention. I start reading.

> As you might recall, late last year I covered the case of Tarla Dawes, an eighteen-year-old woman who left her trailer in the sticks outside of Wolfhunter, Tennessee, to get groceries . . . and vanished into thin air. Dawes had a history of drug abuse and more than a little tension at home; the police were quick to dismiss it as a voluntary departure, though how she departed with just a secondhand purse and no extra clothes is a question the Wolfhunter PD (such as it is) seems to want to avoid. Tarla's mother doesn't believe that Tarla would have left of her own accord, even though there are plenty of reasons to believe that Tarla and

her unemployed nineteen-year-old husband were on the verge of divorce. At least one domestic violence call is on record.

But what eighteen-year-old disappears without posting or texting a friend? At least calling her mother?

Now we have a second young woman gone. Bethany Wardrip, twenty-one. Another one with a troubled history, some arrests, nothing unusual for around Wolfhunter: drug possession, public intoxication, disturbing the peace. She griped to a coworker that night that she wanted to leave this town and never come back. Did she? Bethany didn't own her own car; she often walked or hitchhiked with friends and neighbors. But no one reports seeing her that night, or giving her a ride out of town. Bethany, like Tarla, left with only a purse. Her clothes still hang in her closet. Her three extra pairs of shoes—an old pair of Converse high-tops, a heavy pair of hiking boots, and a pair of worn black high heels—were all left behind. More significantly, so was a coffee can found in her small kitchen cupboard with a roll of cash inside: $462.

That's a decent amount for a woman who works for minimum wage. The careful savings of a woman who bought little, and according to those who knew her, rarely went out with her old crowd.

Maybe it's just me, but I feel like something's rotten in Wolfhunter.

I read through it twice, and feel my heart rate speed up. This blogger could be onto something. Maybe it's the same thing that Marlene felt she needed help with. I don't know how or why that might have led to this horror show with the daughter, but this *feels* like something. "Thanks, baby," I tell him. "This is good information."

"I know it is," he says, with not a small amount of smugness. "Told you I could find stuff."

"Yes, you can," I tell him. "That's your job from now on, okay? Head researcher. Tomorrow I want you to find out if there's any more posted about either of these two ladies, okay? *Tomorrow*, not tonight. Don't stay up. Promise?"

"I promise," he says. "Can I borrow Lanny's laptop?"

"Ask Lanny," my daughter says without taking the hoodie off her face. "I'm right here, doofus."

"Okay," he immediately says, and turns to her. "Can I borrow your laptop tomorrow?"

"No."

"Mom?"

"It's your sister's laptop," I say. "If she doesn't want to help finding missing young women who might be in trouble, that's her business."

That brings Lanny bolt upright, clawing the hoodie back and glaring at me. "*Mom. That's not fair!*"

"If the two of you work together, you can get things done. You always do," I say. "I'm going to have to be at the police station tomorrow. Sam will stay with you guys. I know he'd appreciate the two of you getting along for a day."

"We get along," Lanny says. "Mostly."

"Work *together*."

That pleases neither of them on the outside, and both of them on the inside. Lanny rolls her eyes. Connor sighs.

I know they'll seize the chance to do something useful for me.

Sam comes out of the office, gets back in the SUV, and moves it into place in the parking lot. The headlights shine directly on two doors: numbers five and six.

"Okay," Sam says, and holds out a key to Lanny. Wolfhunter hasn't progressed to modern electronic key cards; it's an elongated plastic tab with the room number on it. "Lanny is the keeper of the key. Lose it, you both chip in for the fine. Got it?"

"We won't lose it," Connor says. "Why does she get the key?"

"I'm older," she says, and takes it. "We're in six. So you're—"

"We'll be in five," he says. "Breakfast at eight a.m., okay?"

"Do we have to hunt for it out in the woods?" Lanny sighs. "Bring home a squirrel or something?"

"There's a McDonald's half a mile down. But if you want squirrel bacon . . ."

"Ew. No. Gross, Sam."

We make sure the kids are stowed away, and locked in, before we take the room next door. It does have a connecting door, and I make sure it works before I can relax. At least there's no arguing from the other side.

"Two beds," he says. "Romance isn't dead." There's nothing familiar about the room, and yet it reminds me strongly of one we shared many months back, after Melvin's escape from prison, before things ended in the green hell of a tumbledown mansion. This one is clean, neat, utterly plain. I put my duffel bag down with my purse. Sam has tossed his bag on one of the beds, and is unzipping it to get out his toiletry kit.

I sit in the single, stiff armchair crowded in the corner next to the air conditioner. It's just blowing out barely cool air. "Do you want me to ask?" I keep the question calm, and soft. "I won't if you don't."

He freezes, and is suddenly intent on the kit he's holding. "About what?"

"Jesus, Sam, really?" I keep my voice low. My kids are right next door, and I definitely do not want them to hear any of this. "You know exactly what I mean."

"Yeah," he says. It sounds grim.

"Meaning?"

"Meaning I want you to ask. But I don't."

I stand up, take the leather bag from his hands, and put it on the bed. Then I put my hands on his cheeks. The stubble's sharp against my palms. No space between us. "What did he write in her journal?" I swore I'd never want to know anything else about Melvin Royal, especially when he was dead and buried in an unmarked pauper's grave, but Sam needs to get this out like an infection from a wound. I've got the name of the person who might have sent it, and we'll put a stop to any more of Melvin's posthumous torture.

He pulls me into an embrace, as if he wants to keep me sheltered from what he's about to say. "He gave me the whole story," he says. "How he abducted her. How she fought back. How he—how long she—"

My mouth goes dry, because it's as if Melvin knows, even dead, what will hurt us most. What destroys us. "Stop," I tell him, and turn my head so that my lips are resting on the soft skin just beneath his ear. "Sam, this is what he wanted. Did I tell you that one of the detectives who interrogated him committed suicide six months later? That's how toxic Melvin was, like breathing nerve gas. You can't let him inside, Sam, you *can't*. Everything he wrote down could have been just his sick, lurid fantasy. We can't know. We *shouldn't* know. And I wish to God you hadn't read it."

I feel the breath he takes in. It's like a hand grasping for a life preserver. "I had to," he says. "Everything he said feels true, Gwen. If she went through that level of pain . . . I don't know what to do about it. He's dead. I don't have anywhere to put this . . . sickness."

I'd wept through the medical examiner's testimony of each of Melvin's victims at my own trial. I'd forced myself to listen, to *know* what they'd suffered at the hands of a man who sat at my kitchen table and slept in my bed and was the father of my beloved children. I'd forced myself to endure it the way their families must have. I already know what happened to Callie, and it had been bad enough then as a clinical report; I've never heard it in Melvin's own emotionally predatory words. He'd revel in the details. In every word choice.

"Put it on me," I tell Sam. "Tell me."

We sit side by side in the blank, empty motel room, and he tries. Outside, the sky is dark over the trees, the stars blaze, and I stare at that view with tears welling up and dropping cold down my cheeks. It's awful, listening to the quiet rage of what Sam is feeling and what Melvin did. I wish it was beyond my comprehension, but it's so familiar. I can picture every step of it, every cut and scream and horrific detail. After he's done talking, he's short of breath and shaking. I wish we had drinks. I feel filthy and heavy and unspeakably sad now, but I know it was important for him to share it, and not to hold it by himself.

Despite our best intentions, Melvin is still reaching out from the grave to hurt us. And I don't know when that will stop. That's probably his plan, to make us dance to his tune for as long as he can. Maybe the man in Richmond is the end of it.

And maybe there are more of them. Melvin always did have fans.

"The last thing he wrote," Sam says, "was that she begged him to kill her. Begged him for hours. He recorded it. He says he'll send me the tape." He swallows. "I'm talking like he's still alive. But he must have planned this out, and there's somebody out there mailing things for him. So it's like he *is* still alive."

I flinch, because once again Melvin's found some unspeakable cruelty to inflict. I wait until my voice is steady, and then say, "I found the name and address in Richmond. Kez is on top of it, and we'll stop him from doing more damage. Melvin hoped to make you his last victim. Don't let him do that to you."

He nods slowly.

I'm not sure he can resist.

After a few silent moments, he stands up, gets his toiletry kit, and goes into the bathroom. I hear the shower start. I lie back on the bed and stare up at the ceiling. It's clean, no water stains, which is a wonder. I hate this. I hate that Melvin is standing invisibly between us, grinning like a skull.

I strip down to a light tee and panties and climb into bed; it's so hot and humid that I toss the comforter back and leave just the top sheet. The shower runs a long, long time. It's easier to stay in there; I remember all the times I tried to wash away the pain, the guilt, the unspoken rage. He needs to feel clean again, but I doubt he'll find it in the bath.

When he comes out, finally, I hear him stop for a moment. Trying to see if I'm asleep, I think. So I say, "It's okay if you want to take the other bed. I understand."

He switches off the light that sits between the two beds. I feel his weight settle in next to me, then the gentle heat of his body as he moves close. I'm on my side, and I look back at him, then turn to face him. The kiss he gives me is gentle, almost regretful. I curl up against him, never mind the heat of the room, and his skin smells like the lemony motel soap that will always, from this moment on, remind me of grief and loss.

We hold each other in the dark, and we don't talk. I'm almost afraid to breathe. There's something so fragile between us that the slightest tap might shatter it.

It might be the most intimate we've ever been.

◆ ◆ ◆

After the promised morning breakfast, and an argument with my daughter about whether or not pajama pants are appropriate for McDonald's, Sam drives us into Wolfhunter.

It's not much to look at, after all. The downtown—well, the whole town, really—is just about a ten-by-ten-block grid, with dirty-fronted shops along the main drag and faded clapboard houses leaning beside rusted fences.

It looks like a town that long ago surrendered. I doubt if more than a thousand people call it home. The only real virtue to it is that it's close to the large, lush national park, so I suppose the transient visitors keep the place on life support, if not alive.

The main street contains the same you see in every southern small town . . . a junk accumulation masquerading as antiques; a kitschy tourist store with lots of Confederate flags and bumper stickers designed to offend; a café that proclaims BEST PIES IN TENNESSEE and is probably lying. Pickup trucks and old SUVs with bumpers wired on, and nothing that's been washed in a year. Judging by the weather-beaten look of everything I can see, there's a paint shortage. Keeping up appearances requires some kind of aspiration.

The police station is just one street off the geographic center of town: a storefront operation that reminds me of old westerns, complete with a hand-painted star on a big plate-glass window. Not exactly the hardened, terrorist-resistant bunker of modern urban centers.

After my shower this morning, I took Kez's advice: I wrote phone numbers on my inner forearms in black permanent marker. It seems like a little too much paranoia, but better too much than too little. When I walk into this place, I'm essentially stepping into a dark room without a flashlight. I don't know who to trust. I don't even know if there's going to be a floor underneath me, metaphorically speaking. Best to be prepared for a fall.

Sam parks right in front, and says, "I'm your one phone call if you end up needing one. Right?"

"And my bondsman," I say, and try for a smile. I don't feel too good about this suddenly. "Okay. Everybody, get back to work on Operation Wolfhunter. I'll call when I'm ready to leave the station. Deal?"

"Deal," Sam says, and kisses me. He brushes hair back from my face. "Be safe, Gwen."

"Be safe," I tell him in turn, and then I lean over the seat and kiss my kids before sliding out into the thick, humid air of morning. The smell of the trees is powerful, overcoming any kind of car exhaust; there aren't that many cars on the road. It's a good smell at first, but then when I become accustomed to it, there's a dark undertone of dead things rotting under leaves. Of a stagnant river, ripe with mosquitoes. I'm not imagining it.

This town smells like death.

I try not to breathe deeply, and manage to smile and wave at Sam and the kids as he backs the SUV up into the street. I watch them until they're up over a hill, heading back toward the motel. There are a few people on the street, and I realize I'm drawing stares. Or glares. It's hard to tell the difference, but they're definitely noticing me.

I push open the door to the police department and head inside. The reception area's small, barely the size of my living room. There are some old wooden chairs up against the wall, and a bench that started life as a church pew. There's also a wooden counter, and a woman sitting on the other side of it typing away on a computer that's just barely aware of the internet age. She's fiftyish, white, with no-nonsense graying hair, perfect makeup, and cat-eye glasses. "Help you?" she asks without stopping her typing.

"I'm here as a witness," I tell her. "For the Marlene Crockett case."

The key-clicking stops. She spins her chair to face me, studies me with care, and then rolls forward to reach a phone. "What's your name, sugar?"

I resist the urge to tell her not to give me endearments when we just met. "Gwen Proctor."

She recognizes the name. I see the slow blink, the sudden shift in expression. Like a castle gate coming down. "Have a seat," she says. "I'll let the detective know."

I claim one of the wooden chairs, which look marginally more comfortably than the bench. She murmurs things I can't catch into the phone, hangs up, and gives me an entirely insincere smile. "Just one minute," she says, and goes back to her computer. If she's got email on that thing, she'll no doubt be spreading word of my arrival everywhere.

I'm glad I have the numbers of lawyers on my arms. I have no idea what might happen in here; they probably won't charge me with a crime. But I've learned the hard way that being innocent doesn't mean handcuffs don't go on.

It's something less than a minute, all in all, until a solid old wooden door in the back wall opens, and a man comes out who has to actually stoop to pass underneath the top of the frame. I stare, which I imagine isn't an unusual thing, because he's got to be approaching NBA heights . . . six foot seven, nine, maybe even more. Thin, too, with long legs; he must have his suits custom-tailored, because this one fits him well. It's light gray, a concession to the heavy heat.

"Ms. Proctor? I'm Detective Fairweather, Tennessee Bureau of Investigation." He holds out a hand as I get up, and I feel miniaturized when we shake. He's careful and professional about it. His skin's the kind of pink that doesn't take to the summers around here, and his hair's Nordic blond, cut military short. "How are you, ma'am? I hope that drive wasn't too difficult."

I have to give him points for using Ms. instead of Mrs. or Miss; I usually have to correct people at least once. His accent is definitely southern, but not so much Tennessee. Virginia? Hard to say.

He holds the door open for me and gestures me inside. I don't immediately obey. "So you're not actually with the Wolfhunter police?" I ask him.

"We're working together on this," he says. "I'm the lead investigator. After you, ma'am."

He's painfully polite. I suppose that should comfort me, but instead it makes me warier. But I don't have much choice; he's not going to let me walk out of here without a conversation. I go past him and into a narrow, dim hallway. It's as scuffed and beaten up as I would have expected. He leads me into a room off to one side and shuts the door behind me.

Typical interrogation room. I settle on the side that I know he wants me to take, the one that captures me best on video. Might as well be cooperative when it's easy.

Detective Fairweather takes the chair on the opposite side of the small table and settles on it like he's afraid it might break. "Ma'am, you don't mind if I record our conversation, do you? It's for my records." He puts his cell phone down. It's entirely unnecessary, unless the camera isn't working properly . . . or he's afraid Wolfhunter PD might not be entirely reliable. I nod in reply, and he presses the red button on the screen. "Okay, so just for the record, ma'am, please state your name."

"I'm Gwen Proctor."

"Originally Gina Royal? Wife of Melvin Royal?" Cheap shot, Detective.

"That's my former married name, yes."

"And just for context, ma'am, where is it you live?"

"On Stillhouse Lake, near Norton."

"In Tennessee."

"Yes."

"And do you live there by yourself?"

"No," I say. "I have two children, Lanny and Connor. And Sam Cade also lives there."

"Sam Cade." He leans forward now, resting his long forearms on the table and lacing his fingers together. "And lives there how, exactly?"

"I'm not sure I understand the question." I do, perfectly. But I want him to ask straight out.

"Is he renting a room from you, or . . ."

"We share a bedroom," I tell him. I suppose a more normal thing to say would have been *We're lovers* or *We're partners*, but even now, I hate to push it that far. Dumb, I suppose.

It doesn't matter how carefully I parse my words, because the detective gets exactly where I'm going. "Well, that's a little unusual, isn't it? Considering your ex-husband brutally murdered his sister?"

I let that sit for a long few seconds. My silence has thorns. When I do answer, my tone's gone sharp and, against my will, defensive. "How exactly is any of this relevant to what I heard on the phone?"

Fairweather holds up his hands in either surrender or apology. "Apologies. Just background questions." No. That was a deliberate ploy to throw me off-balance, and we both know it. "Okay, let's go ahead and move on. I need to ask you some questions about Marlene and Vee Crockett."

"Don't know them," I say. Absolutely true. I force myself to relax. Body language speaks as loudly as words, especially on camera.

Cameras.

I glance involuntarily up toward the one set in the corner. It's disguised, but not very well, with a paint job to match the bland walls. There's no lit-up indicator to show whether or not it's recording, but I can still feel its blank, impersonal stare.

I blink back images of nightmares and try to focus directly on Fairweather again. He's asked me a question I missed. "Sorry?"

"You did speak to Mrs. Crockett, we know that. That call she made to you went on a bit. Wasn't just a wrong number."

"I didn't say she didn't call me. I said I don't know her."

His straw-colored eyebrows round up. "You usually have conversations with some stranger as you don't even know?"

Despite the antique rural phrasing, I recognize the shark gliding under the surface of that question. "Sometimes," I say. I keep it placid. "When they're in trouble."

"And what kind of help can you offer them, exactly?"

"Advice." I'm tempted to leave it there and make him chase the rabbit, but I don't. "Look, you know who I am and who my ex was. People—mostly women—sometimes reach out in dealing with difficult situations."

"Such as?"

"One woman had a husband who was about to be arrested as a child molester. She didn't know how to deal with it, or the fallout. Another woman wanted to do what I did: change her name to protect her kids from harassment. Sometimes I can help them. Mostly I can't. Occasionally I get ones that just need to talk it out."

"And Mrs. Crockett?"

"She wasn't specific about what her problem was. She clearly felt like there was trouble, though I didn't get the impression she thought it was danger to *her*. She wanted me to come up to Wolfhunter. She said she'd discuss it here." I take in a breath, let it out. "To be honest, I thought maybe she suspected someone around her of some crime. That's normally the case."

"Did you? Meet with her?"

I see the spark fly through him, like a pilot light flaring up. How much of a career boost would it be for him to somehow pin a woman's murder on the ex of Melvin Royal?

"No, I did not," I say. Still calm. "I'm happy for you to look at my cell phone records, which should show you exactly where I've been since then, and I'll give you a detailed timeline in writing. I've never been to Wolfhunter before we got here late last night."

If he's disappointed, he doesn't show it. His helpful expression never shifts. "If you could write that all down for me, that would be real helpful," he says. He opens a drawer on his side of the table and comes up with a lined yellow pad and a felt-tip pen. "I'll need to ask Mr. Cade for his timeline from when Marlene first called until you got that second call too."

"Of course. He'll be happy to do that, and give you access to his cell records as well." I wouldn't normally make that kind of promise on Sam's behalf, but obviously this detective's not stupid; he's going to get court orders and pull them whether we like it or not. Acceding will give us the edge on credibility.

"So what exactly did Mrs. Crockett say when she called you?" he asks me, and shifts a little forward. An invitation to share confidences, just between the two of us. He's got a good command of body language, I'll give him that.

"Not much. She called after we got back from Knoxville, after dinner."

"Knoxville," he repeats. "And why'd you go to Knoxville again?"

"I had an appearance on the *Howie Hamlin Show*. It's filmed there." My tone goes sharp again. He gives me a little nod.

"Yes, ma'am, I do remember that now." He must have Googled me already, that would be standard procedure before taking an interview. "And what exactly did she say when she called?"

I think back. My memory's not perfect, but it's reasonably good, and I think I recount it well enough for him. He listens without comment. When I pause, he says, "And why didn't you come to Wolfhunter when she asked you to?"

"Because I'm not stupid," I say. "I don't go running off to meet in secret with people I don't know. Not unless I do it on my own terms. It might have been a trap."

"A trap?" He sits back now. "Set by who, exactly?"

I start ticking off the list. "Fans of my ex. Absalom members who slipped the net. Random internet stalkers, of which I have dozens. Not to mention the families of my ex-husband's victims, some of whom still believe I'm complicit. Oh, and all these crazy people stirred up by that mess on the Howie Hamlin train wreck, because now I've got Miranda Tidewell's *documentary crew* stalking me. So . . . plenty of suspects."

"Sounds like your life is difficult, ma'am."

"Not nearly as difficult as the people who lost their loved ones so horribly," I say. "Damn sure not as difficult as the lives of my children, who've had to endure more than I can imagine. I'm not wallowing in self-pity or paranoia. I'm just realistic about the number of people who want to see me humiliated or hurt. Maybe dead. But I'm not the one dead, am I? Can we get back to Marlene?"

He lets me shift the ground. "Okay. So after that initial call, you had no further contact with her, is that right?"

"That's right."

"Until the call came from her phone."

"Yes." I remember the sick sensation of realizing just how badly things had gone on the other end of that phone.

"I'd like you to describe that call in detail, ma'am. Be as specific as possible."

So I do. I tell him what Vee Crockett said, as best I can recall it; I describe the unsettling way she said it. The panic of the shotgun blast, and thinking that she'd been killed as well.

"Ah," he says. "Well, that was the postman on the front porch, delivering a package. Good thing he was bent over putting it down when she let loose with that shot."

"He wasn't hurt?"

"Ran for his life," Fairweather tells me. "Punched a hole the size of his head through the door just above him. He was damn lucky."

I agree. Vee had meant to kill whoever was on the other side of that door. "That doesn't necessarily mean she killed her mother, though."

"I haven't said anything about that," Fairweather says. "And I'm not here to tell you what I think. Go on. What happened after that?"

"I told her to put the shotgun down, switch the phone to speaker, and hold up both hands after she opened the front door."

"Why not tell her to hang up? Or hang up yourself?"

"Because I felt like she shouldn't be alone," I tell him. "She's *fifteen*. She'd been through a trauma."

"You just described how little that bothered her."

"You know that sometimes people react to trauma in odd ways. She called *me*. I felt I needed to see it through as far as I could. I was afraid . . ." I pause, thinking about whether or not to say it. "I was afraid she'd make a mistake and somebody would overreact."

"Or she'd provoke them into it? Suicide by cop?"

"I can't say. I just felt she wasn't thinking clearly. She needed help."

He changes tack. "Folks around Wolfhunter said that Marlene had a sour relationship with that girl," he says. "She was into drinking and taking some pills. Trouble at school. She tell you anything about that?"

"No," I tell him. "No specifics, like I told you. I can't help you with that. But honestly—that describes a lot of kids, right?"

"Yours?"

Well, that's a precise little stab. "No." Not the drinking and pills part, at least. "Let's stick to the subject, please."

He veers back into timelines, and I tell him point by point up to the minute the phone dropped from Vera's hand, and then add what I've done since. Some of it, inevitably, will be unverifiable, but when paired up with cell records, I think I'll be okay.

He asks me then to write it all down. I do. I know the ploy: Ask the questions aloud, then match the written timeline and identify discrepancies. Then double-check everything.

"Detective," I ask, "how is she?"

"Marlene? She's dead."

"Vera."

"Hospital checked her out. She's just fine. Just not cooperative."

"Have you charged her?"

"I'd be an idiot not to," he says. "Nothing she said to you on the phone says she didn't do it; even then, the physical evidence shows her with fingerprints on the weapon, blood all over her, and gunshot residue."

"The gunshot residue comes from the shot I heard."

"Maybe. Maybe that was her second target. Two shells, and the gun was empty when we collected it."

Even I am not convinced of the kid's innocence, but this bothers me. "Does she even have a lawyer?"

"Ma'am, I caution you not to get too involved in this. We may never know why her mother called you; maybe it was because of the very thing that happened, and the person she was afraid of was her own daughter."

"That wasn't my question."

"The court appointed someone," he says. "Hector Sparks. He's local."

He'll be one of the two numbers on my arms, most likely. "Can I see her?"

He leans back, as if he wants to get as far away from that question as possible. "Why would you want to do that, Ms. Proctor? You don't know this girl. You didn't even know her mother."

"She's my daughter's age," I say. "And . . . and she might talk to me. She did on the phone."

He thinks it over, and I believe he's tempted, but then he shakes his head. "Can't allow someone without legal standing to visit until she's been held over for trial."

"What if her lawyer's present?"

"Well," he says, "if her lawyer's present, and you have his permission, then it's privileged communication as long as you're working with him in some capacity. Otherwise, no decent lawyer would allow it."

There's a strange emphasis, the way he puts that, and something I can't quite unwrap. I let it go. "Okay," I say. "What if she asks to see me?"

"Don't put ideas in that girl's head," he tells me. "She's not the fragile little thing you seem to think she is. And I guarantee you she doesn't need your protection."

"Funny," I say, "I remember the same things being said about me when I was in jail, waiting for my trial."

Fairweather doesn't respond to that. He stops the recorder on his phone, pockets the device, and stands up to open the door. "All right, ma'am." he says. "Well, I thank you kindly for your assistance. Would you mind if I contact you again, if I have some more questions?"

"No, sir, I don't mind at all." Aren't we just the picture of southern cordiality?

He gives me his business card. "Don't forget to email me permission to get your cell phone records, and have Mr. Cade send me a timeline and the same letter granting permission. It speeds things up considerably."

"I'm not sure speeding things up is in that girl's best interest," I tell him. "You seem to be moving awfully fast already."

"Just because it looks like an open-and-shut case doesn't mean I won't put in the work. But I don't expect any twists in this story, Ms. Proctor. Bad blood between them, Marlene even reached out to you for help on her situation, and it blew up before she could get it." His expression loses a little of its aw-shucks-country-boy charm. "And the longer I'm on this case means the less time I put in looking for that little girl."

"Ellie White," I say. "The kidnapping. You were on the task force?"

"Until this mess," he says.

"I hope you find her."

"With respect, ma'am, I'm almost hoping I'm not the one who does," he says. "Because that girl is almost certainly dead."

8

SAM

After we drop Gwen off—and I hate leaving her there alone—I take the kids back to the motel. Connor is fidgeting with the desire to get at his assigned job: tracking down the case of the missing young women of Wolfhunter. Lanny tries to pretend she's massively uninterested, but I know she is.

She also asks a lot about Vee Crockett, which worries me a little. Normally Lanny can be skeptical and a pretty good judge of character, but there's something about Vee's situation that seems to have gotten past her natural defenses. Maybe it's the fact that she's afraid Dahlia Brown's getting tired of their relationship; teens run hot as hell, then cold as ice, and that's normal. But Vee's not someone I'd like her to be fascinated with. Not, I remind myself, that I have any say in the matter. I may be in the household, but I'm not family.

No matter how much I'd like to be.

Lanny, predictably, tells Connor he's going to have to wait an hour, grabs her laptop, and asks me if she can use my room to call Dahlia. I tell her yes, and leave her alone for whatever drama plays out. Connor, grumpy, loses himself in a book, and I check messages on my phone, leaning back in the armchair in the corner of their room.

◆ ◆ ◆

It's under an hour when Lanny comes through the connecting door and hands her laptop to Connor. "Here," she says. "Keep it." She flops onto the other bed and rolls over on her side.

She sounds angry and hurt, and I turn my attention to her as Connor shrugs and starts mining for internet gold. She's been crying, no question. Her eyeliner's a mess, her cheeks flushed, and from the red in her eyes, she's been at it a while.

I sit down beside her, but far enough away that she doesn't feel like I'm in her space. "So?" I say. "What's up?"

"Nothing." She sniffles wetly and shoots me a sidelong glance. "Have you ever been dumped?"

Hoo, boy, this is that conversation. I briefly wish her mom was here, but she isn't, and I am. So I say, "Yeah. Absolutely."

"And?"

"There was a girl. Her name was Gillian."

"When was this?"

"High school."

"Was she beautiful? Did you love her?"

"She was gorgeous, and yeah, for a while. Then one day she just wasn't interested anymore. Next thing I know, she's dating someone else on the same baseball team."

"Well, that's awkward," Lanny says.

"Especially when she told everybody I'd been sleeping around on her."

This time I get the whole stare. "Did you?"

"No. But that's what she said." I shrug. "It happens. My foster mom once told me she got thrown out of a car on a date with her boyfriend and had to walk a mile back to town, in heels, in the dark. That's how her breakup happened."

"Seriously?" Lanny blinks. "He just *left her*?"

"When you say dumped, she got *dumped*. Right by the side of the road," I say. "She told me she never wore high heels on a date again. So I didn't feel so bad after that."

"I guess." The way she says it means she doesn't believe she'll ever feel good again. I remember those years, where everything came in overwhelming waves and was destined to last forever. There's a lot great about it. Even more that's dangerous.

"Something happened with Dahlia," I say, which isn't a genius guess.

She takes a deep breath and lowers her voice to a tense whisper. She doesn't want to say this with Connor in the room, clearly. "Dahlia says she can't see me anymore. Her mom's pissed off about the rumors going around, the documentary, all that crap, and she thinks I'm a bad influence or something. It's not even my fault!"

"It may not be permanent. Let things settle." But that's adult advice, and I know it feels useless to her. "Did she say she'd still talk to you?"

"Yeah." Lanny blinks back more tears. "When her mom wasn't home."

"Then maybe it'll work out."

"Maybe." Lanny doesn't sound too optimistic. She scoots closer and leans her hand against my shoulder. I put my arm around her. "Thanks."

"Anytime, kid. These rumors she mentioned. Like, what kind of rumors?"

"That mom helped Melvin kill people. That she's some kind of sicko." She swallows when her voice falters on that last part.

"Your mom had a fair trial. She was acquitted. Not guilty."

"Yeah? Tell that to the Sicko Patrol that follows us around on the internet," Lanny says. "They *still* believe she's guilty. It ruins everything."

I think about Miranda. The Lost Angels. She's absolutely right. Some things leave a stain, even after all the scrubbing in the world. I feel it like a slow knife to the guts, because I also know how much guilt I bear for that.

"Sam?" Connor's voice. I look over at him. "Uh, maybe you should look at this?"

I kiss the side of Lanny's head and go over to him to see what he's got. He swivels the laptop toward me.

"That's something, right?"

A third young woman, reported missing not from Wolfhunter, but from the Daniel Boone National Forest that Wolfhunter clings on the edge of like a burr. I pick up the laptop.

It's another entry like the ones he found before. Same blog.

ANOTHER WOMAN MISSING
FROM NEAR WOLFHUNTER

Earlier I covered the suspicious disappearance of Tarla Dawes, eighteen. Then Bethany Wardrip, twenty-one.

Now there's another one. Sandra Clegman, who lives in Sioux City, Iowa, but was vacationing in the nearby Daniel Boone National Forest. Her friends saw her zipped up in her tent one night, and she was missing the next morning, leaving behind everything she'd brought with her, including wallet and cash.

People get lost in the woods. But Sandra Clegman was a country girl with a history of camping in forests, and the idea that she wandered off to be eaten by bears without a trace is pretty sketchy, if you ask me. Forest rangers conducted a thorough search, along with the state police and even some FBI. No traces were found: not a drop of blood or a snag of fabric on a branch.

Sandra Clegman, like Tarla and Bethany, just vanished.

If you draw a circle from the center of Wolfhunter, Tennessee, with a ten-mile circumference, you'll find all three of these disappearances fall inside that circle. I made a phone call to the Wolfhunter PD and asked what they thought.

They told me I was talking about two runaways and a hiker who'd probably had a bad fall and died in the wilderness. Nothing to see here, move along.

Well, I'm not moving along. Because something's off.

"It's weird, right?" Connor says. "Three women now. That can't be just luck, can it?"

"Strangely enough, it can," I tell him. "Weird things happen. But more than that, the police may actually believe something's wrong and not want to put the word out to the public just yet. There could be an investigation going on that this blogger doesn't know about."

He doesn't seem thrilled with that. "I still think it's weird."

"I'm not saying it isn't," I tell him. "Keep looking. You could be onto something."

He nods, a little happier, and I give him back the laptop. I check my watch. Gwen's been at the police station for two hours now, and I haven't gotten any calls from her. I wonder if she decided to use the traditional one phone call (presuming they offered; they're not required to) for a lawyer, and she trusts me to call and ask after her.

"I'm going to check on Mom," I tell the kids, and walk into the other room. I close the connecting door and dial her cell.

I get voice mail. I leave a message asking her to check in, and then I look up Wolfhunter PD's central number in the tiny phone book on the nightstand. I get a smooth southern voice asking me how to direct my call, and I ask if I can speak to Gwen Proctor.

She hesitates, then transfers me without another word. This time, a male voice. "Detective Ben Fairweather. Who's this?"

"Sam Cade," I say. "I was looking for Gwen Proctor."

"Hello, Mr. Cade, nice to talk to you. I had a good chat with Ms. Proctor, but she left out of here about ten minutes back."

I don't like that. "Heading where?"

"Most likely to see Vera Crockett's defense lawyer," he says. "You got time to stop in and give me a statement? I understand you were in the room when Ms. Proctor took that call from Vera. I'd like to get your account of it, and a timeline for the past forty-eight hours or so."

He sounds friendly and reasonable. I don't like it, and I don't trust it. "Sure," I say. "Later today, once Gwen's back. I can't leave the kids."

"Of course." He pauses. "So you all came up."

"Family trip," I say. "We might visit the forest." Almost certainly not, but it gives a decent excuse. If Gwen hasn't mentioned it, I don't want him digging into reasons we left Stillhouse Lake. Miranda's crew is, I hope, still in Norton. They'll have a lot to say. Some of it might even be true.

"Okay," he says. "How about two? That okay for you?"

"I'll give you a call," I tell him. "I just need to find Gwen first."

We end it politely, and I find a note from Gwen with two lawyers' phone numbers that Kez had texted her sitting on the bedside table. I call the first one, and I get a recording by what sounds like an ancient man who says he's out of the office.

The second one gets a pickup and a crisp greeting. "Hector Sparks's office. This is Mrs. Pall. May I help you?"

There's something about it that sets me back a little, and it takes a second for me to identify what it is. *Mrs. Pall.* Not many women answer the phone with that form of address in the office anymore. They normally use their first names. "Hi, I was wondering if Mr. Sparks might be having a meeting with a woman named Gwen Proctor? She was heading over to talk with him. Is she there?"

"May I ask who's calling, please?" She sounds *very* uptight.

"Sam Cade," I say.

"I'm very sorry, Mr. Cade, but Mr. Sparks's meetings are strictly private, and I won't be able to confirm that for you."

"Then can I speak to him?"

"I'm afraid not," she says. "He's asked not to be disturbed. But I will give him a message that you called."

"And if Gwen is there, please ask her to call me," I say. She doesn't acknowledge that at all. "Thanks."

"You're welcome," she says, but not in any way that makes me feel it, and hangs up the call.

I open up the connecting door again. Lanny's lying on her bed, headphones on, looking miserable. When she sees me, she turns her back. I don't push it. "Connor," I say, "can you look somebody up? Get a little background?"

"Sure!"

"Hector Sparks," I say. "He's an attorney here in town. I just want to know a little more before . . ." Before what, exactly? There's no real reason for it, but something about that conversation set me on edge. Just like the one with Ben Fairweather. Maybe it's this town. Missing women. A dead mother and a jailed daughter. Wolfhunter just doesn't seem safe for Gwen. And I feel like having her out there on her own is dangerous.

"Okay," he says. "I'm on it."

It takes him about fifteen minutes to report back that Hector Sparks is an attorney who lives in town—he gives me the address—and his father was a lawyer too. Connor's found a couple of local newspaper articles he shows me—old ones, since the local newspaper expired years ago—and it all seems normal enough. One of the articles has a picture of a surprisingly nice, large house that seems like far better construction than the normal Wolfhunter real estate. Old, too—maybe built in the early 1900s. A family posing in front: an old man in a wheelchair, a son standing tall next to him. A mother and daughter are also in the photo, but they're off to the side, definitely just bystanders to the men's special moment. The mother's expression is blank. The daughter's looking away. It's an odd photo to put into a newspaper, even one as amateurish as this publication obviously was. The write-up is clumsy, but it's apparently celebrating the retirement of the father—Donald—and the takeover of the attorney business by the son, Hector.

The women aren't even mentioned in the caption beyond "accompanied by wife and daughter." The dateline is 1992, but the sentiment is pure 1950s.

But the point is, Hector Sparks is legit, and I shouldn't be worrying about Gwen.

Yet I am.

I text her. Even if she has her phone on silent, she usually answers within a few minutes.

Then I sit straight up, staring, because I have a voice mail that's come in while I was on the phone.

I know that number from memory. It's Miranda Nelson Tidewell, and immediately on seeing it on my screen, I'm plunging off a cliff into an abyss.

"Hey," I say to Connor, "got to make a call, okay? I'll be right next door."

He nods, not even taking his eyes from the page, but I think he looks when I turn away. He probably notices my tension.

I leave quickly and take some deep breaths standing in the room I'm sharing with Gwen. The connecting door is shut. I realize it feels warm in here, so I get the air-conditioning going again.

Then I place the call that will send me straight to hell.

Miranda doesn't say hello. She never does. "Sam. Did you even listen to my message?"

"No," I tell her. My voice sounds different when I talk to this woman. I can't remember if that's always been true. "What the hell are you doing?"

"I think the real question is, what do you think *you're* doing, Sam? You're living in her house. In her *bed*. That is, without any question at all, the most monstrously perverted thing I've heard in years, and my God, that's quite saying something."

Her voice. It's both honey and ice. A hint of huskiness, still; while she was being treated for a breakdown after her daughter's murder, she screamed so much she permanently altered it. Her damage starts there, but it's just a hint of the chasm underneath.

Miranda is rich. A multimillionaire, the ex-wife of a hedge fund manager. A former Junior Leaguer who'd had life handed to her on a succession of silver platters . . . until the day her daughter, Vivian, disappeared at the mall. The second of Melvin Royal's known victims.

She'd met me at the airport coming home from deployment. I'd still been in my fatigues. She'd looked like a perfectly composed mannequin draped in designer fashions holding a sign with my name printed on it.

We have something in common, Mr. Cade, she'd said. *My daughter, and your sister. Let me drive you. We'll talk.*

I'd been shell-shocked, raw, angry, devastated, and vulnerable at that time in my life. And Miranda had been far worse than I was. The toxic relationship we'd formed . . . I've seen her unkempt, messy, wearing clothes that stank of days of drinking bouts. I've carried her back into her three-story, six-thousand-square-foot mansion and helped her to the toilet when she needed to vomit. I've listened to her rages. I've taught her to shoot a gun.

We've done awful things together.

"How did you get this number?" I ask her. That's not the most urgent question, but it's the only one I can stand to ask at the moment.

"Money and contacts," she says, and I hear the amusement in the words. It's her answer to most things. "You're not at home. I know. I visited there yesterday, along with my film crew. I did leave a note. I even signed my name, remember? Did you tell her that?"

I hadn't. I'd taken the goddamn note and run it through the shredder.

When I don't respond, she keeps going. "Where exactly are you hiding, Sam?"

"I'm not hiding," I tell her. It's half-true, anyway. "And we've got nothing to talk about, except how you're going to back the fuck off and leave us alone."

"Us." The contempt and scorn in the word feels like a lash against my back. "My God, Sam, really? This is insane."

"It's not your business," I say. "Go home to Kansas City, Miranda. Let it go."

"I sold the house in Kansas City. I'm . . . What's the popular phrase these days? *Property surfing.* Though I have to admit, I had to spend a very unpleasant evening at that local bed-and-breakfast in Norton, and I won't be going there again. I understand there are some reasonably adequate houses for rent out at Stillhouse Lake. Maybe you can recommend the one you used to have."

I don't answer. I can't. The idea of Miranda, with millions to spend and the leisure to indulge her hate, holing up like a venomous spider within striking distance . . . it's honestly horrifying. I know Miranda. I know she was out of control when I left her. If she's abandoned her old life in Kansas City, all her creature comforts and enablers and sympathetic friends . . . then God only knows what she's planning.

"You didn't answer me," she says. "Is this some kind of game you're playing, pretending to be in a relationship with her? I really hope it is, because the alternative makes me want to vomit."

"Let's not do this," I tell her. "Come on."

"So it's true? You're actually sleeping with her. She was *Melvin Royal's wife*, for God's sake. Hurt her, yes, by all means. But don't debase yourself."

I don't want to talk to Miranda about Gwen. My past is a wrecking ball. I've always known it was out there, rushing toward me. I just never imagined how much it would hurt when it finally hit. "I'm only going to say this once," I tell her. "So believe that I mean every word. If you come for her, you come through me. You make even a move toward hurting those kids, and I will end you. They don't deserve any of this. Gwen, the kids—they're innocent. Just leave it alone. Just *stop*."

She's silent for so long that I think I've actually gotten through to her. Then she says, "She's really turned your head inside out. My God, she's good at making otherwise-sensible men believe her, including the ones on her jury. We swore to make her pay. I thought you believed in that." She sounds almost . . . sorry for me.

She's right. I'd believed every word of that at the time I'd met her. I've moved past it, but nothing's changed in Miranda's life. She's frozen in the amber of her grief and rage, obsessed with reliving her dead child's last moments.

Revenge is not my life. I don't want it to be, not anymore. Even after reading Callie's journal . . . especially after that, because I can see myself ending up like Miranda: broken, cored hollow, filled with rage if I step off that cliff.

I don't mean it to hurt when I say, "I'm sorry for you, Miranda. I really am." But from the sharp intake of breath on the other end, it does sting. Deeply. "Please stop. I'm asking you. Please. If we ever had any kind of feelings between us, *please don't do this.*"

"I'm only talking to you because we *did* have that," she says. "One chance. You're better than this. Just walk away from that woman, even if you don't help me. Or I swear to you, the price you pay for it will be very, very high."

I think of Gwen, sobbing in my arms. Waking from nightmares that she can't talk about. Defending her kids despite her own danger. And saving me too. Gwen isn't perfect, by any stretch. But she's a damn sight more real and alive and human than Miranda, whose malevolence is the only thing keeping her broken heart beating.

"Okay, you can say you gave me a chance, if that makes you sleep at night," I say. "If you're coming at me, do your fucking worst."

I hang up on her. That probably drives her wild; Miranda's used to cursing, but only when she's the one doing it, and she's a narcissist. She hates to be ignored. She's lived in a padded box her whole life, handled carefully like a breakable treasure; when reality crashed in on her, she could only believe that her pain, her loss, was bigger and more urgent than anyone else's. And that will never change.

I felt something for her once. Not tenderness. Not love. But a shared delusion that expresses itself in violence is almost more intimate than love.

Miranda Tidewell is back. I know she's not going away.

And everything I've built, everything I love, is about to come crashing down on top of me.

"Sam?"

I look up. Lanny's standing in the doorway of the room that Gwen and I are sharing.

She's got her phone in her hand. Holds it up. I see there's a call open. She hands it to me.

I lift the phone to my ear, and Miranda's voice says, "Did you really think it would be that easy?"

I know Lanny can see me flinch, and I quickly turn my back to her, and say, "You just called a *child's phone* to make a point. Well, I get it. Trust that. What the hell do you want? What is your endgame here?"

"I have all your numbers," she says. "Would you rather I call Gina next, or are you going to come out and talk to me face-to-face?"

She refuses to call Gwen by any name other than her old one. I swallow hard. I'm shaking; I can feel it. "Where are you?"

"Outside in the parking lot of your motel," she says. "I'm in a rented Buick. Definitely not my style, I know, but this isn't Lexus rental territory."

Shit, shit, shit. She tracked our phones. Of course she did; we got careless about changing them. If she got our numbers, it'd be easy as hell for her to pinpoint our locations. Norton's not that far away. And we're sitting ducks inside this room.

"I could have you arrested for stalking," I say.

"Really?" She laughs. It sounds half-crazy. "And are you going to explain what we are to each other to the police? Maybe you should also confess all the illegal things you got up to while you were with me. Stalking, as I recall, was also involved."

I look over my shoulder. Lanny's still there, frowning, trying to listen. I walk over and close the door. I'm struggling just to keep it together. "Leave," I tell Miranda.

"No. You didn't just screw me over, Sam, oh no. You fucked over your dead sister and my dead daughter and all those other dead girls too. That's how low you are. And how much of a gullible coward. *Come out and face me.*"

I go to the door that opens out to the parking lot. Put my hand on the knob. It's as warm as blood, easy to turn. I make myself stop, and I crouch down still holding it, breathing hard against the impulse to go out there, break her windows, beat the holy living shit out of the car, if not the woman inside it.

Because that's what she wants. A confrontation. One that gives her something to use.

"Sam?" I can barely hear her over the ringing in my ears. *Christ.* She knows how to push my buttons. She learned that over those years we nursed our grudges together, hand-fed them on diets of hatred and booze and still-bleeding wounds. She remembers. "The longer you wait, the worse this is going to get. Understand?"

I stand and pull open the door. There she is, Miranda, unmistakable behind the wheel of a running blue Buick, and she's right, the car's too pedestrian for her even on this trip to nowhere. Her hair looks perfectly styled. Her makeup perfectly applied. I've seen her raw and desperate and agonized, stumbling and screaming, but this Miranda is her public face. Rich, entitled, and proud of it.

I don't go out. She sits in the car. We stare at each other for a long, long moment as heat shimmers up between us, and I lift the phone back to my ear and say, "I'm done."

I shut the door and hang up the call. I turn to put my back against the wood and slide down until I'm sitting, a human shield between her and the kids, because she'll come for me first; she'll have to. I don't know what I'm expecting. Gunfire through the door, maybe. I know she's got it in her.

But I hear a change in the pitch of the Buick's engine. It's backing out. Then I hear it drive away.

Lanny's knocking on the connecting door, urgently. "Sam? Sam, are you okay?"

I get up and open it. I hand the phone back to her. "Block that number," I tell her. "Do the same for Connor's phone, okay? I don't want you talking to her."

"Who is she?" She's eyeing me warily, and I can't say I blame her. I probably don't look like the same man who listened to her breakup story. "Is she—she's not—"

"An old girlfriend?" I finish for her, because that's naturally where she'd go. She nods. "No. Someone . . . someone I used to work with."

"You sounded so angry, though."

"Yeah, the job didn't end well." Not that it's ended at all. Miranda's right about one thing. Sooner or later, I'm going to have to face her.

And sooner or later, I'm going to have to tell Gwen what I've been holding back from her, before Miranda does it for me.

9

GWEN

Everything in Wolfhunter is a short walk, even in the heat. Hector Sparks has a lush old place, probably one of the nicest in Wolfhunter. It's a private home with a carefully tended garden bursting with flowers. Bushes trimmed to precise measurements. Trees that don't have a leaf out of place. Since I can't see a lawyer—even in this little burg—having the leisure to tend such a thing, he either has a brilliant full-time gardener, or a spouse with a green thumb and lots of free time. There's a shiny—but discreet—polished brass plaque on the lawn that says HECTOR J. SPARKS, ESQ., and beneath that, even more discreetly, ATTORNEY AT LAW. This isn't a guy who feels the need to plaster his face on a park bench or advertise on late-night television. He has to be very high priced to afford this lifestyle. And living in Wolfhunter?

Interesting.

I stop and check the address on my phone, and realize that I've missed a couple of calls—coverage in this town is shitty, dropping in and out every block or so. One is from Sam, and one is from Lanny. I listen to Lanny's voice mail first. She's sobbing her heart out about Dahlia, which is what I was afraid would happen; I want to call her back, *go* back to her, but first I switch over to Sam's voice mail. He sounds worried about where I am. So I call.

He answers on the first ring. "Gwen?" He sounds tense as hell.

"Yeah," I say. "I'm okay. About to go in to talk to Vera Crockett's attorney."

"Thank God," he says, or I think he does. It's fast and almost a mumble. "Okay, well, I tried to call there, and the dragon lady who answers his phone wouldn't confirm whether or not you were there. She'd only say he was in a meeting."

"And you're concerned because . . . you don't think I can look after myself?" I'm strangely touched.

"No, I'm concerned because we're in a town where women disappear," he says. "And I don't want you on that list, Gwen."

Now I'm charmed, and also a little annoyed. "Do you seriously think I would end up there?"

"No." He pulls in a deep breath and lets it out, as if struggling with what he wants to say next. "Connor's working on stuff for you to look over. Anything you want me to do?"

"Just watch out for them," I say. "Thank you. I know you'll protect the kids, whatever might come."

I don't say that about many people—two others, to be exact, and in truth I only entrusted Connor and Lanny to Javier and Kezia because Sam couldn't stay to do it. He thought my safety was just as important . . . and that's something I need to remind myself of more.

"They're okay, though?" I ask when he falls silent.

"Lanny's got a bit of a broken heart," he says. "Connor's enthusiasm for researching crime is scaring me a little. They're great, though. As they always are." I feel my throat tighten. I have strong kids who care about others despite everything that's been done to them. They're watchful and guarded, but beneath that they have real empathy. It's a gift that must have come from heaven, because I'm not arrogant enough to think it's something they got from me.

"Hey, Sam?"

"Yeah?"

"Everything okay with you?" I ask because I can feel him holding back. I can hear the tension even when I don't see it. "Did something happen?"

"No," he says, and this time he almost sounds normal. "It's just . . . I have a bad feeling, so watch your back. Please."

"I will," I tell him.

"I'd like to leave tonight," he says.

"We already paid, though."

"I know. I just—" He makes a sound that's all frustration, no words. "Dammit. I don't know that going home is much of an answer either. The documentary crew isn't going to give up."

Fucking Miranda. No wonder he's edgy. "Okay. Let's stay here tonight and decide tomorrow," I tell him. "Sam. It's okay. I promise."

He doesn't ask how the hell I can promise, and I'm really glad because I damn sure don't know. I tell him I love him. He says he loves me too.

I carry that inner warmth on the walk up the broad, clean sidewalk and up the front steps onto the wraparound veranda. Bees drift lazily between the flowers, drunk on nectar, and the thick smell of hyacinth and roses mixes in a powerful cloud.

I ring, and the door's answered in ten seconds by a rawboned woman of middle age who seems like she'd have been more comfortable in a farmhouse on the prairie during Westward Expansion—or, to give it the real definition, Westward Invasion. She's got long hair piled up on her head and a sharply angular face, and is wearing—of all things—a full apron, the kind that loops around her neck and goes down to her knees. It looks like a costume. Beneath that, she's wearing a flowered dress with a high collar and long sleeves, even in the summer.

"Yes?" she says doubtfully, looking me up and down as intently as I'm appraising her.

"Hi, I'm here to see Mr. Sparks," I tell her.

"Mr. Sparks is not currently seeing new clients—"

"I'm not a new client, ma'am. I'm just in town for the day, and I need to talk to him about Marlene Crockett's daughter, Vera. Vee."

"Mr. Sparks does not speak with journalists without an appointment."

Oh, come on. "I'm not a journalist." I hate to do it, but there are times when my dark celebrity comes in handy. "My name is Gwen Proctor. I'm the ex-wife of Melvin Royal. Perhaps you can ask him if he'd like to see me?"

She blinks, blinks again, and without a change in expression, says, "Please wait a moment." The door shuts again, but it is more of a gentle motion than a slam, and I do as instructed. After less than a minute, the door opens, but it's not the housekeeper/dragon lady. It's an older man with silver/gray hair, slightly darker on top than on the sides. He's wearing a nicely pressed, blazingly white dress shirt, a paisley tie, and suit pants. He even has suspenders to match the tie. And all of it probably costs more than I've ever spent on my entire wardrobe.

He smiles and holds out his hand. "Ms. Proctor," he says, and raises both eyebrows. "You do prefer Ms., am I correct? I confess, I've read up about your . . . ah, history. I never thought we'd meet face-to-face."

I shake, and nod. "I'm here about Marlene and Vee Crockett."

The smile vanishes, and it's his turn to nod. "Yes, please come in. It will not be a long conversation, I'm afraid."

The hallway smells of fresh lemon-scented polish, and the hardwood floor is spotless. There's surprisingly colorful art on the walls, mostly of gardens, but I don't get time to admire it as I follow Mr. Sparks down the hall and into a spacious office. This one has a gigantic red Persian rug covering most of the floor, gently holding a large antique desk and three matching leather-bound chairs. The room has a reassuring smell of furniture polish with a faint undertone of tobacco, and against my will, I breathe it in deeply. My mother used to use the same lemon-scented polish. My childhood memories are drenched in it, along with my father's sweet pipe smoke.

Mr. Sparks congenially offers me one of the chairs and sits behind his desk. He rocks slightly for a moment before he says, "Where are my manners? Can I offer you coffee? Iced tea? I believe Mrs. Pall has made up a cream cake, if you'd like some."

"Thank you, no, I'm fine." I'm tempted by the cream cake.

"Very well. Please explain how you became involved in this matter, Ms. Proctor."

Like any good lawyer, he's asking me to verify what he already knows. "Her mother called me," I say. "And I'm concerned about what's happening here, because from what I got out of the phone call, Marlene didn't seem frightened that her own daughter was going to kill her."

"You were also an earwitness, so to speak, to what happened with Vera, isn't that the case? Detective Fairweather told me he intended to take your statement." His accent has its roots in the Wolfhunter drawl, but it's a little less antique. He must have gone away to school and consciously struggled with it. Southern accents can be a real barrier in some places. I look around for the degree; almost every lawyer has it framed and on the wall. And there it is, off to the right of his desk, but there's a glare on the glass from the window. I can't tell what school he attended.

"Yes, and I gave a statement this morning," I say. "I assume they'll share it with you."

"Always nice to know what to look for, in case someone overlooks it. And let me ask you a pointed question: Do you think the girl committed this awful crime?"

"I don't know," I tell him. "Detective Fairweather wouldn't let me talk to her, which is too bad, because I felt like . . . like we had something of a rapport on the phone. At least, enough to get her through it alive."

"You likely did save her life," Sparks says. "Our local police are not exactly highly trained. She was lucky, especially since—"

"Since people already knew there was trouble between her and her mother?" I finish it for him, because it seems like he's trying to imply without committing himself. "I know that."

"Interesting," Sparks says. He rolls his leather chair a little forward and folds his hands together.

I'm struck by his incredibly neat, precise desk. An in-box (or maybe an out-box) with just one folder in it. A miniature bronze of Lady Justice, complete with blindfold and scales. A small gavel with some kind of memorial plate. A desk set of penholder and leather desk protector, both looking impeccable. There's only one pen in the container. I don't know why, but that strikes me as eccentric, bordering on odd.

"So let's back up. When Marlene Crockett called you, she seemed afraid of someone?"

"Yes. Or some situation. She wasn't specific," I say.

"Not even a guess?"

"Just that she seemed to be having a crisis and wouldn't give me details unless I came up to talk in person."

"Which you did not do."

"No."

He cocks his head slightly. "Why not?"

I think of a million defensive excuses, but I say, "Honestly? I didn't want to put myself in the middle of something. After the business last year . . ."

"Yes, I can understand your wanting to stay out of the spotlight." He doesn't mention the disastrous Howie Hamlin TV appearance, though I'm sure he's aware of it. "I assume you also considered that it might be a trap set to lure you to Wolfhunter . . . an out-of-the-way place where you might well be caught without support."

"Well . . . yes, I did."

"But you don't think that's the case now?"

I blink. "Marlene's dead. She clearly *did* have something to fear."

"That doesn't mean it isn't still a trap. Just that the bait is bigger." Hector Sparks sits back in his chair and lowers his chin as he stares at me. He's about to say something when I hear a distant banging. Rhythmic, like someone hammering in a nail. Banging a pipe? Annoyance flickers across his face. He picks up the phone sitting at precise angles in the corner of his desk and dials. "Mrs. Pall? *Please* get on the intercom and ask maintenance to keep the noise down, if you please." He hangs up. "Apologies. It's an old house. Repairs are simply never-ending."

"Of course," I say. "It is beautiful. You keep it in great condition."

"Thank you. Well, it's been in the family for a very long time." Something about that seems to give him a flicker of amusement, but then it's gone, and he's back to seriousness. "I just want to be clear about what Vera Crockett is facing in this county. They intend to arraign her for first-degree murder, and try her as an adult. She may not have much of a defense unless I can find some alibi witnesses to show she could not possibly have done the deed."

The banging comes to an abrupt halt. Mrs. Pall is efficient. Mr. Sparks visibly relaxes. "Ah, that's better. Ms. Proctor . . . I have a somewhat unusual request to make."

"About . . . ?"

"I'd like you to speak with Vera. I'll accompany you; everything she tells you will be covered by attorney-client privilege, and you will be acting as my agent in this matter. You're purely there as a facilitator. I'm willing to pay you a generous fee as an assistant to help me get her full story." He shakes his head, a chagrined look coming over that kindly face. "She just doesn't like me, I'm afraid, but I'm all she's got. She talked to you. Reached out to you, in fact. I don't have a lot of time if I'm going to start tracking down an alibi for her."

"Wolfhunter can't be *that* big," I say.

"You don't know this town. Vera's reputation was already . . . let's call it damaged. This place is quick to make judgments and close ranks.

If I don't find her witnesses quickly, then I might not be able to get them on the record at all."

I don't want to be drawn into this any deeper; I'm not sure I actually *want* to help Vee Crockett. She unnerved me on that call. But she's fifteen, and alone, and he's right: small towns like this don't forgive, or forget. "Mr. Sparks, this case could draw media attention, and I'd rather not get caught up in it."

"Understandable, given your, ah, current notoriety. It will only be one conversation, I promise, and then our business will be done, and you'll leave her defense in my hands. Does that sound all right?" When I don't immediately answer, he drops his voice a little into a warmer, slower register. "She's your daughter's age, more or less. And she's trapped in a nightmare, all alone except for what help I can offer. And if I'm to give her any hope of avoiding a conviction, maybe even the death penalty . . . I need your help. All I've got to work with right now is a girl who was in the room with her dead mother, covered in her mother's blood, with her prints on the shotgun that killed Marlene. And I'm assuming she didn't say anything to you that would have exonerated her."

I shake my head. "And even with all that, you still don't think she did it?" I make it a question. Sparks's expression stays carefully neutral.

"I believe she deserves a chance to prove she didn't," he says. "But she won't speak to me to assist in her own defense. You could be the key to helping her."

"I don't think the police will welcome me back."

"I can't imagine you're a great deal concerned with what the police want. I'll get you inside. If you make a good-faith effort but Vee still refuses to talk, then keep my payment and be on your way with a clear conscience."

I think about it and then ask, "Why did you take her case? You must have known the town would be against you."

He's silent for a moment. A long one. Then he slowly leans forward with a creak of springs in his leather chair and spears me with a look I can't read. "I didn't choose it," he says. "I was assigned the case. Believe me, I'd rather not be responsible for it, but here we are. Do we have an agreement?"

We do.

When he writes me a check from a thick leather ledger for $1,000, I get the oddest feeling that he's buying more than my time. But a grand is nothing I can refuse, especially now. I have no idea how he's going to be reimbursed for this—if he ever is—but I'm not going to turn it down if he's willing to offer. And besides, I do want to get Vera to tell her story. I want to know.

So I take the check, and now I'm hired.

"May I have your cell number?" he asks, and I write it down for him. As I hand it over, my sleeve rides up, and he sees the Sharpie marks on my arm. His silvery eyebrows climb. "Is that my phone number?"

"In case I was detained by the cops," I tell him.

"How enterprising. I expect to have our interview set for the afternoon," he says. "Thank you, Ms. Proctor. I appreciate your willingness to help."

As I leave, Mrs. Pall is standing in the foyer, as if she's a robot who plugs into the socket there. Her gaze follows me. I can't resist. "I hear you have cream cake," I tell her. "Any chance I can get some to go?"

She glares at me without answering, but then, I didn't expect a gracious parting gift. I'm just enjoying twisting her tail.

Suddenly she smiles and says, "Have a *very* good day, Mrs. Royal."

"Proctor," I tell her.

"Oh yes, of course. I quite forgot." In a pig's eye.

Then the door shuts, and I can't work out which of us won that. I frown at the shiny surface for a long moment. Something's off with that woman. I have no idea what it is, other than general weird unlikability. Not really my problem.

The only reasonable thing to do while I'm waiting for Hector Sparks's call, though, is to go to the motel, talk to Sam, and maybe get some clarity on what's making him so twitchy.

◆ ◆ ◆

When I call him, he sounds clipped, but normal, and it's a brief call; I wait outside on Hector Sparks's perfectly ordered lawn for five minutes until the SUV glides up. Sam's in it by himself, and I get in quickly and stare at him while I fasten my seat belt. "You left them alone?"

"Yeah, I did," he says. "I needed to talk to you. It's ten minutes, Gwen. Lanny's on guard."

"Okay," I say, but it isn't, not really. "Private talk. This sounds dire."

He plunges right into it. "Gwen . . . I need you to seriously think about moving away from Stillhouse Lake. Because Miranda Tidewell is not going to give up on this."

"You sound like you actually know her." He doesn't answer immediately. "You *do*." I'm taken aback. I don't know how to feel about that. It's certainly not my right to police who he knows, but *that* woman . . .

"I do." He says it quietly, and I can read how reluctant he is to admit it. "We connected after I got back from my last deployment. She met me at the airport. Helped me reacclimate to civilian life, and . . . figure out how to deal with Callie's murder."

I feel a real twinge of anger, and I bury it. Or try to. "Sam, if the two of you were lovers, just come out with it already." I hate that I feel a surge of jealousy. But I can't deny it either.

"No, it wasn't like that," he says. "Look, we talked before about how I was part of the pack of stalkers that came after you online, but . . . not the full extent of what I did, or how. She knows. And she's going to use it."

"Use it how?"

"To destroy us," he says.

I turn and give him a really long look. "Can she?"

He doesn't do more than glance my way, then turns his attention back to the road. We're making a turn onto the main street already. Five blocks, more or less, to the motel. It seems a long way suddenly.

"She's capable of doing anything to fill that bottomless hole where her soul used to be," he says. "Melvin did that to her. She's dangerous, Gwen. To you, to the kids, maybe. I need you to understand and think how we're going to protect against that."

"Is she *physically* dangerous?"

"I honestly don't know. I feel like I don't know where to look for trouble anymore. It's not just watching my back, your back; it's watching *everything*."

"We've always known that," I say. "Always. Three sixty, three sixty-five." That means 360 degrees of awareness, 365 days a year. Our personal code. And it hasn't failed us yet. "It feels like there are still things you're not telling me. Am I wrong?"

"No," he says, and takes in a deep breath. "I also got an outreach from a company in Florida. They're looking for a private pilot to work standby. Good salary, benefits, the whole package."

I'm ashamed that the first thing I feel is a deep fear that he's found a real reason to leave me. Leave *us*. I quickly throttle that back and say, "Congratulations. Are you thinking about taking the job?" That sounds accusatory. I can't help it.

"I wasn't, not seriously," he says. "Not until Miranda showed up."

"Do you really think she can't find you in Florida? She tracked us down at *Stillhouse Lake*." I turn and look at the ramshackle, fading town of Wolfhunter as it glides past the window. The despair it emanates burns down my nerves. "I said I wasn't going to run anymore."

"I know you said that. But circumstances have changed."

"Have they? Do you really think I'm more afraid of an angry, grieving mother than I was of my murderous ex who *skinned women*? I said I'm not running. I won't." I talk tough. I feel like I need to right now, because the undeniable truth is that if Sam *does* take that job in Florida, if he leaves us . . . I don't know what that means. We've been so careful about not putting names and labels on what we have that I don't even know what I'd be losing, except . . . everything.

I swallow hard. "Sam—I can't do this. Not now."

"We can talk about it later," he says, and I know he's struggling with this too. Probably more than I am, if that's possible. "Okay. How'd this morning go?"

"Interestingly," I say, and I'm a thousand percent relieved to change the subject. "I'm going back with Vera Crockett's lawyer to see her this afternoon. He's having some trouble getting a statement, and I might be able to get her to talk more freely."

"Okay." He doesn't seem thrilled. "So we leave tomorrow?"

"Yeah." I pause. "Is that all right?"

"Fine," he says. I don't know why, but I think he's lying. Or at least suppressing something important. "Lanny will be glad to talk to you. I did my best, but broken hearts—"

"Sort of a mom thing?" I finish. "Probably." I don't tell him that for me, the only broken heart I've ever really had was from the first man I thought I loved. After the monstrous betrayal of my ex, nothing else can compare, and certainly never hurt as much.

Though thinking of Sam leaving comes very close. So does the thought that he and Miranda Tidewell were . . . whatever they were to each other. I wonder if he's lied to me about the sex, or lack thereof. Sam doesn't lie that often, but when he does, he does it disturbingly well.

By then, we're passing the McDonald's where we had breakfast, and then making the turn into the motel. We park. Most of the other cars that had been in the lot are gone—campers heading for the forest, I assume. Or couples who rented by the hour. The doors to our two rooms are closed, but I see the curtain tweak in the one occupied by my kids. That eases some tight knot in the center of my chest. Ten minutes seems like a long time for them to be on their own right now.

I feel as if there are enemies all around, and I no longer know who the hell they are.

We both start talking at the same time. "Sam, I don't know—"

"I'm sorry that I—"

When our words collide, we both fall silent, waiting for the other to proceed. He doesn't. So I finally do. "I don't know if I even want to think about moving away from Stillhouse Lake right now. The kids— they only just started to feel safe, and . . ." I trail off. He nods. "I'm not saying you shouldn't go after that job. You should if it's what you want to do. I won't get in your way."

I get out of the SUV before he can think of an answer. I don't want to hear it. I go straight to the door of the kids' room and knock, and before I hit twice, the door's open, and Lanny throws herself into my arms. I walk her inside without breaking that embrace. "I was worried," she says, and sniffles. "You were gone a long time."

"I'm fine," I tell her. I push her back a little and study her. She's been either crying or fighting not to, and she looks puffy and miserable. I hug her again and smooth her silky, multicolored hair. "You know me. I'm not going to leave you. Not even when you want me to, because I'm the most annoying mom ever."

She laughs a little and hugs me tighter. I look over at my son, who's quietly watching us above the edge of the laptop. "Hey, kiddo," I say, "how's it going?"

"Fine," he says. "*I'm* not the one who's freaking out."

"Don't be mean," I chide him.

"Yeah," Lanny says, and turns her face toward him, still pressed against me. "Don't be mean, jerk."

"And you." I bop her gently on top of the head. "Quit name-calling."

"She's been like that all day," Connor says. "I don't care."

He does, though. He and Lanny were each other's everything while I was in jail, then on trial. Even when I came back, they stayed close.

They had to. It was us against the world. I know that has to end eventually . . . but not yet. I can't bear it.

"Anyway, this town's really weird, Mom. It was started because they trapped and killed bears and wolves and things; then they had an iron mine. But some of the histories say there were gangs of thieves here, too, who used to rob people and bury them in the forest."

"Okay." I sit on the edge of the bed where he's propped up. "That's interesting background. Anything more recent?"

"Three women went missing," he says. I like that he's so particular about his nouns; even at his age, he's not falling into the trap of calling adult women girls, or worse, *females*. "And there are a couple of younger ones who maybe ran away but maybe not too. And a disappearing wreck! It's cool, Mom, check it out."

He swings the laptop around toward me, morbid delight all over his face. It's a paranormal website talking about recent accounts of a devastating wreck near Wolfhunter—two cars, a head-on collision. A hunter apparently witnessed it from the trees on the hill above, but by the time he was able to get a signal and call the cops and make his way down to the crash site . . . there was no wreck. No bodies. The tire tracks and crash debris that was left along the shoulder could have been there for days. The article segues into a discussion of a local legend about a deadly crash in the 1940s that left several dead, and a ghostly car that has haunted the road ever since.

Odd. Marlene mentioned a wreck.

"When was this?"

"Last week," Connor said. "But even years back, there was a story about a ghost car that drives that same road. Some people think that's where the missing women went. Maybe the ghost car picked them up and took them away."

"Really, Connor?" Lanny's face twists in a mask of disdain. "Ghosts, now? For real?"

I see the spikes come out in my son. "Like you didn't say Bloody Mary three times in the mirror at midnight."

"I didn't!"

"I saw you!"

"Stop!" I shout it this time, over the rising volume, and glare at each of them until they look away. "Enough! Connor, thank you. I'm not sure the ghost car is going to help, but anything's possible. Come on, you two . . ."

"I want my laptop back," Lanny says.

"Fine, take it," Connor snaps. "About time you did something useful; all you've done is cry about your stupid girlfriend not liking you anymore!"

The color drains from my daughter's face, then comes rushing back in. She snatches the laptop away, runs into the adjoining room, and slams the door hard enough to vibrate the floor. I turn to my son. "Did you think that was necessary?" I ask him.

"Well, it's true. She's been moping around for days and acting like she's the only person in the world. I'm sick of it!"

"Do you remember how it was after she found out you talked to your dad?" I ask him. "What did she do?"

He looks away. "But that's different—"

"No buts. What did she do when she found you'd gone to meet him?"

His voice drops. "She came after me. Helped me get away. Kept me safe."

"She fought for you, baby. She's your big sister, and she'll always protect you. And you should protect her too. Even from yourself when you're not happy with her."

"She started it."

"And she's the one hurting right now. So let it go, okay?"

He nods and crosses his arms. Defensive, but I know my kid; I can see he's thinking. And regretting. I give him a hug, a big one, and whisper "Thank you" to him.

"She's still being stupid," he grumbles.

"She's entitled to be stupid sometimes. So are you, but right now I need you to support her, okay? Thank you for looking this up. It's going to help." I have no idea *how* it will help, but having more background information about Wolfhunter can't possibly hurt. If Marlene actually saw something—something real—then it gives us something to look into. "Listen, I'm going to go see if I can talk to her. Okay?"

He nods. I look up at Sam beseechingly, and he says, "Tell you what, Connor, I could use an extra pair of hands to help me get lunch. Come on. Let's take a ride."

"Okay." Connor slides off the bed and follows. Sam gives me a look as he closes the door. I mouth *Thank you*, and he nods. We have a lot to discuss, but his love for my kids is beyond priceless to me.

I tap on the connecting door. When there's no answer, I go around through the door of room six and use my own key to open the door to room five.

Lanny makes a frustrated sound and throws herself on her side to put her back to me as I close the door. "Do you want to tell me about it?" I ask her.

"Why? You don't care."

"You know that isn't true, honey."

She's sobbing quietly, and I pretend that I can't tell. My heart does ache for her, but at the same time I know she has to get past this. Grow the armor she needs to protect herself for the next heartbreak, and the next.

When I lie down on the bed next to her, she turns and rolls into my embrace, and I stroke her hair and tell her it'll be all right, and she cries like a wounded child. Finally, she hiccups back a sob, and I say, "Did you talk to Dahlia today?"

"No," she says. "Not really. She just did a voice call, not Skype, like she promised, and now . . . now she won't even text me back. Her mom—her mom doesn't want me around anymore." She swallows hard. "Is it because she doesn't want Dahlia to be gay?"

"I don't know," I tell her. "Maybe. But also maybe it has nothing to do with you. Maybe it's about me, and this documentary thing. If it is, I'm really, *really* sorry, Lanny. And I'll do what I can to make that better, okay?"

She gulps back more tears, nods, and after a moment mumbles something I don't catch. I ask her what it was.

She says, "How could I have ever *loved* my dad? What's wrong with me? How could I do that?"

I feel the freezing anguish in my chest tighten. I know these questions. I've asked them of myself every day.

I hug her closer. "He was your father," I say. "We all loved him, at least for a while. The darkness inside him belonged only to him, and we couldn't know it was there. Nothing's wrong with you. Okay?"

"Okay." She gets up and goes into the bathroom. I hear her blowing her nose, washing her face, and then when she comes back, she looks steadier. "Sorry."

"It's all right. I'm sorry things aren't good right now. I wish I knew how to make it better."

She lets out a long, shaking sigh. "I need to do something and get my mind off it. Can I go with you? I don't want to stay here."

"No, Lanny. I'm going to the jail."

She perks up. "You mean, to see Vera Crockett?"

I wish I hadn't said anything at all. "Yes. But—"

"I can help!"

"No, honey, I'm sorry. I don't think that would be allowed."

"But I could be your assistant! I could take notes and everything."

"No," I tell her. And I mean it.

"Really? *Really?* Now you're going to tell me to sit here and wait around like some . . . some child? Like Connor? Vee is *my age*, Mom! And she needs help! I want to *help*!"

"And you can," I tell her. "I promise you. But not—"

"I'm going with," Lanny interrupts me. "And I'm not going to argue about it."

I know that tone, I realize with chagrin. It's the same one I use to end an argument. Lanny gets up from the bed, walks into the bathroom, and shuts the door. I hear water running. She's going to take a shower.

There's a knock on the closed connecting door. I open it to find it's Sam and Connor, loaded down with food. Fast food, of course; there's nothing else in town except one small diner that looks like it caters exclusively to locals.

I don't intend to take my daughter with me to do this. No way in hell.

Until my phone rings, halfway through my hamburger, and I step away to answer Hector Sparks's call. "I've set up the interview," he tells me. "Detective Fairweather isn't very pleased, but I think this is a good idea. She's more likely to give us better information if she feels comfortable, and obviously she feels more comfortable with you."

I take in a breath, and before I let myself think about it too much—and talk myself out of it—I say, "My daughter's coming with me."

"Your daughter?"

"Atlanta. She's fifteen, around Vera's age. I think having her in the room might be useful and put Vee more at ease."

"You're not, ah, concerned about exposing your child to what Vera might say?"

"She's heard worse," I tell him. "Trust me."

"Well, I certainly wouldn't want *my* daughter to be involved. But . . . this is a child's life we're talking about. They'll almost certainly decide to try Vee as an adult. And Tennessee has a death penalty."

"We'll be there. Just to be clear: My daughter won't be talking. I will. She's my—assistant."

"Understood," he says. "Thank you, Ms. Proctor. This is a great relief. They'll expect us at the county lockup at three p.m. It's about a half-hour drive. I will meet you there."

I check the time. It's one o'clock. I turn and look at my family: at Sam, smiling at something Connor's saying, watching my son with real love. At Lanny, picking fussily at the amount of lettuce on her burger, her hair still dripping from the ends. At Connor, with that light in his eyes that tells me he's talking about something he cares about, passionately.

"Meet you there," I tell Mr. Sparks. I hope I'm doing the right thing. At this point, all I can do is pray I haven't made a serious, maybe fatal, mistake.

10

GWEN

Sam readily agrees that we should all take the trip together, and check out of the room while we're at it; he seems a little *too* eager, to be honest, but like him, I find the motel oppressive. Connor's found a place called Wolfhunter River Lodge that's closer to the forest; it sounds nice, and looks comfortable.

The pictures don't lie. It sits about five miles outside of Wolfhunter, and it's a modest-size rustic place with big rooms, a breathtaking view of the forest from the windows, and a cheerful proprietor who seems happy to have us. Once we get to our adjoining rooms, Sam pulls me aside for a quick conversation.

"I'm taking Lanny with me to this interview," I tell him, first thing. "Trust me. I think it's important, or I wouldn't do it. Right now, Lanny needs to feel useful."

Sam doesn't like it, I can tell, but he lets that go in favor of something else. "Give me your phone."

I do, baffled, and he hands me a brand-new one. I look at it with a frown. Another disposable cell. "What's this?"

"Time to change out," he says. "I might be a little paranoid about the documentary crew, but we haven't changed numbers in a while. Trust me?"

"Of course. The kids too?"

"Yeah, I already swapped theirs. I preprogrammed in the numbers they might want to call, plus both of these numbers. You've got mine, Connor, Lanny, Kez, Prester, Javier, Mike, and your mom already in there."

"I should probably put in Sparks and Fairweather," I tell him. "Just in case."

He hands my phone back, and I add them into my contacts list. Then I hand the old one back. "You'll get rid of them?" I say. He nods. "Sam . . . what's wrong?"

"Not now," he says. He glances down at the phone he's holding. "We'll talk about it tonight."

I check the time. He's right; I need to grab Lanny and get moving if we're going to get to the jail on time. Assuming Sparks's directions are accurate. I knock on the connecting door, and Lanny opens it. She's reapplied her makeup, and she looks much more together than before. "Time to go?"

"If you're ready."

"I'm ready." She glances backward and drops her volume. "Connor apologized, by the way."

"He didn't mean to hurt your feelings. Not that badly, anyway."

"I know." She sighs. "He's like hugging a tumbleweed, Mom."

"So are you."

She grins, and I can't help but smile back. "It's a family trait," she says. "You're more barbed wire though."

"Damn right," I say, and hold up a fist for a bump. She rolls her eyes. "Not cool anymore?"

"Let's just go," she says. "Connor says Sam's taking him for a walk in the woods."

"You're sure you don't want to go with them instead . . . ?"

"Duh. I put on makeup, didn't I?"

She's right, half a mile in this heat would melt that carefully applied shadow and eyeliner into a streaky, sweaty mess. "Then let's go."

I second-guess myself through the entire drive to the county lockup. Strong and capable as she is, my daughter isn't an adult. If the last year and our brushes with Absalom and the father of my children have taught me anything, it's that my kids are brave, and smart, but they don't always do the wise thing. The *safe* thing.

And they probably get that from me.

The county lockup is more secure than the Wolfhunter PD office, and I have to present identification at a guard gate before I'm given a parking permit and waved into the lot. There are at least thirty other vehicles in the parking lot; most seem to have gotten rough usage. I pull in as close as I can to the front row and turn to my daughter. "Okay," I say. "Now you have to get very serious, do you understand me? This is not a game. And this is not a safe thing to we're about to do."

She nods slowly. "I know."

"Do you?" I search her expression. "I'm not joking around with you, Lanny. You need to do what I tell you, the guards tell you, the lawyer tells you. No arguments and no hesitation. If there is any trouble, you get down and stay safe, and *do not* stop for me. Understand?"

I'm scaring her, I can see that. Good. She needs to be scared right now. She doesn't say anything, but she nods again.

"Okay," I say. "Let's go. Don't make me sorry I agreed to this, okay?"

We make the short, hot walk from the parking lot to the heavy doors of the county jail. Once inside, we find a well-lit reception area with a massive, intimidating counter that runs the entire length of the room. It's old wood, with a more recent addition of bullet-resistant glass stretching from the counter up to the ceiling. There's just one window open, and a line of four people ahead of us. It takes a while.

I don't see Hector Sparks anywhere, and there's no sign of Detective Fairweather. We get credentials—though the woman behind the counter gives my daughter a long, judging stare—and go sit on one of the benches. It doesn't take long before our badge numbers are called, and we're directed to a door at the end of the counter that buzzes. A sign says PULL ONLY WHEN BUZZING OR ALARM WILL SOUND. I wonder how often they have to deal with that? Often enough to put up a sign.

Detective Fairweather is waiting in the hall. He does *not* look pleased, and when he sees that Lanny is with me, for a moment he looks downright pissed off. It doesn't last long, and then he nods to both of us. "Ms. Proctor. And who's this?"

"Lanny," I say.

"Her assistant," Lanny says, and dares him to deny it. He gives her a long stare, then transfers it back to me. Placing the blame where it belongs.

"This is no place for a kid," he says.

"Odd, because you're keeping a girl the same age here," I reply. "My daughter may be valuable if we need Vee to really open up about what happened inside that house."

"And you think your daughter should hear that?"

I don't even blink. "I guarantee you, Detective, she'll be fine."

At least he doesn't bother to argue, not that he could block her if he wanted to, because just at that moment I see Hector Sparks coming down the hall behind him. The lawyer is in his shirtsleeves, no coat, and he looks a little overheated. "There you are," he says, and pauses. I see him take in my daughter standing behind me. It's only a second, and then his attention returns. "Come this way. Our visiting time is limited."

"By what?" Lanny asks before I can.

"My appointments," Sparks says, which is an odd thing to say; surely the rest of the cases he's handling can't be as urgent as a fifteen-year-old girl with her life at risk. But he turns and walks away before I can ask, and we follow. Detective Fairweather doesn't.

"I'll talk to you later," he calls after me, and I hold up my hand to acknowledge that I've heard him. If he tries my cell phone, he'll get nothing; I'll have to call him instead. I prefer that, really.

As we go down the long, straight hallway toward the locked gate, offices open up on the left—bare, windowless rooms with desks and filing cabinets and virtually nothing that allows any humanity. Not a single Beanie Baby or fluffy unicorn calendar. No pictures of families. I suppose it's smart; it keeps everything strictly businesslike and deters any kind of personal ties that employees might be tempted to form, especially with inmates.

But it's depressing.

At the gate, the three of us are buzzed through by a guard on the other side; it's air-lock protocols, with another gate beyond, and the guard inside protected by a bulletproof office. The county might be small and poor, but the cops here aren't taking chances. Once we're through that, there's just a row of cells to our right. The first one contains an older woman in a neon-yellow jumpsuit who's apparently asleep on her bunk, face to the wall.

Vee Crockett is in the second cell.

She's sitting on the small, thin bed, but she slowly gets up when she sees us. Her gaze fixes on Hector Sparks, but then moves to me. Then to Lanny, who's standing a foot farther back than I am from the bars. Not going to lie; the girl looks broken. I know that stare, equal parts dumb confusion and numbness. She has a shock of messy dark hair, and her eyes are the clearest green I've ever seen. Clear of *everything*. I don't know exactly what I'm getting us into, and right now, I can't even hazard a guess.

A guard has accompanied us this far. "All right," he says. "Step back, all three of you, against the far wall. Stay there."

I'm pleased to see that Lanny immediately obeys, and I'm half a step behind her. It's Hector Sparks who seems to not understand the instructions. The guard advances on Vee's cell, ready to unlock it, but he pauses to repeat what he said to the lawyer. Sparks joins us against the wall.

I get the feeling this might be the first time he's ever been told what to do.

"Here's what's going to happen," the guard says to us as he stands next to Vee's cell. "I'm going to unlock her cell, shackle her, and we will go ahead of you to the interview room. You stay ten feet behind me at all times; you're being watched on video camera. Violate the rules and you'll be immediately escorted out."

"We understand," I say.

"She'll be shackled to the table in the interview room. You will not be permitted to go to her side of the table, pass her any items, or touch her in any way. Do you understand my instructions?"

"Yes," I say, and my daughter echoes me. Sparks takes his time, but finally agrees.

We do it by the book. I take the lead; I don't want Lanny getting overexcited, or Sparks arrogantly assuming that his legal status means he's exempt. So they follow behind me, and I make damn sure that there is more than ten feet of hallway between the guard's heels and my toes the whole way. That's easy enough to track, as there are markings on the floor every ten feet anyway. He stops at another gate, and I freeze immediately; I feel Lanny almost run into me.

"Hey, sweetie," says a voice from the cells to our right, "ain't you a little peach?"

Lanny edges closer to me. The woman's soft southern drawl has an edge to it, and I have no doubt the comment's aimed at my child.

"You look like you like a good time."

Without looking at the prisoner, I say, "Shut up or I'll pull your tongue out through your ass."

"Jesus, bitch, calm the fuck down," the woman says sulkily. I look over at her. She's a bleached-blonde white woman, ragged and unkempt, thin as a medical skeleton. It doesn't take much imagination to guess she's in for a drug offense.

"Sit down," I tell her. There must be something in my tone, or my eyes, because she holds up her hands and backs away from the bars. I've been in prison. I understand how this works.

The gate at the end opens. The guard ushers Vee into the air-lock chamber, and we have to wait on the other side.

Nobody else catcalls my kid.

By the time we're through the double gates, we're in an area with small rooms. Vee's in the first one we come to, already shackled down with ankle chains to the floor, and her wrist shackles run through a thick metal hasp on her side of the table.

The guard runs through the rules again, sounding blank and bored, and then he leaves and locks the door. There are three chairs on our side of the table. I take the one on the far end from the door, and put Lanny in the middle. Vee just stares at me, then at Lanny; she ignores Sparks as if he doesn't even exist. Under it I see a hint of something stirring. Anger, maybe. Hope. Something deep and visceral.

"Miss Crockett, I'm Hector Sparks, we spoke before?" Sparks says. Nothing. Like she's gone deaf. "I should say, I spoke, and you pretended not to listen. I thought I'd bring in someone you already know to help us both through this process."

Suddenly she turns her stare to him. "Go away," she says.

"He can't," I tell her. "He's your lawyer. If he leaves, we have to leave too."

She doesn't like that; I see a flash of petulance in her face, and then once again it goes blank. "Fine," she says, and sits back. Her chains drag noisily on the table. She looks up at some point above her head. I wait, but she doesn't say anything else.

"Is it okay if I ask you some questions, Vee? I want to understand what happened to you, and to your mom," I say.

"You heard," she says. Still looking two feet over my head. "I know you heard what happened."

"Part of it. But only after you called me. I need to find out what happened before."

Vee adjusts her gaze to meet mine for a bare second, and then she skips away to focus on Lanny. "This your daughter?" The girl's got a quiet, oddly normal voice.

"Yes," I say. "She's helping me today."

"Doin' what?"

"Taking notes," Lanny says. She reaches into her bag and takes out a pen and paper. Writes down the date. Her hand is shaking, but damn if she doesn't sound calm. "Go ahead."

"Y'all ain't neither one from around here," Vee says, and it's a velvety-smooth, uniquely Tennessee drawl that I don't have, and neither does my daughter. "Where from?"

"We don't have long with you," I say as Lanny opens her mouth; I don't want this girl-prisoner to know any more about us than is strictly necessary. Just in case. "What happened the day your mother passed, Vee? Imagine yourself waking up in the morning, and just tell me about that day as you remember it."

I say it as kindly as I can, because I'm trying to be generous and believe the weird blankness in her is shock and trauma, and I don't want to make it worse. I imagine the police weren't nearly as considerate.

Vee says nothing. *Nothing.* She just shakes her head and looks down toward her feet, with the mess of tangled hair tumbling forward to shade her face.

"I promise you, I am trying to help," I tell her, even more quietly. "Nothing you say to me is going to be admissible in court, it's only for your attorney to use to try to help you. It'll be okay. You can trust me."

If she even hears me, she gives no sign of it at all. She sways a little, like willow branches in a cold wind, and I feel a prickle of gooseflesh on the back of my neck.

Then Lanny suddenly says, "It's the wrong question, right?"

I send her a look that I hope clearly says *don't lead the damn witness,* but it's worked. Vee is looking up at us again. No, at Lanny. She even pushes some hair back from her face.

"You're right. I didn't wake up 'cause I never went to bed. I was out over at the cutoff near the river."

"Which river?" I ask.

"Wolfhunter River, ain't no other one around here."

"Were you with anyone?" I ask.

"No," she says, and I know that one is a lie, because I see her clear green eyes dart away and come back to fix on my daughter again. I don't like that look. I don't like it at all. "Well. Maybe some others, but we don't pay no mind to each other. We do our thing, that's all."

"So what's your thing?" Lanny asks. I bite my tongue on an impulse to tell her to *be quiet*, because I have the strong guess that if she stays quiet, I get nowhere.

But even Lanny just gets a dull shrug of Vee's prison-uniformed shoulders to that question.

Hector Sparks is avidly following all this. He's staring over his glasses at Vee Crockett with an expression that seems intent and very interested. It honestly makes me a little uncomfortable.

She ignores him totally. Like she's had practice.

"So," I say, "tell me about the night before, and keep going up to when you found your mom."

I think she's going to shut down completely, but instead she finally says, "I went out to score. Tyler had some Oxy he bought off some old lady as needed the money, so I got a few. Sharon had a nice bottle of whiskey and some vodka. So we built a fire and shared all round. Dicky came around with meth, but I didn't have none of *that* shit." She sounds briefly superior. "Then Tyler said I needed to blow him for the Oxy, the dickhead. I stretched out by the fire after. The Oxy and whiskey made me kinda sick, so I stayed. Tyler and Sharon was gone when I stopped flyin'. Fire was out."

I feel my daughter flinch at the too-casual mention of the sexual transaction, thrown out by a girl her own age.

"So what did you do after that?" I ask. Another shrug, even more apathetic than the last.

"Went to school for a hot minute," she replies. "Then I got bored."

"Where'd you go?"

"Nowheres."

"Wolfhunter's not that big," I say. "Not a lot of places to go. Try to remember."

She rolls her eyes. "Hung out at the abandoned glass factory a while. I got a sleeping bag there and some stuff for when I don't want to go to class." *Stuff*, I imagine, is some hoarded pills, or booze, or both.

"Did you see anybody else there?"

"No."

"So what were you doing?" Lanny says. Vee suddenly smiles. It's a smile that shocks me, because it looks so . . . normal. Like the two of them are just having a friendly conversation, without bars all around. Without one of them being accused of matricide.

"Good times, girl. Drank, took the last of my Oxy," she said. "Just sort of drifted awhile."

I don't like that answer. "And then what?"

"Walked home. It ain't far." She turns her face away again. I can't tell if the smile is still there, but I imagine it is, and fight off another wave of misgivings. "Momma was on the floor. Gun was right there next to her. Guess they got her, just like she thought they might. I picked it up 'cause I heard somebody outside. So I fired it to warn 'em off. Thought they might kill me like they did her." She laughs. *Laughs*. "Anyway, it were just the postman, and I missed him."

"Detective Fairweather said you had blood on you. Can you tell me how it got there, Vee?" She doesn't answer that. She freezes up. I let it go, because the clock is ticking. "You said *they*. Who are you talking about?" Vee shakes her head.

"Momma never really said. Just that something weren't right, and she needed to get help. I never paid her much mind. She was always on about something or other. She liked all them conspiracy-theory people." Her voice sounds slow, almost sad. I wonder if she's feeling some regret.

I ask a few more questions, but Vee seems tired now. Almost sleepy. She doesn't respond with more than one-word answers or shakes of her head. Not even Lanny can get a rise out of her.

Finally, Hector Sparks says, "Ms. Proctor, I think we need to wrap this up. I really do need to be somewhere." As if his client is keeping him from something more important. I feel a bright surge of resentment, and have to remind myself that he is, in fact, my boss at the moment. Company rules apply. He nods to the guard outside, who unlocks the door. Sparks gets up and walks out. Lanny hesitates, looking at me.

We're out of time. I lean across the table as far as I dare to. "Vee, look at me. You need to tell me the truth. Did you kill your mother?"

She slowly turns her head and brushes her hair back. No smile now. "No, ma'am," she says. "I wouldn't do that. She weren't a bad woman. She weren't really there, mostly. Not for me."

I don't know if I believe her. I don't know who I'm looking at. Or what.

"Are you going to be okay?" Lanny asks Vee.

Vee gives her a sad little smile. "Nicest bedroom I ever had is here."

It's more than a little sickening, because I'm pretty sure she means that.

"Time to go." The guard's impatient voice. He's holding the door for us.

Lanny and I get up to leave. We've gone a couple of steps toward the door when Vee says, "Wait. Your name's Lanny, right?" I turn toward her. So does Lanny. Vee is leaning forward, picking at a torn fingernail. A bright scarlet drop of blood wells up, and she lifts her finger to let it slither down her skin.

I instinctively put myself between her—even shackled as she is—and my daughter.

"I know who you are, Lanny," Vee says. She's staring past me. "Your daddy was a raper and murderer. Everybody knows that. They likely think you're bad too."

"And what's your point?" Lanny, to her credit, doesn't sound shaken.

"Just that you know what it's like. I didn't do this. I'm not a good girl, but I ain't a killer. Not my *momma*. Not like . . ." Her eyes suddenly fill with tears, but she doesn't cry. She blinks, and they roll down. I wonder if she has a born actor's ability to cry on command. "It was dark in the house. I tripped. I fell over her and got her blood all over me. *I put my hand in her.*" I feel that like a gut punch. She pulls in a breath that sounds painful, and she bows her head. "That's what happened. You wanted to know. That's the truth."

"Ms. Proctor." The guard's voice from the door is stern. "Let's go. *Now.*"

I nod to Vee, and usher Lanny out. I still keep myself behind her, a shield between my daughter and a girl I'm still not sure I can believe.

"Mom?" Lanny turns to me while we're in the air lock between the cells and the open hallway. "Do you think she's lying?"

"Lying about what?" Sparks asks. He's checking his phone.

He'd missed the last exchange. Too damn busy. I say, "If you want something to exploit for the defense, she says she tripped over her mother's body in the dark and fell on her. That's how she got the blood on her clothing," I tell him. "Which you'd know if you weren't in such a hurry to get to your next *appointment.*"

He blinks. "Ms. Proctor, she's hardly my only client."

"You got another one on trial for murder?"

He pulls himself up indignantly. "That's not quite fair—"

"Unfair is being innocent and locked up in a place like this," I tell him. "Look for high-impact spatter."

"What?"

"Close shotgun blasts make high-impact spatter patterns, which might not even be visible to the naked eye. If she doesn't have that pattern on her skin or clothes, it wouldn't have been possible for her to have shot her mother at close range." I pause. I lower my voice. "She says when she fell on the body, she—put her hand inside the wound. So it had to have been a pretty close-range shot to punch with that much force. Pellets spread over distance."

"Thanks." He makes notes. "I'm afraid to ask how you know this."

"I make it a point to know a lot of things. Especially about forensics."

I ask him about the people she mentioned who saw her the night before, and he says he'll follow up. I'm not so sure.

"Mr. Sparks," I say, "are you really going to fight for her? Or are you just checking a box here?"

He stares at me, and behind the oh-so-inoffensive glasses perched on his nose, his eyes look . . . cold. I've often heard lawyers referred to as sharks, but I've rarely seen one who looks quite so open about it. Then he blinks, and it's gone. "I'll do my best. And what's important is that we believe in her innocence, isn't it?"

Do I?

I honestly have no idea.

◆　◆　◆

Sparks gets a phone call. His conversation is brisk and brief, and I look back toward the interview room where Vee Crockett is being unlocked from the table. She lifts her head and looks at me, and in that instant, I *do* know.

I know that Vee Crockett didn't kill her mom. It's a gut-deep judgment. I don't like the kid; she's got a boatload of problems to deal with, and the weird crush she seems to have on my daughter makes me deeply nervous. But I'm looking at a girl in shock, reacting in strange and unpredictable ways. Underneath that is deep, traumatic pain. I can see it.

"Ms. Proctor?"

Sparks is suddenly beside me. I hadn't heard him coming, and it makes me flinch in surprise. I see him note it, but he doesn't apologize.

"What are your plans now?"

"Grab my kids and Sam, get out of town," I tell him. "I did what I said I'd do. I helped get Vera to talk to you. You have her story now."

He seems relieved, which is somehow not what I expected; I'd thought he would have been desperate for *more* help. But he doesn't ask. He just nods.

"Well, drive safely," he says. "I wish you the best of luck, Ms. Proctor."

"You too," I say. "What do you think her chances are?"

"Better than her mother's were," he says.

I don't like it. I don't like how unengaged he seems. A fifteen-year-old deserves more than that. I can tell by the look on Lanny's face that she feels the same.

Sparks goes ahead of us. Watching him, Lanny says, "We don't have to leave *today*, do we?"

I don't answer her, but inside, I'm thinking maybe there's one more stop we could make to get a few things cleared up.

Problem is, I think that nobody in this town's going to welcome me, or my questions.

◆　◆　◆

There's no sign of Fairweather when we emerge from the cell area and head back down the dull office hallway. Not in the reception area either.

So once we're in the car and have the AC going to mitigate the stifling heat, I take my new phone and dial his number.

"Fairweather," he answers.

"Proctor," I respond. "Sorry. New number. I apologize I didn't have time to talk earlier—"

"That's kind of you, ma'am, but things have changed. I've been reassigned."

"Reassigned?" I go blank for a second. "But . . . you just got started."

"I'm sorry to tell you that sometimes that's just how this goes. The evidence stacks up and stands on its own. We don't have any other suspects than Vee Crockett. Given that, my lieutenant is pulling me off to work the Ellie White kidnapping, so I'll be out of Wolfhunter in a couple of hours."

"But—"

"Ms. Proctor, I know you kind of have a personal stake in this. But nothing you told me in your statement gives me any reason to believe Vee Crockett didn't kill her mother. On the contrary, it leans toward the idea she did."

"She just told me she fell over her mother's body in the dark," I blurt out. I know I shouldn't disclose that; it's attorney-client information. But I know, for some gut-deep reason, that I do not want Fairweather to leave this case. Not yet. "It explains the blood on her clothes. Her trauma explains why she picked up the gun and fired it at the noise outside. She was *terrified*, Detective."

He's silent a moment. "Does it occur to you that she might have tailored that explanation to fit the evidence we found on her?"

"Yes. But when I was on the phone with her . . ."

"You said she sounded disconnected. Like she didn't care about her dead mother."

"I know I did. But detachment like that can be a side effect of severe shock. Remember the case of the girl in Texas whose whole family was killed by an intruder? She coped by going out and feeding the farm animals. People *cope*. I think Vera did it by shutting off any kind of emotions. It looks bad that she was probably high and drunk, but it also helps explain her off-center reactions."

"Maybe," he says. "But you're talking about theories. I deal in evidence."

I shift a little, not daring to look at my daughter. "If I find some, will you follow up on it?"

"I can't make you any promises. I've got a kidnapped child to find. Vera Crockett might be a lost cause, you know that."

"Maybe," I agree. "But I'm not the kind who gives up."

He sounds briefly amused. "Yeah, I certainly see that. I can't promise anything."

"Did you ever talk to anyone at Marlene's job?" I ask.

"Marlene worked in the garage pretty much alone, answering phones and doing paperwork," he answers. "Nothing there. She wasn't popular in town. Not a lot of friends."

"Why not?"

"Her daughter's behavior, for one thing, but before that, her grandfather swindled a bunch of people back in the sixties."

"Grandfather."

"Small towns," he says. "Long memories."

"I'm guessing the whole reason you were sent to take charge of this case is that the TBI has zero confidence in the abilities of the Wolfhunter PD. This girl still needs your help."

The amusement is all gone when he finally responds. "God help her, then. And you. If you want my advice, Gwen, just let it go. This town isn't a good place. It never has been. My advice . . . don't stay here." He pauses. "I wouldn't. And I've got a badge and the force of law behind me. This town's sour. Just leave."

Then the call ends, and I sit with the slowly cooling air blasting over us, thinking. My daughter turns to me and says, "He doesn't want to even try to help her, does he?"

"I don't know, sweetie," I say. "I honestly don't know what he's thinking."

◆ ◆ ◆

Downtown Wolfhunter River, at 4:00 p.m., is not exactly jumping. Most stores—those few still in business—are already closed down. A few people are on the streets, mostly clustered near the diner we pass on the way to the garage where Marlene worked. I don't need to look up the name; there's only one garage—a ramshackle, fairly large place built of cinder blocks. Amateurish hand-painting spells out GARAGE in uneven block letters above closed bay doors. There are a few windows in the place, but they're covered by graying mini-blinds. An apparently ancient tire special is still in force, from the price painted on the one larger window up front.

"This looks deserted," Lanny says. The sunbaked sign in the window still says OPEN, and as I check my watch, we're still an hour before the posted time to shut down.

"Stay here," I tell her. "Doors locked."

"Usual drill," she says, and sounds put out. "I could be your backup, you know."

In a strange place, walking into what is essentially a cave full of blunt objects and people with unknown motivations . . . no, she can't. "If I'm not back in fifteen minutes, call Sam," I tell her. "If anyone tries to get you out of the car for any reason—"

"Call Sam, yeah, I get it," she says. "Mom? You've got your gun, right?"

"I got it back when we left the jail," I reassure her. "I'll be fine. Lock up. I'll be back soon."

As I wait outside the SUV to hear the locks engage, I scan the streets. We're near the edge of town, maybe a couple of miles out to the motel where we were so recently staying. Nothing seems out of place . . . and then I back up and look again.

There's another SUV on the street. It's parked near the courthouse, a couple of blocks down, and it doesn't look like it belongs here, especially this late in the day. Day-trippers to the forest would already be headed home. Those camping out would be settling in. This looks like a rental to me; it's clean and polished, with dark tinting on the windows that makes it nearly impossible to see in. Could be visitors, I tell myself. But it feels off.

I can't deduce anything from a car, and turn away. I head for the door, swing it open, and step into dimness that smells of old oil, rust, and mold. I blink. The overhead light is dim in the office area, which is small and plain—a dirty wooden counter, an old 1970s-era cash register bolted in place, a wooden bench under the shaded window. No modern amenities like coffee or water. The jail looked more welcoming.

There's nobody in view. No bell on the counter either. I step up and lean over; the counter has a doorway out into the shop, which is also dimly lit—not ideal for a place to do precision work. Maybe it's better with the doors open and sunlight bathing the bays, but I wonder just how often they air this place out like that. It smells like an abandoned building, with a nasty edge of sewer backup.

I'm about to call out a hello when I hear voices. There's a plain wooden door to my right that must lead out to the work area; I try it, and it opens. I expect a creak, or an alarm chime, but there's nothing.

Definitely voices. I'm facing a sign on the wall that says **WORK AREA—WATCH YOUR STEP**, with a jaunty cartoon worker in a construction helmet pointing at the words. It looks as ancient as this place feels. It's hard to tell where the voices are coming from—somewhere to my left, I finally realize—and when I look that way, I see there's an office behind the reception area that has another door into the work area. It's shut now, but light is leaking around the uneven, warped edges.

I head that way.

I stop when I can hear what they're saying.

"—goddamn girl is talkin'," a deep, raspy voice I don't know says. "You said she didn't know nothing about it. So what's she got to say to that bitch?"

That bitch has to be me. *Goddamn girl* must be Vee Crockett. I guess that's not unexpected, in one sense; either Vera, Marlene, or my involvement must be the topic of most Wolfhunter conversations right now. But it feels alarming.

"No idea," another male voice says, and it sounds familiar. I've heard it somewhere before, but I can't nail it down. Maybe at the police station. "Damn county idiots wouldn't listen in, so we don't know."

"You never should have let them move her to county, Weldon."

"I didn't have a choice! That TBI man, he did it. If I could've kept her here, we'd have been done with it already."

A new voice now. "Boys, boys, calm down. We're fine. Chances are Vera didn't say anything that makes any sense anyway, and Marlene knew better than to run her mouth, didn't she?"

"Well," Weldon says bitterly, "she damn sure forgot, because why did she call that stranger in the first place? Now we got that damn woman to deal with. *And* her boyfriend and kids. It's a damn mess, Carl. This was supposed to be easy."

"It *is* easy," Carl replies. He sounds . . . well, like he's used to being in charge. "It's containable."

"Well, then, you'd best get to it and fast," the original voice says. No one's given him a name yet. "When's our money comin'?"

"Tomorrow or the next day," Carl says. "I told you. It takes time for the transfers to process. If you want it untraceable, then it'll take three or four offshore banks."

My mind's working furiously now. *What are they talking about? What money? What did Marlene know?*

Doesn't matter. I've heard enough. We need to get the hell out of here. Now.

I back away toward the door, and ease it open behind me. It runs into something.

It hits a man about six feet tall wearing oily mechanic's overalls, wiping grease from his hands. He's more than twice as broad as I am, and tops me by several inches; his biceps look enormous beneath the sleeves. I notice those more than I do his face, which is mostly in shadow. As is normal in this town, he's a white guy, and he looks like he crushes metal for a hobby.

"What you doin' here?" he asks me sharply. "Customers ain't allowed out there!"

"I was just looking for someone to help me," I say, and try a placating smile. I'm not sure it works; his body language stays militant. "Maybe you can? How much for an oil change?"

It's the first, most normal thing I can think of. It works, because he relaxes a little and steps back to let me come back into the reception area. "You should talk to—" He glances toward the counter, then looks grim; I don't know why until he says, "Well, ain't nobody working the counter these days. The boss, I guess."

"Who's the boss?"

"Mr. Carr," he says. And he raises his voice, "Hey, boss? Got a lady out here wants to talk to you!"

It's the last thing I wanted, but I can't bolt; the mechanic is between me and the outer door. I try edging over. He moves to block me.

And I hear footsteps behind me, heavy and quick.

"Ms. Proctor," says the voice I first heard from that office. The deep, raspy one.

I turn to face him.

He's almost as tall as his mechanic, but thinner. Lanky, the way only some country folk are. Older, maybe in his early sixties, with a wild explosion of white hair that ought to soften his long, lean face, but doesn't. Paler than I would have expected, and with shocking blue eyes that look like a doll's eyes.

He's smiling, but I can tell that's just a muscle movement, not emotion. There *is* emotion in him, but it's banked and burning behind those eyes.

"Mr. Carr," I say. I extend my hand. He ignores it, so I drop it back to my side.

"You been waiting long?" he asks. Meaning, have I overheard his conversation with the other two in the office.

"Not long," I tell him. Let him make of that what he wants. I don't say anything else. I wait to see what he's going to do. I'm aware, acutely aware, that I might not leave this room without a fight. Or alive. I'm fast on the draw, but even the fastest can go down before they get off a shot, and all he has to do is signal the mechanic behind me to put me in a bear hug. But I have a hole card.

"And what is it you came for? Car runnin' rough?" He's playing with me. I hear the mechanic move away from behind me. Checking out the window, probably. I see Carr's eerie blue eyes move from me to him, then back. *Oh God.* They know my kid's in the SUV. I know Lanny, I know she won't open that door for anyone but me, Sam, or Connor . . . but they could break a window. Drag her out. Would they do that? Right out in public, on the main street?

"I heard Marlene Crockett used to work here."

"Yeah?"

"I really just came to ask if she ever mentioned her daughter, Vera, threatening her," I say. I know he'll take the easy answer. He doesn't disappoint.

"Marlene was scared to death of that damn girl," he says. "No discipline in that house without a man to lay down the law. Vera did as she wanted—drugs, drinkin', whorin' around. That all you wanted to know? Coulda asked anybody."

His chuckle sounds like a knife scraping concrete.

"Thanks," I tell him. "Cops been by to ask about it already?"

"That's my business. Y'all best be going," he says. "Mrs. Melvin Royal. Be careful on those dark roads out there on your way home."

I turn my back on him and walk toward the mechanic, who's still blocking the door. I don't stop. I see the man squint past me at Carr, and he moves at the last second.

I walk out of the dark shop and into the clean sunlight. That place. The *smell*. Rust and oil, sewage and baked-in rot.

And those men, unafraid to threaten me. My word against theirs, sure. But I could feel the odds being calculated, the cold decisions being made.

We need to get out.

Now.

I unlock the SUV from the key fob and climb in. In ten seconds I've belted in, started the engine, and have it backed out onto Main Street. Carr's right. The woods get dark early. And I can see him watching now from his window, blinds pulled up to follow our progress. I check behind us. The black SUV's still parked a couple of blocks away. Now another one has joined it on the other side of the street. I watch, but they don't follow us.

"Mom?" Lanny's watching me. "What's wrong?"

"Everything," I tell her.

That's when my phone rings. It's Connor.

And he tells me Sam's under arrest.

11

SAM

The manager of the lodge tells us the best path to follow for a safe, unchallenging hike—one that'll last a couple of hours at most and bring us back in a loop. Connor doesn't seem that interested at first, though he's happy to be tagging along. But the quiet of the forest turns out to be just what he needs, and it eases some of the vibrating tension inside me too. Something about the green, fresh smell of the air, the flickering shade, the sound of birds singing. Makes you forget all the bullshit for a while. Even if it's bullshit of your own making.

We walk up the trail a bit, and I stop to point out an almost-invisible snake—nonpoisonous, so I let him get closer than I would have otherwise. The snake flees without any show of anger, and we keep going.

"That was cool," Connor says.

"It was."

"I'd like to have a pet snake. That'd be interesting."

"Sure," I say. "You know you have to feed him what he'd eat out here, right? Bugs, mice, things like that."

"I could catch them around the lake," he says. "It'd be okay."

I try to guess how Gwen would feel about that and fail. Though odds are, if Connor really is interested, she'd be 100 percent behind that enthusiasm, even if it means having live mice in the house.

Lanny might not be quite as accepting. I don't enjoy thinking about the epic battles, or the inevitable Save the Mice campaign.

While I'm thinking about that, though, Connor says, "Can I ask you a real question? For real?"

"How do you ask a fake question?"

He gives me a look that tells me he isn't amused. And he's serious. "Are you and Mom staying together or not?"

"Wow."

"Will you tell me?"

"Buddy, I would if I had a good answer for it."

"Don't say *It's complicated*. It's not. You either love her or you don't. And if you don't, you shouldn't make her think you do."

I think about that. We walk on in silence for a while. Connor silently points out a frog by the side of the trail, watching us with unblinking eyes. It hops off into leaf litter as we pass.

"Okay," I finally tell him, "it's not complicated. But it is *hard*. You get why, right?"

"Because of your sister," he says. "Yeah."

"And because she can't forget it. Neither can I. So . . . long term, will we be together? I hope we will. But I can't make you that promise." Especially now. Especially with Miranda and all that ugly, stained past coming back like a sewage flood to sweep us away.

"Well, you should promise," he says. "Because then you'll stay no matter what. You don't break your promises."

I feel a fist close around my heart and squeeze. "I want to," I tell him. "And it'd be a real easy thing to do, because I love your mom, and I love you and your sister."

"But you won't promise," he says, and kicks a rock.

"Not yet," I say. "Ask me again at the end of the week."

He gives me an odd look. Wary. "Why? What happens at the end of the week?"

"That's just it," I say. "Hell if I know. That's the point."

He gives me a little shove. I give it back. I get a rare, clear laugh from him. "You're kind of dumb, did you know that?" he says.

"Only kind of?" I make a snap decision. "Come on. Follow me."

"But—" He points straight ahead as I veer off. "The trail's that way."

"Yep," I say. "Come on. Let's get lost for a while."

We go for about fifteen minutes, and then Connor spots a deer. He starts to speak, and I put a finger to my lips and slowly sink into a crouch behind the brush. He follows suit, carefully mirroring me. I stay very still as the deer comes closer. Closer. I wonder if anyone's ever taken this kid hunting; it was something that bonded me and my adoptive father closely in my teen years. Then I think again about whether or not that would be a good idea, given the inevitable associations with his dad's murders. And the *way* he killed.

This kid's already had enough death in his life.

We sit crouched in the brush and watch the deer as it crops plants and scrapes at the ground for more. She's a pretty doe, and we just appreciate her for a while. When she wanders off, we stand up, and I realize that there's a new path, barely used, going in a different direction. It's not an officially marked trail, more likely a game trail.

"Can we?" Connor asks, and points to it.

"Sure," I say. "And if we get lost, what are you going to do?"

He pulls a compass from his pocket. It's attached to a small key chain with a carabiner on it, and he clips the carabiner onto his belt loop. "Go southeast," he says.

"Why?"

"Is this a test?"

"Yeah. So?"

"Because the nearest place is the lodge, and the lodge is southeast from us right now. Right?"

The kid's got a good sense of direction and spatial awareness. Good. "And what's in your backpack?"

"Trail bars, flashlight, water, map, my first-aid kit, and a book," he says. "I know you didn't tell me to get the book."

"Good man. Nothing wrong with a book. Let's find a good spot to sit and read."

I have a light pack with me too: compass, food, water, map of the area. And a slender volume of Garrison Keillor, but I don't tell him that yet. I also have my Glock 9 mm and a hunting knife, a pocket fishing kit, and insulating blankets in case we get stuck out here for the night, because one thing my time in Afghanistan taught me was don't go if you're not ready to face what's out there.

And though this ought to be friendly territory, I never assume anything. Gwen and I are alike in that.

We've followed the game trail about thirty minutes when I pick up the smell of something dead. It's strong and sweet-sour in the back of my throat. Connor gets it, too, and covers his nose. "What's that?" he asks. "Is it a skunk?"

"Hope so," I say. But it isn't. The wind shifts, and the smell's gone. I check the direction the leaves are bending. The breeze has quartered, so I make a turn off the path to find the smell again. It hits me like a pan in the face: hot, greasy, sickening. Not a skunk, alive or dead. This is something bigger.

We're off the path. I stop. "Connor, check the map," I tell him. He obediently pulls it out of his pack. "Mark where we are right now."

He does, and I check it. We're close to Wolfhunter River, which is an offshoot of larger waterways; these days it's more of an oversize creek, but it's likely dangerous in flood stages. We passed over it on the way to the lodge. The sky is blue and empty of clouds, but flash flooding can happen miles upstream, and it's nothing to mess around with.

"Are we going to find it?" he says. "The dead thing?"

"Do you want to find it?"

He has to think it over, but then he nods. "Yeah."

"You know what we find might be terrible, right?"

"I know," he says. And I'm sure he does. He's old enough to Google and turn off the parental controls without Gwen noticing. He looks up at me. "It's the right thing to do, though. I mean, it might be an animal, but what if it isn't? There are people missing."

Gwen's going to hate me for it, but I'm not about to treat this brave kid like he's made out of glass. "Okay," I tell him. "Mark the trail on the map as we go." I take the marker out and swipe it along the trunks of trees as we go; they're heavy here, but the underbrush is fairly light, and we're able to push through. We startle birds that take off in a rush of wings and cries, but it's almost lost in the thrashing hiss of the trees. It's getting darker in the cover, and for safety I stop Connor and get him to take out his flashlight while I retrieve mine. The halogen beams slice the gloom like scalpels. I widen the output on mine. It doesn't go as far, but I like to see what's coming on the sides.

It's still and silent, except for the sound of the trees and now-distant birdcalls. No traffic sounds. No planes overhead. The farther in we get, the more isolated we are, and I start worrying about wildlife. Dead bodies attract scavengers. Particularly bears.

But we don't have to go far, and we don't see a bear. Just a small, dappled bobcat that slinks silently away the instant I spot him.

The smell continues to increase in intensity, but I don't initially see the body—or at least recognize it for what it is. It's by the bank of the Wolfhunter River, and the green water laps at the edges of the thing lying there. I think for a second, *It's a deer*, because it's unnaturally shaped and splayed and dark even in the glow of our combined light beams.

But a deer doesn't wear sandals. Or have braces on exposed white teeth.

"Get back," I tell Connor, and I step in front of him. "Ten feet back, right now."

"That's—" He sounds shaken. "That's not—that's not a body, is it?"

"Connor, do as I say. Walk back ten feet. Don't look." I cover my nose and mouth with the bend of my arm and walk a little closer. She's not dressed, except for the shoes. *He made her walk here,* I think. Maybe she begged to keep her shoes on, and he allowed that small mercy. I don't see any sign of other clothes scattered nearby. I can't tell how she died, what she might have looked like, or even what race she might be; the body's so bloated and distorted it looks like a Hollywood monster prop. She has—had—blonde hair, though. Tufts of it have been pulled out and are caught on bushes nearby, and strands wave gently in the river water. Animals have been here, and I rise quickly when I realize how many maggots are around the body. An army of them, squirming. Flies everywhere.

Her eye sockets are empty, staring straight up at the dark trees, as if she might be searching for the sky.

"Sam?" Connor sounds even shakier. "Sam?"

I move back to him. He's clicked his flashlight off, and he's breathing too fast. I turn him toward me.

"Connor, I need you to listen to me. Deep breaths, okay? This is a good thing. It's good we came here and found her. Now we need to go back and call the police."

"Did somebody kill her?" He's shaking. I put my hand on his forehead. He feels clammy and cold. I pull out one of the metallic insulated blankets and drape it around him. "Did somebody leave her there? The way my dad—"

"It might not be that at all," I lie to him, because I think he needs that comfort. "She could be a hiker who got lost, had a heart attack, something like that. But it's good that she's not out here all alone anymore, right?"

That steadies him a little. He nods and pulls the blanket closer.

"Okay, let's follow our trail back out," I tell him. I pull out my phone and check for a signal. There is one, but it's low and slow; I dial 911 anyway as we start walking. Connor stares at his map like it's a GPS; he's not really thinking right now. I use my built-in UV light on the other end of the flashlight to check the trail markers I left. It's clear enough where we need to go.

"Wolfhunter Police Department. What is your emergency?" a voice asks me. It's tinny and ghostly, a fragile connection.

"I need to report a dead body," I tell her. "On the south bank of Wolfhunter River, about two miles from Wolfhunter River Lodge."

"I didn't get all that, sir. Can you please repeat—"

The call drops. *Shit.* I try again, get the same voice. "I'm calling to report a dead body. South bank of Wolfhunter River, about two miles from—"

"Sir, I need your name please."

"Sam Cade. About two miles from Wolfhunter River Lodge."

"Was this person breathing, sir?"

I think about the bloating, the blackened skin. "No."

"Did you try CPR?"

"No. She's decomposed." I know they have to ask these questions, but it's infuriating. Like Connor, I'm still dealing with the sight, but unlike the kid, I've seen worse, and in person. "Heading back to the lodge. Send the police; I'll walk them out to the body. We left trail markers."

I hang up before the call drops again, and am slipping the phone back in my pocket when I hear a branch snap. Then rustling. Something's out there.

Maybe there is a bear, after all.

I silently bring Connor to a halt. His metallic blanket rustles, but there's nothing I can do about that. I slowly lower my pack to the ground and get out my pistol. Flashlight gets stowed. I crouch down, and Connor mimics me.

I put my finger to my lips. The kid's face is pallid, and he's shaking even more, but he nods.

I'm first aware of the shot because the tree next to me explodes splinters in all directions, and one of them digs into my arm. I process that, the flat slap of the shot an instant later, and the realization that we're in desperate trouble at the same time. I grab Connor's arm and drag him right, get him safe behind a big, gnarled oak, and tell him, "Stay here. Stay down. Understand?"

"Was that a shot?" He's shaking. A little distant.

"Stay," I order him. I need to lead them away from this kid. He can't make it right now. He's in shock. "Connor! Understand?"

He nods. I move to the next tree and listen for footsteps. I don't hear anything. Whoever's taken a shot at us, he's now stationary. Waiting.

So I give him something to shoot at. I take off the neon-orange cap I'm wearing and fling it like a Frisbee; it sails a good twenty feet, and then it changes course and flies off at an angle. I don't see the shot that shreds it, but I hear it an instant later.

He's a pretty good marksman, but he's slow. Maybe the first shot he took was a little too quick, a little too adrenaline filled, because he rushed it and missed my head by a couple of inches. If he'd been steady, I'd have been out like a light.

I look at Connor again. I hate leaving him here alone, shivering, but right now it's the only choice. I need to draw this guy off. And I need to deal with him, because he's threatened my kid. *My* kid. I've never felt it quite so strongly as I do right now, this need to defend Connor at all costs, but it's there, and it's dug deep into my guts.

I go low, racing for the next cover, betting that he's not good at snapping off quick, accurate shots. He isn't. His shot comes late, and buries itself in the tree I'm already behind. There's a thick crop of underbrush between this tree and the next, and I flatten out and do a combat crawl, resting my weight on forearms and toes as I slither along. It's quick and quiet, and I come up to a crouch as I make the turn. This is a thick stand of trees, and it appears impenetrable from that side. On this side it's clear, and I quickly make my way around in a wide arc that should bring him into view.

It does.

There are two in forest camouflage, no hunter's blaze colors or vests: shooter and spotter. They don't want to be noticed. It crosses my mind that they might have military experience. If they do, the spotter will start scanning the perimeter . . . now.

Right on my count, the smaller one looks away from downrange and does a slow, meticulous sweep. I don't move. I'm pretty confident he'll miss me.

I snap a twig. A small one, something that sounds like it *might* be a vole or shrew. I add a tiny rustle with the tip of my boot.

The second man has to cover the sniper's ass; that's his job too. And he comes to check. I could shoot both of them from cover, no problem, and I'm sure that's what Gwen would have done. But if I do that, I don't find out who set these assholes on us.

I wait, and when the man's passing, I step right and press the barrel of my gun to his neck. He freezes up for a bare second, and it's just enough time for me to jam the back of his knees and send him sprawling. "Stay down," I tell him, and grab his rifle. Then I turn and fire at his friend, who's rolling to get a bead on me. I fire three shots, marching toward him in a neat, straight row. Clear warning. He's a big, bearded man, and I'm hoping that if he's a pro, if he understands his situation, he'll drop the gun and give up.

He doesn't. He raises it toward me and fires. It's a wild shot, off target, but he's made that choice, and eliminated mine too.

I shoot him in the head, and I don't even blink. His death is just about instantaneous; I see his eyes flicker, then roll back, and his body goes limp. One spasm, and nothing.

I turn back to his friend, who's stayed sensibly still, and I press the barrel to the back of his head. Hair sizzles. "Do not move. Understand?"

"Yeah, yeah, sure," he says. He's flat on his stomach, hands now outstretched. I search him from the back, roll him over, and put the still-hot muzzle against his forehead while I check for another weapon. He winces. When I finish and back off, he has a small, perfect red circle burned into his suntanned skin.

"You a marine or somethin'?" he asks me. Local accent.

"Air force," I tell him.

"Damn. Didn't know they taught that shit in flight school."

"Army?" I guess. He nods. "Sorry, brother. Who sent you?"

"Who says anybody did?"

I shrug. "Not open season on kids, as far as I'm aware."

"Man, we mistook you for a doe, that's all."

"Bullshit. Somebody sent you."

"You shoot Travis?"

"If that's your buddy, yeah. Didn't have a choice," I tell him. "He's dead."

"Then fuck you, man, I ain't tellin' you shit." He's a lean, tough guy in his midthirties, a war vet, but his eyes fill with tears, and I see genuine rage behind them. "You just killed my cousin."

I point the gun again. "Who hired you?"

"Fuck. You."

He's hardened, I can see that. Grief does that to some people. I was hoping it might break him open, but instead: concrete. Maybe the cops will get something out of him. I won't.

I hear a little metallic rustle and turn my head in that direction. Connor's discarded his blanket, and he's coming around the trees. I hold up a hand to stop him there. I take out my phone and dial 911 again. I tell them there's been a fatal shooting, and I have one man held at gunpoint. That'll get them moving, I hope.

"Won't do you no good," the prisoner tells me. The 911 operator's telling me not to hang up, so I don't. I put the phone down on the ground next to me.

"Why not?" I ask him. "You got friends in high places, man?"

He doesn't stop glaring. He *really* wants to kill me; I can feel it coming off him like steam. "Not me," he says, and suddenly bares his teeth in what is only technically a grin. "Travis was a *cop*. And you just fucking murdered him in cold blood. I seen it, you piece-of-shit murderer!" He's raised his voice.

"He didn't murder anybody," Connor says. "And you tried to kill *us*."

"You're crazy, kid. Why the hell would two men out huntin' try to kill you? This asshole just straight up went crazy!" I realize what's happening. He wants it on the damn 911 recording.

I reach down and hang up the call. Too late. We're kind of screwed. Sure, I can point to the shots Travis fired, including my shredded hunter's orange cap, but there's always benefit of the doubt in these things, and it weighs heavily in favor of locals, and cops. Travis is both.

I point the gun at my prisoner again. "What's your name?"

"Fuck off."

"Okay, Fuckoff, here's how this is going to go. You're going to tell the truth, because if you don't, I'm going to bring down all the hellfire in the world on you. State police, FBI, whatever I have to do to prove you're a damn liar who was hired to put a bullet in my head, which will get you twenty to life if you don't get smart, fast. Who paid you?"

He shuts his mouth, lowers his chin, and gives me a hard stare that tells me he's never going to cooperate, not with me, and probably not for any price. Paid well enough to keep his lips zipped about it. Or else he's scared that he's next on the list. Either could be true.

Connor says, "Can we go back to the lodge now?" He sounds exhausted, and far too shaky.

"I'm sorry, but no. We need to wait here," I tell him. "Wrap up. Stay warm, okay? Sit down and eat something."

He nods. In a few minutes he looks better after consuming a trail bar and washing it down with water from the canteen. He's wrapped himself in the blanket like a shiny foil burrito. Jesus, it hits me all over again: he is a *kid*. And in one afternoon, he's seen a gruesomely dead body, been shot at, and been at the scene of a killing. Even if he didn't see me shoot Travis—and I hope he didn't—he knows it happened.

I was supposed to protect him. This was supposed to be a walk in the woods.

I can imagine what Gwen's going to say . . . which reminds me that I'd better call her. Now. But when I call her number, I get nothing but rings and voice mail. I don't leave a message. I don't have any idea how to tell her about this yet. She'll call when she sees I've tried to get her.

I hope she's safe. It hits me with sick, brutal force that if someone tried to take me and Connor out, Gwen and Lanny are also at risk. I should have come to that conclusion earlier, but like Connor, my brain's not working at peak efficiency right now. I just killed a man. The calm and focus I feel in combat is starting to wear off now, and the consequences are mounting.

Call me back, Gwen.

But she doesn't. I want to tell her I did my best. I want to tell her . . . tell her I love her.

But I don't get a chance.

When the cops arrive, I put the gun on the ground, kneel, lace my hands behind my head, and get body-slammed to the ground anyway. Knee grinding my spine, voices shouting over each other. The guy on the ground is yelling, too, that I'm a stone-cold murderer, that I killed his cousin. I can't see Connor. I'm praying they don't treat him roughly, but there's nothing I can do now. Nothing.

I hear Connor yelling, "Let him go!" in a voice so raw it makes me hurt.

I turn my head in that direction. "Hey," I call to him, "Connor, stop. Relax. It's okay. Everything's okay."

"You killed a cop, you prick," the cop says. "Trust me, that ain't okay. You're getting the needle. Shut the fuck up."

Something hits me in the back of the head, and the world goes soft and loose around me. I try, but things slip away.

My last thought is for Connor's safety before I plunge off the cliff, into the dark.

12

GWEN

When I arrive at the lodge, it's chaos, the parking lot a staging area of four police cars, two ambulances, and one unmarked vehicle. My heart is hammering, my mouth is dry; Lanny's asking me questions I can't answer, and I park and bail out fast. My daughter catches up during my run toward the lodge. "Mom! Mom, what's happening?"

I don't know. And it terrifies me.

My path is blocked by a uniformed policeman—a big one, scowling at me from under the jutting bill of his hat. "You can't go in there," he tells me. "Lodge is closed."

"Where is my son?" I know I should be calmer, more logical. I can't be. "Connor Proctor! Where is he?"

"Back up," he orders me. I don't. When he comes toward me, we bump chests. He pauses, because he can tell he's going to have to make me back off, and he's struggling to do the math of how badly that will go.

"Mom!" Lanny grabs my arm. "Where's Connor? Is he arrested too? What's going on?"

"I'm trying to find out, honey," I tell her, and for some reason that makes the cop take a step back. Maybe the fact that I have an anxious, frightened daughter hits home with him. I turn my attention back to him and try to start over. "I'm Gwen Proctor—"

"I know who you are," he says. Hard eyes, like pebbles in water. "Step back."

"My son is back there! He's *a child!*"

"And he'll be brought out—" He breaks off, because right at that moment a group emerges from the trees. Paramedics, rolling a gurney with someone on it. I see the bright flash of blood and my heart just . . . stops. I sway. Lanny grabs me tighter than ever, and I make myself, somehow, stay upright.

It's not Connor. But it is Sam. He's unconscious. There's blood on the sheet under him, and I don't see a wound. *God*, did they shoot him in the back? The cop holds me back again, but as soon as the gurney's past me, I rush to it. There's a cordon of cops, but I break through for a second and see that he's breathing.

And he's handcuffed to the railings.

A cop pushes me back. I ignite. "Take your damn hands off me!" I shout. "Did you shoot him?"

"Ma'am, calm down; he was injured a little bit in the struggle," the cop says, and when I focus on him, I realize that he's just a kid, really, barely old enough to buy a legal drink. He seems earnest and out of his depth, so I dial it back. Slightly. "He's going to be okay."

"Don't promise," I say. "Where's my son? Connor Proctor?"

"Mom?"

Connor's voice from behind me. I see him coming, with a single police escort. He's wrapped in a metallic blanket, far too pale, and I rush to him and take him in my arms. He's not in handcuffs, at least, which is good because if he were, I might have to take on the entire police force. He looks like he's in shock. "Sweetie?" I kiss his cheek and push him back to look him over. No sign of injury. "Did they hurt you?"

He shakes his head. "No, I'm okay." His voice sounds lower than it usually is, and deeper. "They hurt Sam, though. I saw it."

The cop next to him frowns, and I quickly say, "We'll talk about that later, okay?" I draw Connor back into the protective hug and meet the officer's eyes directly. "I want to take him to the room. Now."

"Ma'am, he needs to come to the station and give a statement."

"Look at him! He's not in any shape to—"

"No." Connor steps back. He takes the blanket off. It seems to me that my son grows inches in that moment, that he ages years, and it breaks off pieces my heart. "Mom, I need to go. Sam needs me to tell the truth. I'm okay." He isn't, but I know I can't protect completely from this.

I focus back on the cop. "He's a minor," I say. "I'm going with him. My daughter comes too; she's not staying here by herself." He can't really argue with me about any of that, but he seems to be searching for a way. I don't give him time. "I'll drive him to the station."

"Ma'am, he's going to have to come with me." He isn't yielding on that point, I can tell. Because that's something he can enforce, petty as it is. "He's a critical witness to the murder of a police officer."

"Fine," I snap. "Then you take all of us."

He can't find a good reason to refuse, so we crowd into the backseat of the cruiser. There's steel mesh between us and the policeman's front seat, and—I know from experience—back doors that won't open from the inside. We're in a cage now. Right where they want us.

But there's nothing else to be done, except start making moves of my own.

As we're driven back to Wolfhunter, as night starts to close in on this depressing, devastating town, I start texting my contacts.

Every one of them.

◆ ◆ ◆

I sit in the interview room while Connor gives his statement, and I am speechless to hear the scope of it . . . the discovery of the body. The ambush on the way back to the lodge. Sam's actions. Connor doesn't lie, as far as I can tell; he's straightforward and open, even when he tells the detective—a local one I don't know—that he didn't see the actual shooting that Sam's been accused of; he only looked around the tree when he heard the shot.

That doesn't help Sam much, but I'm glad he doesn't make up a story. It would be too easy for them to trip up a kid his age.

Brave as he's been, Connor still drops his chin when the detective leaves the room, though, and I realize he's crying. *Finally*, I think. I grab tissues and pass them over, and just let him work it out. I'm glad my son can cry.

When he's finished, I say, "Don't feel guilty, baby. Sam doesn't want you to lie. You told the truth. That's what matters."

"I know," he says. "But, Mom, they—the way they treated him . . ."

He still remembers how I was treated when I was arrested. It was probably gentler than how these local cops handled things, but it was traumatic enough to leave lasting marks on my children. "He's going to be okay," I tell him. "I asked Hector Sparks to show up at the hospital and protect him in case the cops want to get a statement too soon. Mike Lustig is on his way to Wolfhunter as soon as he gets free. Kezia and Javier know what's going on. Things will be fine. I promise."

"Don't promise," he says, and gives me a sad little smile. "Sam doesn't." I wonder what that's about, but I don't let it take root. I can't right now.

"I'm sorry you had to go through all this," I tell him. "I know it feels bad. I know it reminds you of things that are hard to deal with."

"It's okay," he says, though it's obviously not. "I'm glad we found her. It wasn't right for her to be just . . . left there. Like nobody cared at all."

"She's found now," I tell him gently. "You and Sam did that for her."

"She's probably one of them. Those missing women."

"She could be," I say. "But we don't know that."

He just shakes his head. "I think she is."

I don't try to talk him out of it. I ask if he wants something to drink, and when he nods, I knock on the closed door and ask for a bottle of water. The bottle comes back in the hand of the same detective from before. He brings a printed-out statement with him, and he puts the bottle, the statement, and a pen in front of my son.

Connor automatically picks up the pen. I grab the paper. "What's this?"

"We transcribed his statement, ma'am. It just needs his signature," the detective says. I start reading. I don't get two sentences in before I take the pen from Connor's fingers and start marking up the paper. This *transcription* is more like a free paraphrasing. I shove it back at the detective. He's not happy. "Ma'am, we took this directly from the recording . . ."

"I'll bet," I say, and take my phone out. "Here. Let's play that game, shall we? Because I had *my* recorder running too."

He clears his throat, stares at me for a few seconds, and then stands up and leaves the room without a word. Connor gives me a look. "Wow. Seriously? You recorded that?"

I don't confirm or deny, just in case. I only smile.

When the statement comes back this time, it compares to what I remember from Connor's account. I ask him to read it and correct anything that's wrong. He does on one sentence, and then signs it. Before he passes it back, I take a quick picture of it.

That gets an even less happy response from the detective. I'm fairly sure they were going to try something else shady, but now that I have the picture, they can't. Especially if I have the recording. Which I don't, but they can't be sure.

We exchange stares. He leaves.

Connor cracks open the bottle and drinks thirstily, like he's been without for a day. I want to tell him to slow down, but I don't. When the bottle's drained, I take it. I don't throw it away. The last thing I want is for them to fake some DNA thing to implicate my son down the line, and from what I've seen so far, I'm convinced that the police chief is probably behind this ugly push. It's not really about my son.

It's about showing me who's boss.

I realize that I'm indulging my natural paranoia again—they could get touch DNA from the pen he used, or the paper he's just signed—but I have to try to keep him safe. The fact that even now we're locked inside this room makes me feral.

My cell phone rings. I check the number. It's from Hector Sparks. "Ms. Proctor? Yes, I wanted to let you know that I'm here at the hospital. Mr. Cade is awake. They've just taken him for an X-ray of his skull, but he says he feels all right. He has five stitches in his scalp. Knowing Chief Weldon, I'm sure he has some story about Mr. Cade violently resisting arrest. There's really no point in trying to challenge that, not in this town when the only witnesses are fellow police."

I breathe a little easier, not that it doesn't make me angry all over again . . . and then I freeze. "Wait. The chief of police is named *Weldon*?"

"Yes," Sparks says. "Why?"

Weldon was one of the voices back at the garage, along with the owner, Carr. I don't like where this is going. Not at all. "You'll stay until I can get there?"

"I can stay for another"—I can almost hear the watch check—"two hours. However, according to Officer Helmer, as soon as the hospital clears him, he'll be taken straight to the police department. I assume you're there already?"

"Yes."

"Excellent. Then as soon as he's released, I'll be on my way. I wouldn't want Mrs. Pall to have to wait dinner."

Heaven forbid, I want to snap, but I somehow manage not to. Sparks's legal help is probably superfluous right now, but I can't afford to alienate the only lawyer I know.

I knock on the door again. The same cop opens it. "My son's just turned twelve. He's had a traumatic day. He's given his statement. Either give him some food, or let us go."

"Wait inside," he orders me, and shuts the door in my face. I do, pacing; I'm like a lion in the cage, while Connor is calm and quiet. I want to force their hand before Sam gets here.

I get my wish, because the cop opens the door in five minutes, and says, "You can go. But orders of the chief: don't leave town."

That's bullshit and I know it. Connor's not a suspect; he's a witness, and they can't pull that on a minor child. I don't push my luck, though. I get Connor out the door, into the hall, and out into the reception area. Lanny's slumped in a seat, headphones on, but she jumps to her feet the second she sees us. She runs to Connor and wraps him in a bear hug. "Don't scare me like that," she whispers to him. And he hugs her back. I feel a burn in the back of my throat that might be tears, if I let myself go there. They'd be good tears for a change.

Lanny rushes to give me a hug too. "Are we leaving? Can we go see Sam? Is he at the hospital?"

"We should wait here," I tell her. "Sam's going to be brought in as soon as they're done with him. I'm hoping that they'll be in a hot rush to charge him."

"You hope what? Why?" Connor looks mystified. I give him a smile.

"Because the sooner they charge him, the faster his bail can go through," I say. "And the sooner we can get the hell out of this town."

"But . . . what if he doesn't get bail?" Lanny asks anxiously. "What if—"

"One crisis at a time," I tell her.

◆ ◆ ◆

Sam is brought in—and we're not allowed to get near him, but he's walking, and our eyes meet and lock for a priceless few seconds, and he mouths *It's okay* at the same time I say, "I'll be here"—and then he's taken straight back to the cells, for questioning. We wait until I overhear at 10:00 p.m. that they've arrested Sam for manslaughter.

The arraignment comes at midnight. Lanny's proven correct. There is no bail. And no chance to talk to him. I shouldn't be shocked, but I am, and horrified; I don't want Sam in jail tonight, in this town. I should have realized they'd get the judge onside for this and planned accordingly. But I'm tired. And scared. And I'm feeling very, very exposed.

The saving grace is that Mike Lustig arrives at the courthouse just as Sam's taken away. Mike's a good man. And a black man with an FBI badge, which will be—I'm pretty sure—Chief Weldon's worst nightmare. We spend ten minutes huddling, and I give him every piece of solid information I have, including the conversation I overheard in which Chief Weldon played a role. I tell him my speculation, too, that Marlene Crockett knew about a wreck that was quickly made to vanish by the police, Mr. Carr, the garage owner, and some third party named Carl that I can't identify yet. There's payoffs in the making, big enough to kill for.

"I wonder if it's . . ." He starts that thought, but he doesn't finish it. "Never mind that right now. Let's just get through the night. Listen, I want you to get those kids out of this town. Take them home."

"But, Sam—"

"Leave Sam to me. I'll make myself real useful around here for the night. He won't be alone, promise you that." He pauses for a second. "Don't stay around here tonight. I know you're tempted, and I understand that. But I need you and them out of danger."

He's right. The motel wasn't safe; the lodge wasn't either. We need to get back home, where we have friends and allies who can watch our backs.

Hard as it is to go and leave Sam behind.

"Can I write a note?" I ask Mike, at the end. "Will you give it to him?"

"Voice mail's faster," he says, and hands me his phone. "Use the recorder. I'll make sure he hears it. That way they can't accuse me of trying to pass him a shiv or some bullshit like that."

Mike's read on this place is just as dire as mine, I realize; that's ominous. "If you need help, call this guy," I tell him, and send him Fairweather's number from my phone. I feel his phone vibrate as it arrives. "He's with the TBI. I don't think he likes the way things smell around here either. He got reassigned yesterday. I wonder how that happened."

"It's a damn mystery," Mike says, and gives me a grim smile. "Go on and whisper sweet nothings to your man. I won't listen."

"Liar," I say, but I don't mean it. He walks a couple of feet away, and I press the "Record" button. Then I'm temporarily voiceless. What *can* I say? What makes up for the fact that I'm about to drive away and leave him here, in Wolfhunter, when he came up here determined to watch *my* back?

"Sam," I say, and my voice sounds strange and emotional, and that's not what I want. I take a breath. "Sorry. I need to get the kids out of here, into a safer place. So I'm going to go home until tomorrow, but I'll be back as fast as I can. I'm hoping that Javier or Kez can step in for them temporarily until we can both get the hell out of this town and decide what we do next. Mike's here for you, meanwhile. And I'm coming back for you. I promise." I hesitate, close my eyes, and say it. "I love you, Sam Cade. I'm sorry that . . . I'm sorry. I love you. Don't forget."

I end the recording and take the phone back to Mike, who gives me a long, considering look. "You going to break my friend's heart?" he asks.

"Depends," I say. "Is he going to break mine?"

He doesn't answer that. "You get those kids safe. Sam'll never forgive me if they get hurt on my watch."

I watch him walk away, and then we go to the waiting police vehicle that gives us a ride back to the lodge where we left the SUV. I don't like going back in for our stuff, but Lanny's adamant that she's not leaving her laptop. I make damn sure the clerk knows I'm armed and ready for trouble, and we gather everything in less than ten minutes. Then we're on the road, heading home.

We're going to sleep in our own beds, and whatever tomorrow brings, at least we'll have that much comfort.

I'm just turning onto the main road when my cell rings. The kids grumble and fall back asleep almost instantly once I answer it. "Yes?" My tone is guarded. It's late, I'm exhausted, and I'm in the woods on a dark, twisting road. It's black as a hole out here, except for the wash of my headlights across the asphalt, the jump of the yellow center line, the green from the trees flashing past.

"Ms. Proctor?"

I recognize that careful Virginia voice. "Detective Fairweather. Pretty late to be calling." It's almost 1:00 a.m., I know because I've checked, and I can count the time by the ache in my bones at this point.

"It is," he says. He sounds as tired as I feel. "I just got back from a fingertip search of a field about fifty miles from Wolfhunter. We had a tip Ellie White might be there. All I got to show for it are dirty hands and a sore back."

"But you're calling me . . . ?"

"Because I heard about Mr. Cade's situation," he says. He sounds grim. "Did you bail him out?"

"I couldn't. No bail."

"County lockup?"

"No," I say. "He's in Wolfhunter."

"Well, hell." It's mildly shocking to hear even that much of a curse from him. "I can cook something up in the morning, but I'm worried he's going to have some trouble tonight in that jail."

"Are you telling me they're that bad? Wolfhunter PD?"

"Accidents happen," he says flatly. It's not exactly agreement; most cops won't cross that blue line, and I'm not surprised. "I might be able to work something in the morning, but—"

"But you're worried he might, what, hang himself from a bedsheet in the middle of the night?"

"Something like that. Are the kids all right? I heard one of them was with him during the shooting."

"Connor," I say, and glance over at the rearview mirror. My son is leaning against the side window, fast asleep. "He's okay. We're heading out for the night, back to Stillhouse Lake."

I can hear an infinity of weariness in his voice as he says, "Then I guess I'd best head back to Wolfhunter and find some excuse to visit the prisoner for a while. Let them know the TBI has an eye on this."

I'm deeply grateful . . . and then I'm wary too. I don't know Fairweather that well, and though he *seems* trustworthy enough, maybe he isn't. Or maybe Wolfhunter has gotten under my skin and is poisoning my view of everyone I've met since coming into its dark borders. "No need. Sam's friend is FBI, and he's there helping out."

"Friends in high places?"

I don't acknowledge that. "Sam will make it through the night. And I'll be back in the morning as soon as I can. We *will* get him out of there. He shot a man who was trying to kill him and Connor. Self-defense, pure and simple."

"It's never so simple when the victim's law enforcement. I hear he's charged with manslaughter. You might have tough sledding making a self-defense case. You going to hire Hector Sparks?"

"Do I have much of a choice?"

We flash past a mile marker that tells me we're now five miles outside of Wolfhunter. I start to relax a little. Got a tense drive to make, and a short sleep coming, but just being out of that town's shadow makes me feel better. "Thank you for reaching out, Detective. It means a lot to know you're paying attention to what's going on in this town."

"Oh, trust me, I am," he says. "Okay, Ms. Proctor, you drive safe, and I'll talk to you—"

A rifle shot explodes through our back window and out the front. I register the icy fracture of the glass an instant before I hear the hot crack of the shot.

The first impulse that shoots through me is red, urgent, and it makes me pull the wheel to the side. The car lurches sickeningly, and even as I consciously form a plan, I'm pressing the gas to the floor and straightening out to avoid running off the road. I hear Lanny screaming something, and that's when I focus on the round hole that's been punched in our front window, and the thick spiderweb of cracks still expanding out from it. The back window is worse. I gasp and check my side mirror.

We're being chased.

There's a truck behind us, and a guy standing in the bed of it leaning forward and bracing himself. He's got a hunting rifle of some kind, and he's taking aim. We're going fast, but our pursuers are gaining.

"Connor!" I shout. "Are you okay?"

"Yes," he says.

"Lanny!"

"Mom, they're *shooting at us!*"

"Both of you, get down and *hold on!*"

It takes a precious couple of seconds for them to be concealed, protected, and I compensate by swerving over the line and back to spoil the bastard's aim. Once I'm sure my kids are okay, I take another deep breath, send off a microsecond of prayer, and hit the brakes as hard as I can.

My SUV screeches, fights, tries to slide. I leave a long trail of thick rubber on the road.

The pickup behind me is forced to brake hard, because they'd been accelerating to get closer, and the rifleman gets thrown against the cab so violently that he loses his rifle. It clatters to the road and bounces off into a ditch. Before they're fully stopped, I'm flooring the SUV again and reaching for my phone. I intend to dial 911, but I realize that I've forgotten all about Detective Fairweather. He's shouting in my ear. "Gwen! Gwen what the hell is—"

"Call 911," I tell him. "We're just past five miles out on the main road. We're being followed by a pickup, and a man with a rifle is in the bed shooting—"

Another shot shatters more glass. *He has a backup gun.* I can barely see the road ahead, but I can crouch and look through a clear patch. Keep us on the road. I don't dare slow down. Fairweather's saying something, but I can't understand him. My attention is fixed on the problem behind me. I finally realize he's saying *license number, description.* Yelling it, actually.

"I can't see it," I tell him. "There's no light out here! Pickup, definitely. One shooter in the bed of the truck, Jesus, my kids are here . . ."

I can hear him repeating what I've said. He must have two phones going. "Okay, dispatch is sending a county sheriff cruiser your way; he'll be coming from the opposite direction. They want you to pull over when you see it coming at you; do you understand?"

"I'm not stopping until the pickup does!" I tell him. "Ben, my *kids . . .*" I take a deep breath. "The driver's a white male, clean shaven, looks thin, maybe thirty . . ."

More shots ring out. I look back and see the shooter is up again, a bearded asshole in an old camo jacket and trucker hat. He doesn't have his rifle anymore, but he's got a semiautomatic handgun, and he's pumping off shots as fast as he can. There's a curve, and I have to slow down or risk a wreck, and multiple shots land in the metal of the car. I hear it, and feel the impact. But at least he's not as good a shot with the handgun as he was with a rifle. I accelerate again once we're grooved into the curve. My SUV has better running power.

I can't see any cars coming. We're completely alone.

"How long until the damn cruiser gets here?" I shout it at Fairweather.

"Five minutes," he says. "Hold on, Gwen. They're coming."

In five minutes we're going to be dead if the shooter manages to hit a tire, which is what he's trying to do. "Kids? Are you okay?" My voice is shaking. I'm not sure if that's from rage or terror or both.

There's a second of silence, and I feel a sick drop of horror, but then Connor says, from somewhere near the floorboard in the back, "I'm okay, Mom."

"I'm okay," Lanny says. She's in the footwell of the passenger side, curled up in a protective ball, but she looks up at me with a clear question on her face. *Why is this happening to us?*

I honestly don't know, and I try to swallow my fear, but my mouth is as dry as Death Valley. I try to focus completely on the road ahead, the truck behind. My kids are all right, we're going to be all right, *we have to be all right.*

I see the curve coming. It's not as sharp as the others. It's perfect.

"Hold on," I tell Fairweather, who's trying to talk to me. "I have to try something." I drop the phone on the seat next to me.

Then I swerve wide, and the truck follows me over the double yellow line. The firing had paused for reloading, but now it resumes, a staccato pop-pop-pop as fast as the man can pull the trigger. I ease off the gas and let the truck roar up fast.

Then I floor it and veer off sharply around the curve.

They don't see it coming. The driver is fixated on me, and he's accelerating too hard to easily change course, and as I pull away to the side, he finds he's headed straight for the ditch. When he tries to correct, his back tires lose traction. I see the whole vehicle shimmy violently, and then the spin begins as the lighter truck bed torques and flings the cab sideways.

The man in the back is thrown clear, and I see him flying through the air in the sweep of the truck's headlights as it spins before I hear a short, panicked cry. He vanishes from view. I hear him land; it sounds unforgiving. I keep driving, gaze riveted on the rearview mirror and the truck that has ended up stopped in the wrong lane, facing the wrong way. After a long second or two, the truck suddenly accelerates, straightens into the correct lane, and screeches off in the opposite direction. Back toward Wolfhunter.

They don't stop for their friend.

I look ahead, but I still don't see flashing lights or hear the reassuring sound of sirens. *The truck could turn around. They could come back.* I don't think they will, though. They've lost a rifle, a handgun, and at least one of their buddies on this road, and they can't know if they've wounded one of us, but they *do* know we can keep on running.

I ease off the gas, alert for any sign of headlights coming for us from behind. Nothing. The darkness here is breathless. Oppressive. And I know I should keep moving. The asshole who was shooting at me is back there. He might even still have his gun.

But he also might be bleeding out on the road, praying for help. I'm a paranoid asshole when it comes to the survival of my family, but I'm also human. I don't want to leave someone to die alone. Not even someone who tried to kill us.

Especially not if he can answer questions about *why*.

"Mom?"

I look down at my daughter.

"Are they gone?" She sounds tough and calm. I see tear tracks on her face gleaming in the dashboard light.

"Yeah, baby, they ran away. It's okay. Connor? Sweetie? Are you all right?"

He's already scrambling up in the backseat and staring out the cracked back window. I'm looking at the side mirror. I see no movement at all. "Yeah," he says. Nothing else. I think it's so I don't hear how frightened he really is. My son's already been shot at once today. My temporary wave of empathy recedes, and I want to kill these assholes, including the one lying in the road.

"Both of you, strap in." I check the speed. We're still doing half again the posted rate, but I don't give a shit. I *want* the police. And finally I see the red-and-blue flashers bleeding through gaps in the trees. The road must curve again up ahead.

I finally remember Fairweather was on the phone, but when I look for the device, it's gone. Thrown into the well between the passenger door and seat, most likely, but definitely out of reach.

I slow down and pull over. I have to wait for a few seconds after I switch off the engine to try to get control of myself. My hands are shaking so badly I almost drop the keys when I hand them to Lanny. "Find my phone; it should be somewhere over on your side. Detective Fairweather's on the line, hopefully; if not, call him back. Tell him what happened and is happening. Lock these doors and *stay alert*. If I get arrested or something happens to me, you get Connor out of here immediately; just *drive*. Understand? Call Javier and Kez for help, and get somewhere safe. Do *not* stop unless you think you're safe, I don't care what else happens."

She nods. I'm asking a lot of her, but I know Lanny. I know she can do it, and will.

"Mom?" she says as I start to close the door. Our eyes meet and hold. "I love you."

"I love you too. Both of you, so much. Connor, please listen to your sister until I get back."

"I will," he says, which is rare. "I love you, too, Mom."

I shut the door. I feel the locks engage as I lean against the SUV and hold up both hands. The county sheriff's cruiser comes hard around the corner and immediately slows, pulls over, and brakes. There's a short delay—reporting their position and my license plate, I assume—and then the lone deputy gets out and slowly comes toward me, taking in the SUV, the two kids in the car, and that my hands are up. He has his hand on his gun. "What's your name, ma'am?" he asks. Not "Are you the one who called for assistance?" That's actually smart.

"Gwen Proctor," I say, and I see him physically relax, but he still asks to see ID. I provide it. He's a potbellied man of middle age, African American, with a shaved head and close-trimmed beard. "I don't know what happened, but we were chased and shot at with a rifle, and then with a handgun."

"Is anyone injured?"

"No. We're all right."

"Can you ask the children to exit the vehicle, please?"

I don't want the kids out of the car. Not yet. "I'd rather leave them inside until you've secured the area."

He frowns. "Ma'am—"

"The man shooting was thrown from the bed of the truck toward the end of the chase, but I don't know if he's still capable of firing. Until I know he's disarmed, they need to stay safe."

He accepts that, and says, "Where was he thrown?"

"Back there at the curve." I point. "I'll go with you. It looked like he was tossed to the northbound side."

"No, ma'am, I want you to stay here with your vehicle and *do not move*. I'll be back as soon as I can. There should be a second response vehicle coming in another couple of minutes; you wait for him." With that, he's off into the dark, only the jerky motion of his flashlight beam marking his position.

I knock on the window. Lanny, now in the driver's seat, rolls it down. "Phone," I tell her. She hands it over. "Thanks, sweetie. Close this now."

I check for a signal and find two bars, thank God. And even better, Fairweather's somehow still on the line. "Gwen? Christ almighty, you scared me."

"Yeah, sorry," I say, which is just reflex. I'm *not* sorry. I'm happy as hell that luck made him a witness to all this. "I had to make some defensive moves. The truck's gone now, headed toward Wolfhunter. We're okay; the first cruiser is here. The deputy's looking for the shooter who was thrown clear."

"You ever get a clear look at the make and model?"

"I did, when it spun out. Red Ford F-150, I'm pretty sure. It can't be too hard to find; it looked new-ish."

"How are the kids?"

"Scared to death," I say. "And my kids have been through enough without this on top of things. If they want evidence, my SUV is full of bullet holes, and maybe there's an actual bullet they'll be able to salvage and match. This wasn't just some random country harassment. They wanted me dead, Detective. And I want to know who, and why." I think I already do know, but I'm not completely sure about Fairweather. Not enough to tip my hand to him, anyway.

I realize that my voice is rising, and I'm shaking hard. The adrenaline is being flushed out of my system now that I know things are calming down. My head is full of horrible visions of my children wounded, bleeding, dead. And where I was calm before, I can't control the rage that's rising. I want to kill these men for threatening my kids.

Detective Fairweather is talking, and I try to catch up on what he's been saying. "—license plate?"

"No," I tell him. "Like I told you . . . it's dark out here on the roads. And I had headlights in my rearview most of the time."

"Did the truck wreck? Any body damage?"

"No. Spun out, got straight. It headed back toward Wolfhunter."

He covers the phone and talks to someone, probably the dispatcher again; I can hear the voices but not the message. "Right," he says. "The BOLO is going out now for the truck. Anything distinctive about it that you noticed? Bumper stickers, dents, rust?"

"It's got some mud on it, but it's in good shape," I say. "American-flag sticker in the back window, I think. But I didn't have a lot of time to study it. I was trying to stay alive."

The second county cruiser's flashing lights are starting to strobe the trees, so I finish with Fairweather and put the phone away. I repeat the ritual of holding up my hands as the second deputy steps out. He seems more aggressive than the first. "Keep those hands up!" he shouts. His halogen headlights are washing harshly over me, the SUV, and the road. "Higher!"

If I go any higher, I'll dislocate a shoulder, but I try. I stand perfectly still, since he seems like the type who'll kill me for a twitch, and he spins me and plants me against the hood of the SUV.

I'm instantly somewhere else, my palms against the searing-hot metal of the old Gina Royal mommy van, my vulnerable young children staring wide-eyed through the windshield. The demolished garage wall of our old house. A dead woman swaying at the end of a wire noose inside the broken wall.

It's a flashback. A bad one. The urge to slam backward against the invasive hands of this deputy is almost overwhelming. *Breathe,* I tell myself. *This is different. This is now. You're safe. You're safe.*

It doesn't feel different.

He finally steps back, but keeps one hand against my back. "Don't move," he orders. "Get those kids—"

. . . *out of the vehicle,* he's about to say, but he doesn't get that far. The other deputy calls to him, and he emphasizes staying in place with a last shove to my spine before I hear him moving off with heavy footsteps. I turn and watch as he clicks on his flashlight and directs the beam on his African American colleague.

I realize the two of them are standing over a man who's lying crumpled off to the side of the road, his top half dangling down into a ditch. He must be dead or deeply unconscious, because he's not moving at all, even to recover from an unnatural position. The two men silently look down on the body. Finally, one deputy crouches down and leans into the ditch, with the other holding his belt for stability, and I presume he checks for signs of life. It's obviously futile from the shake of his head when he's pulled upright again.

Then both men are headed back toward me. This time I don't raise my hands. I cross my arms.

"Check her car for front-end damage," the white deputy orders, and I see the black one give him a long side-eye, but he decides this isn't worth it and goes to look.

"Nothing," he says. "No sign of any damage here."

They're looking for evidence that I ran the guy down, I realize. "He was thrown from the bed of the truck when it spun out. I didn't hit him or the truck," I say. "I guess you can call it an accident in commission of attempted murder."

The deputy sent to check for front damage proceeds around the car toward the back, and says, "Jesus, come look at this. Must be five shots that hit here, not counting the window damage."

The white deputy joins him, and I see the flashlight playing over the cracked and broken glass. "Huh," he says. "Don't know that those weren't there already." I hear the resentful mistrust.

That's when it becomes clear to me that this man knows exactly who I am. Unlike the first deputy, he didn't ask for my ID, didn't ask what happened. He's already made up his mind that I'm somehow to blame just for existing. And I feel a sick, metallic taste forming in the back of my throat.

Gwen Proctor. Gina Royal. Whoever I might be, there will always be someone who thinks the worst of me and tries in petty ways to make my life more difficult.

"Look, there are shell casings all over the road back there," the black deputy says, and I can tell he's growing impatient now. "She was on the phone with Detective Fairweather the whole time. I could hear the shots when I was hooked up on the call. Couldn't you?"

"We can have this discussion later. I'm calling out the detectives. Let them sort this mess out."

On the one hand, that's good news; I'd been afraid he'd send the first deputy on his way, and then claim I'd gone for his gun and shoot me dead somewhere out of sight of the kids. Paranoid? Sure. But then, someone's clearly out to get me.

On the other hand, having detectives in the mix can mean anything. They won't necessarily be on my side either.

I can only hope that Fairweather will show up for me.

◆ ◆ ◆

Fairweather does, in fact, show up. The detective takes me and the kids to the county sheriff's station, which is about half an hour away. My SUV's towed in for evidence processing.

I know I'm in for long, dark hours of saying the same things over and over again. And so are my kids. I don't tell them what to say. They know to tell the truth.

I look up at the black sky on the way inside. *Sam,* I think.

Please be okay.

I'm not wrong about the long hours, or the exhaustion that takes hold; after my statement I catch a catnap with my head down on my crossed arms on the table, and when I wake up, I find that the kids are camping out on a fold-out couch, sound asleep. "They're okay," Fairweather tells me. "A couple of minor scratches from the broken glass. You?"

"Sore," I tell him. "But that's from stress and lack of sleep. I'm sure you feel that way too."

He silently offers me a bottle of ibuprofen, and I take two with a swig of not-great coffee. "How's Sam?" he asks me, and for a second I wonder when, exactly, our guarded relationship progressed to first names. It was *Ms. Proctor* and *Mr. Cade* with him, but now it's *Gwen* and *Sam.* I suppose around the time he had to listen to me being shot at, which was a vivid demonstration of just how far people will go to actually get me. I've been moved to a category of persons he actually cares about.

"Mike texted me," I tell him. "Peaceful night, seems like."

"Mike's the FBI agent you talked about?"

"Yeah. Mike Lustig."

"He's the one broke the Absalom case," Fairweather says. I raise my eyebrows. "I follow the news, time to time. He got some kind of commendation too."

"That's him," I say. "Big Man on Federal Campus right now, at least. That must have registered with Chief Weldon."

"Yeah. About Weldon." Fairweather stirs his coffee. "He was a pretty straight shooter when he started five years back in the office, but lately he's been . . ."

"Shady," I say.

"Let's just say that there are some people in town who can do no wrong, as far as the locals are concerned."

"But not Vee Crockett."

"No. Nor Marlene."

I take a risk. "She worked at the garage, right? For Mr. Carr? You know anything about him?"

"Carr's a weird old duck. He's got a place out of town. A compound."

Compound is a telling choice of words. "I'm guessing visitors aren't welcome."

"He's got a wall," Fairweather agrees. "It's topped by cameras and floodlights. I don't think he likes visitors much. I've never had any cause to go inside." But I get the idea that he'd like to nose around in there.

"And he's friends with Chief Weldon."

"Cousins."

"They have any other relatives around here?"

"It's a small town, Ms. Proctor. And cousins abound."

"Any of them accountants? Bankers, maybe?"

He stares at me for a few seconds before he says, "Carl Weldon works at the bank. His father is Chief Weldon's daddy's brother. Why do you ask?"

I don't think I want to tell him any more details; if I do, and I'm wrong, my kids are in even more danger. He has enough to be on his guard about if he's not in on all this. I just shake my head and leave it there. "How long before they let us leave?" I glance at the clock hanging over the coffee machine; it's now three thirty in the morning. Despite the coffee, I feel like I'm running on empty, and my stomach rumbles to remind me that it's been many hours since I last ate. I made sure the kids had something, but I've skipped a couple of meals now, and I'm suffering for it.

"Well, you can go anytime you want, but your SUV's going to be in evidence processing and held here. You got another way home?"

I don't. And I'm not even sure it's worth going home at this point. "I'm not sure where to go from here," I tell him. "I'll be honest: I'm so exhausted. And I'm really afraid that the place we were staying—the lodge—might have been part of this attack on Sam and Connor. Can't go back there."

"There's always the Motel 6 . . . it ain't fancy, but I can guarantee you that it's not owned by one of the Weldons. I can send you back there in a cruiser and ask them to stick around, make sure you're okay. At least you can get a few hours of rest."

I hate it, but he's right. "I still need transportation for later, if I can't get my SUV back."

"I got a buddy with a garage out of Fountain Ridge; he can get one of his loaners out in about an hour. He'll want a good-faith deposit, though."

"Okay." I feel immense relief, honestly; being without some means of escape feels awful. "Hook me up with that. I'll give you a credit card number. Thank you." He nods, clearly wanting it to be No Big Thing. I leave it there.

I sit and nurse my coffee while he makes the calls. My kids are still sleeping, and I just want to crawl in and join them, but I can't. Even here, surrounded by supposedly impartial county deputies, I can't really relax. I'm not even sure why, but I just feel like there's more to this. More coming.

I need to find a way to bail Sam out of this mess, fast. And I need to protect my children from this circling, dark storm. Right now, those two feel like opposite goals. But something in the back of my mind is telling me that they aren't, not really. That the solution to everything is in a town I'd rather not go back to, and people I'd rather not face again.

Wolfhunter isn't finished with us yet.

◆ ◆ ◆

The cruiser takes us to the Motel 6. The officer walks in with us and, once we're in the two adjoining rooms, tells us that he'll be out in the parking lot until we're ready to go back to the county sheriff's office for that rental car. I intend to sleep. I do.

The kids definitely are worn out; they crash in the two beds in their room, exhausted as they've ever been. But not me. I can't stop. I'm worn to a thread, but I keep moving. Thinking about Sam. Thinking about Vee Crockett. Thinking about the spiraling disaster of my life.

I keep the connecting door open for a while, but the mounting panic inside me needs an outlet, and finally I shut it, go to the bed, and curl up on my side. I put the pillow to my face.

I shatter.

The pillow stifles the sound that boils out of me like steam. It's pure grief. Pure anguish. Pure hell.

When it finally stops, it isn't because I don't hurt inside; it's because I just can't find the breath to scream anymore. I gasp for air. I tuck myself into a protective ball and pray, pray, *pray* that I can find a way to live through this one more time. I meant what I said to Sam: I'm not running away from Stillhouse Lake. I can't. Whatever comes, we have to meet it here in the house that we made a home, in a town that doesn't want us. I thought the lake would drown the last traces of Melvin Royal forever. But he's not gone. He's never going to be gone. The damage he did to me, to *us*, is permanent.

Melvin would laugh to see me like this. Paralyzed. Traumatized. It's what he would have wanted.

I put the pillow aside. I'm still shaking. I'm raw and bleeding inside. But the thought of Melvin's satisfied grin makes me sit up, take deep breaths, and get myself the fuck together. The path out of this might be black and full of sharp edges, but I'll find my way.

And Sam? What about Sam? I know he's wandering the same dark territory that I am. He's hiding something from me. But he's also the man who came after me when I was alone and hurt and desperate. The man who helped me find my children when they were lost. The man who cracked Absalom. Who saved Connor just yesterday.

Doesn't that count too? Can't there be some way, *any* way, back to the light for both of us?

My head aches from the emotion and stress, and I get up and go to the bathroom. I study myself in the mirror. Fine lines etched lightly on my forehead, at the corners of my lids. A distant, shocked look and reddened eyes. I look like someone who's seen hell and lived.

That's something to rest on for a moment.

My cell phone rings, and I put it on the bathroom counter to see who's calling. I don't know the number, but I answer it anyway.

"I need to talk to you," a cool, elegant voice says. "I'd like to come inside."

Inside?

It's a second later that I realize who it is, and the ice inside me grows into a glacier. I hang up the call. I look at myself in the mirror again.

Then I go to the door and open it to face Miranda Nelson Tidewell.

Out in the parking lot, the deputy gets out of his cruiser and comes toward us. Miranda must know he's coming. She doesn't turn to look. She's taller than I am. Thinner, in the way that some rich people are, as if she's dieted away half her rib cage. Dressed in a black shirt and jeans. A brooch with a gold bird is the only jewelry, and I know she wears it because her daughter loved birds and was in school to become a vet.

"Everything all right, Ms. Proctor?" the deputy asks me. He has his hand on the butt of his gun. He can't figure out what's going on between the two of us.

I'm not sure I can either.

Miranda raises her perfectly shaped eyebrows. A cool, calm challenge.

"We're all right," I tell him. "She's going to come in for coffee."

He doesn't like it, but he nods and goes back to his cruiser.

"Coffee," Miranda says. She sounds amused. "I can't imagine what kind of trash this place must have available, but by all means. Let's be civilized."

We just stare at each other for a long moment. She has haunting eyes, the kind of blue that seems like arctic ice, with color that shifts with her mood. Pale-blonde hair, going gray in graceful swoops.

I move back, and she steps inside. I don't take my eyes off her as I shut and lock the door. She's the one who ought to be afraid. After all, she's now locked in here with *me*.

But she's not, in any way I can detect. She examines the room clinically, and while she seems mildly revolted, she says, "Are your children here?"

"Not in the room," I say. "Next door."

"Good." She suddenly meets my gaze. "I'm sorry they're been made part of this."

"Well, that's a lie," I say. "You want me to feel *your* pain. The pain of a mother losing her children. You think I don't know that? I saw it

225

on your face every day during my trial. I admit, I thought you moved on with your life. But here you are. Still."

"Here I am." She's studying me, trying to read me. "I find it obscene that they let you keep those children, considering what you've done."

I still haven't raised my voice, though I want to. "And what is it I've done, besides survive a man even you have to admit was a monster?"

"You enabled him. You supported him. You helped."

"I. *Survived.*"

"My daughter didn't." Her expression doesn't alter. I'm not sure that it can. The plastic surgery is brilliant, but the effect is unnatural. Nevertheless, I see something move underneath, like a creature shifting in its shell.

"How far are you going to go with this . . . documentary?" I ask her. "Coming after me is one thing. Involving my kids . . . that's not okay. Are you planning to hound Sam too?"

"Sam. Well. He chose his bed. Literally, it seems." The distaste just steams off her words. "Sam certainly knew who Gina Royal really was, at least before he went to Stillhouse Lake. And yet you were still able to twist him all out of shape."

"I'm very tired, Miranda. Why are you here?" I ask it bluntly, because I'm already sick of playing her game. And the urge to rip out a handful of that perfectly ordered hair is pretty strong.

"You helped kill my daughter. And I want to know why a mother would do that. *How* a mother *could* do that, and not slit her own throat."

There it is, finally. Right out in the open. A naked statement, not even clothed in anger. She's stating a fact, as she sees it. And demanding an explanation.

"Melvin Royal killed your daughter," I tell her. "Melvin Royal didn't need or want my help. He was a *serial killer*. He fantasized and planned and stalked and abducted and murdered all by himself. I'm alive because I was stupid. Because I believed him when he told me he was working late, or making tables in his workshop, and do you know why? Because on some level, *he frightened me*, and I was afraid to even begin to find out why." I catch my breath. "You have no idea how much that hurts when I look back at it. How sorry I am that I didn't—didn't become what I needed to be, when it would have saved lives."

If she was expecting a full confession, she's disappointed, but I can't tell what Miranda is feeling. She's a frozen lake of a woman, with something dark swimming deep beneath the surface.

She turns and walks to the tiny desk. I feel myself go still as my instincts and training start to kick in. "Do you know how long I've wanted to do this? Talk to you face-to-face?" she asks me. She holds up one of the cheap foam cups. "I believe you mentioned you might make some coffee?"

I put in a filter, tear open a packet, add the water. It takes time, and we don't talk as the coffee slowly brews into the two-cup pot. I pour. She stands to drink it, sipping with elegant little motions. Her gaze moves around, missing nothing.

"I wanted to see your face when I asked you about Melvin," she says.

"And what did it tell you?" I ask.

"That you lie very well." She drinks. I wait. "Well enough you even convinced Sam, and I never thought that would be possible. If you'd known him when I met him, you'd have been shocked how angry he was. How bitter. And how dedicated to hurting you. Has he told you that?"

She leans against the counter. Hot coffee in her cup, no other weapon I can see except the brooch she wears. It's strange, but I can *feel* her violence. I can feel the boundless hate inside her, blackening the space between us. The worst thing about Miranda is that I know her hatred comes out of an even greater grief. It makes it very hard to want to hurt her. And so easy for her to want to see me dead.

"Why did you let me in?" she asks. "You could have left me standing on the doorstep. You didn't have to acknowledge me at all. Yet you did."

"My husband murdered your daughter," I tell her. "I do acknowledge you. I know you blame yourself for not being able to protect your child; I've spent years trying to protect mine. I understand your rage perfectly. I just wish it wasn't aimed at me."

She doesn't answer. But she puts down the half-finished coffee. I watch her hands. One goes in her pocket. I tense all over. I can't imagine she has something *in* her pocket; I can't see any outline of anything dangerous. But I can't afford to be wrong.

"Do you even understand why you obsess about me, instead of Melvin?" I ask her.

"Your husband's dead. I can't hurt him."

"You didn't target him even when he was still alive," I say. "You came after *me*. Why do you think that is?"

"Because you got away with it."

"Because in your narrow little world, it was my job to keep my husband happy, right? My duty to satisfy him in ways that kept him away from your daughter. And I didn't do that. But I wasn't Melvin's keeper. His sins were his own."

She flinches. It's a small thing, but I see it. "You knew. Your neighbor saw you helping him. There was video of you with him taking a girl inside."

"The neighbor lied for attention. The video was faked; the FBI proved it. Do you really believe every wild theory that you think proves your case?"

"I'm going to see you destroyed."

"Get in line, Miranda. You don't even rate the time it takes to get a restraining order."

Now she's glaring. "The Lost Angels will carry on making your life a misery. If I can't have justice for Vivian, then at least I can have some comfort knowing you'll suffer the rest of your life for what you've done."

She's quick, I give her that. I'm looking at the welling fury in those cold eyes, and her hand comes out of her pocket. I see something in it. I dive sideways, hit the floor as I pull the gun from the shoulder holster, and I bring it into line, dead center on her heart.

I cannot die here. My children need me.

I'm a fraction of pressure from killing her when I realize that though both her hands are raised in a stabbing motion . . . she has no knife. She has a cell phone. Her face is bone white, but she looks exultant, like a martyr giving up her soul. She intended this. She walked in here ready to die. *Glad* to die if it sends me to prison.

I ease off the trigger.

The exultation fades from her face. She shuts down, and for a second neither of us moves. Then she says, "I really thought that would work." It's a mild, careless observation. She lowers her hands.

It terrifies me how close she came. If I'd shot her, it would have looked like cold-blooded murder; she wouldn't have had a weapon. Chances are I'd have been convicted. I myself told the deputy to let her inside. I'd only have my word to back up a justified shooting. And no proof at all. They'd play the TV-show confrontation at my trial.

Case closed.

I shake off the adrenaline rush as I holster the gun again. "Well, it didn't, did it," I say. I climb back to my feet. "Now you can leave, and I never want to see your face again. Not here, not near me, not around my kids. Whatever sick thing you and Sam might have had once, it's over. Leave him alone too. Understand?"

"We don't forget," she says. "The Lost Angels are never going to stop. Never, until you get what you deserve. If Sam gets in the way of that, so be it."

"The only thing Sam and I deserve is peace," I tell her. "So do you, by the way. I hope you find it. Now get the fuck out of my room."

Her mouth tightens a little at that. "Still a vulgar mouth on you," she says. "Good. I wouldn't want anyone to feel sorry for you." Before she leaves, she delivers the lowest parting blow she can. "Tell Sam I miss him."

I want to pull the gun and empty the magazine into her straight, arrogant back. I don't. I wait until she's gone, and then I collapse back to the bed, shaking.

She came so close.

No.

I did.

13

SAM

I don't like being in jail. It's my first time, and it feels worse than I imagined it would. I'm not claustrophobic—can't be a pilot if you are—but the walls close in anyway. Despite what I said to Gwen before they led me out, I feel lost now. Very much on my own in a place that feels like the belly of the proverbial beast.

Two hours in, I'm trying to close my eyes, and not daring to really sleep, when a voice from outside the bars says, "Opening number six."

I'm in number six. I hear the rattle of the lock, and I sit up fast, already reaching for the makeshift blackjack I've put together.

I feel pretty stupid when Mike Lustig ducks under the too-low opening and steps inside. The cell locks behind him, but he doesn't seem to notice. He nods toward the weapon. "That soap in your sock, or you just happy to see me?"

"Jesus, man." I put it down and sink onto the narrow, shallow bunk. The mattress feels like it's filled with crushed scorpions. "The hell are you doing here?"

"You're in *jail*. Dumb question."

"I didn't think you'd want to risk your new, shiny rep associating with a felon."

"First off, I'm not associating. I'm *investigating*. Second off, shut your damn mouth. Did you talk to them?"

"Facts only," I tell him as he leans against the wall. He's a big dude, Mike, bigger than you'd think would fit into a pilot's cockpit, but he's damn good despite his size. He takes up a lot of this small space. "Nothing but facts."

"You know better," he says. "Any word comes out of your mouth they can twist. And right up in here, they will."

I stop and look at him. Really look. He's tired. He's come all the way from DC, probably on his own dime, to help me. "Gwen called," I say.

"Hell, yes, she did. Good thing, too, because I guarantee you that in this snake pit you'd have some episode by morning and end up either dead or beaten half to it." He puts scare quotes around *episode*. "Killing a cop's bad enough, but killing a small-town cop in a town that thinks of the Civil War as being waged last week? Only way it gets worse for you is if you're black. Which you're lucky you're not."

"But you are," I say. "Maybe this isn't the place for you."

"Oh no, son, it's exactly the place for me," Mike says. "I'm your best friend until the judge I woke up gets your bail hearing done."

"I had a bail hearing. I didn't get any."

"We're revisiting."

"Oh." I shake my head. "Thanks, but don't you dare put up the cash."

"Why? You planning on cutting out on me?"

"Not unless they say I can't leave town. I mean it, though. Don't." FBI agents are not wealthy, and Mike's putting himself in debt for this already. "Gwen and the kids. They're okay?"

He changes position, and I'm immediately on guard; the dread sets in when he speaks, because he's changed tone too. He now sounds pro-fessionally comforting. "They're fine, man. Listen, there was a problem, but they're okay, I want to say that up front."

I stand up. It isn't voluntary; I need to be on my feet. "What happened?"

"Someone came after them on the road," he says. "The car's shot to shit, but they're not hurt."

"Who?" My knuckles hurt, and I realize I've balled my hands into fists. "Who the *fuck*—"

He's held up his hands to fend off the anger. "Don't know yet," he says. "We've got a description of a truck, and a guy dead on the road. She didn't kill him; he got thrown out of the truck when it spun out. We'll find the driver soon enough and ask some questions."

"Who's we?"

"Me, for a start. Plus, there's a pretty decent TBI investigator."

"Fairweather?"

"Yeah. Got a good rep. We'll add people when we find decent ones. Not that we're likely to find many in Wolfhunter proper. Rot spreads, and this town smells like it's got it in the bones."

Mike's getting almost lyrical about it, but I don't doubt his instincts. Not for a hot second. "Tell me again that they're okay."

"Yeah, man. They're okay. They're at the county sheriff's substation, about half an hour out to the west. They'll be there all night, most likely. Soon as I know more, you'll know."

I slowly sink back down on the bed. It doesn't feel any better, but I stretch out anyway. "They need protection."

"Fairweather's on that. I asked."

"You should go."

"Ain't going nowhere until you are."

I sigh. Feel it deep, like the exhaustion. "Thanks, Mike."

"Yeah, remember me at bonus time."

"Like I'm ever going to be able to afford you."

"Another charity asshole." He digs a phone out of his pocket, and a pair of earbuds. "Here. Listen."

I send him a look and put the earbuds in, not sure what the hell he's doing, and then he plays Gwen's message. I close my eyes, listening, hearing, the real emotion in her voice, and when she says *I love you*, my eyes open and I stare at the dark ceiling. The ghostly light of the phone throws everything into sharp relief.

She doesn't know how much I don't deserve that. And how much I needed to hear it.

I strip off the earbuds and hand back the phone. "Don't delete it," I tell him. "Send it to me."

He doesn't ask why. Proving, once again, I can pick good friends when I try.

We make up a chess set out of spare change and random junk, and play until the guard comes back to unlock the door. "Judge is ready," he says. "Let's go."

"I've got him," Mike says, and takes my arm. To be fair to the guard, it looks like he's capable of ripping the arm off, which is probably why I don't get shackles like I did earlier; it makes walking easier, at least. "Try to look pitiful. Oh, wait, you nailed it already."

"Shut up."

He walks me through the gates.

The ride to the courthouse is about two minutes. I wonder if Mike's as alert as I am, because it's a chilly predawn now, mist rising up from the ground like escaping ghosts . . . and we're alone in a police car with two of Wolfhunter's Finest, neither of whom look friendly. We could disappear, end up dead on the banks of Wolfhunter River like the woman Connor and I found. Or never be found at all. Still, making a prominent FBI agent disappear is probably too big a magic trick for this town to pull off.

Hopefully.

The only cars on the street this time of morning are three police cruisers . . . and a surprising number of black SUVs. I point at one that's parked near the courthouse. "That yours?"

Mike nods. "Why?"

"You bring company?"

He gets it in the next second as he takes in the other, similar vehicles. "No," he says. "They don't look too local."

"They don't," I agree. "I count three of them in view right now."

"That's a lot of strangers."

"You're sure they're not FBI? TBI?"

"I'm sure," Mike says. "How many people you think it would take
to secure this town?"

"The whole town?" I think he's kidding for a second. He isn't.
"Uh . . . one main road in and out, so . . . couple of cars ought to do
it. If you mean locking down resistance, you'd want to hit the police
station first. Right?"

"Right," he says.

"But that hasn't happened."

"Not yet."

He doesn't say anything else. We're not close enough to read license
plates in this dim light, or I'm sure he'd be jotting them down or taking
a picture.

Mike's got a theory, I think. He's just not telling me what it is.

Once we're out of the car and inside the courthouse, I breathe a little easier. The judge is a grumpy old man from out of town. He's made
all the more angry by the hour, and the fact he must have been rousted
out of bed by someone at the highest state levels to get this done. He
gestures to the yawning court clerk, who calls the case, and I realize my
lawyer isn't here. Well, shit. It doesn't seem to matter; the judge just
makes a pronouncement that seems like he's reading it from a card.

"Based on my review of additional evidence, I'm amending the
earlier decision and granting bail to the defendant in the amount of two
hundred fifty thousand dollars. Usual conditions apply."

That must be shorthand, because the court clerk keeps typing as if
more's been said, and for quite a while. The judge waits until she stops,

then bangs the gavel and rushes out. He's still got on pajamas under the robe, looks like. I can't imagine his next defendant is going to have a very good time of it.

"Two hundred fifty thousand?" I say to Mike when he comes to claim me. "Yeah, don't bother to tell me you haven't got it handy."

"Man, I don't got it at all. But you're in luck. Someone does."

It's not Gwen. She does have some cash socked away, but definitely not *that* much. Mike walks me out, and I don't know what I'm expecting when we hit the sidewalk, but I balk when I recognize the car. It's a rented Buick.

Mike opens the door and gestures me in to sit beside Miranda Tidewell.

"Are you fucking kidding me?" I ask him. "Mike. Come on."

"Just get in. You needed an angel."

"She's the opposite."

Miranda leans out and says, "Sam, don't make me regret my investment in you. Please. Get in. Listen to what we have to say."

I look at her, then at Mike Lustig. "So it's *we* now." I feel doors shutting inside me. Ties being cut. I've counted on Mike and his friendship for a long time, longer than I knew Miranda; I never thought anything could shake that trust, or break it.

But I feel that chain coming apart now, link by link.

"Get in, man," he tells me again. I could walk away, but fact is, where would I go? Gwen isn't here. And she's dealing with worse than this.

I get into the car. Mike climbs in on the passenger side up front, and the entire sedan groans and settles a little. "Well," I say to Miranda, "at least you didn't make him your chauffeur. Even for you, maybe that's a bridge too far."

"Fuck you," Mike says. "You think I did this for *money*?"

"I don't know, Mike, why don't you tell me why else you colluded with a woman you know I hate?"

"Mr. Lustig has your best interests at heart, Sam," Miranda says. She pulls the car out from the curb and starts driving. I don't know where we're going. And I don't like it. "Someone needed to help save you from yourself. If Mike and I colluded, I promise it's because we both still care."

"Oh, you care now." I say it flatly, and I hope she can feel the slap. She sinks back into her seat and stares straight ahead.

"Yes," she says, "I do. Somehow. Even with everything you've done to push me away." I remember that tone, that voice. Low and with a faint rasp to it, like a cat's tongue. It's like falling back into the past, and it scares the hell out of me.

Miranda doesn't look quite like herself. Her hair's down, spilling in smooth waves over her shoulders; she's wearing a plain black shirt and blue jeans. Expensive, of course; she wouldn't be caught dead in some regular store brand. But she's as casual as I've ever seen her when not under the influence . . . and then I realize she's drunk. Not wildly drunk, like she used to get. But enough. "What did you do?" I ask her. My voice sounds tight now.

"I saw Gina," she tells me. "Don't worry. I didn't spill your secrets. I just wanted to . . . to test her a little."

"Did you hurt her?" I don't realize how angry I am until I hear the sound of my voice. Mike's hand clamps down on my shoulder; he recognizes that tone. The way I've shifted forward, ready to lunge. "Don't, Mike. *Did you hurt her?*"

"No," Miranda finally says. "She's fine. And so are the children, apparently; I didn't see them."

That's something. It lets me step back from a very long drop. "Why would you do that?"

"She's dragging you right down with her," Miranda says. "That doesn't have to happen. I don't *want* that to happen, Sam. I never did. I care too much to watch you . . . debase yourself like this."

"Then don't watch. Go back to KC and leave us alone," I tell her. "Let it go."

Her face flushes, little hard dots of red in her cheeks and forehead. She can't keep herself quite as icily calm when she's drunk. "You're not a mother. I had a child I carried in my body, and she was absolutely destroyed. Someone has to pay for that."

"Someone did," I say. "Melvin Royal got a bullet in his head."

"You of all people knew she was guilty too. And now you're letting her get away with it."

"Yeah, I was angry and deluded. I got better; you should try it."

"The documentary will be made," she says. "Your lives will still fall apart, because Gina coming out of the shadows was the beginning of the end for whatever you think your relationship was. You ought to be smart enough to realize that." She reaches into her pocket and brings out a folded piece of paper. She hands it to me.

It's a printed article from the internet. In it, someone is earnestly talking about Gwen Proctor as a full partner in her husband's crimes. It's not from five years ago. It's brand-new.

"I didn't print the comments section," she says. "But I can promise you there are thousands posting, and they're just as full of rage as they ever were, if not more so. No one believes in her innocence. No one but *you*. And once the documentary is out, no one ever will again. She'll have no peace from now on. But we will have some measure of justice."

Jesus. The monster in this equation isn't Gwen. It's sitting next to me, and I helped create it. "Call them off."

"You started it, Sam. You're the one who founded the Lost Angels. The one who made up the wanted posters with her picture we used around the neighborhoods every time we found her. You pushed us to follow her every move, track her aliases, keep showing up and driving her away. The one who came up with the idea to prove, once and for all, just how guilty she really is by moving in next door to her at Stillhouse

Lake. Why would I call them off? I trusted you to finish this for all of us. And instead, you *fell in love with her*."

The edge sharpens on the last of that. Ah, God, no. Don't tell me that's what this is really about. I see the red rims of her eyes, the barely controlled grief and rage. This is about how she feels about *me* as much as her loss. I'd fooled myself into believing that we were just allies, but for her it was always more. It was a *relationship*.

I just never saw it that way. She was a means to an end. And she used me in the same measure.

I turn to stare in disbelief at Mike. "And you're in this with her." He's got his stone face on, but I know he's feeling guilty behind that. He has to be.

"Look, man . . . I like Gwen. I do. But I have to put my brother first, and Gwen is never going to shake her past. It's just too heavy. I don't want you going down with her."

"So you're okay with her being harassed, stalked, maybe killed. And the kids along with her."

"No," he says, "I'm not. But I'm also not okay with you being collateral damage. Hear this woman out. That's all I'm asking."

"You don't know her," I tell him. "Jesus, Miranda, don't you get it? I never loved you. I barely *liked* you. We had our losses in common. And now it's over."

She doesn't answer immediately; she's slowing the car, and now she's making a turn into a familiar parking lot. The Motel 6. "I'm giving you a choice, Sam. You have a job offer in Florida, a chance to start over and do something positive with your life. Just . . . take it."

I get it then. Finally. And it *sucks*. "Mike didn't recommend me for the job, did he? You twisted some corporate arms. Got me a nice, cushy position far away from Gwen."

"I did recommend you," Mike says. "I want you alive, man. And I don't see that happening if you stay on this path." He sounds genuinely unhappy about this. I think he really is. He never liked Miranda and her crusade; he never liked who I was when I was part of it, though he never gave up on me either. I understand why he's done this now.

But he's completely fucking *wrong*.

I listen to the engine idle. I count pulse beats because it keeps me calm when I want to rip this car to pieces.

"You have a choice to change your life," Miranda says. "I'm driving Mike back to the Nashville airport. If you say yes, I have a private jet ready there to fly you to Florida. Mike and I will get these charges dropped against you, because it's obvious you're not a murderer; you were defending yourself, and the state police's investigation will fully bear that out. You take that job. You find someone else. You heal from what she's done to you. And you never, ever come back."

"Or?" I ask tightly.

"Or you get out of the car and wait for Gina. I swear to God if you make that choice, I will make it my personal mission to destroy you both," she says. "I will make you and Gina Royal so toxic, so poisonous, that everyone that touches you is destroyed by association."

Scorched earth. She means it. I hear Mike protest that, but I'm not listening; he might not have realized what she intended, but he bought into this, and he stays in for the full ride.

"You can't do that," I tell her. I even manage to be gentle about it. "You can't punish innocent kids like that."

"I look forward to the day someone destroys those children the way Melvin destroyed mine. Then I can rest, because the last trace of Melvin Royal will be gone from this earth."

It's horrific, but she means it. I know this woman. I cared for her, once. And seeing the fanaticism, the cruelty . . . it's like looking into a mirror and seeing myself two years ago.

"You're insane," I say. I'm actually sorry for her. And frightened of her. "You'd go that far."

"I would go to hell to punish Gina Royal," she said. "And if you get out of this car, Sam . . . that's where you're going too."

I look from her to Mike. He looks nakedly appalled now. He didn't know she'd do this, or take it this far. I feel sorry for him for a tiny second, before I remember that he's trying to pull me away from the people I love.

"See you both in hell, then," I tell them, and I open the door and get out.

I watch the car drive away. Dawn's showing on the eastern horizon, but the morning is oddly cold for the season. Ghosts escaping the ground.

I sit down against the wall of the Motel 6, and I wait for whatever will come for me now. If it's the Wolfhunter PD, I'll be dead before I see the sun.

But if it's a choice between watching Gwen suffer, or suffering with her . . . I'll be with her, every time.

I'm sitting there half an hour before they show up. Three men, not here to mind their own business because they look around, see me and head right over. The one in the middle of the trio is a lanky red-haired man with a thick, unkempt beard; the other two are shorter, both with dark hair and beards. Under all the hair I see a resemblance. I don't know them. And they damn sure shouldn't know me.

"Fellas," I say. I don't get up. I'm tired. "We really have to do this right now?"

I expect them to lead with the obvious, the killing of their local hero Travis, but they surprise me. The big redheaded one says, "Where is she?"

"Gwen?" I shrug. "Why?"

"We got a date," he says, and laughs the way a donkey brays. "Bitch is gonna suck my dick, I hear." He stops laughing, because he sees it's not working. I really don't want to do this. I really don't. I feel sick and lost and utterly not in the mood. Until he says, "Not the mother, I wouldn't do her with a thousand condoms. I'm talkin' about that fine daughter."

Everything else stops. The exhaustion. The depression. The fear that I can't quite suppress. I stand up. "You mean *my* daughter." Because she is. And I'm not letting this asshole get away with it. "Nice mouth you got. You kiss your brother with that?"

Not surprisingly, they come for me. They were only waiting for the excuse.

It's not like the damn movies, where two wait politely while the first one has a go at you; they rush me in a jumbled, stumbling group, and two of them keep my right arm pinned back while the third—the big one—slams a fist the size of a coffee can into my stomach so hard I feel it up my spine. I take it, because I'm trying to spot their weaknesses, other than lack of discipline. The big one's ungainly, and listing his weight to the right. Easy fix. I gag back the pain of his punch, raise my work boot, and slam it into the side of his right knee. I feel the crunch of tearing cartilage, and his high-pitched scream echoes off the concrete bricks of the motel court.

He hops backward, howling and crashing into the wall, where he leans and keeps making noise. Not down, but for now, out of the fight.

The two limpets locked onto my right arm stare at their friend in shock. All I have to do to shake them off is punch my left fist into the side of the first guy's head, grab him by the hair, and introduce him to the point of my knee, which breaks his nose and sends him reeling back to fall in the corner.

One left. Nobody holding me back. I don't feel pain right now. I feel a deep, almost sickening joy that I'm laying these guys out. And he can see it.

He holds up both hands and backs off.

I'm surprised that when I speak, my voice sounds pretty even. "Hey, fellas, let me ask you a question. Who put you up to this?"

The one with the broken nose tries to curse at me but breaks into a coughing fit that sprays blood. I wince, and also feel a savage rush of satisfaction.

Redbeard says, in a voice that sounds like he's grinding rocks in the back of his throat, "Asshole." He manages to give it the Tennessee twang even on two syllables. "Everybody knows you're part of it."

"Part of what?" I'm expecting it to be about this town, about Travis getting shot. But it isn't.

"You're Melvin Royal's little errand boy," he says. "Everybody knows that. You and her, together, helping him get those girls. You're fucking *dead*."

After he says it, I hear a white-noise buzz, like I've taken a blow to the head. I just look at him without any real comprehension. Then the sickness creeps in. *Jesus Christ*. I take a breath and let it out. I feel unsteady now. "Where did you hear this?"

"Bar," says Redbeard.

The man still holding up his hands says, "Somebody said it on Facebook."

I turn on him. "Who the hell said it?"

"Why?" The man whose nose is ruined spits blood and grins with pink teeth. "You gonna go fuck her up too?"

Her. My immediate, sickening thought is this comes directly from Miranda. This is the kind of thing she'd launch, pure propaganda with no truth in it at all. An accusation without backup, without merit, spreading fast . . . and one thing I know about people from deep personal experience: they're happy to jump on the hate train if it makes them feel like fucking heroes.

I grab the uninjured man by the shoulder and say, "Show me." He pulls out a surprisingly good cell phone and navigates with shaking fingers, then thrusts it toward me.

I read the post. It isn't by Miranda. Or, at least, it doesn't *seem* to be. It's attributed to a woman who says her name is Doreen Anderson, and the picture is of a blonde, plump woman whose address is listed in Atlanta. Here's Doreen at a bake sale with her kids. At a church social. Posing with two men, one of whom looks familiar to me, though I can't immediately pinpoint why until I see the white panel van in the fuzzy background. They're all beaming and giving the thumbs-up sign.

The circuit clicks. She's part of the film crew. I check her employment details. She's a bank clerk who's been laid off, as so many have, by the advance of automated tellers. Current occupation is listed as "Documentarian."

Her post strongly implies that I'm some acolyte of Melvin Royal's, moving in with Gwen because we have that in common. But nothing is strong enough or directly stated enough to take to court, which I wouldn't do anyway; it would only fan the flames. Lots of *What if he* and *Maybe the two of them were* kind of speculation. What passes for journalism in today's world.

Tar sticks. If she meant to cause trouble, mission accomplished. And like Miranda told me: it's just beginning.

I flip the phone back to the man, who fumbles and drops it. I hope the screen's cracked. "You idiots spread the word at that bar you were talking about: you come for me, or for Gwen or our kids, and you won't walk away next time. You're lucky I didn't kill all three of you. Now fuck off."

"Faggot." Redbeard spits at me. Misses, because my reflexes are still pretty good.

"Pretty pathetic that's still your go-to insult, big man. That ligament's fried, by the way. You'd better get it fixed if you ever want to walk without a limp."

"My nose is broke," the second man volunteers, like it's not obvious. He doesn't sound so much combative as sad. "It's fuckin' *broke*."

I just nod. The three of them shuffle off around the corner, with the still-whole third man helping Redbeard hop along, and Broken Nose trying to stop the streaming blood with the sleeve of his denim jacket. Unsuccessfully. There's a good chance they'll go straight to the police and get my bail revoked, but I can't help that. If the Wolfhunter police want to find me, nothing I can really do about it. At least I'll cost Miranda her quarter of a million. That's petty revenge, but hey. Revenge.

I'm starting to walk off toward the woods to find a place to piss when a white, boxy sedan I don't recognize pulls into the motel parking lot; I don't pay a lot of attention to it because I'm starting to feel the adrenaline wearing off and exhaustion setting in again, until it pulls in abruptly in front of me. I step back, reaching for a gun I don't actually have anymore, and then I realize that Gwen's driving the car. We look at each other for a long, telling moment, and then I glance into the back. The kids are inside. Quiet and subdued.

"Get in," Gwen says. "Let's get out of here."

"There's no place to go," I tell her. "And we need to talk. Now."

14

GWEN

Sam doesn't look right. He seems pale, and tired, and deeply unhappy, lines on his face I haven't seen before. I don't know what he sees when he leans down to look at me through the open door of the car, but he gets in and slams it shut. I immediately start driving.

"Where are you going?" he asks me. He even sounds exhausted. Hasn't slept, I'm sure. Like me, he's worn thin with it.

"Away from all this bullshit and this damn town. Mike called me. He said you were out on bail and where to pick you up. Where is he?" Sam doesn't answer. "Never mind. Let's go home."

"Home isn't a refuge," he says. "Stop the car."

I haven't pulled out of the motel parking lot yet, just made the turnaround. I pull the rental into a space. "What?" I have the feeling I'm not going to like this. At all.

He hesitates for a long moment, and then he says, "I don't want the kids to hear this."

"I'm pretty sure we need to," my daughter says. "Enough with the secrets! We're not babies."

But they always will be to me; tiny little bundles of sweet, new skin and kicking feet and waving hands that need protection from the world.

I feel breathless, because Sam wouldn't have said that if it wasn't serious. If it wasn't something that would change *everything*.

But he takes Lanny at her word. He leans up against the passenger side door to look at me, and at them too.

Then he tells us the truth.

"Miranda Tidewell and I used to be close," he says. "I lived with her for a while. Before you assume anything, it was just . . . I needed a place to stay, and she provided a room in her house. A guest room."

"For how long?" I ask him.

"From the time I got back from deployment until I moved to Stillhouse Lake," he says. "I told you that I went there thinking I'd prove that you had something to do with Melvin's crimes. That was true. I just didn't tell you that I had funding."

"Funding," I repeat. "From Miranda."

"And I guess she's finally realized she's not getting value for her investment."

I feel something catch inside me, sharp as a fishhook. He's only ever talked about it as his own decision, not that it was any kind of shared secret. Shared with *her*. "She knew you were coming to Stillhouse Lake. To hurt me. Put me in prison if you could do that."

"Yes."

Connor says, "The woman on TV? *That one?* You lived with her?"

"I did." His voice breaks. He doesn't want to admit this to Connor. "There's more. I put together the Lost Angels group. It started with the two of us, then pulled in the families and friends of Melvin's other victims. If we didn't get everyone, we got close. It was meant to be a place to heal. But that's not what it turned into."

"Sam . . ." I know about the Lost Angels group. And I feel a crawling horror beneath my skin. "No. *No.*"

"I started it," he says. "Miranda and I did that to you. God, Gwen . . ." I can see how long he's carried this secret, and how much it hurts him. I can feel sorry for him even as he's cutting my heart in two. "At first it was just talk, just internet bullshit to make ourselves feel better. Then . . . then I made the wanted posters. I found out where you were living after you changed your name." He looks ill now. "We came back every day to put them up. For weeks. We tracked you."

I want to throw up. I brace myself on the steering wheel. I remember how happy I was to get my kids back with me, how safe and warm our new refuge felt after my acquittal. We'd started over. I believed in the goodness and forgiveness of people then. I'd really thought we could move on without the stench of Melvin's evil following us.

And then wanted posters with my picture went up around our neighborhood, accusing me of rape, torture, and murder. They were stuffed in our mailbox. They were nailed to our *front door*. To the doors of my kids' school.

To hear that Sam did that . . . it burns something to ash inside me. *He* destroyed our safety. *He* pushed us to run for our lives, because after that first time it all went viral, beyond anyone's control. Reddit went mad with speculation about how deep my involvement went in the murders and concluded that I was the *mastermind*. That Melvin was just my patsy.

We were relentlessly doxed from that point on. No safe spaces. The Lost Angels, and the army of rabid assholes who followed after them, began sending us more and more violent imagery and fantasies about our deaths.

I realize, with a horrible jolt, that *Sam* sent those too. He must have, in the beginning. It's never stopped. Every day, the Sicko Patrol floods my in-box.

Sam is the real author of our misery.

I don't even know how to process the depth of that betrayal, even if it was done before we ever really met.

There are tears in my eyes now, cold enough to freeze. It hurts. Everything hurts. *How could you not tell me? How could you make me trust you? What kind of sick game are you playing now?* I can barely feel my body. I'm sick enough to faint, but I don't. I cling grimly to the world, this ugly, broken world, and I say, "You *asked me to marry you.* Did she tell you to do that? Marry me, then break me? Or maybe just kill . . ." I can't continue; it hurts too much. My voice is shaking. I'm shaking. And I realize, *Oh God*, that I've not told the kids he proposed, that my children are witnesses and victims now, that I should have done as he asked and stepped out of the car to listen to this confession because this . . . this is going to destroy them. They trusted him.

I turn to look at them. Connor's head is down, and I know that posture; he's guarding himself against the pain. Lanny is staring at Sam, and there's pure horror on her face.

It sharpens into rage. "You *bastard*," she says. "You *monster!*" She's quoting her father's letter. *You don't know who he is, Gina. You don't know what he's capable of doing. I'm laughing at the thought that you only bring monsters into your bed. You deserve that.*

Maybe I do. My children don't.

Sam's face has gone starkly pale now, his gaze still on me. "I came here to hurt you in the beginning, and yes, Miranda knew, but then things changed, they *changed*, and when I say I love you and I love these kids, I'm telling you nothing but the truth. I understand why you said no to me. I get it. But please. *Please believe me.*"

I hear the pain in his voice. I see it in his eyes, glittering with tears like the ones running down my cheeks. All this is said in quiet tones, but I want to scream and keep on screaming until the world stops. I've never imagined Sam as the kind of monster Melvin was until this moment, but now it's all too clear. All too *real.*

Because he's hurt us just as much.

"I don't believe you," I tell him. "Miranda just paid your bail. Didn't she?"

He makes a sound like I've gutted him. For a moment he doesn't move, except to bow his head. He just breathes. I wait. If he reaches out toward me, toward either of my children, I will grab that arm and break it. I will keep twisting, and he'll bend forward and I'll crush his throat with a hard, straight fist. The sequence is clear to me, but his face isn't there when I try to imagine it. It's just a blank space. Because right at this moment, I can't fathom who the man sitting across from me really is.

He opens the car door and lunges out, like he can't wait to get away from me. But then he staggers and has to lean against the car, on Lanny's side. He doubles over and braces himself with palms on his thighs and gasps for air.

"Go," Lanny says. "Just drive, Mom." There are tears running down my daughter's face. "I want to go home!"

I've failed them. Again. I don't know how to ever make this right. "Okay," I tell her. "We will."

Before I can put the car in gear, Connor opens his door and gets out. I freeze because I don't know what he's doing until he walks around the car, faces Sam, and says, "Are you telling us the truth now? Everything? Are you sure?"

Sam nods. He's still trembling and trying to breathe. I can't imagine what my son is feeling, but I don't want to stop him. I can't.

"Mom!" Lanny hits the back of my seat with a hard fist. "Do something! Get him back in the car, and *let's go!*"

"Connor!" He's not listening to me. I climb out of the driver's side. "Connor, get back in the car!"

But my son's ignoring me—and Lanny, who's going ballistic in the car. He's watching Sam with steady focus.

Then he says, "I understand." He's not talking to me. He's talking to Sam. "They're mad. I'm mad too. But it's easy for somebody to tell you what you need to hear. I listened to my . . . my father even when I knew better." He swallows, and I can see how nervous he is. And how much it takes for him to do this. "We knew who you were before. It's not different. It's just . . . more."

"Kid . . ." Sam hangs his head. "You should get back in the car. Your mom and sister want to go home."

I want to say something, but I can't. There's something happening here, and it's important.

Connor says, "You hated us once. Then you got better. I still believe you."

It hurts. Everything's in chaos inside me now, whirling edges of steel that cut and cut and cut. *Connor's a child, he's just a child, he can't understand.* But in some ways, my son understands more than I ever will.

Sam lets out a tortured gasp, and he grabs my son into a hug so fierce it makes me ache. Connor hugs him back. And I know that look. I've felt it, all the way down. I know the loss and the fear and most of all, the love.

Sam loves my son.

He really does.

"Mom!" Lanny gets out of the car now. She's pale and frightened and unsure what's going on, and I put an arm around her and pull her close. "Mom, Connor can't just . . . he can't just *forgive him.*"

But she's wrong, and I see it like a sudden flash of sunlight. There's something beautiful in front of me. Something precious. Nobody earns this. But Sam deserves it.

"Lanny," I say quietly. "Connor's right."

"Mom, we can't trust him!"

I know that. There's not a reason in the world to trust him except . . . except what he's done since coming to us. At no point has he hurt us except when his past has come to light. At no point has he done anything but be my partner, protector, champion. That isn't an act. It *can't* be an act, because I am seeing the consequences right now, in real time, for being truthful. He knew this would happen. And he told us anyway.

That's brave. That's the Sam I know.

Rachel Caine

Sam kisses my son on the top of the head and says, "I love you, Connor. Remember that, okay?"

Connor steps back. "You can't leave."

"But I have to," Sam says. "Don't I?"

Sam and I look at each other from opposite sides of the car. I catch my breath on another surge of real pain; I can see the heartbreak in him. The damage done.

"Sam," I tell him, "get in the damn car."

He blinks. I see the flash of hope, and then it's gone. "Miranda . . ."

"You said she'd destroy us. Don't let her."

"It's too late. Isn't it?"

I honestly don't know. "You can't just . . . go. You don't have money, or any way to get out of town. Unless Mike—"

"No," he interrupts me. "Mike's with her."

I don't know what to say. I'm not the only one who's been betrayed today. He was already hurting. Now it's worse. He's as alone as he's ever been, I think.

"You're right. She did bail me out," he says. "She and Mike gave me a choice. I chose you. I chose this."

If he's telling the truth, it's the biggest thing that anyone has ever done for us. And despite the gulf between us, despite the pain of what he did that feels new and raw even if it's years past now . . . I can't ignore that.

Lanny whispers, "Mom? Mom, but . . . what he did . . ."

"It's what he's doing now that counts," I tell her, and turn to look right at her. "Do you trust me?"

She nods. Unwillingly. There are tears glittering in her eyes. She's confused and hurt. I understand that.

I turn back to Sam. When I speak again, my voice is gentler. "Please get in the goddamn car."

He stares at me for a second, frozen. He drags in a breath and wipes the heel of hands across his face. "I'm sorry," he says.

252

"I know that."

I wait until he's getting back in before I join him. Connor gets in behind us. That just leaves my daughter. She hesitates, glares at me, and then slides into the backseat.

"Thank you," I tell her. Lanny crosses her arms and looks away. Not ready yet, but she will be. I hope.

We're not a family. But we're together, and that's a new start.

"Please tell me we're leaving this damn place," Lanny says.

"Can you?" I ask Sam. He shrugs as he fastens his seat belt. "The bail . . ."

"It's Miranda's money."

That's enough to make me accelerate.

We are fifteen minutes out when my phone rings.

I look at the name. I intend to blow it off, but it's Hector Sparks, and I feel obligated to answer. I put it on speaker. "Gwen Proctor."

"Ms. Proctor, I need your assistance immediately. You have to find her!" He sounds breathless.

"Find who?"

"Vera Crockett," he says. "She's escaped. And I think she's in very great danger."

"What? How the hell did she—"

"The police claim they were careless," he says. He sounds nervous, and it sounds like he's pacing the floor. "But I think they were very deliberate in allowing her to get away; she was left unattended in the van at the courthouse. I believe this is a plot to have her silenced. Now that she's on the run, she can easily be killed."

"Because of what she knows?" I sharpen my tone. "After talking to her, my whole family is on the same list, don't you realize that? Did you know this would mean whoever killed Marlene would also come after us? Or are you just that stupid?"

Sparks is quiet for a moment. Then he says, "I can turn to no one else in this town for help. Not a single person. If you find Vee and bring her to my house, I promise you that I can and will keep all of you safe. But she has to be found. *Now.* Ms. Proctor, I am not exaggerating when I tell you that this girl has no chance without our help."

Dammit.

I should keep going. I don't owe this girl anything. I don't.

I look at my daughter in the rearview mirror. Her lips are parted. All her defensiveness is gone. She's staring at me as if she expects me to do something.

And right now I can't bear to let her down.

I turn the car around.

"I know where she's going," Lanny says.

"How could you possibly—"

"She's going to her mom's house. She's scared, and she knows they'll kill her. That's where she'd go, right?"

My kid's smart. Smarter than I am, because it makes perfect sense, and it makes me wonder if Lanny's thought about ending things. If she's ever been that desperate and alone. Then I know, from the look in her eyes. She has. Of course she has, with the life she's been forced to live. That's a wound that Sam and I inflicted together, for very different reasons.

I have to make damn sure I don't let her down.

◆ ◆ ◆

The police are doing a grid search, fanning out from the courthouse; it won't take them long to make it to the taped-off Crockett house. I head straight there and slide to a stop at the curb. No police cruisers in sight so far. I see that the tape that once sealed the front door—the one with the shotgun blast through it—has been ripped off and is flapping in the breeze by one corner.

"Stay here," I order, and I'm directing it at everyone, but no one listens to me. As I run for the door, I look back. Sam's coming. And worse, so is my daughter. I slow as I come up the front steps. Vee tried to kill the last person who surprised her. I gesture for the other two to stay back, and I enforce it with a scorching look.

Sam grabs Lanny and pulls her to a halt. I proceed carefully. Slowly.

The house is worse than I'd imagined. A leaning, neglected thing, with a half-rotten porch with no railing. The front door creaks as I ease it back. The stench of old blood hits me, and I try not to gag. "Vee?" I say. "Vee, are you here? It's Gwen."

I look back at Sam, who's still holding Lanny back. I point to the car. To Connor, who's hesitating next to it. I mouth *Look after them*. Sam nods and goes back. No hesitation. I send him a silent thanks for not second-guessing me, and I realize that he rarely does. That's a gift he's been quietly giving me this whole time, and I never saw it.

I step inside. The place is dim, rank with the smell of death, and yet oddly neat. Marlene tried, I think; the carpet is worn but clean. Pictures of Vera as a little girl hang on the wall, along with a set of plaster praying hands and a simple cross.

Vera is sitting in an old rocking chair, hunched over, motionless. She's still wearing the jail jumpsuit we saw her in before. Her hair hangs lank over her face. As my eyes adjust, I see she's got something in her hands.

A knife.

That's when Lanny slams breathlessly through the front door. "I'm not waiting in the car!"

Oh God. I step between the threat and Lanny. "Vee. Please put the knife down."

I hear Lanny slide to a stop. She realizes the situation, and at least she holds back from doing anything *more* impulsive.

"You can't help," Vee says. She sounds different. When she raises her head, she *looks* different. The frozen lake has thawed. She looks like a girl who's finally starting to feel something, and it's hellish. "They killed my momma. And they're going to kill me too. I'd already be dead except you tried to help me, and I'm sorry, I heard them talkin', and they say you're next. *I'm sorry.*" She's crying. There are tears running down her cheeks. She's shivering. I want to wrap her in a blanket, but I can't; I can't even comfort her as long as she's holding that knife. "I was just so *scared.*"

"This isn't your fault," I tell her. "Come with us. We can help you."

She shakes her head, and she puts the edge of that knife to her arm; it's set to cut upward, tearing open the long artery. People bleed out quickly from that. I hear Lanny gasp. I see the skin indent from the pressure of the knife. There's a tiny, tiny impulse that's holding Vee back, and anything can tip things in the other direction. I don't dare say anything.

My daughter does. "My dad was a murderer, did you know that? And they thought my mom helped him. They wanted to take her away from us forever. And"—Lanny gulps air—"I didn't see any way out. I was twelve, and so many people hated us, Vee. *So many.* I just wanted . . ."

Vee hasn't moved, but she's listening. "Did you try?" she asks when Lanny pauses.

Please say no, I think. But my daughter says, "Yes. Once. When I was living with my grandma. I got scared after I took the pills. I threw them all up. She never knew."

I never knew, either, and it shakes me to my core.

"You can change your mind," Lanny says to the girl in the chair, the girl who is one-quarter of an inch away from death. "I did. You can be braver than this. You aren't guilty. My mom wasn't either. Look at her. She fights every day, and you can too. I believe in you, Vee."

"Why?" Vee's crying harder now, and it's a quiet, wrenching wail. "Nobody else ever did."

"Well, then, somebody should," Lanny says. "Come on. Stay with us. Fight. Do that for your mom."

Vee gasps. She drops the knife, and it bounces away. I quickly pick it up, and my daughter heads straight for the girl; she wraps Vee in a hug, and Vee shudders and relaxes into that embrace like it was all she ever wanted. Someone to believe, for just a moment, that she was worth saving.

"Come on," I tell them quietly. "Vee, you're coming with us. We'll take you to Mr. Sparks."

She nods listlessly. It's like she's back to a passive state again, but it's not as eerie. More like relief.

We make it outside. I wipe the knife and toss it out into the weed-covered yard. Best not to have my fingerprints on anything here, or Vee's either.

We switch around. Connor comes up front. Sam and Lanny bracket Vee in the back, in case she suddenly decides to bolt again. And I accelerate away from the house and round the next corner just as one of the Wolfhunter PD cruisers turns down the street. It doesn't follow. It stops at the first house.

Grid search. It's helpful right now.

Hector Sparks's home office looks like a safe harbor. I pull up to the immaculately kept house and stop the engine. Then I turn to look at Vee Crockett. "Before we go in, I need you to tell me something, okay? What did your mother know? Because I think you *do* know, or you wouldn't be so afraid they'd kill you."

"If I say, they'll kill all y'all," she says. "You know that, right?"

"Well, they already tried anyway," Sam says. He sounds calm and strong, and it's just what she needs, I can tell. She nods slowly. Lifts her chin. This kid has problems, there's no doubt about that; she needs help. But she's got something inside, I can see that too. Trauma leaves a mark. So does character.

"My momma saw the wreck," Vee says.

Connor turns and stares at her. He gets it first, I think. "The *ghost car* wreck?"

"Wasn't a ghost car," she tells him quite seriously. "Ghost car's an old Tin Lizzie as drives out on the road by the river. This was two cars that hit head-on. One was an old man who drinks and lived up in the hills." She swallows hard. "He died. Momma told me she saw him with his head all crushed in."

The supposed ghost car wreck, I remember, was just about a week ago. "Vee," I say, "your mom worked for the garage dispatching wreckers. How did she see it?"

"They was shorthanded a driver, so she drove one of the two trucks. She helped haul them off to where they got buried."

"You said the old man from the hills died. What about the other driver?"

"He died too," she said. "But he weren't the only one in the car. Mom said she heard somebody crying in the back. She thought it was his ghost at first. But then they opened the back and . . ."

"And what?" Lanny asks, and takes her hand. Vee seems to steady again.

"And they found the little girl," she says. "She's still here, I guess."

"What little girl?" Sam asks, but I already know.

"Ellie White," I tell him.

It all fits. Marlene, seeing the wreck. The involvement of Carr, who owns the garage, plus the police chief and cops, plus the banker to demand another ransom payment to their own offshore bank. No wonder they want us all dead, if they're this close to getting paid. They've already assumed that she told us in prison during that interview.

And they're all implicated. Most of the cops, if not all. Everyone at the garage. Maybe it stretches further than that.

"Vee? Did your mom say what happened to the little girl?" I ask.

"Mr. Carr took her away," she says. "He told Momma she'd get ten thousand dollars if she kept her mouth shut."

But Marlene hadn't kept her mouth shut. She'd called me instead, worried that she was in over her head. Worried that a little girl's life was on the line. She must have heard something to make her doubt the child would be returned safely.

What we need to do now is call the FBI. Let them descend on this town like locusts until they get to the truth. The problem is, if we do that, there's no guarantee that Ellie White won't be dead and dumped at the first sign of a federal badge. They didn't seem afraid of the TBI, which is obviously looking in the wrong place.

I follow that trail to the end, and I realize I've forgotten something.

They *have* seen a federal badge. Mike Lustig's. He flashed it last night in the process of protecting Sam from whatever was coming for him. *Oh Jesus.* They have to believe it's all coming down on them.

We might have killed this little girl already.

"Mom?" Lanny says. I realize I've been silent too long. "Are we going inside? We shouldn't be out here too long, right?"

This has suddenly gotten very, very complicated. There's only one road through Wolfhunter that I know of. All these people have to do is wait for us to try to leave town, and they can close their trap and get us all at once. I suddenly wonder what's happened to Mike Lustig. And Miranda Tidewell, if she was with him.

If these people want to get away with collecting a fortune in ransom, they have a lot of people they need to eliminate. Fast.

And we're high on the list.

"Out of the car," I tell them. "Let's go."

15

GWEN

I bang hard on the door, and Mrs. Pall greets me with a grim look. "He's not here," she says. "You should have called. You'll have to come back later."

She's already shutting the well-polished door. I ruin the shine by putting a hand flat against the wood and pushing back. "Where is he?"

"He's not available."

"I don't care. He called *us*," I tell her. My tone tells her not to screw with me. I'm not about to be left outside, exposed, with Vee and my kids at risk.

Mrs. Pall gives us a sour look, but stands back. She's wearing what I would swear is the same dress as before, but in a different color, and another nineteenth-century–style apron. She stares out at my rental car while I move past her, and finally says, "Do I have to watch over your children now as well?" There's a strong implication that Social Services should have taken them away long ago.

"No, thank you," I say. "What a kind offer." I head straight for the hallway that leads to his office. I can see Sparks behind the desk. He's rising from his seat when Mrs. Pall suddenly cuts in front of me, and

I have to stop or run right into her. "You'll have to wait in the parlor," she says. "It's behind you to the left."

Hector Sparks is swinging his door shut. "I'm sorry," he says. "I'll need just a few minutes to finish a phone call."

I heard nothing on a speakerphone, and he hadn't been holding a phone either. But before I can tell him that we have his missing client, he's slammed the door on me.

If this is a trap . . . Paranoia surges back. But the fact is, we have few options left. Yes, I've got a gun; I'm guessing that Sam doesn't because it would have been held as evidence by the police. My extra weapon is locked up in my SUV, held at the county sheriff's substation. I'm no longer sure that Mike can help us. I remember those black SUVs in town. If Carr and his coconspirators hired outsiders to come in and blockade the road, take anybody who wasn't part of the plot . . . then help is very far away right now.

"What the hell was *that*?" Lanny asks. She's still holding on to Vee, or Vee's holding on to her; it's hard to be certain. "I thought he wanted us to come here!" She sounds both outraged and nervous. I don't blame her. I'm still facing Mrs. Pall. The dislike radiates off her like a dark cloud.

"Behind you," she says again. "To the left." Each word is overly enunciated. I'm not really tempted to comply, but I can hear the others turn and head in that direction. I'm the last to move, but I finally follow.

"Seriously, a *parlor*," Lanny says, as Mrs. Pall slides doors shut on us. "Didn't those go out, like, ages ago?"

She's right. It's severely dated: a formal receiving room with stiff Victorian horsehair sofa, a leather chair by an empty fireplace, antique wallpaper, glossy curio cases filled with teacups. There's a poker by the fire. I take note of it, just in case. Sparks had sworn we'd be safe here, but how is he planning to defend this house? *If* he is.

"You're sure about this guy?" Sam asks me. He's looking around as if he finds this as strange, as alien, as Lanny does. Vera is huddling close to my daughter, and Lanny, after turning up her nose, leads the other girl to the sofa. They sit. There's a knitted blanket sitting on a chair, and Lanny retrieves it to drape it over Vee, who's still shivering.

"I'm not sure about anyone right now," I tell him. "We need to find something for Vee to put on. That jail jumpsuit has to go."

"But . . . I thought you had to take me back to jail?" Vee seems dazed. I don't blame her. "Why should I change?"

"I'm not here for Sparks to turn you back over; I'm going to convince him we need to get you out of town. So we'll need a different car, one that can't be traced back to us, and we need a disguise for you."

"Mom, that's . . . What do they call it? Aiding and abetting a fugitive? Can't we go to jail for that?" Trust my son to know the proper statutes we're about to violate.

"We can," I say. "But the thing is, if we can call in the TBI and FBI, and get Vee safely out of here and into their custody, we can make the case that we weren't aiding and abetting; we were all working on the side of a kidnapped child. All of us. Including Vee, who has direct knowledge even if she didn't know it."

"And you think *this* guy's going to help?" Sam says. "We should call Mike."

"I thought you didn't trust him," Lanny says. I can tell by the way she frowns at him that she's not completely Team Sam anymore either.

"I don't," he tells her. "But that's personal. This is a kid's life. I can trust him with that."

I don't want to admit my suspicion that Mike—and Miranda—might never have even made it out of Wolfhunter. "Then text him what we know," I tell Sam. "The faster they're on this, the better. But don't tell him where we are."

Sam, I'm relieved to see, has his phone; I suppose they had to give it back when he was released. He quickly texts. While he does, I slide the parlor door open. Mrs. Pall is standing in the entryway as if she's been listening, or waiting. It's creepy. "Do you have anything we can give Vera Crockett to wear?"

She thinks for a moment, and then smiles. I don't think I like that expression any better than her usual sour one. "Why, yes, I think I do," she says. "I'll be right back. Please wait there."

She marches off down the hall on the other side of the stairs. I look toward Sparks's closed door. I can't hear any conversation, but I suppose he could be on the phone, after all.

"Mom?" It's Connor. I close the sliding doors and look at him. "Won't the police search here too?"

"Sure. He can refuse them entry, though, unless they have a search warrant specifically for this house . . . which they won't," I tell him. "It all depends on how much the chief of police wants to push things. But we better find a place to hide that car. It's not registered to me, but they'll trace it eventually. Once they do, we'd better be out of this town."

Sam finishes his text. Without looking up, he says, "You've got Fairweather's number, right?"

"Yes. Why?"

"We should probably cover all the bases."

He's right. In case my suspicions are right, we should have a local backup plan. Fairweather isn't local, but at least he's relatively close. And so far, everything about him tells me he's not in bed with the good ol' boys of Wolfhunter.

Mrs. Pall rattles the sliding doors back and holds out a set of clothes. They're ruthlessly folded into perfect squares. I can't say I'm surprised. She probably knows how to fold fitted sheets too. "These should fit," she says, and thrusts them into my hands. She's gone before I can summon up a thanks, for which I'm actually relieved. I shake out the clothes: a pair of jeans shorts. A faded T-shirt, rust red. A jean jacket to match. No shoes included. I wonder if they're relics of her own younger years, but they seem newer than that, and she doesn't seem the sentimental type.

I hand them to Vee. "Okay, let's get that jumpsuit off," I tell her. "Try these on. There's a closet over there if you're shy, but Connor and Sam will be gentlemen about it."

They've already walked over to the other corner, in fact, and are looking out the heavily curtained window at the street. Vee nods, and under the cover of the blanket, she unsnaps her jumpsuit and wiggles it off. Lanny hands her the shorts, and she gets them on, then reaches for the T-shirt.

I send a text to Fairweather telling him that I need him to get to Sparks's house as soon as possible. I debate putting more into the message, then text, ELLIE WHITE IS IN WOLFHUNTER.

That will bring him fast.

Lanny pauses and looks at me. "What is that?"

"What?"

"That noise?"

I listen, and at the very edge of my hearing, there's an irregular thumping sound. Something with a metallic edge. It sounds familiar, but I'm not quite sure.

I've heard something like this before in the house, but Sparks said it was some kind of maintenance work being conducted. Surely it's not the same thing.

"Maybe it's that girl," Connor volunteers from across the room, but he doesn't turn. Vee's getting up from the couch by then and discards the blanket. The shorts are too large, and sit loose on her hips; they're not flattering on her, but they'll do. The tee is a little tight, but it works. So does the jacket she pulls on. Her laceless shoes and socks are still prison issue, but unremarkable.

"What?" I ask my son. "What girl?"

"Ellie," he says. "Maybe she's here."

I freeze. *Is she? Did I completely misread Sparks?* Not that the man isn't eccentric, and Mrs. Pall isn't terrifying. If he is involved, maybe he's on the phone right now with the corrupt local police. Maybe all of us are sitting in the jaws of a trap that's about to snap closed.

The hammering could be Ellie White trying to get our attention. *Oh God.*

I slide the doors back. I can't tell where the sound is coming from. Somewhere in the basement? Down the other hall? I try to follow it, but I only get as far as the stairs. I can't tell where it is.

Everyone has followed me, which I didn't intend . . . even Vee, who's crowding in against Lanny. Lanny has an arm around her shoulders. Vee no longer looks like the empty, defiant girl I met at first; she's scared, vulnerable, and *my responsibility.*

"Sam," I say, "text Javier, Kez, and Prester. Tell them we're in trouble in Wolfhunter, and we may have evidence that Ellie White is here."

That's when Sam says, in a very calm but urgent voice, "Gwen."

I turn.

Hector Sparks is standing in the doorway of his office. I hadn't heard his door open. Mrs. Pall is standing in the opening to my left that leads to what I believe is a dining room. I have the eerie feeling we're caught in a cross fire . . . and yet neither one is armed.

"Ms. Proctor, I don't know who you're referring to," Sparks says, "but there is no Ellie White here." He sounds sorrowful, and utterly unbothered. "What you're hearing is, I'm afraid, the washing machine. If you'll go with Mrs. Pall, you'll see what I mean."

Mrs. Pall says, "If you'll follow me, please?" and leads us through the formal dining room—a gleaming table, lots of chairs, I don't spare any attention for it—and off to a small room off a neat, glistening, magazine-clean kitchen.

There's a washing machine, and it's shimmying back and forth. It's off-balance. Mrs. Pall reaches out and opens the top; the load spins down with shaking thuds until it finally stops.

The house is silent.

"I'm afraid the sheets sometimes clump to one side," she says. "And the machine is old. I'm sorry for the disturbance; I'm sure that seemed very, ah, significant to you." Her dry tone suggests I'm hysterical for even suggesting it. "You're completely free to look around, of course. I wouldn't want Mr. Sparks to think I wasn't assisting you in your *investigation*." The weight on the word is brisk and unmistakable. "Whoever this Miss White is, you won't find her here. As Mr. Sparks said."

Funny thing is, I believe her. And yet there's something wrong here. I can smell it.

Sparks has followed our little entourage, and as we gaze at the quiet washing machine, he says, "Ms. Proctor. I deeply apologize. I was discussing a very private client matter. I couldn't compromise that confidence. I see you've found young Vera. That's very well done. My dear Vera, you'll be safe here. I can promise you complete protection. If you'll follow me . . . ?"

We do, back to his office. Sparks listens to Vera's story, and I'm deeply relieved to see that the story of what Marlene Crockett knew seems completely new to him. And disturbing. He sinks into his chair, staring first at Vee, then Sam, then moving his gaze to me. "You're telling me that you believe this poor kidnapped child might actually be held in Wolfhunter? By Chief Weldon and Mr. Carr?"

"I don't think Marlene would have any reason to lie about it," I tell him. "You know them?"

"Of course. My family goes back generations in Wolfhunter. I'm acquainted with everyone." He does seem really distressed. "The poor girl. So *young*. We do need to get out-of-town authorities involved. I can make some calls."

I look over at Sam. "Anything from Mike?"

"Nothing," he says. "I texted Miranda too."

I want to snap at him, ask him why, but I know why. If he last saw Mike with her, he wants to find out if they're both missing. I make sure my tone is calm when I say, "No reply from her either?"

He shakes his head. That is not good news. Surely one of them would have gotten back to him. Miranda would have jumped at the chance.

I turn to Sparks. "Make the call," I tell him.

He looks at his phone, but doesn't pick it up. "I'd much rather get you all safely out of town and arrange a meeting elsewhere," he says. "Perhaps at the county sheriff's office. Where is your vehicle?"

"My SUV's in the county sheriff's forensics lab," I tell him. "You know about that?"

Sparks looks ill. "I thought—I hoped, at least—that it would turn out to be an attack by your own personal enemies, not something related to this town. But I'm afraid the truck used in the attack has traced back to a local man, who claims it was stolen. Of course. And unfortunately, he's the uncle of Mr. Carr, so unfortunately it supports your theory—"

"We can worry about that later. Do you have a place to store our rental and get it off the street before the police see it?"

"Yes. Immediately." He opens his desk drawer and takes out a remote control. "That will open the carriage house out back. There are two open spaces."

"Sam?" I hand him the keys and the remote. He nods and is gone, fast. I'm starting to relax a bit, because I read Sparks as being happy to help us. Eager, even. "How are you planning to keep Vera safe?"

"Don't worry," he says. "I promise, the chief knows better than to trespass on my property without my permission."

"You may be relying on normal situations," I tell him. "This isn't that. Weldon dispatched one crew to shoot Sam and Connor earlier yesterday, and followed up with the ambush on the road last night. I get the sense that whatever's going on, he's desperate to keep a lid on things. You'd better have a backup plan other than just good manners."

"Trust me, this house is very defensible. We can keep you safe." He suddenly turns and holds his hand out to Lanny. "You are Miss Atlanta, is that correct?"

She shoots me a panicked look, but shakes his hand. "Uh, yeah. Sir."

"And Mr. Connor?" Connor awkwardly shakes the offered hand, and Sparks moves around the desk to take his seat.

"And Miss Vera," Sparks says. "I'm glad you're safe. I truly am. You've been through an appalling time, child, but I promise you this: I'm going to make sure you're secure. No one will hurt you anymore."

Vera suddenly begins to weep. Lanny hugs her. It's both heartbreaking and beautiful to watch her melt, to see all the nerve and fight go out of her, and let herself feel—at least for the moment—really, finally safe. But we're not safe. Not yet.

I can't see Sam or the garage from where I'm standing, though the carriage house is behind us; the windows are all curtained. *He's okay. We're all okay now.* I allow myself a deep breath. My phone buzzes, and I pull it from my pocket to look at the message.

It's Kezia Claremont, short and to the point. WHAT TF IS HAPPENING?

I start to enter a message, a long one, explaining everything.

I'm in the middle of it when Mrs. Pall says, from the hallway, "Mr. Sparks? The police have pulled up in front. They're coming to the door."

"See to them, please," he says. "Ms. Proctor, perhaps you could, ah, back up Mrs. Pall? Stay out of sight, though."

"We're okay," Lanny tells me, and gives me a really lovely smile. She's still hugging Vera, as if she never intends to stop. That's complicated. I can't deal with it right now.

I follow Mrs. Pall out, and grab the fireplace poker from the parlor as she opens the front door. The text will have to wait.

I get to see the backstage view of Mrs. Pall's intimidation; it's more than equal to the two policemen who are standing on the doorstep.

They tell her they need to search the premises. She icily says, "You may not." When one of them dares to put a hand on the door, she says, "Would you really *like* to be sued for a million dollars? Because I'm quite sure Mr. Sparks can easily arrange that. If you'd prefer. Where's your warrant?"

One of the police says, "Ma'am, we're going to check this house, or we'll have to call Chief Weldon down to sort this out. Orders."

"Well," she says, and butter suddenly wouldn't melt in her mouth, "you tell Chief Weldon that I'll be most happy to make him his favorite tea, and I have cream cake, and he's welcome to visit. But he's still not searching this house without an official warrant, and that is final."

She closes the door, locks it, deadbolts it, and looks at me. I feel stupid holding the poker. I put it back where I found it. When I do, I realize that something's changed down the hall. Sparks's office door is now shut.

Well, that's sensible. In case the cops get past me and Mrs. Pall, he'd want to have the kids behind yet another barrier.

I try the knob. It isn't locked, so I open it. "Mrs. Pall sent them packing," I say, but I'm talking to no one.

The room is empty.

That's impossible. I know Lanny, Vee, and Connor didn't come past the parlor. And where would they go? Sparks isn't here either. What the hell . . .

They're just . . . gone.

I turn around, and Mrs. Pall is standing there with a shotgun in her hands. Before I can react, she reverses it and slams the butt into my head.

And I fall.

16

Sam

I drive the white sedan into the first open space in what Sparks calls a carriage house; I suppose it was, a hundred years ago, before the horse stalls were removed and Model T Fords took their place. It's a big, spacious barn of a garage with three metal doors, each allowing access to two cars. This remote only opens one of them.

I leave the keys in the car, and as I'm standing beside it, I check my cell again. Nothing from Mike. Nothing from Miranda, either, and that's ominous; she'd jump at the chance to reestablish contact, I know that. Something happened on their way out of town; I can sense it like blood in the wind. And I don't know if they're alive or dead. That all depends on just how far the people in this conspiracy are willing to go.

Well, they went far enough to blow a hole in a woman's chest for even thinking about betraying them. Killing one person is hard, but once they've done it, killing the next will be—in their minds—inevitable. I'm worried for Mike. And even Miranda. Neither of them has any clue what they've gotten into.

I'm just turning off my phone when I hear a scrape of shoes behind me, and something cold presses against the back of my neck. Heat tears through me, followed by chills, followed by rage—at myself. Why the *hell* didn't I hear this coming? Why did I think we were safe here?

"Easy," a voice says from behind me. It isn't Sparks, or Mrs. Pall. I've never heard it before. It sounds calm, cool, and utterly in control. "Hands behind you."

It isn't the police, or they'd have already announced themselves. I try to take a look. The gun barrel presses closer.

"Nope," he says. "Hands. Now. Or I leave you dead right here. Where is she?"

"Where's who?"

"The kid."

"You mean Lanny? Safe. Where you can't find her." I'm lying. All he has to do is walk up to the house. *Jesus*, why are they after Lanny? I can't let this happen.

"Who's Lanny?" He sounds impatient now. "The *girl*."

"Vera Crockett?"

"Jesus. Shut up. We'll sort this later. *Hands. Now.* If I need to blow your skull across this room and go get your woman in there, I will. And her kids. Understand me?"

He means it. I put my hands behind my back.

He clicks handcuffs on. *Shit.* "Ellie White. You're going to catch a beating if you lie to me."

"Not Vera?" I'm honestly surprised. I thought we were the only ones who'd figured out the Ellie White connection.

"All I care about is the girl. Everybody else is collateral damage, you get me? You, your girlfriend, those kids. I know you know where Ellie is. And you're going to tell us."

Us. He's not alone. I need to get this guy out of here, fast, before he gets the bright idea to search inside the house. I don't want him anywhere near our kids.

"Who told you I knew?" I ask him. Because someone had to. I figure it'll be the police, Carr, someone involved in the conspiracy.

But instead he says, "Your buddy."

Mike. They have Mike. "I'm not saying anything until you take me to him."

"Works for me," he says. "We're going to need some privacy anyway."

He prods me to the back of the carriage house. I hadn't seen it before, but there's a small door back there, and on the other side, a carport. A black SUV is idling there. He puts me in the backseat. For the first time, I get a good look at him; he's definitely not from around here. He's tall, lean, olive-skinned, with neatly trimmed dark hair and a devilish goatee and mustache. I'd think he was a hipster, except for the Sig Sauer in his hand. He's wearing a leather jacket, and under that he has a shoulder holster he uses once I'm in the SUV.

There's a shorter, paler carbon copy of him in the backseat who has his gun on me from the second I get in. He's got the calm, dispassionate eyes of someone who's killed before, and I believe he will again. *They need me,* I tell myself. *And I'm getting them away from Gwen. Lanny. Connor.* Right now, that's a good enough reason to stay quiet and cooperate. Opportunities will come. They always do.

"Who hired you to find the kid?" I ask, as the man who caught me gets into the driver's seat. He straps in and backs out of the drive without answering.

"Word of advice," he says, and fixes me with a look in the rearview mirror. "Keep it zipped."

"Was it the parents?" Best I remember, the parents are rich. And desperate. I'm really hoping these slick sons of bitches are hired guns working on the right side of this, however sketchy their tactics.

The man next to me, who hasn't spoken yet, just puts the gun against my knee in a silent promise. I shut up.

Beyond the tinted windows, Wolfhunter glides by. The cop cars are grid-searching, but they're ignoring us; that's too bad, because I'd love to hear these assholes explain having me in handcuffs in the back. *Except the cops would probably just kill us all anyway.* Jesus, this town. I can't be sure of anything anymore. Everything is wrong here.

At least Gwen and the kids are somewhere that is—hopefully— safe. I can't do anything about it now, but I know Gwen; at the first sign of danger, she'll be a grizzly bear for our kids. She'll fight *anyone* to the end.

Just keep it together, I tell myself. I'm sweating, and focusing too much on things I can't control. My world has to be here, in this car. With these two armed men.

I pay attention to where they're taking me. The cordon of police cars is moving out; we're heading in the opposite direction, toward the center of town and then beyond it, to the outskirts on the other side. Not a long distance, but long enough. This section of town is sparse, lots of thickly weeded lots, boarded-up decaying houses. I don't see anywhere I could even hope to find help. I don't see a single person outside.

The SUV pulls to a stop in a bare dirt alley lined with weathered wood fencing on both sides. The driver gets out and opens my door with his gun drawn. My backseat companion speaks for the first time. "Out."

Always an opportunity.

Getting out of an SUV in handcuffs is a naturally clumsy business. I put my booted foot down on the running board, and as the driver reaches for me, I let myself lean too far, and my foot slips off. I crash into him, and he isn't quite prepared for it; he staggers back and nearly goes down. Nearly. I'd hoped he'd drop the gun, but he doesn't; he's lithe, and as I roll to my feet and dodge behind the SUV, I know I haven't bought as much time as I'd hoped. My backseat companion is already scrambling to get out; I can feel the shift of the vehicle against my back. I have a split second to look around and decide. *Are they going to shoot me in the back?*

Probably not. Mike's succeeded in making me seem valuable. They want me. Doesn't mean they won't try to hit me in the leg, the shoulder—something nonfatal.

I run anyway.

"Hey!" I don't know which of them yells that, but it doesn't matter; I don't hear a shot, but I do hear heavy footsteps behind me. Running in handcuffs slows me down. I dodge behind a fence and press myself flat against the rough, leaning wood; as the first man—the hipster—blasts past, I catch him with an outstretched foot on his shin and he goes sprawling. This time he does lose the gun. I dive, roll, and manage to get one hand around the grip. It hurts like holy hell, but I brace on my left and aim the gun right-handed at an angle from behind my back. Feels like I'm about to dislocate my shoulder, and thick bolts of agony come off the joint, but I meet the eyes of the second man through the fence break, and I see him calculate the odds. He can kill me, sure, but wounding takes a slower, more meticulous calculation at this distance, and his buddy's in the way as he tries to get up. I have a clear shot. He does, too, if he wants to kill. But I'm betting he doesn't.

"Drop it," I tell him. "Fucking now."

He shrugs and bends down to place the gun on the ground. "How do you think you're going to get up, man? There's two of us, one of you. You're handcuffed. All we have to do is kick your ass."

"Harder to do if you're dead," I tell him. "I'm a good shot."

"From behind your back?" Hipster says. "Doubt it, my man." He's up now, mildly pissed off but uninjured, and he slips another gun out of an ankle holster. He aims it at me and sights on my shoulder. "*I'm* a good shot too."

He's got me, and he knows it. So do I. They still need me alive and talking, or he'd just go for it and shoot—and he will, if I make him.

I let the gun fall and roll over on my back; the release of tension on my shoulder feels like a shock all its own. I don't fight when the two men haul me up to my feet and march me back out into the alley. The shorter one is putting some cruel pressure on my elbow, as if he means to tear something. The taller one seems more willing to forgive and forget.

We don't talk. They take me around the SUV and into an open back gate in an equally dilapidated wooden fence, through waist-high weeds to a cracked back porch of a shotgun shack that looks like it saw better days in the 1950s. There's a significant lean to it. The back door, though, swings open, and they shove me in.

It's a kitchen. I immediately lunge forward, pretend to stumble, and fetch myself up against a dirty counter. This place has been empty a long time. There's a raw hole where the stove would have been, and the fridge is gone too. They're only a step or two behind me, and I can't find anything useful in grabbing range. They spin me, and walk me down a filthy, peeling hallway with holes in the ceiling where light fixtures once lived. The place stinks of mold and unflushed toilets.

And it isn't empty. In the cramped living room—at least, I guess that's what it was once, because there's a sagging sofa against one wall, and the gap-toothed remains of a brick fireplace—there's another man waiting.

On the sofa are Miranda Tidewell and Mike Lustig, and for a sharp second I think *they* are on the crew . . . but then I see the gag on Miranda's mouth, and the bruises and cuts on them both, and the way their arms are pinned behind their backs.

They're prisoners.

Somebody kicks the bend of my knees, and I hit the floor hard, but I barely feel it. I'm looking at the fear and desperation in Miranda's eyes. She's been crying. Black trails of mascara down her cheeks stain the off-white cloth of the gag. There are lots of shallow, bloody cuts on her arms, blood staining her blue jeans where cuts were made on her thighs. Her left eye is swollen shut and dark red.

She's in her worst nightmare, facing a helpless, tortured death. How many nights did she drink herself into a weeping mess over her daughter's murder, and tell me she never wants to die that way?

Mike's gagged, too, and if anything, he looks worse than she does. They didn't hold back with him.

"You bastards," I say. "Let them go."

The new man directs his question not to me, but to the two on the couch. "Is this him?"

Mike ignores the question. Miranda nods. More tears break free and slip down her cheeks.

"Okay." The new man is older, harder, skin like varnished walnut. He's wearing a plain black suit, something off the rack at Sears, and I think, *Prison issue*, because he looks like a convict, someone who's survived the toughest kind of time and come out distilled to a violent essence. He has a wicked combat knife in his right hand. He turns to face me, and there's *nothing* in his eyes. "They say you know where Ellie White is. You're going to tell us."

They tried to beat it out of Mike, the sons of bitches. Mike didn't talk—not that he knew where to even begin to look for the girl. Miranda talked, but she lied. She did only what she thought would help her get through this alive: send them after me, in the hopes I'd be able to find a way to stop them. I don't blame her for that.

I blame them.

"Let me guess," I say. "You're the original kidnappers, right? The real crew who took the girl in the first place?" The longer I can keep this as a conversation, the more relaxed they'll get. I need them complacent.

A tiny expression bends his lips. Distaste? Amusement? I can't tell. "What makes you say that?"

"You're organized. You clearly know what you're doing," I say. "How'd you lose the kid?"

"Not sure," he says. "GPS died on the car close to this shit town."

"Maybe your driver disabled it and took the kid himself."

"I know my guy." In a flash, that knife is at my throat. I instinctively try to pull back, but two more sets of hands grab my arms and hold me in place. Walnut's face hasn't changed. It probably won't when he cuts my throat. And he will. He's just admitted a federal crime to me, not to mention the abduction of the federal agent sitting across from me. The three of us aren't walking out of here alive. In the back of my mind, I'm scared, but I can't let that rule me. Panic won't help.

"Now," he says, "who has Ellie White? Where's she being held?"

I have zero downside to telling him, but the fact that I do, in fact, have an idea where the kid might be means I have a card to play. It's a low-value card, but I have to try. "There was a two-car wreck about a week ago," I tell him. "On the outskirts of town, in the dark. Two men died. You want me to tell you more, you let the woman go. Have your guy drop her at the hospital."

He stares at me for a second, then nods. "Okay." Something's wrong; I sense it like a sudden heat on my skin. "That's a deal." He calmly takes the knife away from my throat, slots it in a sheath on his belt, and in the same smooth motion draws a gun from a holster on the other side. It's a semiautomatic, but that's all I see as he turns away from me, sights, and fires.

He shoots Miranda Tidewell in the head.

It's a kill shot. She's looking at me, not him; she's fearing *my* death. She never sees it coming, and so I get to see that the last look in her eyes is anguish. Anguish for *me*.

The bullet he's fired leaves a small beveled circle in her forehead. Prefrontal cortex, her ability to learn: gone. Memories, gone with her hippocampus. Bone shrapnel cascades through the soft tissue with the bullet, shredding her brain. A high-velocity bullet, like this one, leaves damage ten times its diameter in its wake.

I hear the shot while all this useless information burns through my own brain, but by then Miranda's already dead. Her limbs are relaxing.

Her eyes blank as empty glass. The bullet doesn't exit, so the only visible damage is that small, ragged circle, and a trickle of blood.

Her body slumps back on the couch. It's an empty sack now.

Mike's thrashing against his restraints.

It hits me: a flash of shock, horror, and then I scream. It's a roar of pain and rage I can't stop, and neither can the two men holding me down; they've flinched in surprise at the shot, and I lunge up and into the man who's killed Miranda, drive my head into his chest, and bull-rush him back onto the fallen bricks around the fireplace. He goes down. His head hits the corner of a jutting brick and breaks it off with the impact, which dazes him. He swings the gun down and tries to shoot, but I raise up, sweeping his gun hand with my shoulder, and when the shot comes, it's already past me, headed for the other end of the room. I hear one of his men cry out. They can't be far behind me. The wild shot he fired has hit one of his own.

I don't know what Mike's doing and don't have time to look. I lower my chin and lean in as I explode upward with all the power in my legs, and the bony top of my skull connects with his chin and keeps going. The impact jolts through me like a train coming off the tracks, but it's worse for him, a stunning hit that travels through bone to slam his brain against the top of his skull. Lights out. I feel his knees buckle.

As he goes down, I feel one of the other guys at my back. *I can't die here.* That would be a bitter damn irony, with Gwen thinking . . . no, *knowing* . . . that I chose Miranda over her at the end. So I charge backward into him. It's reckless.

It's also effective. He yells. We both slam to the floor, and I'm lucky: the impact is mostly his. He's my cushion, and as he squirms and tries to buck me off, my fingertips skim the gun that's still gripped in his right hand. I grab his wrist and force it down hard. I feel something break in his hand, and he lets out a burst of a yell just as the spasm pulls the trigger, and a bullet goes into his side.

My tunnel vision is fading now, and I take in that Walnut Face is lying unconscious, but the gun's still next to him; the hipster is the one who's just inflicted his own wound. His shorter buddy is now leaning against the wall, gasping for breath, and half his shirt is red. I can't tell where he was shot, but it's bad. Mike has lunged up off the couch and is on his feet now, though he's swaying and dripping blood. I only have time to take note of that before Hipster throws me off him in a convulsive thrust, and I topple over on my side.

Hipster's still got the gun.

Mike draws his leg back in a powerful kick. It connects with the side of Hipster's head and snaps it sharply to the side—not a killing thing, but it definitely makes the man forget what it was he was doing for a while. As he rolls over and tries woozily to get up, I kick him too—in the wounded side.

He goes down, curled in a fetal position. I toe the fallen gun away from him and slide it under the couch, then go back to Walnut and do the same for his. Mike, unasked, kicks the third gun away. It's not really necessary; that guy has lost consciousness and has slipped down the wall to a sitting position. He's left a broad red streak behind him.

We have a second to breathe. Mike sits down on the floor and, despite his bulk, works his handcuffed hands under his butt and under his feet until they're in front. He searches pockets. Hipster has the handcuff keys, and Mike undoes mine, then his.

The first words out of his mouth when he pulls his gag off are "Mother*fuckers*." It's pure fury. He presses his fingers to Miranda's throat. It won't do any good. I could tell him that, but I don't. Maybe I'm wrong.

I'm not wrong. He eases back with a sigh and shakes his head. I squeeze my eyes shut and try to erase the image from my head, of her *worrying about me* while the bullet enters her skull. God*dammit*. The pain twists and tears inside me, but I have to push it aside.

I try to tell myself that she's beyond all of this now. All the pain, the fear, the fury. It's true, but it's a cold truth with no comfort. "How'd they get you?" I hear myself ask. I shouldn't sound that normal.

"Spike strip on the road out of town," Mike said. "Five minutes after we dropped you off. Real efficient and professional. Once they had us covered, I gave up. Figured it might save her life." He glances toward Miranda, and even though his face is badly swollen, I see the grimness underneath. He falls silent for a second, then forges ahead. "They wanted to know where Ellie White was."

"Which you didn't know."

He shakes his head. "Miranda guessed Gwen would have told you whatever she knew. And she knew you were pretty much our only hope. They'd have gone after Vera Crockett if they could have, but she's locked up, so . . ."

"She's not," I tell him. He stops and looks at me in surprise. "She broke out. More likely they let her go so they could hunt her down and kill her."

"The *cops*?"

"Some of them, for sure," I say. "They're grid-searching for her right now. Maybe ten minutes until they reach this street. Faster, if somebody in this wasteland called in the shooting."

He suddenly bends at the waist and coughs. Spits out some blood, and it scares the shit out of me. He waves off my bracing hands. "I'm okay. Had worse. Cut in my mouth, my lungs are okay."

"There's an SUV out back," I tell him, and roll Hipster—who's still unconscious, but definitely not dead—to grab the keys from his pocket. I leave him on his side and handcuff him with the same bracelets he used on me. He's bleeding, could be going into shock, but the police will be here soon enough, and I can't summon up much in the way of sympathy for him. I check the pulse on Walnut, lying by the fireplace.

He's still breathing, but his skull injury looks bad. I search him and find a set of zip ties in his pocket; I use those to pin his limp arms behind him. I resist the white-hot urge to kick him, and go to put handcuffs on the second henchman, who's also still breathing, by some miracle. I check all of them for extra handcuff keys and pocket what I find.

Then I stand up and say to Mike, "Time to get the hell out. Get a couple of those—" I'm about to say *guns*, because he's closer to them than I am; we slid all three under the couch while our hands were still pinned.

He pauses me with one massive, upheld hand that he folds into a fist. I freeze. Then I hear the creak in the floorboards. *Shit.*

I meet Mike's eyes. We silently have a conversation, and he nods. I'm faster.

I throw myself flat on the floor, noise be damned, and sweep my arm under the couch. I only find one of the guns and a pile of dead cockroaches. My fingers crunch a couple as I grab the gun, but I barely notice. I stay on the floor, braced against the couch, and am dimly aware of Miranda's motionless legs beside me; my focus is on the hallway that leads into the room.

A face appears in a blur, checking corners, and it's about six inches above where I was looking. It draws back fast, and it takes me a second to place it, and then I try to slow my racing heartbeat. *Shit.* "Fairweather?"

"Cade?" he asks, and when he comes around the corner, he's holstering his gun with careful, obvious motions. "What the *hell* is this?" He takes it in with a cop's precision, stopping for a second on each still form to absorb information. "Is she dead?"

"Yes," Mike says. I can't answer. The past wraps us together in red-hot barbed wire, a painful trap that I knew I'd never quite escape, but I never wanted *this*. I never wanted her to die afraid and imprisoned like this. She deserved better. Everyone does. "That one shot her." He indicates Walnut, over by the fireplace. "They're all alive."

Fairweather nods and takes a small compact radio from his belt. He recites the address into it and says he has two wounded. Then he hesitates, looks at the two of us, and says, "I'm bringing two men in who have information. Headed in now."

He puts the radio back. I realize I'm still aiming the gun at him, and I wonder for a second just why I haven't put it away, but that flash is paranoia, not rational thought. I hand the gun to Mike, who puts it in the small of his back. I dig under the couch and grit my teeth, because there are living cockroaches under there too; I shake them off and pull out another weapon. Too late, I realize that I'm probably putting my fingerprints on the gun that's killed Miranda; odds are, it's either this one or the one I held earlier. *Shit.* Not that I think Fairweather's on the Wolfhunter PD's payroll, or Carr's, but . . . it nags at me.

Fairweather crosses the room and checks each of the still bodies. Then he looks at the two of us and says, "Come on. My sedan's out back, official TBI car. I'll get you somewhere safe out of here. I'll send the county cavalry out here for these men, but not until the two of you are safe."

"We need to get Gwen and the kids," I tell him. "Stop at the Sparks house, get them out, and head for the border."

He doesn't like that, I can tell, but he nods. "Let's go," he says. When I hesitate, he sighs. "Come on, Sam, do you trust me or not?"

His gaze is on me and the gun in my hand.

I don't want to, but I put it away.

We follow Fairweather out of the house, and he takes appropriate precautions before waving us to the cruiser. "Down," he tells me and Mike as we pile in. Mike groans. He's still bleeding from cuts, and badly bruised from a beating. "Low as you can get."

I slide down into the passenger-side footwell. Mike, with difficulty, stretches out on the backseat. "Don't tell any of the locals," I tell Fairweather. "We don't know who to trust."

The detective glances down at me. "You'd best start at the beginning," he says. "Because last I knew, you all were looking to clear Vera Crockett. Who are *they*?"

"We still are. Marlene was killed by either Weldon or Carr," I tell him. "She knew about a wreck that happened out on the highway outside of town, right near the forest. She helped clear it all up."

"And?"

"And there was a dead driver, and a tied-up little girl in the back."

He looks grim. "Jesus. Ellie White."

"The kidnappers' plan didn't include a bad-luck head-on collision, and the police chief and tow-truck operator deciding they'd just struck gold. When was the ransom paid?"

"Thirty million dollars, paid four days ago," he says. "Wire transfer to an offshore bank."

"My guess is two geniuses here organized that and got some local banker in on the scheme to clean the cash. They could provide proof of life. The original kidnappers couldn't." There's a siren coming. Getting louder.

"Stay down, cruiser's coming." Fairweather slows, stops, and rolls down his window. "Hey, what's the commotion about?" He has to shout to be heard over the siren. It cuts out.

"Escaped prisoner," I hear another voice say over the idling of two engines. "Vera Crockett, if you can believe that."

"Haven't seen her, but I just got back in town," Fairweather says; it's a classic mix of truth and fiction. "Just heading for the station right now."

"Watch your back. People around Vera Crockett got a habit of dying on us."

That's slick, I think; the cop is already laying the groundwork for getting rid of all of us.

The chat goes on a minute or so, and then Fairweather rolls up his window and drives on. I hear Mike groan in the backseat. "You okay?" I ask.

"Fine." He isn't. Mike's voice goes a little deeper. "If I'd just stayed with you, Sam—"

"It probably would have gone down the same way," I say. Ironic that Miranda's dead in a fight that had nothing to do with her, or Gwen, or Melvin Royal. A fight over money, pure and simple. But I'd like to think that she would have protected that little girl to the end. Miranda was a mother first. Always.

Having her gone from the world now feels inexplicable. Love, hate, that no longer matters. She's been such a presence in my life that coming to terms with that vast absence will take time.

"You think Carr and Weldon are behind this," Fairweather says. "That they've got the kid?"

"Likely," I say. "Unless the poor kid's already dead."

"Proof of life came in, but that was before the ransom was paid. Time's running out, if it hasn't already," he replies. He's silent for a while. "I'm not going back for Gwen."

"Hang on," I say, and start to get up.

"Stay down. Got another black SUV like this one, coming up behind us," he says. "It's the original kidnappers, right? Come to find their prize. They still want their cash."

"Don't care," I say. "We have to go back."

"They're safe where they are, right?"

"I don't know that. They're with the lawyer. Sparks."

"Then they're safe for now. Stay the hell *down*." He's watching the rearview mirror, and I can read the tension in him. He finally says, "Carr's got a compound outside of town. He claims he's a farmer, but word is he's some kind of sovereign-citizen nut too. It's a perfect place to keep the kid secret. I'm making the call."

Mike says, "Could local PD pick up that call? Listen in?"

It makes Fairweather hesitate as he reaches for the radio. "Yeah. Shit. We need a good head start."

I care about that, but not as much as I care about finding my family right now. "Gwen and our kids. Right now. Or I jump the hell out of this car."

"Do you want to die?" he asks. "If I don't get you two out of town, *that will happen.* Not just to you. To Gwen and the kids too."

I don't like it, but he might be right. "Be honest. Is Sparks part of this?"

"Don't think so," he says. "He's a screwup, but not in with Carr and Weldon. Sparks is a loner. Not a very good lawyer either. He passed the bar after—what was it—three tries? He's been pretending to be a big shot around town for many years, but he never tried a single criminal case before."

That's a jolt. "Never? Why give him Vera's case?" But I know. They'd arranged for Sparks to have the case because Weldon knew Sparks would flail around and let Vera down . . . which he probably would have, if Vee hadn't called Gwen the day that her mother died. Nobody had seen that coming. So I ask the question that really matters to me. *"Are they safe with him?"*

Fairweather takes time answering that, which doesn't make me feel any better. "I know he can't be part of any kidnapping scheme. Weldon doesn't trust him. Neither does Carr," he finally says. "Doesn't mean I like him. What kind of man makes his sister work as his housekeeper and calls her by a made-up name?"

It takes me a second to realize that he's talking about Mrs. Pall. "You're kidding."

"Wish to hell I was. It's like a Gothic nightmare in that house. It's possible the two of them are—" Fairweather stops and shrugs. "Who the hell knows."

"We need to go back," I say. "Right now." It's more urgent now than ever to get to my family.

"We're already out of town," he tells me. "And we're not turning around." He takes out the radio and keys it on. "10-34, 10-34, dispatch immediate county assistance, Detective Fairweather with FBI agent Lustig and one civilian outside of—"

The shot comes almost head-on. It punches through the windshield; I don't see that from where I am, but I hear it. Fairweather drops the radio. "Shit!" Fairweather yells, and jerks the wheel to the left, then right. For a second I think the shot's missed him completely . . . but it hasn't. It's hit him right below the collarbone, dead center, and punched a hole right through. It's a big entry wound. Blood starts pouring down his shirt front, wicking through the cotton. Bright red taking over the starched white. He looks down at himself as if he's not quite getting the idea of what's just happened. I lunge up and grab the wheel as his hands come off it, and I struggle to steer the car as it starts to veer wildly back to the other side. He's pulled his foot off the accelerator, but that instinct is dead wrong; if we stop now, we're dead. Someone's in the trees, and if we don't get past, they'll keep firing until we're swiss cheese.

Fairweather's eyes have rolled back. No breath, and the pulse of blood has already stopped from his chest. He's dead. I hate the calculus.

I don't have time to honor him. I open his driver's-side door, slam my fingers down on the seat-belt release, and shove him out as I scramble into the blood-drenched seat. It's warm. His blood soaks into my pants, the back of my shirt. I try not to think about that, or the fact that I'm leaving a good man behind us.

I floor it.

"Mike!" I yell. "Hold on!"

"Yeah," he says. He sounds quiet now. No jokes. This is Mike Lustig in combat, steady as a rock.

The windshield is a cracked, crazed mess of webbed glass, but I don't have time to deal with that. I ignore the damage and try to see past it. Sharp turn coming up five seconds. Four. Three.

Another shot drives through the windshield, and another. Both miss me, because the angle's growing more and more acute. The cracked glass doesn't help the shooter either, and I'm cramming myself into the far left corner as I drive. I swerve and keep my foot down; the back tires scream and shimmy, and I correct as it fishtails.

"Incoming from your six!" I yell, because now we're past the shooter's position, and he's got time to swing around in his perch and try to get me from the back. He might be able to see Mike from that position, depending on his elevation. He'll take whatever target he can get, and maybe just spray and pray at this point.

I sink down into the seat and keep the gas pedal jammed to the floor. I hear more shots thunking into metal, breaking more glass. "Call out!" I say.

"Present!" Mike yells back over the roar of wind streaming in. Pieces of glass are breaking free and whipping into my face. I can't slow down. This asshole is a pretty good shot. If I can make it to the next curve . . .

I can't.

A tire blows—whether it's from a bullet or just the stress, I don't know—but the whole car jerks sideways as physics rips the rubber apart. I can't slow down. I keep the thing moving. But I can't keep it straight.

"Brace!" I yell, and set myself, because I know we're going into the ditch. I can't stop it in time, and something in the steering feels loose and shattered. We're screwed.

And then the car rolls.

17

CONNOR

When Mom goes with Mrs. Pall, Mr. Sparks smiles at the three of us—me, Lanny, and Vera—and puts his finger to his lips. He goes to the door and quietly shuts it. "There," he says in a low voice. "Now. We need to get you somewhere safe in case the police demand entry, regardless of our wishes."

He takes a remote control out of his desk and presses a button, and the bookcase over on one side silently swings out from the wall. The only thing I can think is, *That's really cool,* because I've never seen anything like that except in the movies. It's like a Batman trick.

It *sounds* like he's doing something good for us, but I'm not so sure. Why wouldn't he do this when Mom could see? I don't want her not knowing where we are. So I look at my sister. "Lanny?" I'm asking her because I don't know for sure, and she will.

She looks at the hidden door, then at Hector Sparks. She's frowning. "Maybe we should wait for Mom," she says.

"There's no time," Sparks says. "Do you want Vera to be caught? Perhaps killed?"

Lanny shakes her head. She gives up and heads for the hidden door. I don't like it. I'm not sure why, not at all, but I just *don't*. So I go to the office door to tell Mom.

I hear something click in the door before I get there. When I try to open it, the knob won't turn. "Mom!" I bang on it. Hard.

"Quiet!" Mr. Sparks snaps. "Go with your sister, boy. You'll be safe down there."

I turn around. He's standing behind his desk, still. "Open the door!"

Lanny's turned around now, and she and Vera are standing there watching. "Connor?" my sister says. "Come on. We should do what he says."

"Not until we tell Mom!"

Mr. Sparks sighs, opens a drawer, and says, "I truly did not wish this to be difficult. But you brought this on yourselves." He takes out a gun. It's an old one, a revolver, like something you'd see in an old black-and-white movie. But it's a gun, and I freeze. So do both the girls. "I need you all to go downstairs at once."

"You *do* have her," I blurt out. "Ellie White! You kidnapped her!"

Mr. Sparks frowns at me, as if I've said something really dumb. "Don't insult me. I'd never hurt a child."

"My *brother's* a child!" my sister says. She sounds angry and terrified at the same time. "You leave him alone!"

"He's over twelve," Sparks says, like that makes sense. "I didn't abduct that poor girl. I wouldn't. And if you three are good and obedient, I promise that you'll be perfectly all right. But right now, *get in that room*, or I promise you, I will shoot one of you right now."

He scares me.

I want my mom to break down that door and find us and take that gun away and *kick his ass*, but I think she doesn't even know we're in trouble. I'd yell, but I'm afraid that would make things worse. So I keep my voice quiet. "Mom will come for us," I tell Lanny. "It's okay. Do what he says."

My sister doesn't argue with me. It's just about the first time that's happened, but I don't get to enjoy it. She leads Vee into the opening of the bookcase.

"Boys should be seen and not heard," Mr. Sparks says. "You'll have to be taught how to behave. But I believe you have some promise, young man. Once you're removed from the influence of your mother . . ."

I'm scared now, really scared. I look at him. I don't blink. "If you hurt my mom or my sister, I'm going to kill you. And I can. I know how. My dad taught me."

It sounds good. Scary. I've been practicing that since I learned it frightened off some of the bullies in school.

It doesn't work on Mr. Sparks. He shakes his head, like I've said something stupid, and hits a remote control on the desk. I hear the office door unlock, and for a second I think he *is* going to let me talk to Mom . . . but then he grabs me by the wrist and drags me into the opening behind the bookcase. I yell and pull back, but he's bigger and stronger and shoves me inside the opening. He reaches to grab a hand-hold that swings the bookcase closed behind us. I hear a click. I don't think I know how to open it again. I think about my mom not knowing about any of this, just walking in. She won't *know*. And if Mr. Sparks has a gun, then Mrs. Pall will too.

Lanny's got to be in here—but she isn't. It's a small space, and then there are stairs going down. I can't see her, but it's dark at the bottom. "Lanny!" I shout. She doesn't answer. I try to get free. I can't. Sparks puts his hand around my throat and squeezes until I'm on my toes, gasping for air, and it *hurts*, it hurts really bad. He shoves me forward and keeps his grip on my throat. I stumble down a couple of steps, then a few more.

He keeps pushing me on. "I'm going to let go now," he says when we're in the middle. I can hardly breathe, and I've stopped fighting him. "You be a good boy or your sister will suffer."

The pressure lets up, but he grabs my shoulders. Still pushing me down, step by step. "My mom is going to come get us," I tell him. "She'll find us!" I can barely say it. My throat hurts bad, and I'm shaking all over.

"No, I don't think Mrs. Pall will allow that," Mr. Sparks says. "Watch your step, it's a little dark at the end, I must get that bulb fixed. Three, two, one . . . and we're here."

The lights come on, really bright and hard.

We're in a cave. The second I realize that, I start feeling like I'm suffocating, because Lanny and I, we were in another cave once as prisoners, and all of a sudden it feels like the walls are moving in on me, the dark is *too* dark, and I *want my mom*. I want her so bad that I feel like I'm going to start screaming. I *hate* this, I *hate* that Mom is up there without us, and Mrs. Pall might kill her, and I *hate* this smiling man with his ugly, mean eyes.

I see Lanny and Vee huddled against the wall at the bottom, and the second I do, I run into my sister's arms. She shoves me behind her, and as she does, I realize she's found a weapon. It's a piece of rock, and it's not very big, but it has a wicked sharp edge on it.

"What is that?" Lanny asks, and nods toward the other end of the cave. There's a locked steel door on that end with a window in it at the top, and a bigger dark window next to it, like you'd see inside a house. Only it's blacked out. Mr. Sparks pauses where he is, and that smile gets wider.

"It's going to be your new home, girls." He has the remote control in his hand, and he presses a button.

The black window has a metal shutter on the other side, and it raises up, and I see the three beds in the other room. There are only two women in the room, though, and as soon as the window slides up, they both get up and stand there, staring straight ahead with their hands folded together. They're wearing white dresses. And they have long hair.

I recognize their pictures because I looked at them online: the missing women of Wolfhunter. The sickly-looking blonde is Tarla Dawes; she's the younger one. The other one is Sandra Clegman, who I think is older.

There's one missing. Bethany Wardrip. I remember the awful body we found at the river, and I want to throw up when I remember her picture from the website. That was her. It had to be.

"You killed her," I say, and look at Mr. Sparks. "Bethany."

"No, of course I didn't," he says, and for some reason I believe him. He sounds offended. "I take very good care of my girls. She just got very sick. There was nothing I could do for her."

"You threw her away. Like trash!"

"I left her for God and nature to purify," he says. "You'll understand how dirty women are when you get older. I'll teach you."

"Like you taught them?" I swallow back more vomit when I see that those women on the other side of the glass haven't moved. It's like they're afraid to breathe. *He's going to put my sister in there too. And Vee.*

But he hasn't said anything about me. Which is scary. "Are you going to kill me?" I just ask. I'd rather know now.

"Of course not! I won't put you in there with them; that wouldn't be appropriate. I'll teach you how to be responsible for them. Be their *father*," he says. His cell phone buzzes, and he takes it out to read a message. He looks grumpy when he puts it back. "Stay down here with the girls. I will be right back."

He points the remote at the window, and the shutter comes down. I can imagine the two women in there slumping over, sitting down. Maybe crying. They're so frightened. I could see it in their faces—that they're scared all the time.

Mr. Sparks is a monster, and I never saw it, just like I never saw it in Dad, and I hate it, *I hate it* that I can't see it. Monsters shouldn't look normal.

If he touches my sister . . . *No. No, you won't let him. Mom won't let him.*

I'm still staring at the black window when I hear footsteps. When I turn around, I realize that Mr. Sparks is halfway up the stairs again, moving fast. *Mom!* I turn and rush for the stairs; I get there ahead of Lanny, who's running for it too, but we're still only halfway up when I hear that bookcase swing shut again, and the lock snaps in place.

"Wait," she says, and drags me to a stop. "We can't get out that way. We need a plan. There must be another way out of here."

"But Mom—"

"Help me look!" I hear the shake in my sister's voice, and when I look at her, she's crying, but there's something hard underneath the tears. That's how Mom looks when she has something to fight against, and fight for. "Come on!"

We're only partway down the stairs again when we hear the lock disengage. Lanny freezes, and so do I. We turn to look.

Mr. Sparks is dragging our mother down the stairs, holding her by one wrist as he slides her down. She's lying on her back. She's leaving a trail of fresh blood behind. I've never seen my mom hurt, not like this. She's not moving. *She's not moving.*

I let out a scream, and I break free of Lanny, and I charge up the stairs right at him. My sister's right behind me. Sparks seems like he has no idea what to do. Just a shocked old man. But that's just his mask. Like my dad's words. Like his smile.

He hits me so hard I smash against the wall, and for a second I can't pull myself up. I find myself stumbling on the stairs, and I realize that Mom's eyelids are fluttering. Lanny's struggling with Sparks. "Mom!" My voice comes out as a croak, so I try again. *"Mom! We're in trouble!"*

Her eyes fly open, and for a second they're vague and confused. Then they fix on me, and they're not confused at all.

"Get your damn hands off my kids!" she shouts, and she spins around, still flat on her back, and kicks Mr. Sparks from behind. Not in the ass, like I would have, but right up between his braced legs. She kicks him like she means to score a field goal.

He screams. He lets go of Lanny and stumbles down two steps. Then misses a step. Then he's falling all the way down, and he hits the concrete floor at the bottom and slides limp for two or three feet before he comes to a stop, facedown.

He isn't moving. The gun slides out of his hand and across the floor. Vera runs to pick it up, and she holds it in trembling hands and aims it at Mr. Sparks.

"Don't!" Lanny's voice is hoarse but loud. "Vera, don't do it!"

"I won't," Vee says. "Would serve him right, though." She sounds tough, but she looks like she's about to cry. "He was supposed to *help me*."

I reach out to my sister. She takes my hand. She's coughing from where Mr. Sparks had his hand on her throat, and I know how that awful burning sensation feels. "Mom?"

I hold out my other hand, and Mom takes it and climbs to her feet. She sways a little, but I feel her get immediately stronger and steadier as she hugs us to her, and for just that moment, everything's okay again, everything's *right*. It only lasts a second or two, and then she lets us go and moves down the steps. She pauses and presses her fingers to Mr. Sparks's neck. "He's alive," she says. "Help me tie him up. Get his belt."

I stop her. "We don't need to." I grab his phone, his keys, and then I pull the remote control from his pocket. It has four buttons on it. The bottom left one opens the window, I remember. He pressed the top left one upstairs to lock his office door so the knob wouldn't turn. One of the others must lock the bookcase—probably the right one on the top.

So that just leaves the bottom right one. I point it at the door and press the button.

There's a harsh buzz, and the steel door pops open half an inch.

Lanny runs down and opens the door wide, and light spills out from the room across the concrete floor. "Hey," she says, "come on. You can come out now. You're safe." She looks back at Mom. "We can put him in here. Right, Connor?"

"Right," I say. "And leave him." To die, I think, but I don't say that. But for a long second I imagine him starving to death in there, falling down, turning to bones and dust.

Lanny looks in the room again. I press the window control so I can see what she's seeing.

The two women are standing, hands folded. Tarla's crying, but she's not moving.

Sandra is the one who breaks. She slumps, gasps, and moves to take Tarla by the hand.

"No!" Tarla says. "No, we can't, we can't, he'll punish us!" She looks scared to death. She keeps pulling away and standing at the foot of her bed.

My mom takes all this in. I see it in her face, in her eyes, in the way she straightens up.

The way she looks down at the man we trusted to keep us safe.

She grabs him by the wrist and drags him limp as a dead fish across the concrete and into the room where the women are. His captives.

The second they see him down and helpless, it all changes. Tarla screams, and it actually hurts to hear it because it's like months of fear just come boiling out of her and turn into fury. She runs. I think she's running for the door, but she stops and starts *kicking* him, hard, over and over, until Sandra grabs her and pulls her on.

They step out of the room, and Tarla staggers like she's been hit. She sags against the rough wall and sinks down to a crouch. I hear her white gown catching on the chipped rock and tearing.

Mom turns and walks back out of the room. Mr. Sparks is starting to wake up, but he's not as quick as she was. Maybe he hasn't had as much experience.

As soon as she's clear, I press the control, and the door swings shut with a heavy, final slam.

Mom takes the gun from Vera, who looks relieved to get rid of it, and she comes to stand next to me. Puts her arm around me.

Mr. Sparks gets up and lunges for the door. We can hear him banging on it. Then he tries the window and smashes his fists into it over and over. Thump, thump, thump.

"That's the sound we heard," Mom says. "It wasn't a washing machine off-balance. It was the two of them, trying to let us know they were here. Hoping for rescue."

I nod. I press the bottom left button.

The window shutter comes down, and we don't see Mr. Sparks anymore. It's like he doesn't even exist, except for the thumping. If he's screaming, we can't hear him.

Vee Crockett starts to help Tarla to the stairs, but my mom stops her. "Not yet," she says. "You stay down here until I come back and tell you it's safe." She turns to me and holds out her hand for the remote. "Which one is it?"

"The top right for the bookcase," I tell her. "Top left for the office door. You're going after her?"

"Yes," she says, and hugs me so fiercely I feel like my ribs might break, but it's good pain, and I love her so much, that hurts too. Then she hugs my sister. "I love you. And I'm so proud of you. *Stay here.*" She hesitates, then hands my sister the gun. "You know how to use this. Protect them if you have to, sweetheart."

"What if you don't come back?" Vee asks her. "What if *she* does?"

"That's my mom," Lanny says. "My mom's coming back."

There's no doubt in her voice.

Sandra Clegman comes over to us as my mom goes up the steps. She looks scared, still, but steady. "Give me his phone," she says. I hand it over. "I can help."

There's a passcode on the phone, but she stares at it for a second and then punches in a number. She must have watched him do it a hundred times, and it works. It unlocks.

"What are you doing?" I ask her.

"Texting his sister," she says. She laughs shakily. "I loved to text. I usually did emojis. People still use those?"

"Yeah. There's even more now. But I don't know if *he* would use emojis."

"No. He wouldn't." She looks thinner than her picture, like she hardly eats. I can see the bones in her wrists. She types out something and hands the phone back to me.

It says TIME FOR DINNER.

I look up at her. She shrugs. "If she's carrying a dinner tray, it means she can't have the shotgun," she says. "He does this every night if we do what he says. We get to eat."

I look at Lanny and Vee. They're listening. "And . . . if you don't do what he says?"

"Then we don't eat," Tarla says. "I nearly died before I learned. Now I eat on the regular." She sounds tired. Almost drunk. "Is there still ice cream out there?"

"Yeah," Vee says. She sits down next to Tarla. "We'll get some."

I hit the "Send" button. Tarla puts her head on Vee's shoulder. I hope Sandra's right. Because if she isn't, if somehow that was wrong to send that message . . .

Mom will be walking into something really bad.

18

SAM

It takes me a while to get my brain working again after the wreck. I run it backward and remember Fairweather, dead back on the road. Shots through the windshield.

The shooter's still out there.

I lunge for the door and tumble out, yank open Mike's door, and grab for him. We lock forearms, and I pull. He's heavy, and nearly dead-weight. I'm aware that I'm going to pay for all this later, but for now we have the car between us and whoever's coming.

Maybe only one or two guys coming for us now. Probably one. They're down at least three from the original kidnapping team back at the house. I try to remember how many black SUVs I've spotted cruising Wolfhunter, but they're all alike, and it's hard to know for sure. At least three, I think, which means three or four guys each. We've accounted for one SUV full. They probably couldn't spare more than one to take Fairweather down.

Mike's bleeding pretty badly now. Shaken up even more than he was already. I prop him against the steaming metal and say, "Hang on, man, back in a second."

He just grunts. That's how I know he's really hurting. I leave him and climb back in the cruiser. The shotgun's broken free of its lock behind the front seat. It's a pump-action riot gun, preloaded with at least six shots. I bring it back and hand it to Mike. "Watch my back," I tell him. "And stay here."

"Can't do both," he says. I'm not listening. I'm starting to feel real pain. The crash jolted everything inside me good. I may be busted up somewhere. I can't tell yet, but it doesn't matter. I have to move.

I need to find this enemy, and I need to end him.

Plans change when I'm a few hundred yards away from the crash site, because I realize I'm not thinking straight, though the haze is finally starting to lift as pain sets in. I'm not up to stalking through the woods. I need to make him come to us. And he will. He can see the steam from the cracked radiator if nothing else.

He doesn't know if we're alive or dead, and he'll need to be sure.

I crouch where I am near a tree and watch. Every second means more blood Mike is losing, and I'm pretty sure I have a couple of broken ribs. I try to breathe shallow and slow. I don't think I've punctured a lung; if I have, I'm in trouble.

I hear Mike moving slightly. Then I hear another noise that comes from another direction. It's soft, well disguised, but in this breathless stillness, it's definitely there.

I see the man before I hear him again. He's wearing hunter's camo, and it's not the cheap Vietnam-era versions that the men who ambushed me back near the lodge had; this is the good stuff, private-contractor quality. He has training and money. He moves like liquid through the forest, invisible when he pauses. I'm not invisible. I'm not a trained ghost. But I'm a smaller target than Mike, who's moving, bleeding, and the best bait to get this man up close. But *close* is a relative term. I don't know the range and power of this gun, and now isn't the time to screw it up.

I have to get closer.

I'm not bad at this, but I'm bad enough. I get within twenty feet, and something—poor foot placement, brushing a branch, the sound of my breathing—alerts the enemy. He's close to Mike. And aiming. Screw it. I rush forward, low and fast, and close the distance to ten feet. No time to aim; he's turning to focus on me.

Mike saves my ass. He pumps the shotgun, even though he's out of range to do anything effective. The sound scares the man just enough. The shot that would have killed me blows a hole in the tree beside me instead.

I drop to one knee, brace, and fire. I can't go for his torso; I can't tell what kind of armor he's wearing under the camo. So I take the dangerous target, and aim for his right eye.

I'm off—nerves, the jolt that hits my broken ribs, whatever reason. Instead of the eye, I hit him in the side of the throat, but it does the job; he reels back, loses his weapon, and rolls on the incline. I scramble after him, ready to shoot him again, but he's lost interest in the fight. When I get to him, the man's got both hands wrapped around his throat, shaking and trying to hold in his blood. It's a minor miracle, but I don't think I've hit anything vital.

He's a slender young guy of Asian extraction, and as much as I want to hate his guts, I can't. He looks too much like a scared kid. I aim the gun at him anyway and say, "Keep pressure on it. You'll live." Maybe.

I hear sirens, but I can't tell which direction. If they're from Wolfhunter, Mike and I are screwed, and as dead as Detective Fairweather. If it's the county sheriff and TBI, we're saved. I can tell that this guy doesn't much care.

"Help," he whispers.

"You help me first," I tell him. "You're with the original crew that took Ellie?"

He nods. He's terrified. "Ambulance," he says. Blood's oozing out between his fingers. "Help."

"You know where the little girl is?"

"No," he whispers. His lips are turning a delicate shade of purple. "Get me help."

I pat him down for more weapons. He's got a hunting knife, a good one, and an even better 9 mm in a Velcro holster I almost miss. I take both, toss them over beside Mike, who's now propped himself up a little. Mike's good eye is open and watching. "You keep that pressure on, and you'll live. What's your name?"

"Zhao Liu," he says.

Mike manages a chuckle. "The John Smith of China," he says. "Don't think so." He turns his head. "Where those sirens coming from?"

"Not Wolfhunter," I say.

"You sure about that?"

Zhao's eyelids flutter. He passes out. His hand falls away from his neck, and blood gushes out.

"Dammit. Shoot him if he tries anything." I crouch down and apply pressure on the wound. I don't have a phone, but Zhao does, and I dial it one-handed to get to the county sheriff's office.

We all live to see law enforcement arrive: two county cruisers, followed almost immediately by a third, and an ambulance trailing. Fairweather's 10-34 got action, after all. He saved us. And I left him dead on the road. *Dammit.* That hurts worse than my broken ribs.

The county sheriff himself arrives in the next hour, accompanied by a full van of TBI agents in identifying windbreakers. By then my ribs are wrapped, I've been allowed to sit down next to Mike against the wrecked car, Zhao's in an ambulance handcuffed to a gurney, and I am so infinitely tired, but nobody's answered my damn questions and I *need to know* that Gwen and our kids are okay. I make enough noise that I finally get the sheriff, who plants his booted feet in front of me, casts me in the shade of his Stetson, and says, "What the *hell* are you going on about?"

"Gwen Proctor and the kids. They're with Hector Sparks," I tell him. "In Wolfhunter. You need to get them out of there."

"Can't do it now. We'll see to that after we get Chief Weldon and that son of a bitch Carr."

"You know about Carr?"

"Fairweather told us his suspicions. We got us a warrant to search his compound. If Ellie White's there, we'll get that poor child back for her folks, alive or dead." The sheriff, who's a beefy old guy with a Santa Claus beard and the eyes of a snake, walks away without another word. Mike and I both watch him go.

"You know," Mike says, "if he's been bought off, none of us are making it out of here alive."

"They can't buy everybody."

"So you say."

"Relax, man. You'll live to print fake money again."

"Do *not* make me laugh." He sighs. "I'm sorry about Miranda. I didn't like her. But I would have saved her if I could."

"I know," I say. I get up to my feet. Everything hurts, and I'll be black-and-blue tomorrow, but for now, I'm steady enough. "Not your fault, Mike."

"Where the hell you going?"

"To find somebody to take me to Wolfhunter," I tell him. "I need to be sure they're okay."

I don't get more than a couple of steps away before the sheriff comes back. He studies us for a few seconds, then says, "Come with me."

Mike, despite the cuts and bruises, stands up too. "Where we going?" All the weapons we took off Zhao have now disappeared, like a magic trick. I don't have them. But Mike's probably a walking secret gun show.

"Carr's compound," the sheriff says. "Then we'll go get your family."

◆ ◆ ◆

It's a ten-minute ride; nothing's far around here. The description of Carr's place as a compound is accurate; it's got fortified concrete brick walls, coiled razor wire on top of them, and some impressive floodlights on top.

The central gate's been wrecked. It lies in pieces.

"What the hell?" I say.

"Our men got here to serve the warrant and drove into the middle of a damn war," the sheriff says. He sounds grim. The situation warrants it. There are two Wolfhunter PD cruisers inside the gate with their light bars flashing, but nobody near them . . . until the sheriff's car rolls farther in, and I start to see the bodies.

Two dead officers lying between the two cars.

There are two burning SUVs, and dead men all over the place, I realize. A guy lying at the base of the wall in old, cheap desert camo, which is just dumb out here in tree country. A cluster of four or five over by what looks like a barracks on the other side of the wall.

"What the hell happened?" I ask.

"Best we can guess right now, these people in the SUVs got here half an hour ago," the sheriff says. "Full-on firefight ensued, with lots of casualties. Then Wolfhunter cops arrived, and they got killed getting out of their cars. We found Carr's wives and kids hiding in a basement."

"You did say *wives*, right?" Mike says.

"Plural. It's a mess. Some kind of redneck doomsday cult going on out here with Carr as their high muckety-muck prophet. Turns out that old shit had himself a fine petty kingdom, until today."

"Is he dead?" Mike asks.

"Haven't found him yet, but this is a goddamn bloodbath. Far as we can tell, the men in the SUVs were hired guns, and they're all dead too. They all shot each other to pieces. No idea who's missing." He eyes the two of us. "You got any info?"

"The men from the SUVs are probably the original kidnappers," I tell him. "The crew that took Ellie White, maybe some extras they hired on for this job. They intended to get her back."

"Maybe they did. We haven't found any trace of her yet."

"Have you talked to the wives?" I ask him.

"They don't say anything. They just stand there, hands together. It's damn unsettling."

"So why would you bring us here?" I ask.

The sheriff sighs. "I hoped you'd have some ideas where to go from here. Nothing?"

"Nope," I say. Mike shakes his head. "What about Chief Weldon?"

"In custody," he says. "Weldon claims he left everything to Carr; he doesn't know where the girl is being kept." He heaves a sigh. "Well. FBI's flying in on helicopters, they can take this with the TBI from here, I guess. It's a real shame we got this close and couldn't find that kid."

It is.

And then I remember something. "Vee Crockett," I say. "Vee Crockett told us her mother said the wrecks were *buried*. What if they buried the girl with them?"

"You mean old-school kidnapper-style, with an air pipe?" Mike considers that. "What's the last place you'd look?"

"C'mon, Mike, look around. Everywhere?"

"That's not how these guys think; they like to have their eyes on it all the time. Control freaks. They *hide* this stuff, but they also watch it. Under houses. Under heavy equipment. Under—" He pauses. "They got any heavy equipment?"

"Yeah," the sheriff says, and points. "A backhoe, right over there, next to the trash heap." Every rural property has its own trash heap.

I lean forward. "Open this door!"

The sheriff hits the "Unlock" button, and I hit the ground running. I'm aware this is a crime scene, and I'm not wearing either a uniform or tech gear, but all I'm thinking at that moment is that minutes are passing, and there's a little girl who's already been kept for far, far too long.

The trash heap is *massive*. It's more of a trash mountain range; that peak on the left is made of white garbage bags. The one in the center is fat tied stacks of decaying cardboard.

On the end, a tangle of rusting junk. Scrap metal, scavenged parts, the bare skeleton of a fifties sedan with no engine.

I look at the backhoe. It's dirty, but that's to be expected. There's nothing remarkable about it.

No. There is. It's sitting in a weird place, too close to the towering pile of garbage bags that might tumble down over it. There's lots of space for the backhoe. Why put it there?

Because it's blocking something.

Mike's limping out to join me. The sheriff's helping him. I reach the backhoe and climb into it. No keys, but they're stuck under the floor mat. I start the engine and roll it straight back.

As I do, I see there's a short length of PVC pipe coming out of the ground beneath it. Grace of God I didn't turn the wheel as I backed up. It only protrudes maybe two inches, and it's been painted to match the dirt around it.

The sheriff grabs a long piece of rebar from the scrap heap and starts stabbing it into the ground. Four inches down, it hits something hollow. He tries again. Another hollow sound.

"That's wood," Mike says. "It's a trapdoor."

We start kicking away the loose ground and finding the edges. There are two doors, and they are heavy wood. From the fading paint it seems like a set of barn doors that have been scavenged from somewhere else. Either that or this was once a root cellar or tornado shelter.

There's a heavy chain and a new lock on them. The sheriff shouts for bolt cutters, and someone comes running with a set. He cuts the lock and sets it aside, careful not to touch it with bare fingers.

"Prints," I tell Mike. He nods, and we wait until the sheriff hands us blue gloves to put on. Then we each grab a side of the doors, and haul. They're damn heavy. Impossible for a small child to push open, even without the lock and chain. I feel my cracked ribs shift, and bite down on the pain. Pain's good right now. Pain is productive.

It's dark as an inkwell down there. The sheriff has a heavy halogen flashlight, and he shines it in, revealing a set of old wooden steps bowed in the middle, a dirt floor, a pile of empty plastic water bottles and shredded snack-food packages.

Ellie White is curled in the corner. She's filthy, her once-pretty pink dress now streaked with mud and torn at the hem; she's not moving. I can't even tell if she's breathing. She looks thin and fragile, like a bundle of sticks.

It's Mike who plunges down those steps, injured or not, and scoops her up. She's tiny in his big arms, and her head rests against his chest. Her hair's out of one of its braids and fluffs into tight spirals that catch and move in the wind. Her arms and legs swing loose.

"Is she alive?" the sheriff asks. I can hear the horror in the question. Mike's about to lay the child down when I see her finally move.

She puts her arms around Mike's neck.

He leans against the backhoe and shuts his eyes. "It's okay, honey," he tells her. "We got you. We got you."

"God almighty," the sheriff says. "That's a miracle. We got us a miracle."

Nobody tries to take her away from Mike until the paramedics come racing up with a gurney. Once she's loaded in and off to the hospital with a racing phalanx of county cruisers, I look at the sheriff. "He goes next," I say. The sheriff nods. "You promised me. Now we get my family."

He sighs and adjust his Stetson to a more comfortable angle. "All right. You've earned that. Let's go."

19

GWEN

When I click the remote to open the bookcase and ease it away from the secret opening, I use it as a shield; I don't know if Mrs. Pall is still in the office with her shotgun. It might blast a hole through the books *and* the case, but it's the best defense I've got right now.

She's not in the room. I shut it, and hear it click as the lock engages.

It's only then that I look at the red-leather collection that occupies the shelves. It's nothing out of the ordinary, just law books like you'd find in any lawyer's office. Specifically, *Criminal Practice and Procedures*, volumes one through eleven, followed by *Tennessee Rules of Court*, volumes one through three.

All of them are dated in gold leaf in the year 1982. Like everything else Hector Sparks has in this house, it's a sham. Nothing but a museum to his father's former glory; surely a real lawyer would have more recent law books. Not Hector. No wonder he needed my help with Vee.

I can't imagine the kinds of twisted things that have gone on here to create the monster we've locked in his own dungeon, or the woman who's been helping him. Serving him. *Celeste. Mrs. Pall.* I don't really know who she is at all, or why she'd be part of this. I can't even imagine the damage that's brought *her* to this.

Because she's what Miranda Tidewell has always imagined me to be: a full and willing participant in a man's crimes against women.

And that makes her very, very dangerous.

I hear Mrs. Pall's footsteps once I open the office door. Sharp little taps of sensible heels on hardwood floors. Everything neat, tidy, clean, perfect. All this outward perfection is nothing but another mask, another shell covering the rot.

I ease out of the office into the hallway. I can't remember if the wood creaks. I need to remember, but nothing's clear suddenly. I have my gun out and down at my side; I realize it's not a magic shield, that if Mrs. Pall steps around that corner with her shotgun, it's a matter of who's got the best reaction time, and even if *I* do, she can still obliterate me with one random, spasmodic trigger pull as she dies.

The floor doesn't creak. It's silent as I carefully move forward. I check the parlor. It's empty. No one is on the stairs leading up to the second floor.

Mrs. Pall's footsteps are coming from the other side of the house. I'm all that stands between my children and this woman, that man in the basement cage. If I go down, they'll disappear. Connor . . . he'll kill my son. He's got no use for him. But he'll kill my daughter in an entirely different way. He'll devastate and destroy her, twist her into the shape he finds most enticing. She'll live and die down there. And Vee, who's now my responsibility, too, just as fragile and vulnerable. And the two anguished women we just set free.

I can't lose. I can't.

Mrs. Pall is humming quietly under her breath as I move through the dining room with a table big enough for a dozen people; the wood gleams, the china in the cabinets looks spotless and in perfect order. The centerpiece is a bowl of fresh flowers that seem to have been cut from the garden this morning, and the heavy smell of gardenia hangs in the air, tickling at my nose. The carpet in here is soft and muffles every step.

She's in the kitchen. I don't like that. Kitchens are deadly places full of weapons. She's got something boiling on the stove that could be thrown on me. A knife block full of options. Blunt objects like heavy pans hanging on a rack that crouches above the freestanding center counter.

The room smells like freshly chopped garlic and baking meat. Same smell as earlier, but stronger now.

Her back is to me. She looks the very picture of the perfect 1950s housekeeper, down to the coiffed hair, the glint of pearls at the back of her neck, the perfect bow on the back of her apron.

I ease into the room.

The floor creaks.

She freezes. I can't see her hands. What I *do* see is that the shotgun is leaning in the corner ten feet from her. I aim my gun at her back. "It's over," I tell her. "The women are out."

"Where is my brother?" Mrs. Pall asks.

Her brother. Of course. I wonder if she was ever really married, or if she was, how long her husband got to live after the wedding.

"You don't have to be like this," I tell her. "I changed. You can change. Whatever happened to you, *you can change.*"

"You have no idea what happened to me." Celeste's shoulders move back, and I can imagine her chin coming up. She turns, slowly enough so that I don't shoot her. Her right hand is up, and she turns in that direction.

She throws the knife with her left. I fire, but I'm also trying to duck; she has the speed and skill of someone who's practiced this move. It's not panicked. It's precise, and even as I move, she adjusts.

The knife buries itself in the skin of my upper right arm, and I feel it hit bone and stick. The shock is the impact, not the pain, but she's managed to fuck up my ability to shoot. I try anyway. I miss, and the agony that races up my arm makes my fingers spasm.

I drop my gun.

Stupid, stupid, stupid.

I don't let that slow me down as I dive for the shotgun. She's almost as fast, but her shoes slip on the highly polished floor. Mine don't. I reach for it. I instinctively grab with my right, and my fingers go hot and cold with pulses of agony. The shotgun tips over with a heavy thud as my whole hand spasms.

She gets hold. I throw myself on it, weighting it down, and drag her with it as her shoes scramble for purchase. She falls to her hands and knees and lets out a shriek that chills me to the core, like some banshee released from a tomb, and she comes at me with sharp fingernails and grasping hands.

I punch her in the face with my left.

She falls backward, and I kick the shotgun away and pile on top of her. She's wiry and strong, but I have more muscle. I get in two more hits before she finally bucks me off, rolls, and scrambles to her feet.

I expect her to go for the shotgun, but she doesn't. She runs toward the door where I entered and scoops up my fallen handgun instead; she doesn't stop to fire at me. She keeps running. I pick up the shotgun and check it. Two barrels, ready to go. The question of how the hell I intend to fire it is another matter. I know I shouldn't pull the knife out of my arm in case it's nicked major blood vessels; the pressure of the blade is holding anything like that mostly shut. But there's no damn way I can hold the shotgun one-handed and fire with any kind of accuracy with a knife in my arm.

I put the gun on the counter. I grab the knife, take a breath, and yank straight out. I feel the blade come free of the bone with a brisk snap so intense it almost takes out my knees; I manage to stay up, and drop the knife into the sink. Blood sheets down my arm in warm pulses. *Fuck.* If I don't bind that, I'm dead, but I have to catch Mrs. Pall. If she goes down to the cellar . . .

I grab a dishrag and stuff it into the wound. Another haze comes over me, but only for a second before adrenaline comes roaring back to erase it. I start to grab the shotgun, but then I realize that I can hear her just reaching the wood of the hallway, heading for her brother's office.

I don't need to catch her. I just need to stop her.

I pull the remote control out and hit the button to power-lock the office door. As I put it back and take the shotgun, I hear her impotent scream of frustration. I try my right hand. My fingers respond—not perfectly, they're shaking and weak, but they'll do. They have to.

I go after her.

I'm not fast enough; by the time I make it through the dining room, Mrs. Pall is at the top of the stairs and running hard to the left side of the house. I follow. If I can get a clear shot, I will take it. I need to bring her down. I *will*.

When I get to the top of the stairs, she's already gone. It's a long, narrow hallway with doors on either side. Dangerous. I take a step. The floor creaks.

She's going to hear me.

I take a breath and run, making it past two of the closed doors.

She shoots through the one on the left, leaving three jagged holes in the wood and flinging splinters onto the floor. I stop, put my weight as close to the wall as I can, and ease back. Then I crouch low and fire a shotgun blast through the doorknob to knock it open. *God*, the recoil nearly sends me sprawling, and the haze comes back in thick, red pulses.

The kitchen rag is soaked through now. Blood is drizzling from the matted fringe on the end of it. I stuff it in harder, and rise up.

I see the blur of a bright pink-and-orange bedroom, the kind a teen girl of twelve might love. Aging Madonna posters on the walls. Stuffed toys. I aim the shotgun around the room, but I don't see her. *She's not here.*

Closet. Or under the bed. Or behind the door.

I check the door and get nothing. She'll shoot for my legs if she's under the bed; I lunge forward and shove hard, and the whole bed slides. Nothing underneath, not even a dust bunny.

Has to be the closet.

I don't want to do this, I don't, but I have to. I'm all there is. For all I know, she's trying to get to another shotgun, or she has another remote she can use to unlock that office and get to my kids. I need to stop this woman. She was once a kid who loved Madonna and fluffy stuffed bears, but that doesn't matter anymore. It can't.

I breathe for a second, building strength I know is ebbing away, and I fling open the door.

It isn't a closet. It's a pass-through to the next room. A boy's room, just as frozen in time as this one. The door's hanging open to the hall; she drew me in here and then she ran for it, and I've missed her.

What I don't miss are the shackles at the corners of the boy's twin bed. They're hanging down, swinging slightly, and they're stained with old blood. I turn and look at the pretty little bed behind me.

There are shackles there, too, hanging from the bedposts.

What happened here? I don't know. I can't imagine.

I check under the boy's bed too. Nothing.

There's a closet full of children's clothing. The girl's stuff is kept on one side, the boy's on another. It's all old and dates back at least thirty years . . . but there's another section. Newer clothing, carefully draped on hangers. A pair of blue jeans. A tank top. A flannel shirt. Another pair of khaki shorts.

The clothing of abducted women. That's where Mrs. Pall got Vee's new clothes. A joke. A dark one.

She almost gets me as I exit the closet. I see a flash of movement and duck; her bullet punches the wood over my head. I want to fire back, but I know I'd be wasting the shot; she was already on the move when she pressed the trigger. I hear her shoes hitting the wood of the hallway. Then muffled thumps.

She's going down the carpeted stairs.

I follow, because if she's going downstairs, she must have a way into the cellar.

By the time I get halfway down, I can see her turning toward the office door, and I aim and fire.

I miss.

The recoil throws me back, jars loose the kitchen rag I'm using as a plug in the wound, and this time the haze descends and buries me in fog. I struggle up again. This isn't a pump shotgun; I have no more shells. I drop it and stumble down the rest of the steps, turn the corner, and see that she's got the office door open.

She's at the bookcase. She has a remote in her hand.

I grab the letter opener from Hector Sparks's desk, and I bury it in her back. It punches all the way through and emerges from the other side, filmed with blood. She screams, drops the remote, and turns the gun on me. I have no choice; I grab for it. We struggle. I hear the bookcase click open, and I think, *No, no*, but she has her way to her brother now, and if I don't get this gun away from her, my kids will stand no chance at all. The fog is thick. My body feels heavy and slow, my brain oddly weightless. But the image of my daughter in shackles on that little girl bed digs one last ounce of strength out of my failing muscles, and I bend Mrs. Pall's arm sharply up and in . . . just as she fires.

The bullet goes straight up under her jaw and out the top of her skull. Her mouth falls open, and suddenly she's deadweight shuddering in my arms. I'm looking into her eyes, and for just a second, I see utter confusion in them. And fear.

I see a child.

"I'm sorry," I tell her. Not for this. For everything that brought her here.

And then I can't hold her, and she's falling, and I'm falling too. I know I should get up. I feel that urgently. But there's a thick, warm pool of blood forming under me and sinking into the expensive Oriental carpet, and I don't know if it's from Celeste or from me, and maybe it doesn't matter anymore.

"Mom?"

Someone's holding me down. There's pain, sharp enough to make me open my eyes. "Ow."

"Tie it tighter!" That's my son's voice.

"I've got it." Lanny. The pain gets worse. "Sorry, Mom, but we have to stop the bleeding." It *really* hurts, and I struggle to make them stop. "Hold her down!"

More hands on me. I look up.

I see Sam, looking stark and calm. Connor's next to him. Both of them are holding on to me as my daughter pulls a leather belt taut over a thick, bulky piece of cloth. She's used her own shirt for the bandage, I realize. She's just wearing a sports bra. *Put something on,* I try to tell her, because I don't like anyone being vulnerable right now, not here, not in this place.

There's a man in a police uniform and a big hat pacing around behind them. He's talking on the phone.

"Quiet," Sam tells me, and puts his hand on my face. "Gwen, help's on the way. The kids are okay. We're all okay."

I think he's lying, but I don't care.

I let it go.

EPILOGUE
GWEN

Four months later

I'm shifting uneasily in a stiff chair and facing an unblinking glass eye. It's not the *Howie Hamlin Show* this time.

It's a video camera, but it isn't on. It's sitting on a shelf along with a bunch of other equipment. Tools of the trade. A trade I hope I'll be joining, if I make it through this interview.

"I usually start by saying, 'Tell me about yourself,'" the round-faced woman sitting across from me says. She's a tanned sort; *outdoorsy* is the word that comes to mind, and she hasn't bothered to dye her graying, practical hair. "That's really not necessary for you, because Lordy, I have never seen so many Google results come up on anyone who's not an actor in my life. But still: tell me about yourself, Gwen. I want to know your view."

"That's the last thing I want to talk about," I tell J. B. Hall. The *J*, she's informed me, doesn't stand for anything at all. The *B* is for Barbara, which she loathes. "I'm not that complicated. I just want to keep my family together, and safe from harm."

"The most basic of things," she says. "Leads to all sorts of nonsense, doesn't it?"

"In my case? Yes."

"I admire what you've managed to do," J. B. says. "Not just surviving, though that's admirable, but the things you've uncovered in the process. Not everyone has these instincts. Or the drive. It's impressive."

"I don't do it alone," I tell her.

"I know that. Family affair, is it?"

"More or less." It hurts to say it, because I'd like to say yes. I want Sam as family. I need that. And maybe that will happen. But there are wounds between us that are going to take time and love to heal before either of us wants to make it legal. We're together. I can't say we're fine. Not yet.

"Instincts and dedication are everything in this business," she tells me. "Everything else can be learned. You've already taken most of the coursework, is that right?" She's talking about the associate's degree necessary to secure a private investigator's license.

"I'm seventy-five percent finished," I tell her. "I'll be done by the end of the quarter. At that point, I can either start as an independent company, or join another one."

"And why did you choose mine?"

"Because the Whites recommended you," I tell her. Ellie's parents have been extraordinarily grateful for her safe rescue, even though I had little enough to do with that. This woman was with them in the greenroom that terrible day on the show, the day everything started to come apart. Smart, calm, competent. I like her. I want her to like me, and that's a relatively new sensation.

"That's odd they'd recommend me," she says, "seeing as I got next to nowhere on that case, and you and your friend Mr. Cade got everywhere."

"They like you," I say. "And you have a lot of positive Google results, so . . ."

She laughs. I like her laugh. Low and raspy. It reminds me a bit of Miranda Tidewell, but I never heard that woman laugh, not with any kind of humor. There is something similar about J. B. Hall, but a cleaner version. A healthier one. Maybe that's why I'm here, trying to make amends to a ghost who—I'm sure—would still be happy to drag me to hell.

Jesus. I need more therapy.

We're in a high-rise office in Knoxville—as high-rise as Knoxville gets, about twenty-seven stories. The J. B. Hall Agency is busy as hell outside of the glass cube we're sitting inside; there are at least a dozen people talking, walking, working on computers, and I know there are twice as many already out and working outside. It's a good place. It has good energy.

"Tell me about the cult in Wolfhunter," she says. "What you know of it, anyway."

"It started in the sixties," I tell her. "Carr's grandfather opened some kind of fringe church. A lot of people joined initially, some left. Those who stayed became a cult, and Carr's grandfather claimed to be the voice of God on earth. He started the practice of . . . training."

"Training women," J. B. says. "To be a man's perfect servants. His goal was to purge them of original sin." She looks disgusted. "I'm just quoting the text they found on the property."

"Some of the women ran. Some died. But enough stayed. The children were brought up in the—I don't want to call it *faith*. Cult." I feel the camera on me again, even though I know rationally it's not watching. "Hector Sparks's father was one of them. And he trained his son and daughter, though they broke from the cult after his death."

"Hector started abducting women, with the aid of his sister. Pretending he was somehow saving them, at least to himself." J. B. nods. "Horrible."

"Yes," I say. "It was. All of it."

"You kept your name out of the papers."

"I tried. I had help." Nobody, it turned out, really wanted to credit the infamous ex-wife of a serial killer with solving a case, so it was an easy answer for the FBI, TBI, and county sheriff's office to give the praise to the dead Detective Fairweather. I was fine with that. So was Sam.

"And . . . Mr. Cade's charges?"

"Chief Weldon confessed to trying to have Sam and my son killed in exchange for his plea deal," I tell her, and even now, that makes my blood boil and my hands shake. "The charges were dismissed. Thank God."

"Good. And I understand the documentary about Melvin Royal is stalled."

I relax, just a little. "Miranda's obsession died with her. It's going to take years to settle her estate, so they have no funding to continue."

J. B. Hall sits back and studies me. It's warm, but somehow analytical at the same time.

"I really want this job, J. B." I blurt it out, and though it's true, I wish I hadn't tipped my hand that far.

"And you'd be good at it," she agrees. "Are you sure you want to stay there, at Stillhouse Lake? I can make a place for you here in the office. You can find a home in town." *She's offering me the job.* My God. I somehow didn't prepare for this moment. I wanted it so badly that I forgot to think what to do if I actually got it.

Sam didn't leave for his dream job. I can't either. Not if I'm really committed to making things work between us. "I thought the point was for me to work remotely."

"If you'd prefer. Most of my investigators work from their homes, or out of suitcases on the road. The ones you see in here are locals who enjoy structure. To each their own, I say." She pauses for a second. "You come with baggage. I'm well aware that you could bring us some . . . notoriety, both good and bad. You've got people on your trail who want you hurt, or dead, and that can be a complication we don't need. But fact is, most of my people have never faced down a dangerous situation. Even most who came out of law enforcement never found themselves in a real gunfight. But you have. And that's valuable. There are cases—like Ellie's kidnapping, or the women in Hector's basement—that aren't about the routine work. They need insight and creativity. I think you have it. I just worry you're inviting trouble by staying back at Stillhouse Lake. I read the police reports. You've got some local trouble with some hill folk from around there."

"We do," I tell her. "But I promised my kids that we won't run. They have a stable life, friends, a real home. I can't take that away from them now."

"You know you may have to fight to protect it."

I manage a smile. "I think you know that's not new."

If she's trying to mother me, she gives it up. "How's your right hand these days?"

I hold it out. It's steady, no tremors. I make a fist. It's fast, fluid, and convincing. The fact that it hurts doesn't mean I can't fake it well.

"Excellent," she says. "We'll get to the important bits like health care and benefits in a second, but I have to ask: How would you recommend we handle the press that comes from hiring you?"

There it is. She means it. She's really offering me a job. And now I feel a golden burst of excitement. It's so . . . strange. Is this happiness, the kind of happiness regular people feel? I'm not used to it. Not for anything outside my family.

But this is mine. Something for *me*. And it's precious, like a breath of air I didn't know I needed.

"Use my controversy," I tell her. "Look, there will always be people who hate me. I can't help that. The Lost Angels—the group founded by families of Melvin's victims . . ." *By Sam.* That still hurts, but it's a distant, familiar pain. "The Lost Angels will always believe I had something to do with his crimes. Conspiracy theorists are everywhere. But I've learned recently that we all make our own hells out of our pasts; I want to use mine to help people. And I hope you'll help me do that."

She smiles slowly and nods. I think she likes that answer.

I think I do too.

SOUNDTRACK

Music gets me through. It sets a mood. It helps define characters and drive emotion through my books. So if you're musically adventurous and mad eclectic, try out these songs . . . and please, buy the music if you can. Artists don't just need exposure, they need real patronage!

- "Year of the Tiger," Myles Kennedy
- "I Get It My Way," Paul Otten
- "The Angry River," The Hat
- "Wicked Rain," Los Lobos
- "How Do You Love," Shinedown
- "You Want It Darker," Leonard Cohen
- "Save Yourself," Breaking Benjamin
- "Violet City," Mansionair
- "I Feel Like I'm Drowning," Two Feet
- "Devil," Shinedown
- "Zombie," Bad Wolves
- "Traveling Light," Leonard Cohen
- "Miracle," CHVRCHES
- "Glitter & Gold," Barns Courtney
- "White Flag," Bishop Briggs

- "Dark Country," Dominic Marsh & Paul Miro
- "Copycat," Billie Eilish
- "Blue on Black," Five Finger Death Punch
- "Blood//Water," grandson
- "Dangerous," Royal Deluxe
- "Unstoppable," The Score
- "Rise Up," Extreme Music
- "Hit and Run," LOLO
- "Dangerous" (Left Boy remix), Big Data
- "Crossfire," Stephen
- "Crossfire, Pt. II" (feat. Talib Kweli & KillaGraham), Stephen
- "Crossfire, Pt. III" (feat. Saba, Ravyn Lenae, The O'Mys, & J.P. Floyd), Stephen
- "Self-Inflicted Wound," Joe Bonamassa
- "Closure," Dommin

ABOUT THE AUTHOR

Photo © 2014 Robert Hart

Rachel Caine is the author of the *New York Times*, *USA Today*, Amazon Charts, and #1 *Wall Street Journal* bestselling Stillhouse Lake series. With more than fifty novels to her credit, Caine is also the author of the Morganville Vampires series and the Great Library series. She's written suspense, mystery, paranormal suspense, urban fantasy, science fiction, and paranormal young-adult fiction. Rachel lives and works in Fort Worth, Texas, with her husband, artist/actor/comic historian R. Cat Conrad, in a gently creepy house full of books. For more information, visit Rachel at www.rachelcaine.com.